Praise For
Semi-Sweet

"I savored every bit of this romantic and deeply true novel, right up to the surprising ending."

—Susan Wiggs, *New York Times* bestselling author

"A charming tale…Author Roisin Meaney cleverly captures the sweet, semi-sweet, and bittersweet manifestations of love in its many forms…[She] has created a delightful version of life's recipe, by blending together ingredients that range from the mundane to the earth shattering, and everything in between. A visit to this small Irish town is a trip worth taking."

—FreshFiction.com

"An endearing, insightful story of self-discovery, empowerment, love, and yes, most deliciously, cupcakes."

—Erica Bauermeister, author of
The School of Essential Ingredients

"Meaney definitely knows how to bake up a tasty story from scratch. The fact that it was set in a small, idyllic town in Ireland was just the frosting on the cupcake!…Roisin Meaney is being moved up to the top of my authors to watch list!"

—GoodReads.com

"*Semi-Sweet* is a heartwarming tale of the yearning for love, the search for happiness, and the importance of friendship—all served up with tea and cupcakes."

—Lisa Verge Higgins, author of *The Proper Care and Maintenance of Friendship*

"A set of characters you can truly care about and a story that has the ring of authenticity make this a novel that you'll be totally focused upon from start to finish."

—BookLoons.com

"Roisin Meaney writes with charm and wit about the characters and stories that make up this community...each story line proves to be engaging, poignant, and appealing to read about...Meaney has truly made this town and its people come alive. This is an entirely pleasurable story to read!"

—RomanceJunkiesReviews.com

"Ms. Meaney has such an easy way of showing fragments of everyday life, both the heartwarming and the unthinkable. She clearly has a marvelous ability for creating distinctive, authentic, and likeable characters...This is one of those books that stays in your thoughts long after you read it. If you are looking for realism, romance, and character growth then this book [is] sure to appeal."

—All About Romance (LikesBooks.com)

Life Drawing for Beginners

Also by Roisin Meaney

Semi-Sweet

Life Drawing for Beginners

Roisin Meaney

five
spot

New York   Boston

Copyright © 2011 by Roisin Meaney
Reading Group Guide Copyright © 2012 by Hachette Book Group

5 Spot
Hachette Book Group
237 Park Avenue
New York, NY 10017

www.5-spot.com

Printed in the United States of America

RRD-C

Originally published as *The Things We Do for Love* by Hachette Ireland, 2011.

First U.S. Edition: August 2012

10 9 8 7 6 5 4 3 2 1

5 Spot is an imprint of Grand Central Publishing.
The 5 Spot name and logo are trademarks of Hachette Book Group, Inc.

The Hachette Speakers Bureau provides a wide range of authors for speaking events. To find out more, go to www.hachettespeakersbureau.com or call (866) 376-6591.

The publisher is not responsible for websites (or their content) that are not owned by the publisher.

Library of Congress Cataloging-in-Publication Data
Meaney, Roisin.
  Life drawing for beginners / Roisin Meaney—1st ed.
    p. cm.
  ISBN 978-1-4555-0408-4
  1. Friendship—Fiction. I. Title.
  PR6113.E175L54 2012
  823'.92—dc23
                            2011049676

For Max and Gae Schjerning, *le gach dea-ghuí*

Life Drawing for Beginners

Four unconnected events took place on the morning of September 21, which fell that year on a Friday. The people involved in each incident were not known to one another at the time, despite the fact that they all lived within an easy walk of Carrickbawn's modest but beautifully designed public park. All four, however, were destined to meet very soon afterwards.

The first incident took place as Audrey Matthews made her way on foot to Carrickbawn Secondary School, having left her house at approximately twenty to nine. Audrey didn't normally walk to work, but her usual mode of transport being in the motorcycle repair shop, and her route not coinciding with a bus one, she found herself left with little choice.

No matter: The morning was fine and Audrey strolled along quite contentedly, humming a tune she'd heard on the radio halfway through her second bowl of Crunchy Nut Corn Flakes. With each step she took, the green canvas bag that was slung across her body bumped gently against her well-padded hip, and as she walked she glanced now and again into the windows of the various shops that lined her route.

And entirely without warning, halfway along a short pedestrianized lane connecting Carrickbawn's two main thoroughfares— a lane she rarely had occasion to visit—thirty-seven-year-old Audrey Matthews saw something that caused her to fall abruptly and profoundly in love. Her heart stopped; everything stopped for a delicious handful of seconds. And when it could move again her pink, lip-glossed mouth formed a soft O of complete adoration.

She approached the shop window and pressed her palms and nose to the cold glass, and her wide, wide smile caused the tiny ragged tail of the tousle-haired brown-and-black pup in the pet carrier inside to wag vigorously as it scrabbled against the grille at the front of the carrier and yapped soundlessly at her.

The second event occurred an hour or so afterwards, in the driveway of Irene and Martin Dillon's redbrick detached home. In her haste to get to an almost-forgotten dental appointment, forty-two-year-old Irene swung her Peugeot out too quickly and clipped the passenger wing against the gatepost, causing a small but definite dent in the metal, and leaving flakes of dark green paint embedded in the nubby concrete of the post.

Feeling the scrape of the contact, Irene swore loudly but didn't stop to inspect the damage, deciding instead to make straight for the dental clinic and deal with the car later. She sped angrily down the peaceful residential street, causing her second next-door elderly neighbor to lower his pruning shears and tut in disapproval before resuming his attack on the overgrown rosebushes that flanked his sitting room bay window.

The third happening took place around eleven o'clock, as Polish immigrant Zarek Olszewski, twenty-five, walked slowly from a newsagent's, blond head bent as he scratched carefully with the edge of a five-cent coin at a silver panel on the little card that nestled in his palm. As each sum of money was revealed—for of course the card was a lottery one—Zarek blew the silver scrapings away.

When there was nothing more to scratch he examined the card for several seconds, running a hand through his hair twice as he did so. Finally he stopped, a delighted grin spreading across his face, and turned and retraced his steps to the newsagent's.

The last incident took place just before morning became afternoon, as Jackie Moore, twenty-four-year-old single mother, stood in a queue in an art supply store, holding two paintbrushes and willing the customer ahead of her to hurry up and decide if he wanted an A4 or an A5 watercolor pad.

As she waited, conscious of the precious minutes of her lunch hour ticking by, her attention was caught by a small notice pinned to the shelf on her right. She read the short message twice, her face expressionless, as the other customer finally made his choice and moved off.

After paying for the paintbrushes, she returned to the notice and skimmed it again before rummaging in her bag and pulling out a pen. She scribbled a number onto the palm of her hand before hurrying from the shop.

Four separate events, four different settings, four strangers. But for all that, the consequences of these happenings would be significant, and more lives than theirs would be affected within a handful of weeks.

The First Week

September 21–27

A new evening class, an important purchase, and a disturbing encounter.

Friday

"May God protect the king," the beautiful man declared, smiling widely.

On the point of making its first mark, Audrey's pen stilled. She looked up. Such incredibly white teeth.

"Pardon?"

"Is my name," he told her. "English meaning of Belshazzar: May God protect the king."

"Belshazzar? But I thought you said your name was—" She suddenly couldn't remember the impossibly foreign-sounding word she'd been about to write. Something beginning with Z— or was it X?

"Zarek, yes, is short name of Belshazzar."

"Oh, I see." Audrey positioned her pen for the second time. "Maybe you could spell that for me?"

She wondered if anyone else was going to turn up. It hadn't occurred to her that she mightn't fill the class; she'd just assumed enough adult inhabitants of Carrickbawn would be interested in signing up for life drawing. But she'd been sitting alone for nearly forty minutes in Room 6, becoming steadily less confident, before the handsome Polish man had appeared.

Forty minutes gone out of sixty, which left just twenty. What if this young man was it? One person's payment wouldn't cover the model's fee, let alone Audrey's time. And could you even hold a class with just one student? Was there a minimum requirement?

Still, as long as he was here, she'd better register him.

"And your surname?"

He looked blankly at her.

"Your last name?"

"Olszewski." He eyed her unmoving pen. "Is better if I write?"

She slid the form across. "Much better, thank you."

In Ireland since May, he'd told her. In Carrickbawn since the middle of June, having decided after three weeks that Dublin wasn't for him. Eyes as blue as Paul Newman's—and would you look at the length of those lashes. A real heartbreaker of a face.

She guessed midtwenties—too young, sadly. Not that he'd be interested in Audrey in a million years, not when he could pick and choose from the pretty young ladies of Carrickbawn. How could a generously built thirty-seven-year-old, not blessed with a particularly beautiful face, hope to compete with a slimmer, younger, more attractive specimen?

Not that she was offering the class in order to find a boyfriend; of course not. Still, you wouldn't rule it out. You'd never rule it out. The man she was waiting for could be anywhere, so why not here? What was to stop him from opening the door of Room 6 in the next few minutes and walking in?

"Is this the still life drawing class?"

Audrey looked up. A couple stood in the doorway. Sixties, possibly older. The man wore a grey tweed cap and held a super-market shopping bag from which a long cardboard container protruded—aluminum foil? Waxed paper? The woman stared openly at Zarek, a look of profound distrust on her face.

"Hello there," Audrey said, smiling brightly at two more pos-sible students. "It's not actually still life, it's life drawing."

The skin on the woman's forehead puckered. "Is that not the same thing?"

"No." Audrey hesitated, wondering how gently she could

break it. "Still life is drawing inanimate objects, like fruit and, er, bottles and things, and life drawing is, well, drawing the human body."

They considered this in silence.

"And would that be a real person?" the man asked eventually. "I mean, are you talking about someone sitting there in front of the class?"

"Exactly," Audrey said. She had to tell them, she couldn't let them sign up and arrive on the first night not knowing. She crossed the fingers of the hand they couldn't see. "And in life drawing, the person is normally…unclothed."

Another dead silence, during which the color rose slowly and deeply in the woman's face. Audrey wondered if Zarek, who didn't seem to be paying too much attention, understood the significance of the conversation.

"Well," the man managed eventually, "I think you ought to be *heartily* ashamed of yourself."

"*Disgusting*," his companion added vehemently, her face still aflame. "Bringing that sort of thing to Carrickbawn. Have you no morals?"

Audrey considered pointing out that the nude human body had been drawn and painted by great artists for centuries, but decided that such a defense would probably fall on deaf ears, and might make things worse. She opted instead for silence, and did her best to look abashed.

Another few seconds of wordless outrage followed. Audrey wondered if they were planning to stand there till eight o'clock. What if more potential students turned up—would the couple bar the door? She smoothed a seam in her skirt and cleared her throat discreetly. Zarek continued to make his way slowly through the enrollment form, hopefully oblivious.

"You haven't heard the last of this," the man said eventually, and to Audrey's great relief they gathered themselves up with a series of outraged tuts. She listened to the sound of their footsteps fading along the corridor.

She should have made it clearer, she shouldn't have assumed that people understood what life drawing was. Come to think of it, confusing it with still life was perfectly understandable. And of course some people would balk at the idea of a nude model; she should have anticipated that too.

As she was wondering if she should scribble out a clarification notice and stick it beside the list of classes in the lobby, a woman appeared in the doorway. Late twenties, possibly early thirties. Hopefully not offended by a display of naked flesh.

"Life drawing? Am I in the right place?"

"Yes, this is life drawing," Audrey replied. Still a good quarter of an hour to go, and the student count was up to two. If just three more came, she'd have a respectable class. Five was fine, wasn't it? Four even, at a pinch. So what if she took home a little less cash than she'd anticipated? She'd never been a big spender.

The woman walked to the top of the room. "I've never done it before," she said. "Not any kind of art, not since school."

Her dark red hair was twined into a fat side braid that hung over her left shoulder. The frames of her small, oval-shaped spectacles were deep purple. Even in her flat tan slip-on shoes Audrey calculated that she must be six feet tall, or as close to it as made no difference. At five foot one Audrey was used to looking up at people—including, sadly, many of her secondary school students—but making eye contact here involved a little more head tilting than usual.

"Inexperience is no problem," Audrey told her. "It's a beginner class, so everyone's in the same boat, and the pace will be very relaxed."

As the newcomer reached the desk Zarek thrust his hand towards her. "I am Zarek Olszewski. I am from Poland. Please to meet you. I also take this class."

Wonderful—a welcoming committee of one extremely attractive man. Audrey couldn't have planned it better.

The woman looked impressed. "Meg Curran," she replied, shaking his hand. "Very nice to meet you. I was in Poland two years ago, on holidays. I went to Auschwitz—very sad."

"Yes," he agreed.

"But I loved *The Pianist*."

"Please?"

"Well, when I say loved, I mean it was terribly harrowing, but very well made, don't you think?"

Seeing Zarek's look of incomprehension, Audrey decided that the time might be right to hop in. "And I'm Audrey Matthews," she said. "I'll be teaching the class." She passed the woman an enrollment form. "If you wouldn't mind filling this in for me—"

Soft footsteps sounded behind her. Audrey turned to see another woman approaching the desk.

Around the same age as the others, maybe a little younger. Petite, boyish figure; pale hair cut so short it was hard to define the exact color. Three tiny silver rings pushed through her right earlobe, one above the other. She wore a white top and blue jeans.

Her brownish red lipstick was startlingly dark—and not, Audrey thought, the most flattering color for her. Overall there was a delicate quality to her features, the tidy nose slightly upturned, the small, almost child-like mouth, the pale unblemished skin. Elfin, if you had to put a label on her—and apart from the lipstick, rather colorless. Next to Meg, she looked positively miniature.

"Hello," Audrey said, smiling warmly. "Have you come for the life drawing?"

The woman nodded. "Fiona Gray," she murmured. "I'm not late, am I?"

"Not at all." Audrey took another enrollment form from the stack. Three students, just another one or—

"Hello?"

Everyone turned. Yet another woman, who unwound a long, narrow, lavender-colored scarf as she walked past the rows of tables. "This is life drawing, yes?"

"Yes, it is, yes," Audrey told her—four, she was up to four; wonderful. "You're very welcome."

The woman slung her scarf over the back of a chair as she reached the desk. "I've been running to catch up since this morning, thought I'd be late for this too." She wore a black leather shift dress that stopped above her knees, and red patent shoes whose heels were high enough to make Audrey think of stilts. How on earth did she walk in them?

Her musky scent was cloying, her white-blonde hair beautifully, perfectly cut in a bob that slanted from high on the back of her neck to just below her chin. Her voice was throaty, the voice of a theater actor. Older than the others, around Audrey's age—or maybe even the other side of forty—but looking after herself.

"I've never done it before," she said, "life drawing, I mean. That's with a live model, yes?"

"That's right," Audrey told her, relieved that the point had been made in front of everyone, but anxious to make it completely clear. "We'll be working with a live, *nude* model."

She waited. Nobody looked shocked.

"Good," the blonde repeated. "Should be fun. Does it matter that I'm a total novice?"

"Not at all, it's a beginner class," Audrey said, handing her an enrollment form.

"We are all in the same ship," Zarek told her cheerfully.

The woman looked at him with interest.

"I am Zarek Olszewski." He stuck out his hand again. "I am from Poland."

She laughed. "You don't say." Letting her hand linger in his, which of course they all noticed. "Irene Dillon," she told him.

"Charmed to meet you, I'm sure. And...?" Turning to the two other women with, Audrey thought, a noticeable lessening of interest.

As they introduced themselves Audrey began distributing the materials list. "As you know, it's a drawing class, so your requirements are relatively few—unless, of course, anyone would care to add color, in which case that's absolutely fine; and while you could stick to pencils for the drawing, I thought charcoal would be a nice—"

"Excuse me."

She stopped. A man had appeared at the door, his head covered in a black woolly hat. "Sorry to interrupt," he said in a soft Northern accent. "I don't know if you're full, or..."

He took in the handful of people. One man who didn't look Irish and four women, the largest of whom seemed to be in charge. He decided this was probably a mistake—what did he know about life drawing, what interest had he ever had in any drawing that wasn't technical?

He'd wanted to enroll in intermediate French, to back up the CDs he'd taken out from the library the previous week, which were already helping him resurrect the words and phrases of his schooldays. He wanted to bring Charlie to France next summer, so she could start learning it too—at her age, she should soak it up. He hadn't ruled out moving to France at some stage. These days he wasn't ruling anything out.

But according to the handwritten message pinned to the notice board in the college's reception area, intermediate French had been canceled due to the tutor becoming ill.

"Can't you get someone else?" he'd asked the man behind the glassed-in cubicle, but the man had apologized and said he was just the janitor, and he had no information about tutors. So James had returned to the notice board and studied the other Tuesday-evening options, and had not been inspired.

Computer programming, Pilates, or life drawing. Not one of those remotely appealed to him. He used a computer at work and hated it—who would have thought an estate agent would have to spend so much time on a damn computer?—and he had no intention of having anything to do with them in his spare time.

He had a vague idea that Pilates involved stretching out on a mat and doing exercises of some sort, which approximated pretty much his idea of hell. Rowing was the only exercise that he'd ever taken any sort of pleasure from, and that was firmly in his past now, like just about everything else he used to enjoy.

Of the three choices, life drawing seemed the least offensive. He had endured more than enjoyed trying to reproduce the collections of objects his art teachers had assembled at school, but he supposed this might be different. Life drawing was people, not things, wasn't it? Might be marginally more interesting—and who cared if he was utterly useless at it? He certainly didn't.

He had to choose one of the Tuesday classes, because Tuesday was the only evening he could make his escape, and he needed an escape, so life drawing it was. He made his way to the room where the enrollment was taking place—and as he walked in and drew attention to himself, he realized that he'd made a colossal mistake.

What had he been thinking? Who said he had to sign up for any evening class at all? Couldn't he sit in a pub for a few hours, couldn't he go to the cinema if he wanted a break from home once a week?

As he opened his mouth to say thanks but no thanks, the large woman beamed at him.

"No, we're not full," she said. "You're very welcome. Do come in." She took a step towards him, putting out her hand. "I'm

Audrey Matthews, the teacher. Come and let me introduce the others."

And she looked so genuinely happy to see him that he found himself ridiculously unable to disappoint her. He stepped forward, his heart sinking.

"James Sullivan," he said.

The name felt odd, but he'd get used to it.

———————

This was going to be a laugh. Irene signed the enrollment form with a flourish. Talk about eye candy, when all she'd come for was a bit of fun, something different to do on a Tuesday night. Pity the Pole wasn't stripping for them—now that would be interesting. Bet he had some body under that tight black T-shirt and faded chinos.

All in all, today had shaped up pretty well. Not that she'd fancy driving into the gatepost every morning, but it had turned out to have its upside.

"Not too bad," the mechanic had said, running his hand along the dent. Oil under his nails. Short, broad fingers. "Not too deep. Could be worse."

The sleeves of his overalls pushed up past his elbows, arms covered in dark hairs, muscles taut. Probably didn't need to work out, plenty of stretching and weight lifting with his job.

"You'll have to leave it with us," he'd said.

Irene had stood close enough to let him get her perfume. Men went mad for musk. "How long?"

He'd leaned against the car, arms folded. A head full of dark hair, cut short the way she liked it. Brown eyes. Bet he tanned as soon as he looked at the sun.

"Thursday at least, we're busy right now. Give us a call Thursday morning."

"You couldn't do it any quicker?" she'd asked, a hand reaching up to touch his arm oh-so-briefly. "It's just that I use it a lot, for work."

Hard muscle, not an ounce of fat there.

"I wouldn't ask," she'd said, flashing her newly cleaned teeth at him, "only it's really awkward being without it."

"I'll see what I can do," he'd said then. "Give us a call Wednesday morning."

"There you go." Irene handed her form to the teacher, whose bright blue blouse with its tiny pink polka dots and horrendous turquoise flowery skirt were probably meant to be terribly artistic—and that must be her yellow jacket slung over the back of that chair. How could anyone seriously wear that collection of colors and patterns all at once?

Must be very liberating all the same, not to give a damn what you looked like.

On the whole, Zarek Olszewski was quite happy living in Ireland. He accepted that the erratic weather system was what you got when you chose to live on a tiny island perched beside a huge ocean quite far up in the Northern Hemisphere. He'd grown accustomed to cars traveling on the wrong side of the road, and after four months he'd learned—just about—to live without his mother's spicy dumplings and sauerkraut soup.

He shared a small flat with two other immigrants, one of whom produced a very edible dinner each evening in return for ignoring every other household chore, an arrangement that suited all three perfectly.

Zarek worked behind the counter in one of Carrickbawn's fast-food outlets. His salary was modest, but his expenses were few. By shopping almost exclusively at Lidl and avoiding the pubs and restaurants of Carrickbawn, he managed to send a small monthly bank draft to his parents in Poland, and he squirreled away what little was left towards his eventual return home.

His single weekly extravagance was a €2 lottery card every Friday on his way to work. By the end of August he'd claimed two free cards and had won €4 enough times to keep investing in them. And just this morning, he'd scratched away the silver covering as usual and revealed *€250* three times. Two hundred and fifty euro!

His first thought was to send the entire amount to his parents—what did he need it for?—but later that day, as he struggled during his fifteen-minute break through Carrickbawn's free local paper, the Senior College's autumn schedule of evening classes had caught his eye. *Life drawing*, he'd read, and his pocket dictionary had confirmed that it was what he thought it was, and enrollment was that very evening. The lure had proved irresistible.

A hundred and fifty euro would be a perfectly respectable windfall. His mother could fill the freezer, his father could get a new pair of trousers. They'd be perfectly happy with €150.

And now he was signed up, and the teacher was friendly and jolly, and he looked forward to the classes. He read the materials list for the second time and wondered again if he could ask the teacher what a putty rubber was.

Audrey bundled the five enrollment forms together and slipped them into her canvas bag. She tucked checks and cash carefully into the bag's side pocket and zipped it closed. She took her yellow jacket from the back of the chair and slid her arms into it and fastened the red toggle buttons.

She locked the classroom door and returned the key to Vincent at the reception desk, who told her that two people had asked him to lodge a formal complaint about the naked drawing classes to the college authorities.

"Lord," said Audrey, alarmed. "What should I do?"

"Nothing," he said. "Some old people just love to have a moan." Vincent was seventy-five if he was a day. "If they come back, I'll say someone is looking into it. See you Tuesday."

In the car park Audrey unlocked the chain she'd wrapped around the front wheel of her newly repaired moped. She placed her bag in the basket and puttered down the short driveway of Carrickbawn Senior College. Five people signed up, five checks paid over—no, four. Zarek, bless him, had paid in cash.

Nice to have a non-Irish student in the class, made it feel quite cosmopolitan. After several months in Ireland, Zarek's command of English was still a little precarious; and of course the language employed during the classes could well be a little specialized, "putty rubber" being a case in point. Maybe Audrey could suggest he bring a dictionary to the classes, to make sure he understood the instructions.

She wondered what he did to earn a living. What did any of them do, these five strangers who'd opted to spend two hours a week in one another's company from now till Halloween? No doubt she'd find out in due course.

Interesting, too, to see how the dynamics would go, who'd get along and who'd have nothing in common. Would the women stick together, or would there be personality clashes? Would any attractions surface? Imagine if one of the three women made a play for Zarek; they'd all looked gratified to have him in the class. There might be a torrid affair—

She stopped. Listen to her, creating drama where there was none. They were simply a group of adults sharing a common interest, planning to spend a couple of relaxing hours together each week, no pressure to be anything else but amiable companions. Torrid affair, indeed.

But it would be nice if they bonded as a group; they might get quite chummy over the six weeks. There might even be a call for an advanced life drawing class after Halloween—if they weren't run out of town before then by Mr. and Mrs. Scandalized.

And purely as an observation, with no hidden agenda whatsoever, James Sullivan had a beautiful soft Northern accent, and hadn't been wearing a wedding ring. And looked to be about Audrey's age.

Oh, he was probably attached, most people were by the time they reached his age, and lots of men didn't bother with rings. She wished he'd taken off the hat—not that it mattered at all what kind of hair he had, but Audrey would have liked to see it. Presumably all would be revealed on Tuesday—he hardly wore the hat around the clock.

And speaking of all being revealed, there was still the problem of a model—or rather, of no model. So far Audrey had had three inquiries over the phone, one male and two female. The male had lost interest when he'd heard what money was being offered, and neither female had shown up for the subsequent face-to-face interview.

On the plus side there'd been another phone call just this afternoon, and a meeting had been arranged for the following day. With the first class looming, Audrey was keeping her fingers crossed that Jackie Moore turned up at least.

She'd sounded pleasant on the phone, and hadn't seemed to mind the pay. Maybe a little unsure about the actual stripping, but that was to be expected. Happily, it wasn't in Audrey's nature to worry unduly—she'd hope for the best, like she always did, and see what happened.

And if Jackie didn't work out and nobody else responded to the ad, there was always Terence, who taught science at Carrickbawn Secondary School and who'd been a little too eager to offer his services as soon as Audrey had mentioned the classes in the staff room. Terence would certainly not have been Audrey's first choice, but he'd do in a pinch—as long as she kept a good eye on him.

She motored unhurriedly along the early-evening streets, still quite bright just after eight o'clock. The thought of the winter months ahead didn't alarm her. Winter brought big coal fires and deliciously spicy curries and rich meaty stews, or bowls of steaming soup to dip soft floury rolls into—not to mention the occasional hot port when she came home wet through and frozen to the bone.

Summer's food and drink, in her opinion, wasn't a patch on winter's. She'd never been a big fan of salads. Lettuce was just too leafy, no matter how you dressed it up. And she'd never really seen the point of cooking out of doors, with everything either burned or half cooked, and always the danger of food poisoning from carelessly barbecued chicken. And chilled white wine hurt her teeth; give her a glass of warm red any day.

And this winter, she remembered with sudden delight, if all went according to plan, there would be two of them sitting in front of the fire. She considered making a detour just to have another look at him—but the pet shop was at least twenty minutes out of her way, and of course he wouldn't be there at night.

And she was starving, having eaten nothing since a tomato sandwich at four, and a steak and kidney pie was waiting at home. She loved steak and kidney pie, admittedly not the most nutritious of dinners—precooked in a tin like that, God only knew what kind of meat you were getting—but terribly tasty. And so handy, just whip off the lid and pop the pie into the oven, ready in no time.

She increased her pressure slightly on the accelerator, causing her flowered skirt to billow out. She'd go there first thing in the morning and get him, she couldn't wait. She'd go straight after her rashers and sausages breakfast.

And maybe a bit of white pudding.

James put the pint glass to his lips and took a deep swallow. As long as he had an hour off he may as well use it. Once he got home he'd be back to being Dad, who got precious few hours off.

So he was all signed up, he'd written his check for €90 and handed it over. He could always stop it in the morning, before the teacher had a chance to get to the bank. He could cancel the check and forget about fooling around with pencil and pad in the company of strangers for the next six weeks.

He drank again, feeling the stout coursing through him, relishing its pleasant malty taste. When had he been able to do this, could he even remember the last time he'd gotten away on his own, even for an hour?

Work didn't count. He was never alone there; always someone around the office asking him questions he couldn't answer, or telling him things he didn't want to know. But he had to pretend, he had to make out it was where he wanted to be, otherwise they'd get rid of him, and he'd have nothing. He hated to acknowledge it, but the truth was he'd been lucky to get any job in the recession, even if it was one he despised. Better surely to be going out to work than sitting at home all day, trying to pass the time till Charlie finished school.

He glanced around the small pub. Two old men in the far corner, sitting side by side and saying not a word to each other. Another man on a stool at the counter, licking a thumb to flick through the pages of the *Carrickbawn Weekly News*. Not exactly the most exciting place on earth.

Which was fine by him: He hadn't been looking for excitement when he'd applied for the estate agent's job, when he'd uprooted Charlie and brought her here. As far as he was concerned, the less excitement Carrickbawn had to offer, the better. But after coping on his own with a six-year-old for over a month,

James realized that he did need some sort of a break—and the drawing classes would probably be as good a way to achieve that as any.

He wouldn't get involved, he'd keep his distance from the others. He'd speak if he was spoken to, but not otherwise. They'd get the message eventually, they'd leave him alone. And if they thought he was an unsociable so-and-so they'd be dead right, for that was exactly what he had become.

He checked his watch and saw that his hour of freedom was almost up. Better not push it, or Eunice might find a reason not to babysit in future. He drained his pint and left the pub.

———————

"So," said Pilar, spreading peanut butter on dark rye bread, "you join the artist class?"

"Yes." Zarek slung his jacket on the radiator and took a carton of apple juice from the fridge. "I join."

"That is good." Pilar arranged banana slices carefully on top. "How many peoples?"

Zarek thought. "Three…no, four, and me."

"Five people, small class." Pilar cut the bread carefully into neat triangles. "You like some sandwich?"

"No, thank you." Zarek poured juice into a glass, listening to the guitar music that wafted softly from the next room. A savory scent still hung in the air, echoes of the rabbit casserole the three of them had eaten earlier.

"I go to have bath," Pilar announced, taking her supper with her. "I come out in half hour."

"Okay," Zarek replied. Left alone in the kitchen he leaned against the fridge and sipped his juice and let the music wash over him.

Saturday

"How much is that doggy in the window?" Audrey tried to keep a straight face, and failed utterly.

The man behind the counter didn't appear to see the joke. He studied Audrey over his steel-rimmed glasses. "You want to buy the pup?"

Audrey's smile dimmed slightly. No doubt he'd heard the line before, but it cost nothing to be pleasant. Thank God she'd decided against singing it—she'd feel even more foolish now. But she had no intention of letting one dour man disturb her Saturday-morning good humor.

"Yes, I'd like to buy the pup," she said, keeping her voice determinedly friendly. "He's adorable—I've fallen totally in love with him."

As soon as the words were out, it occurred to her that expressing such a sentiment might well hike up the dog's price. It was probably a bit like raving over a house you went to view, so the estate agent knew you'd pay as much as you could possibly part with. Ah well, nothing to be done now.

The man continued to regard her as if she were a slightly irritating disturbance to his day. "He's a she," he said flatly, "and she's fifty euro."

Audrey's mouth dropped open. She'd been prepared for twenty, thirty at a push. "But isn't he—she—a mongrel?" she asked. "I mean, she's gorgeous, but she's not a...thoroughbred, or a pedigree or whatever it's called, is she? I mean, she doesn't look—"

"Fifty," he repeated, lowering his head again to the newspaper that was spread open on the counter. "Take it or leave it." He turned a page.

Audrey stood before him, feeling the last of her good humor dribbling away. Was he simply going to ignore her, just read his paper and pretend she wasn't there?

She stood for another several seconds, looking down crossly at his thinning, greying hair. How rude. She should leave, forget the whole thing.

Only, of course, she couldn't.

She turned and walked over to the window and crouched by the carrier. Its occupant began a frantic yapping at Audrey's approach, tiny tail wagging furiously, her whole rear end wriggling, her small pink tongue darting at the fingers Audrey poked through the grille.

"Hello, sweetie," Audrey said softly. The pup scrabbled at the grille, demanding to be released. Audrey yearned to open the carrier and gather the little creature into her arms, but decided against it. Who knew how that disagreeable shop assistant might react?

She returned to the counter. The man continued to read his paper. Audrey determined to stand there until he did something. He couldn't ignore her forever.

The seconds ticked by. Audrey prickled with annoyance. Had he never heard of customer relations? How on earth did he manage to stay in business if he treated everyone this way?

Finally he raised his head and regarded her silently.

"I'll take her," Audrey said curtly, opening her bag. "Have you got a box?"

"Box?"

She was tempted to say, *You know, a container with four sides and a top, generally made of cardboard.* Really, his manner was appalling—but she wasn't going to stoop to his level. She was going to remain polite if it killed her.

"Yes, a box," she replied evenly. "I'll need some kind of container to bring her home in." Probably charge her for that too.

He closed his newspaper without another word and disappeared through the rear door. Audrey was quite sure she was being overcharged—surely they gave mongrels away for nothing at any cats' and dogs' home—but what could she do? She'd fallen for this dog, and no other one would do. And by the looks of it, she'd be doing the poor animal a charity by rescuing her from this obnoxious man.

A minute went by. Audrey scanned the nearby shelves and saw tins of pet food and bird feeders and bags of peanuts and cat and dog toys. Maybe he liked animals more than humans, maybe that's why he worked in a pet shop. She selected a single can of puppy food—just enough to do her until she got to the supermarket—and brought it to the counter.

She returned to the little dog, who set up a fresh burst of yapping at her approach. She lifted the carrier, which was surprisingly light, and held it up so she and the dog were eye-to-eye. "You're coming home with me," Audrey told her. "I'm taking you away from that horrible grumpy man."

"I haven't got a box."

Audrey whirled, almost dropping her load. Had he heard? He must have. Impossible to tell from his distant expression, which hadn't changed since she'd arrived. Oh, what did she care whether he'd heard or not?

"You can borrow the carrier," he said shortly. "I'll need it back on Monday."

"Thank you," Audrey said coolly. "May I ask how old she is?"

He shrugged. "Three months, give or take."

Give or take what? Another month? Audrey gritted her teeth

and waited while he scanned the tin of puppy food and totaled her purchases.

He took her money without comment. He'd probably never heard of "please" or "thank you," but she made a point of thanking him clearly as he handed over her change. At least she could show him that one of them had manners.

To her surprise he walked ahead of her and held the door open. She nodded stiffly at him as she left, vowing not to return unless it was absolutely necessary. Of course she had to bring back his carrier, that couldn't be avoided, but she'd simply deposit it on the counter and leave before he had time to annoy her.

The problem was, his was the only pet shop in Carrickbawn— probably the sole reason for him still being in business—so she wouldn't have much choice if the supermarkets didn't stock whatever she had to buy for her new pet.

Not that she was at all sure what she had to buy. There'd never been a dog or a cat in the house when Audrey was growing up. Neither of her parents had relished the idea of an animal around the place. She'd bought the pup on impulse, and hadn't the first notion of how to look after her. She'd have to get a book—or better still, visit the vet as soon as she could; surely he'd answer any questions she might have. She'd make an appointment first thing on Monday.

In the meantime she had to come up with a name. She'd been considering "Bingo," but that was when she'd assumed the pup was male, so she'd need to think again. Something nice and feminine; "Belle," maybe, or "Daisy."

And Audrey would let her sleep in the kitchen; that alcove beside the stove would be perfect if the log basket was moved behind the back door. She'd have to get a little pet bed, one of those nice furry ones. And a leash for walks, and her own pet carrier. The vet might sell things like that, if the supermarkets didn't.

And a dish for food. Audrey could use her empty steak and

kidney tin from last night until she got a proper one. Lots of things to think of, but where was the hurry? She raised the carrier until she and her new pet were eye-to-eye.

"I'm Audrey," she said, and the little dog yapped back.

She lowered the carrier and turned onto her road, her good humor fully restored, humming "How Much Is That Doggy in the Window?"

Fifty euro. It had been well worth it.

———————

Jackie had almost missed the ad. She would have missed it if she hadn't gotten trapped behind the long-haired man, forced to wait while he dithered about watercolor pads until she was ready to scream. Twelve minutes already wasted out of her precious lunchtime hour, five of those spent rummaging through the paintbrush display, because the single assistant—one assistant, at the busiest time of the day—was too preoccupied behind the counter to help her.

"Would you mind awfully?" Jackie's boss had asked. "I need them for my class this evening, and I've got nobody else to ask." And what could Jackie do but agree to call by the art supply shop in her lunch hour to buy the forgotten brushes? To be fair, she'd been given a fiver for her trouble—"the least I can do is buy your sandwich," her boss had said, and Jackie had silently agreed—but what good was that if she was left with no time to eat it?

And as she'd stood silently fuming, the small card stuck to the shelf beside her had caught her eye. *Wanted*, she'd read, *Model for adult life drawing class. No prior experience necessary. Build immaterial, but must be over eighteen. Tuesdays 7:30–9:30. Relaxed atmosphere.*

The handwriting was ridiculously round. All the *i*'s had a flower above them instead of a dot. A border of smiley faces marched around the card in various colors.

Artist's model. Paid work, presumably. Money for sitting still. Nice work if you could get it. Life drawing, though—wasn't that taking your clothes off? And this was an evening class, which meant not just one artist but lots of them, all looking at her. And not proper artists either—anyone at all could enroll in an evening class.

"Just these," she'd said to the assistant when her turn had finally come. The brushes had been checked out and paid for, and then Jackie had stood aside while the woman behind her handed her purchases to the assistant.

On the other hand, it was only two hours a week—and she could use the money, with Eoin's heart set on a Wii for Christmas. How hard could it be, taking your clothes off and striking a pose? All you needed was a bit of nerve, take a deep breath and just do it.

She'd walked back to the notice and read it again. *Build immaterial*—so you didn't need the perfect figure, which in Jackie's case was just as well. Tuesday evenings, she could manage that. Didn't say where, but evening classes were usually held in the Senior College, weren't they? She could tell her parents she'd enrolled in some other class, whatever else was on the same night.

Might even be a bit of a laugh, sprawled out on a blanket or whatever, like some kind of Greek goddess. She'd found a pen in her bag and scribbled the mobile phone number onto her hand. She could find out how much it paid anyway. She wasn't committing herself to anything just by asking.

She'd bought her sandwich and gone back to the boutique, and plugged in the kettle in the little room behind the shop floor. While she waited for it to boil she'd called the number. The woman who answered had sounded nice.

"I'm the teacher," she'd said. "Let's meet up, and you can ask me all about it. I'll wear an orange scarf so you'll recognize me. What about tomorrow? I'm free anytime after eleven."

"I work on Saturday, but I could meet you during my lunch hour," Jackie had replied, so they'd arranged to meet at ten to twelve in the little café beside the post office, and here Jackie was, pushing open the door at nine minutes to twelve—and there was the teacher, orange scarf wrapped like a turban around her head, waving and smiling from her table by the wall.

"I guessed it was you," she said, standing up and reaching out her hand as Jackie walked over. "You looked as if you were meeting someone, but weren't sure who. I'm Audrey, and thank you so much for coming."

She wasn't someone you'd overlook, with bits of her hair tumbling out of the turban-scarf and her bright pink blouse and full green skirt. She was certainly colorful. But her hand was soft and plump, and her smile was genuine, and her voice was friendly and warm.

"Now," she was saying, picking up the menu, "I fancy some cannelloni—what about you? My treat, of course."

Jackie smiled. She could take her clothes off, she was suddenly sure she could. She'd look on it as an adventure, something slightly risqué to laugh about later. *I used to be an artist's model,* she'd say, watching people's reactions.

"Cannelloni sounds good," she said.

———

As the shop door opened, Michael Browne glanced up and saw a teenage girl holding a small child by the hand.

"I'm closed," he said, dumping the coin bags back into the drawer of the cash register and sliding it shut.

"The door was open," she replied, taking a few steps towards him. "I'm not here to buy nothin', I jus' want to talk to you."

Her accent was flat. Her grammar made him wince. He regarded her over his glasses. Maybe a bit older than a teenager, maybe twenty or twenty-one. Wearing the jeans they all wore, shapeless black top over it. Pale pinched face, looked like a square meal wouldn't go amiss. Or a bath.

"If it's money you're after," he said, "you can forget it." She didn't look as if she was hiding any kind of weapon, but you couldn't be too careful. She could have a syringe up her sleeve, or there could be an accomplice waiting outside.

"I jus' want to talk," she repeated.

"In that case, talk to me on Monday. I told you I'm closed." In future he'd turn the key at five to six.

She didn't move. The child stood beside her, regarding Michael with enormous blank eyes. His red sweater was too small, and frayed at the waist.

"I'm closed," Michael repeated loudly. "Didn't you hear me?"

"Look," she said, "I jus' want to tell you somethin'."

Michael strode out from behind the counter. She barely came up to his shoulder. The child scuttled behind her.

"What bit of 'I'm closed' do you not understand?" Michael asked angrily, folding his arms. "It's six o'clock and I've been here all day, and whatever you want can wait till Monday. Now get lost before I call the police."

"You're Ethan's father," she said rapidly, her pale eyes on his face.

Michael stopped dead, his arms stiffening across his chest. He stared back at her, feeling the blood rushing from his face.

"I had to come here," she went on, the words falling over themselves now, as if his question had unleashed them. "I didn't know where you lived, I jus' knew this was your shop, Ethan told me. I waited till you were closin' up."

"How dare you mention my son," Michael said quietly, dropping his arms and moving towards her, conscious of the child making some kind of a whimpering sound behind her. "How dare you say his name to me."

She stepped backwards but continued to talk rapidly. "We were together," she said, her eyes never leaving his face. "Me and Ethan. I saw you at the funeral."

Michael stopped, his heart hammering in his chest. Knowing, abruptly, what was coming next. "Don't——"

"He's Ethan's," she said—and as the words left her mouth Michael strode past her and pulled the door open.

"Get out," he said, as calmly as he could manage, "before I call the police. Leave this shop now."

She stood her ground, an arm around the boy, who was burrowing into her side. "We need your help," she said urgently. "Please——"

"Get out," Michael repeated, everything tightly clenched inside him. "Stop talking. Leave my shop now."

She advanced towards him, the child still clinging to her top. "Look," she said, "I'm desperate, we got no place to go, we're bein' thrown out on——"

"For the last time," he said, "I'm asking you to leave."

"*Please*, I wouldn't ask only——"

"I'm counting to ten," Michael said.

"He's your *family*," she insisted, her voice beginning to tremble. "I was *dealin'*, but I stopped, for him."

"Congratulations," Michael said. "One, two, three——"

She looked at him in despair. "I've got nothin', no money, no job, nothin'. If you won't help us we'll be out on the——"

"Four, five, six——"

"He's your *grandchild*—don't that mean nothin' to you? Your grandchild livin' *rough*."

"Seven, eight, nine——"

She gave up then, pulling the boy past Michael and turning onto the street. Michael closed the door and locked it, and changed the sign from OPEN to CLOSED. He finished bagging the money and packed it into his rucksack and left through the back way, as he always did.

There was no sign of them as he rounded the corner into the street, no sign of anyone behaving furtively as he deposited his takings in the bank chute. And not once on Michael's way home, which took just over twenty minutes on foot, did he allow his dead son to cross his mind.

But as soon as he opened the door of his house, Ethan came anyway.

———

Irene knew by his breathing that he was awake. She took off her robe and slung it on the chair. She slid naked between the sheets and moved towards her husband, who wore boxer shorts, and who was turned away from her.

She laid a hand on his side, just above the waistband of his boxers, feeling the rise and fall of his rib cage. She began stroking the warm skin gently, pulling her body closer until she could feel the heat from his. The scent she'd just dabbed onto her pulse points wafted around her—she knew he could smell it too.

As her instep connected with the heel of his foot he turned onto his stomach, leaving her palm sitting in the middle of his back.

After a few seconds she moved away from him and closed her eyes and waited for sleep. Before it arrived a wail sounded from outside the room. Irene stiffened. The sound came again, a long, high cry. Irene lay motionless.

Her husband stirred. "Did I hear Emily?"

"Think so."

He slid out of bed and left the room. Irene turned onto her side and pulled the duvet around her shoulders.

Sunday

As Audrey drifted awake she became aware of hot, quick breath on her face. She screamed and leapt out of bed—and her flailing left arm caught the little dog and sent her flying in the opposite direction with a startled yelp.

"Oh—" Audrey scrambled back across the mattress and peered over the side of her generous double bed "—oh, I'm so sorry. Are you all right?"

Her new pet looked none the worse for her abrupt departure from the pillow. She trotted back to the edge of the bed and Audrey scooped her up and settled back against the headboard, pulling the sheet around both of them.

"You gave me the fright of my life," she told the little animal. "I thought I was being attacked. Of course, if you'd slept in your own bed this would never have happened."

She'd lasted forty minutes the night before, determined to ignore the surprisingly loud whines that drifted up from the kitchen. To give in would be a disaster: Audrey's years of experience in the classroom had taught her that. You had to establish who was boss from the start. She would be resolute, and the whining would eventually stop, and a lesson would have been learned.

But the whining hadn't stopped, the whining had shown no sign of stopping. Audrey had buried her head under a pillow, vowing to stick to her guns. The laundry basket was a perfectly adequate bed, and very comfortable with the old cushion in it. Really, you couldn't get better.

As the minutes ticked by, the noise from the kitchen seemed if anything to increase in pitch. In the face of such obvious distress, Audrey's resolve had begun to weaken. *She's only a few weeks old,* her inner softie had pointed out. *She's still a baby, probably not long separated from her mother. Maybe she had lots of brothers and sisters who all snuggled up together at night. No wonder she's lonely now, all by herself in a strange dark room. How can you be so hard-hearted?*

Stop it, Audrey the teacher had commanded—but both Audreys had known that the battle was lost, that it was only a matter of time before victory was declared by the smaller of the two warring factions. When her clock radio showed midnight, Audrey had finally admitted defeat. She'd gotten out of bed and padded wearily downstairs, hearing the whines turning to excited yaps as she'd approached the kitchen door.

Scolding as she went—"You're perfectly safe in this kitchen, there's nothing to be afraid of. I don't know why you're making such a fuss, I'm only up the stairs"—she'd hefted the laundry basket back to her room, the pup scampering delightedly around her feet.

"This is only for tonight," she'd warned, placing the basket in the corner of the room. "In you go." She'd patted the cushion encouragingly, but the new arrival was trotting happily around, scrabbling at the duvet in an attempt to scale the bed, pushing her nose into Audrey's bundle of folded clothes on the chair and sending them tumbling to the floor.

"Come on now," Audrey had ordered, "into your basket. Good dog. Good girl." She'd crossed the room, scooped up the little dog, and placed her in the basket. "Stay," she'd said firmly—but the minute she'd turned towards the bed the pup had leapt onto the floor and padded after her, and Audrey had been too tired to argue.

She scooped up the animal and placed her at the bottom of the bed. "No more whining," she'd ordered, getting in herself and switching off the lamp, "and certainly no barking. And please try to keep to your end."

The pup had padded around the duvet, turning in circles until she'd settled herself squarely on Audrey's feet, dropping her head onto her paws with a satisfied grunt.

Audrey had listened to the tiny, rapid breaths coming out of the darkness, had felt the corresponding rise and fall within the little body at her feet. She'd had to admit that it was pleasant to have another presence in the room, even if a small hairy four-legged creature wouldn't have been top of her list of bedroom companions.

Still, for the first time in her life as an adult she wasn't alone as she'd fallen asleep, which could only be a good thing. The laundry basket would be moved back to the kitchen first thing in the morning, and Audrey would be unrelenting the following night.

She'd begun to consider possible names as she'd drifted to sleep, and somewhere during the night, the perfect one had floated into her head. She lifted the pup now and looked into her face.

"Dolly," she said.

The pup yapped, one of her ears pricking up, her pink tongue darting towards Audrey's face.

"Dolly," Audrey repeated. "I hereby name you Dolly Matthews."

Her first pet, with a name chosen by her, totally dependent on Audrey for food and shelter. She'd look on it as a rehearsal for the real thing—because the babies would come along in due course, like they came for everyone else. So what if Audrey had to wait a bit longer? She was still only thirty-seven, lots of people didn't start having children until they were that age, or well past it even.

Didn't things always fall into place eventually? Hadn't her life drawing model come along, just like Audrey had trusted she would? Within minutes of meeting her, Audrey could tell that Jackie was just what she'd been looking for, and now everything was sorted for Tuesday. Things always worked out if you waited long enough.

"Come on," she said, pushing away the sheet and sliding to the edge of the bed, "time for breakfast—and I suppose you need to spend a penny."

She slipped her feet into the fluffy purple mules she hadn't been able to resist a week ago and pulled on her blue-and-white dressing gown, and she and Dolly left the room and went downstairs.

And happily, the discovery of pennies spent during the night wasn't made until well after the full Irish breakfast.

———————

As soon as James cut the engine Charlie unclipped her seat belt and shot from the car.

"Easy—" he said, but she was already halfway up the garden path. The front door was opened before she reached it, and Charlie was enfolded in her grandmother's arms.

"There you are at last," James heard. He locked the car and walked up the path as the other two disappeared inside. He met his father-in-law in the hall.

"Peter." Timothy shook his hand. "How're you keeping?"

His tone was perfectly civil. If you didn't know either of them, if you were ignorant of their history, you'd swear the two men were as close as any in-laws could be.

"Keeping well," James said. "And you should know that I'm not using 'Peter' anymore, I've switched to 'James,' my second name. Thought it was best."

"Right." Timothy nodded, unsurprised. "I'll mention it to Maud."

"If you would," James said. "It's just for Charlie, so she doesn't get confused. I need everyone to use the same name."

"Of course. I can understand that." Timothy indicated the sitting room. "Come on in. You'll have a drop of something."

They'd been there for Charlie, all through the nightmare. When James was useless with grief and rage, when everyone had been convinced that he'd done it—he must have done it, he was the husband—Maud and Timothy had taken care of Charlie, somehow managing to see past their own devastation to the bewildered little girl who kept asking when her mother would be coming home.

And they'd never once said a word against James to her, never tried to turn her against him—even though they must have suspected him too, they must have had questions they'd hardly dared to voice, even to each other. They must have wondered, lying awake in the night, if James had ended their daughter's life. Maybe they still did.

"How are things?" Timothy filled a glass with room-temperature 7UP and handed it to James. "How's the new job?"

"Fine," James answered.

The new job wasn't fine, the new job was far from fine. Being an architect was all he'd ever wanted, and if the fates hadn't decided to destroy his life, he'd still be an architect, with his own company. But there was little to be gained by saying that now. Timothy didn't want to hear any of that.

"And the house is all right?"

"The house is okay," James answered. The house actually *was* okay, insofar as it was fairly clean and tolerably well furnished. It was the neighborhood that was the problem—but saying that would sound horribly snobbish, and again, it wasn't what Timothy needed or wanted to hear.

"And Charlie? She's settling into the new school?"

"She is, aye. She seems to like it." James sipped his drink, wishing for ice, and a lemon slice to cut the sweetness. "I think she has a boyfriend," he added.

Timothy raised his eyebrows. "At six?"

"Ach no, I'm joking—but she's got friendly with some boy in her class. I'm just glad she's happy."

Timothy poured himself a small dark sherry. "Of course." The mantel clock ticked. From the kitchen they could hear Charlie's piping voice.

"I've enrolled in an evening class," James said when the silence started to stretch. "Art." He wouldn't say life drawing, Timothy might get the wrong idea.

"Evening class? Have you someone to mind Charlie?"

James smothered the stab of irritation. Timothy was concerned, that was all. Just looking out for his granddaughter. "The next-door neighbor," James told him. "Nice woman. Her husband goes out on Tuesday nights, which happens to be when the class is held, so it suits her to babysit."

"That's good…I didn't knew you had any great interest in art, though—I mean, that kind of art."

"I thought I'd give it a go," James said. "You never know."

They passed the time with this idle conversation, this polite chitchat, until Charlie appeared at the door.

"Granny says lunch is ready."

And James saw, with a stab of sorrow, that his daughter looked happier than he'd seen her all month.

———

Michael Browne warmed milk and added a dessert spoon of whiskey to it like he always did. He brought the glass upstairs and sipped from it as he undressed and got into his blue pajama bottoms. He washed his face and cleaned his teeth in the bathroom before putting on the pajama top. He got into bed and set his alarm for half past seven and switched off his bedside lamp and lay down.

So far, so normal. He closed his eyes and waited for sleep, suspecting it wouldn't come.

Why had she turned up? Why had this...*vexation* been visited on him? Hadn't he had enough, hadn't the fates dealt him more than his share of rotten hands? *Leave me alone*, he shouted in his head to whatever malevolent beings might be listening. *Get the hell away from me, go and bother someone else with your nasty little tricks.*

We were together, she'd said. Me and Ethan. Which could, he supposed, be the truth—what had he known about his son's friends in the last eight years of Ethan's life? Not a thing.

Not since you threw him out of the house at sixteen. The voice was back, the voice he thought he'd silenced forever.

Michael turned over, punching his pillow angrily. "He left me no choice," he said loudly into the darkness. "It was his own doing." How many times had he used those very words to Valerie, in tears at the thought of her brother roaming the streets in the rain?

"You can't just desert him, Dad," she'd wept. "It's cruel, he's only a child."

"He's an addict," Michael had insisted, over and over. "We can't help him unless he admits he needs help. You saw what he was like before he left—"

"Before you kicked him out, you mean."

"Valerie, he was out of control. He was stealing from me, he was lying—"

But nothing Michael said had made any difference. Whatever his problems, Ethan was her big brother, and Michael was the monster who'd banished him from the house. So of course Valerie had left too, as soon as she could afford it, and now what little contact they had was forced and polite, more like distant acquaintances than father and daughter.

She visited him out of a sense of duty, he knew that; affection didn't come into it. And he'd never once been invited to her apartment—his only glimpse of it had been on the day she'd moved in, when he'd insisted on helping.

He looked at the clock and read 2:53. A car passed in the street outside, tires sloshing through water. He was sick of this country, sick of the interminable rain, the awful unrelenting greyness. He and Ruth had dreamed of living in the south of Spain, or somewhere equally balmy. Italy maybe, or Greece. You could open a pet shop anywhere. And the kids would love it, growing up with blue skies and sunshine.

But before they had a chance to put their plan into action, Ruth had pulled up at a roundabout on the way to visit her mother, and a truck in the next lane had braked too sharply and jackknifed into her car, and Michael hadn't been allowed to view her body. Ethan had been four, Valerie just two—

Enough, enough of that. Michael shoved the memory away, the pain of it still sharp after more than twenty years, and turned his thoughts instead to yesterday's dilemma.

Who was to say that the boy was Ethan's? There was only the mother's word for it. Presumably she *had* known Ethan, it sounded like that part was true—but couldn't they simply have been casual acquaintances? It was hard to see what might have attracted Ethan to such a downtrodden, pathetic creature.

Much more likely that they'd somehow become known to each other, that she'd discovered by chance that Ethan's father owned a shop, and decided to try passing her boy off as his grandchild. Ethan wasn't around to confirm or deny it, so how could Michael challenge her?

I was dealing, she'd said—and Michael knew all about *that*, how drugs turned you into a liar and a thief, how they stripped you of your self-respect, tore away every shred of decency you possessed. He'd hardly recognized Ethan in the last few terrible weeks before the final row. The surly teenager who went through his father's pockets and stayed out all night bore no resemblance to the little boy Michael had pushed on the swing, or taken to the park to feed the ducks.

The child in the shop was younger than Ethan had been when Ruth was killed, no more than two or three, by the look of him. What kind of a life must he have, with an absent father, whoever he might be, and a mother involved in drugs? Michael dreaded to think what kind of a dump she and the boy shared with other down-and-outs.

She claimed to have given up dealing, which Michael doubted. Why would she give it up if she was making money from it? So easy to prey on the weakest, so tempting to wrest every last cent from them when they were begging for a fix, when they'd do anything for it.

She'd said something about being thrown out of wherever they were living—so the boy would be homeless, not even a filthy bed to lie in.

Stop. Michael punched his pillow again, willing his mind to shut down, longing for sleep—but the thoughts refused to leave him alone, Ethan refused to leave him alone. Michael's only son, his only beloved son, dead two years ago from an overdose, aged just twenty-four. Lying under six feet of earth in the graveyard, next to his mother.

And what if her story was true, what if Ethan had become a father before his death? Because distasteful as it was to Michael, there was an infinitesimal possibility, wasn't there, that she was telling the truth? Maybe Ethan had held that boy as a baby, maybe he'd had feelings for that girl—

Michael shook his head angrily. Nonsense, all nonsense and

lies. Someone trying to pull a fast one, someone trying to con money out of him. He wasn't responsible for a couple of down-and-outs, they were nothing to him.

He heard the wind whipping up, and a fresh rattle of drops on the window. More bloody rain. He remembered lying in bed after Ethan had gone, listening to the rain pelting on the roof and wondering if his son had any shelter from it. He remembered wondering what Ruth would have thought of him kicking Ethan out of the house. He imagined her arguing with him, like Valerie had. Maybe if she hadn't been killed, Ethan wouldn't have gone near drugs.

He turned over again, pulling the covers up to block out the sound of the rain—and at two minutes to seven he finally tumbled into a deep sleep.

Monday

The minute Audrey let herself into the house a high-pitched yelping sounded from the kitchen, accompanied by a frantic scrabbling at the door.

"Yes, yes," she called, dropping her canvas bag at the bottom of the stairs and shrugging out of her jacket. "I'm coming. Here I am."

She opened the kitchen door and Dolly flew at her, yapping joyfully and leaping around her ankles.

"I told you I was coming back." Audrey lifted the wriggling bundle and hugged her, feeling the rapid heartbeat through the warm, rough hair. She'd felt bad leaving the little dog alone in the kitchen for the school day, but what choice did she have? The garden wasn't secure enough to hold an energetic animal, and the shed was much too small.

The kitchen would suffer, of course. Audrey scanned the room and counted five puddles on the floor. The newspaper sheets she'd optimistically laid down that morning looked untouched, apart from one that had been shredded and scattered across a wide area. Kindling that usually sat on top of the logs in the basket was strewn across the floor, along with several fronds from Audrey's asparagus fern.

A corner of the yellow canvas blind on the window above the sink had been chewed and was fraying. The salt and pepper cellars on the table had both been upended, their contents sprinkled over the wooden surface. One of the turquoise-and-orange seat pads on the chairs had an ominous darker patch in the middle.

Audrey sighed and held the little dog at arm's length and regarded her sternly.

"I thought I explained about the newspaper," she said. "I thought you understood about that. And chewing blinds is not allowed either. And *what* have you done to my poor asparagus fern?"

Dolly yapped happily, her whole rear end wagging enthusiastically.

"I know you're sorry, but I still have to clean up."

She needed help; she had no idea how to house-train an animal. Unfortunately the vet was on holidays till Saturday. His answering machine had given a number to use in case of emergencies, but Audrey doubted that learning how to handle a small dog, however disruptive, constituted an emergency. She'd do her best till Saturday.

In the meantime she had to return the carrier to the pet shop, and buy the leash the supermarket didn't stock. She left the house again, ignoring the indignant yaps as soon as she closed the kitchen door, and made her way hurriedly through the late-afternoon streets.

It took her less than a quarter of an hour to reach the laneway that housed the pet shop. The man inside looked as glum as before, and gave no sign that he remembered her. Audrey placed the carrier on the counter, determined to get her business over with as quickly as possible.

"I borrowed this on Saturday," she said, "when I bought a little dog from you." Keeping her voice perfectly civil, but unable to muster up more than a tiny, stiff smile.

He looked tired. He made no comment as he transferred the carrier to a shelf behind the counter.

"And I need a leash," Audrey continued in the same polite tone.

"Second aisle on the left," he said, flicking through pages on a clipboard.

What was wrong with the man? Would it kill him to be pleasant? Audrey crossed to the aisle and selected a red leash. *Don't let him get to you*, she told herself as she brought it to the counter. *Don't let him see you're the least bit put out.*

The transaction was conducted in silence. Audrey took the leash and tucked it into her bag. "Thank you *so* much," she said. "Do enjoy the rest of your day."

She walked from the shop, not waiting for a reply. She wouldn't return, not if it killed her. Whatever else she needed that wasn't available in the supermarkets or at the vet's would be bought in Limerick. So what if it meant a round trip of nearly sixty miles? It would be worth the bother not to have to face him again.

"I hope you realize that I rescued you from a cranky old man," she told Dolly when she got home. "If I hadn't come along, you'd still be sitting in that window making eyes at all the passersby, trying to escape from Mr. Grumpy."

She took the seat pad off the chair and put it into the washing machine. She mopped up the puddles on the floor and tidied up the kindling and swept away the plant debris. Then she set out fresh newspaper and placed Dolly in the center of a sheet.

"*Here* is where you go," she said firmly—and the little pup promptly walked off and squatted on the tiles next to it.

"*No—*" Audrey lifted her hastily and brought her out the back and deposited her on the grass by the hedge. She stood by the door and watched Dolly scampering around the garden, nosing into shrubs, reaching on her hind legs to sniff at the clothes on the rotary line, pawing at the coal bunker, scratching at the shed door.

Caring for a young animal was a lot more complicated than Audrey had imagined. Her bedroom still smelled strongly of Dettol, and she doubted that the duvet would ever fully recover. She hadn't anticipated Dolly's ferocious energy: It was like having a miniature whirlwind in the house. She hadn't been prepared for the upheaval one small creature could cause.

But they'd learn, both of them. They'd cope, given time. The puddles on the floor would become a thing of the past—and hopefully Dolly would grow out of chewing everything in sight. And maybe this evening's walk on the new leash would tire her out. Maybe she wouldn't mind so much where she slept tonight.

Audrey scanned the patio on the other side of the hedge, but there was no sign of life next door. Her neighbors must still be in Cork. She forgot how long Pauline had said they were going for.

Her stomach growled and she turned her thoughts to dinner. She had an idea there was a chicken and rice dish in the freezer. The pack said *serves two* but really, you'd want the appetite of a bird to be happy with just half of it.

She turned back inside just as Dolly discovered the compost heap behind the shed.

―――――――――

Jackie Moore was having second thoughts.

What had she been thinking, how on earth had she imagined that she could do this? It wasn't as if she'd always yearned to be a model: On the contrary, the thought had never entered her head. For one thing, her figure was far from model material. Not that she was overweight exactly, but you wouldn't call her slim either.

And since she'd had Eoin, no amount of sit-ups would flatten her stomach—those muscles were shot forever. And horrible cellulite on her thighs, no matter how much she scrubbed with the loofah, and that awful varicose vein behind her left knee. She was no Elle Macpherson, and never had been.

The trouble was, Audrey had been so nice, so friendly and

chatty. She'd assured Jackie that varicose veins and cellulite didn't matter in the least.

"Imperfections are part of nature," she'd said. "Have you ever seen a perfectly shaped apple?"

"Er—"

"Of course not, because it doesn't exist. Everything in nature is imperfect, including the human body. But nobody will be focusing on that—they'll be more concerned with curves and lines, and getting things like proportions and foreshortening right."

She'd asked how old Jackie was.

"Twenty-four. Everyone says I look younger."

"You certainly do."

"How many in the class?"

"Five, nice and small."

"Is it mixed?"

"Just two men, both very nice."

Jackie had visualized two men sitting in front of her—strange men, checking out her breasts, having a good long look at all her bits—and her earlier confidence had begun to waver.

"Well…"

"Don't worry," Audrey had said, in the kind of warm voice you'd expect Mrs. Claus, or your fairy godmother, to have. "There's bound to be a little awkwardness initially. That's perfectly normal when you live in a society where nakedness is associated with sexuality, where the nude body is regarded as something that should be covered up."

"That's true." Jackie thought of Irish beaches, where people undressed under towels, terrified of showing intimate parts in public.

"The human form," Audrey had declared, "is a thing of beauty, nothing to be ashamed of at all. Not in the least."

And the thing was, Audrey's own figure was far from ideal. Jackie would have said quite overweight, although she carried herself well, her broad shoulders back, her head held high, and she had a pleasant, open face. Surely such an abundance of flesh wouldn't be regarded as a thing of beauty though?

Mind you, most of the nudes in famous old paintings had had pretty generous curves, all wide hips and full bosoms, all big bellies and substantial thighs, and the artists had obviously thought them worth painting, so maybe it was only modern thinking that said you had to be thin to look good.

Really, why shouldn't every human body, whatever its shape, be considered beautiful? The idea was certainly appealing. No more anorexia, no more girls and women starving themselves in the name of beauty. Everyone waddling around happily.

Audrey had poured them both more tea from the pot they'd gotten to follow the cannelloni. "So what do you think? Are you interested?"

The money being offered wasn't great, but it would make it possible for Jackie to get the Wii that Eoin wanted. And it all sounded so easy: just sit there, or lie there, or whatever, and collect your money at the end. Really, what was there to object to? All Jackie had to do was get over her inhibitions, loosen up a bit.

"I think I'm interested," she'd said. And just like that, she'd committed herself.

For the rest of the day she'd felt satisfied with her decision. She'd seen a way to make a bit of extra cash and she'd gone for it. She'd obviously impressed Audrey, who'd said more than once that she thought Jackie would be perfect for the job.

When you thought about it, Jackie was being terribly broad-minded and mature. She was the girl who took her clothes off for art. As she walked home from the café she'd felt acutely conscious of how she was moving. She'd found herself straightening her shoulders, pushing her chest forward, swinging her hips. She was an artist's model. She was a thing of beauty.

But when she lay in bed that night, the implications of what she'd done began to sink in. Taking off her clothes, *all* her clothes? Standing there completely naked, with five people focused on her wobbly bits—did she really have the confidence to go through with it?

And throughout the following day, the whole notion had become more and more intimidating. What if the women were all glamorous and beautiful, the kind of women who enrolled in evening classes just to have something to talk about at dinner parties? How could Audrey be sure they wouldn't sneer when Jackie presented her far-from-perfect body to them, or snigger at her dimpled behind, her pitifully small breasts?

Or worse, what if someone she knew had enrolled in the class, what if a neighbor turned up? What if she had to undress for Mr. MacDonald in Number 20, whose gaze drifted to her fully covered chest anytime she talked to him? Two men, Audrey had said. And if anyone she knew *had* signed up, just imagine her parents' horror when they found out what their daughter was doing on Tuesday nights. They wouldn't see it as art, no way.

Round and round her uncertainties flew, growing and multiplying until now, the night before the first class, Jackie knew that she simply couldn't do it. She felt awful about letting Audrey down by backing out at such short notice, but not awful enough to conquer her fears. Surely a few other people had responded to the ad, surely a replacement could be found?

She checked that her parents were watching television before scrolling through her phone contacts until she reached *Audrey Matthews*. She took a deep breath and pressed *call*, and listened to Audrey's phone ringing.

And ringing.

After eleven rings her son came out to the hall and saw Jackie sitting on the stairs.

"Can I have a biscuit?"

"Just one—and brush your teeth straight after."

She listened to three more rings before the line went dead. No voice mail, no way of letting Audrey know she'd changed her mind. What now?

She hung up and walked slowly into the kitchen. Audrey had been so friendly when they'd met, and so delighted with Jackie. What if she couldn't get a replacement, what if the class had to be canceled because of Jackie abandoning ship at the last minute?

"I need my PE gear tomorrow," Eoin said, replacing the lid of the biscuit barrel.

"Right," Jackie said absently.

Maybe she should give it a go, just once, and see how it went. It mightn't be as bad as she was imagining. Maybe the people who'd signed up would be nice and mature, maybe they'd be totally impervious to the fact that Jackie was naked. Maybe they'd just concentrate on making art.

And if it did turn out to be awful she could say so after the class, and her conscience would be clear because Audrey would have a whole week to find someone else.

She followed Eoin upstairs, just as Audrey climbed, dripping, from her Monday-evening bath.

———————

"You have to go," he said, grinding his cigarette butt into the bare cement floor. Carmel knew he was doing it to annoy her; he knew she hated cigarettes. He could just as easily have flicked it out the open window.

"We got nowhere," she said. "You can't throw us out, we'll be on the street."

"Not my problem," he said. "I told you, you don't deal, you don't make no money, you can't stay."

"You can't make us go," she said. "This isn't your place. We was here before you."

He took a step in their direction and she instinctively pushed

Barry behind her. He reached out and grabbed her wrist and squeezed it painfully.

"You'll go," he said softly, "or your little boy will be sorry. You can't watch him all the time."

She felt something lurch inside her. "You touch him an' I'll kill you," she said, feeling his nails digging into the skin of her arm.

He laughed. "Stop, you're scaring me," he said, dropping her arm. "You got two days to go back to dealing, or you're out." He hawked and spat on the floor, barely missing Carmel's shoe. "You hear?"

Carmel said nothing.

"Two days," he repeated. "Then it's bye-bye." He wheeled and left the room, and Carmel turned and gathered Barry into her arms, her skin still burning.

She'd have to go back to the pet shop. Even though Ethan's father thought she was a liar, even though he'd ordered her out and said he'd call the police, she'd have to go back and try again, because she couldn't think of anything else to do.

"My tummy hurts," Barry whimpered.

She put her hand on it and rubbed round and round, the way her granny used to do with her. "Shh," she said.

She was afraid of going back to the pet shop. He'd be angry when he saw her again, he might get so angry that he'd hit her this time. But she had nothing else, nobody else.

She put Barry on the bed and pulled the blanket up around him, even though it smelled like sour milk. His forehead wasn't hot, so it must be the sandwich giving him the pain. She often took stuff from the bins at the back of the supermarket. She only took things that were still wrapped up, but once in a while something would be gone off and you wouldn't know until later. He'd vomit it up in a while and he'd be okay.

She found a plastic bag and left it by the bed. She sang softly to him, rubbing his tummy round and round.

Tuesday

B ut *why* are you going?"
  James untied and redid the belt of his daughter's red dressing gown. "I told you, because I'd like to try and do some drawing. It's just for a little while."

"But why can't you do drawing here?" She poked a finger through one of his buttonholes.

"Because I want the teacher to help me," he answered patiently. "Because I'm not very good."

"But why can I not come too?"

"Because it's only for grown-ups."

Charlie pulled hard at the buttonhole. "That's not *fair*."

James smiled. "Well, school is only for children—that's not fair either."

"I *hate* school," she said crossly, twirling her finger around, winding the fabric into a creased bunch. "School is a stinky bum."

"Now, now, that's not very nice," he said, extricating the finger. "And mind my poor jacket, you're making it all crumply. Look, you're going to have great fun with Eunice."

"I don't like Eunice," Charlie mumbled. "She's smelly."

"Ach now," James protested—but he had to admit that his daughter had a point. Helpful as their new neighbor was proving to be, Eunice wasn't exactly fragrant. On the contrary, she exuded a peculiarly cheesy odor, which James suspected was emanating from her feet. But what could he do, when she was allowing him these two precious hours of freedom?

Just then, Eunice herself came bustling in from the kitchen. "The popcorn is made," she said. "Will we let Daddy get off?"

Charlie buried her head in James's chest. "Don't want popcorn," she mumbled.

"Now stop that," James said firmly, taking her shoulders and holding her out from him. "Have some manners. Eunice is being very kind to you. Come on now," he added coaxingly, "be nice. Tell you what," he went on, inspiration striking, "I'll phone you at the break and tell you a story." The break should roughly coincide with her bedtime—and would surely last ten minutes.

Charlie looked doubtfully at him. "Not a old story."

"No—this one will be brand-new."

"With a princess. And a pony."

James got up from the sofa. "Princess and pony, got you. And you have to promise to go straight to bed for Eunice afterwards. Deal?"

She considered. "Okay."

"Good girl. Now I need you to find my car keys."

As she left the room James turned to Eunice. "Thanks again for doing this. I hope she'll be okay for you. She's been…a bit clingy since we moved down here."

Eunice nodded. "Of course she has—and all the more reason for you to get a little break. Don't you worry about us, we'll be fine."

James wondered what Eunice and Gerry had made of a man moving into the area with a small daughter and no sign of a partner. He'd made no mention of Frances to them, and thankfully they hadn't asked—assuming, probably, that he was either widowed or divorced. Eunice had offered to babysit before James had even considered going out in the evenings. Feeling sorry for the lone father, no doubt.

"Tuesdays would suit best," she'd told him, "since it's Gerry's night for cards with the boys down at the local. I'm sure you could join them, if you were interested."

James could imagine Eunice cajoling her husband to take the newcomer along to meet the boys. He wondered how long his past would remain a secret in the company of card-playing drinkers. And what he'd seen of the local, with its graffiti-covered walls and huddle of tough-looking smokers in the doorway, didn't encourage closer acquaintance.

"I'm not much of a one for cards," he'd lied, "but thanks for the offer. I'll keep it in mind."

And the more he thought about it, the more he longed for one evening away from the demands a six-year-old could put on you. He loved his daughter dearly, but having sole responsibility for her from five o'clock each weekday, and all weekend, was extremely challenging.

When Frances was there, it had been so much easier. The care of Charlie had been shared between them during the week, and Maud and Timothy, less than forty miles away, were happy to take their only grandchild for at least part of each weekend. James adored his only daughter, but like any parent he appreciated the breaks from her too.

And now her mother was gone, and her father had made a decision that had put real distance between Charlie and her grandparents, and the only break he got apart from work was the once-a-month visit to Maud and Timothy's for Sunday lunch.

James had been uncertain when they'd suggested it. The events of two years ago had prompted a seismic change in the relationship between him and his parents-in-law that didn't surprise him in the least. Their lives had been upturned, their happiness snatched away in a single afternoon, and they had no way of knowing if James was responsible.

The case was still open, with nobody having been charged, or even arrested—for without any evidence, with no proof that any crime had even taken place, how could any arrest be made? James imagined what awful mixed feelings Maud and Timothy must have, how they must wish for an ending, even the worst of all possible endings—for wouldn't that be better than this terrible limbo into which they'd all been plunged?

But whatever they felt for and about James, whatever dark places their thoughts about him might bring them, they were still Charlie's grandparents, and she needed them in her life. They needed each other, with Charlie their only remaining link to Frances. So James had agreed to the monthly Sunday lunches, even though the visit now involved a round trip of over two hundred miles. But the first one had been successful, if only from Charlie's point of view.

His parents-in-law had both been perfectly polite, of course, and Maud had pressed more roast lamb on James, and a second helping of blackberry and apple crumble afterwards. But the strain had been there, he'd felt it in the lightning glances that passed occasionally between the older couple, in the small pauses between remarks, in the forced element of their laughter.

Happily, Charlie had been oblivious to any tension. Throughout the visit she'd chattered to her grandparents, answering their questions about school and friends and the new house. She'd fallen asleep in the car on the way home, and James had watched his daughter's face in the rearview mirror and seen, with a familiar pang, her mother's high cheekbones and pointed chin.

Now, driving the mile or so to Carrickbawn Senior College, James felt a growing sense of dread. He hadn't a clue how to draw, and he had no wish to learn. For the second time he considered absconding from the whole business, driving to a pub and sitting with a drink and the evening paper for two hours. What would anyone care, who would even know except himself and the other people in the class, perfect strangers whose opinion didn't matter a damn to him?

But he'd signed up and paid, and he'd bought the pencils and charcoal, the sketch pad and the putty rubber. He may as well give it a go, at least once. If it was as bad as he was anticipating, he need never return.

He turned into the college car park at twenty-seven minutes past seven precisely.

———————

Zarek was looking forward to his first life drawing class in Ireland. He wondered if there would be any difference between these classes and the ones he'd taken at home. He supposed a nude body was a nude body, whatever the nationality—although he had yet to see what a naked Irish body looked like—and the rules for drawing the human form must surely be the same the world over. Still, it would be interesting to see how this teacher, whose name he'd forgotten, would approach the subject. He hoped his English wouldn't let him down.

Although he couldn't remember her name, the teacher had made a good first impression on him. Her flowing, colorful clothes, her generous, womanly build told him that here was a person who, like himself, enjoyed the sensual, the visual, the beautiful. Of course he had to acknowledge that she was no great beauty herself, at least not in the popular, physical sense.

Attractive certainly though, with her fresh, unlined skin, and brown hair whose curls gleamed with rich, red lights—did he imagine it, or did all Irish people have some red in their hair?—and eyes the color of caramel.

Her personality was appealing too. Her friendliness was tempered with a touching hesitancy; her instincts, Zarek felt sure, tending towards helpfulness. She would make a good teacher, she would guide rather than steer. Her criticism would be kindly meant, and constructive.

He took his jacket from its hook and lifted his satchel onto his shoulder as the apartment door opened and one of his flat mates appeared.

"I have a horrible day," Pilar said, dropping her bag to the floor and yanking off her hat. "I kill that woman if I work for her one more week." She unzipped her jacket, glaring at Zarek. "You know what she say me today? She say I eat too much biscuits. Plenty money, but she count biscuits—*pah*!"

She stalked towards the kitchen, leaving a faint tang of disinfectant in her wake, and Zarek heard her speaking to Anton in precisely the same annoyed tone.

He closed the front door quietly behind him and bounded happily down the stairs, looking forward to two hours of no dramas, no complaints.

———————

The bedroom door opened and Martin walked in. "She's asleep."

Irene slipped a chunky silver bangle over her hand. "Good." She changed her mind and took the bangle off again—it might get in the way when she was drawing. "Did you start the dishwasher?"

He opened the top drawer of his bureau and began rummaging through it. "I did."

He didn't look forty-eight. He had the muscle tone of a man years younger. Irene appreciated how he filled his T-shirt, how hard and firm his body was under that grey marl cotton. She loved the way he moved, the way he strode across a room, any room, as if he owned it.

She wondered again if he was having an affair—and again, she didn't ask.

"You'll be glad to get the car back," he said, still riffling through files.

"Sure will," Irene said, taking a thin gold chain from her jewelry box and wrapping it around her wrist.

"When did they say?"

"Thursday, but I told them I needed it for work. I'll give them a ring in the morning."

"You're an awful liar," he said in the same neutral tone of voice.

Irene shrugged and reached for her perfume. "No harm done—and the guy will get a fine fat tip if he has it ready for tomorrow."

She touched the stopper behind her ears and on her wrists, conscious of his presence behind her. She dipped the stopper back into the bottle and dotted perfume on her cleavage. She stood and took her lavender scarf from the bed and draped it around her neck.

"Have fun," Martin said, pulling out a folder and bending over it.

"You know me." She rested a palm briefly on his back as she passed. Aching to press against him, to feel his solid bulk all along the length of her, to breathe in his spicy smell. "See you."

In the hall she took his car keys from their hook and opened the front door. Now that the first night of life drawing had arrived, she was half regretting her impulse to sign up. Did she really want to stare at another woman's body for two hours? Should she have gone for photography on Wednesdays, or pottery on Thursdays?

The teacher was a mess, with that mop of curly hair and horrendous fashion sense—imagine putting a patterned skirt over those hips. Irene could only hope that she was better at teaching art than dressing herself. If the opportunity arose she might mention the gym, just throw it out to the group, make sure the teacher overheard. She'd be a real challenge, if Irene took her on.

As she drove towards the college she thought she wouldn't mind being a model for a life drawing class. She'd never been shy about showing off what she had, and what she had was in pretty good nick, thanks to her workouts. Breasts that still pointed in the right direction, a behind that would give Beyoncé a run for her money, long lean thighs. Her Brazilian wax might cause a bit of a scandal, though. The view might be a little too revealing.

She thought about the mechanic who was repairing the car. She'd know when she collected it, she'd know by the way he talked to her if anything was going to happen. She wouldn't push herself on him, she'd never do that. But she had a feeling he wouldn't need any encouragement.

Not that she wanted him particularly, not that she wanted any of them. But Martin had put himself beyond her reach, and the emptiness that had caused in her had to be filled. She had to try and fill it, try to put something in its place, or she'd go demented.

She drove through the college gates and pulled into a parking space. She locked Martin's car and strode towards the entrance, her three-inch heels clacking loudly on the paving stones. She passed an elderly couple holding placards and she smiled brightly at the woman, who glared back at her.

As he approached the massive doors that led into the Senior College, Zarek observed a man and woman pacing back and forth in front of the building, each holding a notice of some kind. Perhaps they were advertising the evening classes, maybe they were some sort of Irish welcome.

But as he got closer he changed his mind. Neither of them was smiling or looking at all welcoming. On the contrary, the woman was regarding Zarek with what appeared to be surprising hostility.

"You're one of them," she said as he drew level with her. "I saw you. Didn't you see him?" she demanded, turning to her companion.

The man nodded grimly. "Oh yes, he was there, he was filling in the form. I hope you're thoroughly ashamed, young man. It's not too late to change your mind."

Zarek was puzzled. They seemed angry with him, but he had no idea why. Had they met before? They didn't look at all familiar. He scanned the notices they held, thinking they might offer some explanation.

NO FILTH IN CARRICKBAWN, he read on one, and KEEP OUR TOWN DECENT on the other. Both signs were handwritten with a black marker on squares of white card, and attached to their wooden poles—sections of a broom handle?—with green insulation tape, and their messages completely escaped Zarek.

"Excuse me," he said, "but I do not understand—"

"Oh, you understand all right," the woman told him. "You understand enough to enroll in this *sinful* class. How can you sleep at night?"

"How I sleep?" asked poor Zarek. "Very well, thank you." Had he somehow offended them by being a sound sleeper?

"Is your conscience not troubled?" the man asked.

"My—"

"Hello there."

To his enormous relief, Zarek recognized the tall woman who'd enrolled in the life drawing class. Perhaps she would explain.

"Can I ask what you're protesting about?" she asked the couple.

"You can," the woman answered grimly. "There's a class going on here this evening involving a naked person."

"Really? A naked person?" Behind her purple-framed spectacles her eyes widened. "I didn't hear anything about that. Some kind of publicity stunt, I suppose." She turned to Zarek. "We might get our pictures in the paper."

"Some kind of *filth*, you mean," the woman retorted—before Zarek, who was now completely lost, could attempt a response. "An *art* class, if you don't mind, bold as brass in the middle of Carrickbawn, and my husband and I felt we had to show our disgust."

"Well, good for you," the tall woman said, edging towards the doorway. "Well done, pity there aren't more like you." She addressed Zarek again. "Come on, we'll be late for our...flower arranging."

"No—he signed up for the art class," the older man protested. "We saw him."

"Actually, there was a mistake," the woman told him, lowering her voice. "He's from Poland, very confused, terrible English. He thought he was signing up for flower arranging, poor thing— well, you can see how he could mix them up. It was all sorted out eventually. And now we must dash, or we'll be late. Keep up the good work."

She shepherded the bewildered Zarek briskly through the college entrance. "Phew—let's hope we don't have to do that every Tuesday."

"You not come to life drawing?" he asked her. "You change to other class?"

She smiled. "No, I haven't changed, I'm still going to life drawing. I just said that to get away. Remember, if you meet those two again, you're going to flower arranging, okay? It'll just keep you out of trouble."

Zarek nodded. It seemed the simplest thing to do.

———

"You hardly touched your dinner. Are you all right?"

"I'm fine, I just thought I'd better not be too full for the Pilates. I'll have a bit more when I get home. And thanks for looking after Eoin."

"What looking after? He's no trouble. You should get out a bit more." Her mother eyed the bag on Jackie's shoulder. "What's that you have?"

"Just a towel," Jackie lied. "We were told to bring one, for the cool-down." Amazing, how easily the lies came.

"Bring a dressing gown," Audrey had said, "that you can slip on and off."

Jackie thought of slipping off the dressing gown in front of them all and her stomach lurched for the thousandth time. She hoped to God she'd be able to keep down the bit of dinner she'd managed to eat. She'd been jittery all day at work, her anxiety increasing as the evening had drawn nearer.

A mistake, a huge mistake. She wasn't cut out for this, she didn't have the nerve for it. But it was much too late to back out now, she'd have to go through with it. She'd endure tonight somehow and tell Audrey she'd have to find someone else for the rest of the classes. She opened the front door and stepped out into the cool evening air.

"You can feel the autumn coming," her mother said. "Are you sure Dad can't drive you?"

"No, no—I could do with the walk."

Imagine meeting Audrey outside the college, imagine her saying something to Jackie's father that would give the game away. It would be like Santorini all over again.

"Enjoy yourself, love, see you later."

"See you."

Enjoy yourself—if she only knew what her idiot of a daughter had signed up for. As Jackie made her way to Carrickbawn Senior College she marveled, not for the first time, at how life had returned to normal in the Moore household after she'd turned it upside down over six years earlier. It hadn't seemed possible, in the awful weeks following her revelation, that she'd ever be forgiven.

Her father leaving the room anytime she walked in, hardly able to look at her if they met on the stairs. Her mother's accusatory, tear-filled rants, wailing that Jackie had disgraced them, that they'd never again be able to hold their heads up.

Jackie's friends had assured her that given time, they'd come around. "When the baby is born," they'd said, "things will change, wait and see." But Jackie hadn't believed them. Her friends hadn't a clue, none of them had been in her situation. If anything, the baby would make things worse, would be a constant reminder to her parents of how stupid Jackie had been.

"Your whole life ahead of you," her mother had sobbed, "anything you wanted to do, all waiting for you. And now this, everything gone, the Leaving Cert useless to you."

And Jackie had remained silent, knowing that it was all true. She *had* ruined her life, she couldn't deny it. She'd gone to Santorini with three friends the summer after the Leaving Cert. She'd drunk too much and taken a chance, like so many others, and she was one of the unlucky ones who'd been caught.

She had no idea who Eoin's father was. She remembered he was English, but that was it. They'd met in a bar and they'd made their way to the beach afterwards. Jackie had woken, headachy and alone on the chilly sand as the sun was coming up. She'd never seen him again. They'd been together for a few drunken hours and they'd made a child, and he'd go through the rest of his life not knowing that one summer he'd fathered a son.

By the time Jackie realized she was pregnant, a fortnight before she was due to start college, her holiday tan had long since faded. She'd confessed to her parents—what else could she do?—and all hell had broken loose.

And now Eoin was six, and his grandparents had doted on him from the day he was born. And twenty-four-year-old Jackie, who'd given up her college place, worked in a boutique that was owned by a friend of her mother's, and she couldn't say that she was unhappy.

She rounded the last bend, and the gates of Carrickbawn Senior College loomed ahead of her. She took a deep breath and walked on, willing the next two hours to fly by, telling herself to rise above it and pretend it wasn't happening.

Audrey turned in the college gates and hurried up the driveway, blotting her damp, rosy face with a tissue. She approached the entrance, panting heavily, hardly registering the older couple who were stowing something in a car boot, their backs to her.

In the lobby she waved distractedly at Vincent as she rushed past his cubicle. Hopefully he'd assume she had a good reason for turning up almost fifteen minutes after the starting time, as indeed she had. A moped that wouldn't start, despite having just been serviced, surely constituted a good reason.

But Lord, how unprofessional to arrive late to your first-ever evening class, when you were the teacher and naturally expected to be there ahead of everyone. How bad it must look, how they must all be regretting that they'd chosen her class.

She burst into the room, full of flustered apologies: "I'm *so* sorry"—fumbling at the buttons of her jacket as she approached the desk—"my moped refused to start"—her blouse stuck to her back, her armpits *drenched*—"so I had to *race* all the way"—her face on fire—"you must all think I'm just the most careless person—" She flung her jacket on the chair, trying to catch her breath, doing her best to compose herself, forcing a smile as she panted to a halt.

They regarded her silently. Five faces registering varying degrees of concern, no disapproving expression that she could see.

At least they'd all waited, at least none of them had walked out when she hadn't shown up at half past seven.

Audrey patted her hair, attempting to marshal her thoughts—and as she scanned the room she realized with fresh horror that her model was nowhere to be seen.

———

Michael ran his hand along the row of photo albums on the bottom shelf of the bookcase until he came to what he wanted. He pulled it out and brought it to his armchair.

For some minutes he sat with the book closed in his lap, staring at the framed photo of his wedding day on the mantelpiece. Ruth wore a white fur stole over her dress—they'd chosen New Year's Day to get married—and carried a small bouquet of white flowers. She leaned into Michael's side and gazed up at him—such a little slip of a thing she'd been—and they both looked perfectly happy. If they'd known what lay ahead, how little time they'd have together, what a mess Michael would make of everything after she'd left.

He opened the album and turned the pages slowly. Like all parents, they'd gone mad with the camera for their firstborn. Ethan had been snapped in all manner of poses. Lots of him fast asleep, curled on his side, mouth pursed, clutching Bun-Bun, the little blue rabbit that someone—Michael's mother?—had given him, and that had gone to bed with him for years.

In others he was sitting on somebody's lap, or on a rug out the back, his face and hands covered in ice cream, or standing by the clothesline, podgy hands hanging on tight to the pole. Michael remembered, with a fierce stab, Ruth running in from the garden to snatch up the camera, shouting *Quick, he's standing, he's staying up!*

And there he was later, toddling around by himself, grinning up at the camera in little shorts and a T-shirt with Mickey Mouse on the front, splashing naked in a paddling pool, sitting in front of a birthday cake with two candles.

Michael turned a page and looked at Ethan on a couch, his baby sister in his arms. He would have been three then, or almost. About the same age as the child who'd come into the shop with his mother.

The white-blonde hair was similar—but lots of young children had hair that color. Ethan's had darkened to a midbrown by the time he was six or seven. The faces were different, the boy in the shop was peaky, with none of Ethan's chubbiness—but that could be down to how he was being brought up. A steady diet of junk food probably, and precious little fruit or vegetables.

Michael sat back and closed his eyes. What was the point of this? He'd made his choice, he'd sent them away, and chances were he'd never see them again. He shut the album and returned it to the shelf. He switched on the television and watched as someone tried, excruciatingly slowly, to win a million pounds.

———

"Remember we're just trying to get the overall shape of the body here," Audrey said. "Forget about detail—in these short poses we'll map in the holistic view quickly, so look for the curve of the spine, the angle of the head, the positioning of the legs. And don't worry about getting it right, let's just enjoy the form."

She walked among the tables, keeping up a running commentary of instruction, demonstrating how to produce a rapid sketch, how to use the pencil to gauge proportions, how to relate the various body shapes to one another.

After the first ten minutes she'd picked out Zarek's natural affinity with his pencil, and James's rough, brave efforts. She observed Irene's flamboyant but amateur attempts; Meg's overreliance on her putty rubber; Fiona's hopeful, haphazard scribbling.

Along the way she also noted Irene's cleavage—could that tan be real?—Meg's silver earrings that were shaped like tiny scissors, the small, dark brown mole on the back of Fiona's neck, the flecks of white scattered through James's almost black hair. And as she walked around the room taking everything in, Audrey offered silent, fervent thanks that after the shakiest of starts, her first life drawing class was finally under way.

Once she'd established that her model wasn't in the room, she'd instructed her band of students to rearrange their six tables so that they formed a horseshoe shape. "After that," she told them, pulling rolls of masking tape from her bag, "you can take a wooden board from the table at the back and attach a page from your pads to it with this. I'll be right back."

She'd hurried from the room, praying that Jackie was in the vicinity—surely she'd have gotten in touch if something had prevented her from coming? But what if she hadn't bothered, what if she'd simply changed her mind? Surely not—she hadn't struck Audrey as that kind of person when they'd met.

She might have lost her nerve though, and been too embarrassed to let Audrey know. How could anyone conduct a life drawing class with no model? Audrey wondered wildly if Vincent the caretaker could be persuaded to sit for them.

She pulled her phone from her pocket and jabbed at Jackie's number. It was answered on the first ring.

"Hello?"

Faint, nervous—but at least she'd answered it. Audrey closed her eyes and crossed her fingers tightly.

"Jackie? It's Audrey. Where are you?"

"I'm here, I'm in the bathroom, but I can't—"

"Hang on—I'll be right there."

Audrey dashed towards the toilet block, heart in her mouth. She pushed the door open and burst inside—and there was her model, huddled by the bank of sinks in a blue dressing gown, deathly pale, her shoes and socks still on, a rucksack clasped to her chest, an expression of abject fear on her face.

"I can't do it," she blurted as soon as Audrey appeared. "I'm really sorry, I thought I could, but I just can't. I feel sick. I can't go in there. Please don't make me. I'm sorry, I know I'm letting you down, but I can't."

It was what Audrey had been dreading. Jackie had had too much time to think about the implications of presenting her naked body to a group of strangers. Her initial confidence, which Audrey had bolstered so carefully in the café, had worn off and left her terrified.

Audrey put an arm around her shoulder, searching her mind for the right words, praying for a miracle in the next minute or two. "Jackie, if I had a euro for every model who was nervous before her first time, I'd be a millionaire. What you're feeling is perfectly understandable, but I know you're well able—I wouldn't have taken you on if I didn't think you could do it. The students are lovely, and like I said, there are only five of them. They're adults, they're very professional. You'll have no bother at all."

Jackie looked unconvinced, her head slowly shaking from side to side.

"Imagine them in their underwear," Audrey went on desperately, aware of time ticking by. Would they all have given up and gone home by the time she persuaded Jackie to return with her—if that ever happened? "Imagine them in long johns—or maybe bloomers, you know those ones with elastic and…frilly ends."

"I really don't—"

"And think of what you can treat yourself to, with the money," Audrey said. The money might do it.

"I was hoping to get my son a Wii for Christmas," Jackie admitted. "But I honestly don't think I can go through with it."

Audrey felt a flicker of hope—not that she had the slightest notion what a wee was. "There you go, he'd be thrilled with that—they're all going mad for them now." *Please*, she begged silently, *please*. "Tell you what," she said, "give it ten minutes. If you still hate it after that I'll let you go home, I promise."

And eventually, finally, Jackie was coaxed back down the corridor and into the room, where the group sat in their horseshoe positions, pages taped and ready—and where the clock on the wall read eight minutes to eight.

Audrey introduced Jackie quietly and without ceremony, aware that the girl remained extremely reluctant, that the slightest glitch might still cause her to bolt in fright. She indicated a chair off to the side. "You can leave your things there," she said in an undertone, "and then I'll tell you what to do."

Acutely conscious, as she plugged in the fan heater she'd brought along, as she positioned a second chair facing the horseshoe of tables and covered it with a dark blue sarong, as Jackie crouched to unlace her runners and peel off her socks, that every eye in the room was trained on the girl. *Don't look at her*, she begged silently, *not yet*.

"We'll start with a series of short poses," she told them, keeping Jackie at the periphery of her gaze, aware of the dressing gown being slowly opened. "Two or three minutes at the most, just to warm us up."

The dressing gown slid from Jackie's shoulders and she bundled it quickly onto the chair. "Right Jackie, if you could come and sit over here please," Audrey said calmly, praying silently.

Her model walked slowly to the chair that faced the horseshoe of tables, not looking towards the students, not looking anywhere but down at the seat of the chair, hands held awkwardly in front of her. Audrey noted the small breasts, the rosy pink of the nipples, the full bush of dark pubic hair.

"Good girl," Audrey murmured. "The worst bit is over. Trust me, it gets easier from now on."

Jackie still looked sick. "What do I have to do?"

Audrey positioned her on the chair. Jackie sat as instructed, eyes downcast.

Audrey turned back to the class, feeling the tension of the evening beginning at last to slither out of her. Finally, they were ready to begin.

"Right, everyone," she said, "the first of our short poses. Remember we're just trying to get the overall shape of the body here, don't worry too much about detail. Note the position of the limbs, the angle of the head, the line the torso makes."

———————

"So what about the big protest?" Meg asked.

Irene regarded the plate of biscuits but made no move to take one. "What protest?"

"Two people," Fiona told her, "with placards, out the front."

"Oh yes, I saw them but I took no notice. What were they protesting about?"

"Us," Meg said. "This class. They don't approve. I had to rescue Zarek." Turning to him, on her left. "Didn't I?"

"Please?"

"The angry people outside, before the class. I had to take you away."

"Oh yes; I was not understanding what they say."

"Hear that, Jackie?" Irene asked. "You're causing a scandal."

Jackie, back in her dressing gown, smiled shyly. "Oh dear."

Audrey listened to her students and sipped her tea. All seemed to be well, halfway through the first class. They were chatting, they were getting on.

Or rather, most of them were chatting. She wondered where James had gone. Out for a cigarette maybe. Pity if he smoked though, very off-putting. She'd been pleased to see his nice head of hair when the woolly hat had come off—not that baldness was necessarily a bad thing, of course. Look at Yul Brynner, or Telly Savalas. Well, maybe not Telly Savalas, bless him.

And the height of Irene's heels again tonight: How did she walk in those shoes? They made her almost as tall as Meg, who was in flats, and who seemed far too busy making eyes at Zarek to notice what Irene had on her feet. Maybe there would be a fling after all.

What was that saying about boys not making passes at girls who wore glasses? Not that Meg struck Audrey as the type who waited for a man to make a pass—and anyway, glasses were so trendy now, more like a fashion accessory than a passion killer. And Meg's pair was certainly striking: Audrey approved of the purple frames.

And despite her age, it had to be acknowledged that Irene looked good in a short skirt. Look at those slim legs, those shapely calves. Audrey would have loved to wear minis when she was younger, but at twelve she'd decided that her substantial knees were best hidden from public view, and she'd turned to color by way of compensation.

She took a second custard cream from the plate by her elbow and dipped it into her cup. So far so good, after the shakiest of starts.

———————

"The princess climbed back onto her pony and galloped over the mountain, just in time to put out the forest fire—"

"How?"

"What d'you mean, how?"

"She had no water. You have to have water to put out a fire."

James thought quickly. "Oh, I forgot to mention the magic well she found at the top of the mountain."

"But if there was a well how could there be a fire?"

"I can't understand it," he said sadly, "and neither could the princess. But anyway the magic well had a hose attached, and she squirted it at the fire and put it out in no time at all. Then she married the prince and lived happily ever after."

"With her pony."

"Yes, with her pony. Now, make sure you brush your teeth and go straight to bed, okay?"

"Okay."

"Night-night, poppy. Big hug."

"Night, Dad."

James hung up and got out of the car. He'd kill for a cup of tea, but the princess and her pony had probably put an end to that.

———

"So you enjoyed the Pilates."

Jackie took the plate of leftover chicken from the microwave. "I sure did: It was excellent."

"That's good; and you had the walk to and from the college too. Plenty of exercise."

"I'll be as fit as a fiddle in no time." She filled a cup with tea.

"Eoin was asking again if Charlie can come to play after school," her mother said.

Jackie added milk to her cup. "Those two really seem to have hit it off—he's always talking about her."

"You should have her around."

"I will, as soon as I meet the parents."

She brought her cup and plate into the sitting room and sat next to her father on the couch, pretending to watch a documentary about Irish murders while she replayed the events of the last couple of hours in her head.

When she'd passed the protesting couple at the door of the

college—"no filth": God, that was *her*—she'd looked straight ahead and kept going, and thankfully they hadn't attempted to talk to her. Walking into Room 6 and seeing no sign of Audrey, her nervousness had increased. What was she supposed to do, where should she change?

No, not change, undress. Strip. Get naked. Whatever way you put it, it sounded horribly sleazy.

There were three people already in the room, two women and a man, standing over by the window. They'd glanced around when she'd entered, but Jackie had been careful not to catch anyone's eye. These were the people who were going to be looking at her nude body in a few minutes. She couldn't possibly have a conversation with any of them now.

She'd perched on the chair nearest the door, her rucksack clutched to her chest, the knot in her stomach growing steadily tighter as the minutes had ticked by. Where the hell was Audrey, why wasn't she here, telling Jackie what to do, putting her at her ease?

Finally, she hadn't been able to bear it any longer. She'd gotten to her feet abruptly, her chair scraping loudly on the tiles, aware of heads turning towards her again. She'd fled from the room and stood outside the door, searching the corridor for Audrey, but still seeing no sign of her.

She'd considered bolting, just walking out quickly past the front desk and making her escape. She'd stood there biting her lip, her whole body tense. It had been so tempting.

But she couldn't let Audrey down, not at this late stage, even if the thought of what she had to do was becoming more daunting with every second that passed. Anyway, knowing her luck, she'd be sure to meet Audrey as she tried to leave. She'd turned and walked quickly past the open classroom door and farther down the corridor, willing her nerve not to desert her as she spotted a sign for toilets ahead.

She'd hurried into the nearest cubicle and removed her clothes with trembling hands, her sense of dread increasing with each garment she stuffed into the rucksack. When everything apart from shoes and socks was off, she'd wrapped the dressing gown around her and belted it tightly, and stood quaking by the bank of sinks.

By the time her phone rang a few minutes later she'd been on the point of getting dressed again, having decided that she couldn't, just couldn't, go through with it. She'd waited for Audrey to walk in, bracing herself for the other woman's disappointment, or even anger. Of course she'd be angry, with Jackie letting her down at the very last minute.

But Audrey hadn't been angry, she'd been kind and understanding—and however she managed it, she'd persuaded Jackie to give it a go. And Jackie had given it a go. She'd felt the fear and done it anyway, or whatever that expression was—and it hadn't been half as awful as she'd imagined.

It had taken a while to get over the mortification of it, of course; she hadn't relaxed immediately. For the first couple of poses she'd sat rigidly, acutely conscious of them all staring at her, terribly aware of the imperfections they could clearly see. She kept her gaze fixed on the floor in front of her, frightened to look anywhere else in case she caught someone's eye.

But as the minutes passed and everyone just scratched on the pages with their pencils, and asked Audrey questions about shading and lines, and nobody seemed particularly interested in Jackie, apart from how to get the shape of her hip or the curve of her breast right, she realized that being naked was no big deal in an art class. And slowly, very slowly, she began to relax.

The ice had been well and truly broken at break, when they'd all been so nice and friendly, joking about the protesting couple, apologizing to Jackie for their pathetic efforts to capture her on paper, and generally including her as part of the group.

And by the end of the class, she'd decided that one of the people she'd been so terrified of was in fact absolutely gorgeous.

All in all, the most interesting evening she'd had in a long time. She took another mouthful of chicken and glanced at her father, and decided that sharing her euphoria with him might not be the best idea in the world.

———

For the fourth night in a row, Dolly occupied the bottom of Audrey's bed, lying on a nest of newspapers that crumpled loudly anytime she moved. The room smelled, in no particular order, of Audrey's patchouli bath oil, bleach, and dog urine. Audrey lay awake and listened to the rapid breathing of the bed's other occupant.

She'd failed miserably to get Dolly to remain in the kitchen overnight—some figure of authority she'd turned out to be. And once in the bedroom, Dolly persisted in trying to clamber onto the bed until Audrey gave in and lifted her up, which meant that the duvet's days were numbered—newspaper could only provide limited protection against an enthusiastic canine bladder. Newspapers on the kitchen floor were similarly ineffective, Dolly preferring to leave her calling card on whatever tiles she could find each day.

And everything was chewed, from the kitchen table legs to the log basket to the handles on the floor-level cabinet doors to the blind cords. Nothing was safe—when it came to putting something between her teeth, Dolly didn't discriminate. What on earth was Audrey to do, how was she to stop the house from mini demolition?

She didn't think she'd last till the vet returned on Saturday. Much as she resisted the idea, it looked like she might have to return to the pet shop and seek the cranky man's advice. He surely couldn't object to someone looking for help with an animal he'd sold—wasn't it his duty to provide after-sales service if it was needed? Audrey would be all politeness and civility if it killed her, she'd make it impossible for him to brush her off.

She turned her thoughts to the first life drawing class, and gave thanks again that it had turned out well in the end. Her five students had seemed happy enough, and thankfully Jackie had gotten over her inhibitions and promised to come back.

"My parents think I'm at Pilates," she'd confessed to Audrey at the break. "They'd go mad if they knew about this."

Still living with her parents at twenty-four, and the mother of a child. No mention of the boy's father—and if her son was old enough to know that he wanted a wee, whatever that was, Jackie must surely have been young when she'd had him.

None of Audrey's business. She turned over, trying to ignore the pins and needles in her left foot, on which a small and blessedly sleeping animal was positioned.

Wednesday

Irene picked her way across the graveled surface in front of the garage. Heels were a curse sometimes, but it would take more than a bit of gravel to make her give them up. She pushed open the office door and there he was standing at the desk, writing something on a sheet of paper. He raised his head as she walked in.

"Hello," Irene said, ignoring the girl who sat behind the desk. "I believe you have a car for me."

"It's out the back," he told her, and led the way through the workshop and out the rear door. Irene's car sat in the concrete yard with several others. She crouched and examined the paintwork.

"That's great," she said. "It's perfect." She ran a finger along the metal. "I can't feel a thing."

"That's the idea," he said. "Even rush jobs are done well here."

She straightened up and took a €50 note from inside her jacket. "I appreciate it," she said, folding the money and slipping it into the breast pocket of his overalls. "Where do I pay the bill?"

"Office," he said. "They have the keys. Thanks for that."

"No problem." She began to turn away, and stopped, as if something had just occurred to her. She reached into her bag and pulled out a card. "If you ever want a trial session," she said, handing it to him. "Costs nothing, doesn't tie you to anything, you don't have to join up."

He took the card and read it. "Personal trainer," he said, and she saw the different way he looked at her.

"That's right."

"Weights and stuff, is it?"

"Exactly." She held eye contact for just long enough before turning away. "Thanks again."

She wondered how long it would take him.

———————

"I'll have…"—the girl played with a strand of her hair as she studied the menu behind Zarek's head. Her fingernails were long and purple, with silver stars in the center of each—"…a chicken mega burger—or, no, a cheeseburger." She frowned. "Or will I? I can't decide." She looked directly at Zarek, twirling her hair around her index finger. "Help me out here," she said.

Zarek had never tasted as much as a chip in the café. Being surrounded by the smell of hot fat from the minute he walked in effectively killed his appetite, not that he'd ever been drawn towards fast food. "The chicken is good," he said.

She held his gaze, her hips thrust forward to push against the counter. "Is that what you like?"

A snort from the table behind her, where two of her friends sat.

"Is good," Zarek repeated, keeping his expression neutral. He was well used to the flirtations, accustomed to the young girls who did their best to tease and tantalize.

"Where are you from?" she asked, all pretense of wanting food suddenly gone.

"Poland," he told her, taking a cloth and wiping the counter that was perfectly clean. Her scent, much too sweet, trailed across to him.

She twirled her hair lazily. "You got a girlfriend?"

Zarek was ready. "Yes," he said, injecting what he hoped was the right amount of regret into his voice. "In Poland I have fiancée."

Her hand dropped abruptly, and for an instant Zarek felt ashamed of the lie. But what else could he do, to avoid the blatant propositions? Wasn't an imaginary fiancée kinder than admitting that he simply wasn't interested?

She turned without another word and swayed her way back through the tables, followed by her friends, who completely ignored Zarek as they got up and left. He waited until the door had closed before coming out from behind the counter and clearing their table of shredded napkins and chewing gum wrappers.

Michael looked up as the shop door opened. Oddly, the sight of them caused him no surprise, and he realized that he'd been expecting them to return. He put down his pen and folded his arms and waited.

They were dressed in precisely the same clothing as before. The sleeves of her black top were pushed to the elbows, her jeans so tight he wondered how she got them on and off. The boy stood beside her, his hand in hers, brown trousers several sizes too big, legs rolled up at the bottom, scuffed canvas shoes beneath. He gazed solemnly at Michael, a thumb stuck into his mouth. His hair had been clumsily cut. His face was unnaturally pale.

They approached the counter, the boy moving closer to his mother. A half-full black plastic sack dangled from her free hand.

"Sorry," she said. "I know you don't want us, but we got nowhere else to go, I swear."

Close up, he could see that her chin was pitted with small red marks, and near one corner of her mouth was a cold sore that he didn't remember from their last visit. Her dark blonde hair was pulled tightly off her face.

Michael shook his head. "I told you to stay away."

"I know you don't want nothin' to do with us." She spoke rapidly, in a low voice that Michael had to strain to hear. He winced at the flatness of her vowels, her dropped *th*'s, her deplorable grammar.

"You don't believe what I told you," she said, "but it's true, I swear to God."

Michael's eyes flickered to the boy, who stared impassively back.

"I wouldn't blame you," she said. "You don't know me, you never seen me before, but I'm not lyin', I swear."

The shop door opened then, and immediately she stepped to one side, pulling the child with her, and stood silently, her gaze on a stand of bird food. The customer looked inquiringly in her direction, and Michael said shortly, "She's not buying anything."

As soon as the man had left Michael turned back to her.

"You have to go. This has to stop."

"It's not for me," she said. "I'm not lookin' for nothin' for me, it's jus' for him."

Michael glanced again at the boy who was clutching the end of her top, a dark smudge under each eye, a long thin whitish stain running down the front of his sweater.

"I know you haven't got no proof," she said, "but I'm askin' you to believe me, because it's the truth."

"Why should I?" Michael demanded. "You're a drug dealer, you told me yourself. Truth means nothing to your sort."

She shook her head. "I'm not dealin' anymore—I gave that up, I *told* you, I gave it up for the child. And he is who I say, you can do any kind of test you—"

"Why don't you go back to your family?" Michael cut in. "Why are you bothering me? Go back to them: You're a stranger to me."

Her expression hardened. "No way," she said. "My father…if you knew what he done to me…I can't say it here."

She was tiny, hardly five feet tall, and scrawny with it. Was she twenty? Michael was no good at putting an age on females. His daughter was twenty-four, but there was a world of difference between Valerie and this girl who stood before him.

"It's jus' for the child," she said then. "If you could jus' take him in, jus' for a while till I get meself sorted—"

"Take him in?"

"Only at night, jus' to sleep," she said. "It would only be—"

Michael looked at her in disbelief. "You're asking me to take your son into my house? You'd hand your son over to a stranger?"

"You're not a stranger—you're his grandfather," she shot back, her voice rising, a flush spreading across her pale cheeks. "You're all we got. I wouldn't ask only I'm desperate." Her eyes filled suddenly with tears, and she brushed roughly at them with her sleeve. "Please," she said. "I'm beggin' you. I got nowhere else to turn, we been put out, we're on the street, this is all we got—"

She was willing to let her child off with a strange man, someone who'd shown them the door already, someone who'd ordered her off his property. She must indeed be desperate—that much, at least, must be true. Assuming he *was* her child, and not some ragamuffin she'd commandeered to gain sympathy.

"Can he talk?" Michael asked then.

She frowned, blinking away more tears. "'Course he can talk, he's not stupid." A thumb swiping quickly under each eye, a loud sniff.

Michael came out from behind the counter. "I can't possibly take him," he said brusquely.

She narrowed her eyes at him, defiant now. "Why not?"

"Because," Michael replied through gritted teeth, "you could have some cockeyed scheme up your sleeve. You could say I kidnapped him, or abused him in some way. You could be planning to go running to some lawyer and tell all sorts of lies about me, just to try and get your hands on some of my money."

Her head began shaking slowly from side to side. "God," she breathed, "the way your mind works. I wasn't thinkin' nothin' like that. I'm jus' tryin' to keep him off the streets, that's all."

"Sorry," Michael said, crossing to the door. "It's not a chance I'm willing to take."

"Look," she said rapidly, "I jus' want—"

He opened the door. "Out," he said. "There's nothing for you here. Don't bother coming back, the answer will be the same."

Her face crumpled, the color rising in it once more, tears welling again. "He'll have to sleep rough," she said desperately, "or I'll have to go back to dealin', I got no choice if you won't help."

"He's not my problem, and you're not either. It's nothing to do with me." He held the door open and waited for them to walk out.

"But he *is* your problem, he's your *grandchild*—"

She reached for his arm but Michael pulled it out of her reach. He took his phone from his trouser pocket and began jabbing at buttons.

"*Jesus,*" she cried then, "you're some *bastard.*" She swept through the doorway, tears running unchecked down her face, the black plastic bag bumping against Michael's knee as she passed, the little boy trotting to keep up with her. Michael watched them hurrying down the street—and as he turned to go back inside he narrowly avoided a collision with a woman approaching from the opposite direction.

She looked uncertainly at him as he moved out of her way, and he knew she'd witnessed at least some of what had just happened. He nodded curtly at her and held the door open while she walked inside.

"I was just…" She stopped. "This might not be…"

"What do you want?" Michael attempted to keep the exasperation out of his voice.

"I bought a little dog from you last week," she said, "on Saturday. You lent me a carrier, I brought it back on Monday."

He waited. Probably looking to give back the damn pup, not what she wanted after all. Fat chance.

"It's just," she said, fiddling with her hair, smoothing her skirt, making him almost twitch with impatience—"well, to be honest, she's a bit…unruly, and I just—"

"I'm not taking her back," Michael said. "No returns."

She looked shocked. "I don't want to give her *back*, for goodness' sake—I just wondered if you, um, might have some…I don't know, advice about how I could manage her a bit better, that's all."

"You want some advice," Michael said evenly.

"Just a few pointers. I've never had a—"

"Get a book," he cut in. "Go to the library, or go to a bookshop and pick up a book. That's my advice."

He turned on his heel and walked back to the counter, and by the time he'd resumed his place behind it she'd vanished. He slumped on his stool and rubbed his face.

He'd done the right thing. She was an addict, she couldn't be trusted. They weren't his problem. He'd done the right thing.

After a while he opened his newspaper and returned to the crossword, but for the life of him he couldn't make sense of a single clue.

———————

Audrey banged the frying pan onto the cooker. The *nerve* of the man, the absolute *cheek*. She had a good mind to go straight back to that shop and give him a piece of her mind. How *dare* he take that tone with her, how *dare* he think he could treat people like that and get away with it.

She sloshed olive oil onto the pan and pulled open the fridge, her blood still boiling, nearly an hour after the encounter. And that poor girl, rushing out in *floods*—he'd obviously upset her too, and a young child with her. Audrey tore the plastic from a half pound of sausages and stabbed them with a fork and flung them on the pan. Such an *ignoramus*.

She yanked the lid off a tin of beans and upended it into a saucepan. She couldn't for the life of her understand how he stayed in business. Surely no right-thinking people would willingly shop there? She wondered if there was anywhere she could lodge a formal complaint. There must be someplace consumers could go to report rogue traders, or whatever you'd call him.

She shook the pan and the sausages hopped. When they were brown all over she lifted a plate from the dresser and opened the oven door and pulled out the tray of chips. She tossed them onto the plate and plonked the sausages beside them, and splashed the beans on top.

She took her plate and brought it out to the garden and sank onto the garden seat. She was *not* going to let him ruin the rest of her day. She'd get a little bottle of wine to have with her dinner, even though she never normally had a drink during the week. But this was an exception, this she needed.

She left her plate on the seat and went back inside—and in the thirty-four seconds it took to open the wine, pour it into a glass, and return to the garden, Dolly managed to dispatch one and a half sausages and an impressive amount of beans.

Thursday

When he drew up outside the school, James reached past Charlie to open her car door. She ruffled his hair, as she always did. "Stop messing my hair, you monkey," he said, as he always did.

"Can Eoin come to my house after school?"

Eoin again. "Not today, poppy."

She scowled. "You *always* say not today."

"Well, that's because I have to meet his mum first."

"But how can you meet her if you never come in?"

Good point. James had yet to lay eyes on the famous Eoin. When he dropped Charlie at school, he stayed in the car and watched her walking in, and in the afternoon she was collected from school by someone from the nearby crèche, and taken there till James picked her up again at five. He had no wish to strike up any kind of acquaintance with the parents of his daughter's classmates—not yet anyway—and he figured if the teacher wanted to see him, she'd let him know.

All the same, he wondered how long more he'd be able to get away with distancing himself from Charlie's school life. "Tell you what," he said, "why don't you and I have dinner out tomorrow?"

"Why not today?"

"Because I've already taken the bacon out of the freezer."

She thumped her feet against the seat. "I *hate* stupid bacon."

James kept his patience. "You do not, you love bacon." He

tickled under her arm, and she squirmed away. "Say you love it or I'll tickle you to death. Say it."

Being a parent, he'd long since realized, wasn't so much one job as several, all of them unpaid, and all with extremely unsociable hours. Cook, cleaner, minder, nurse, educator, entertainer, chauffeur, disciplinarian—and doubtless as she got older the list would lengthen, maybe with jobs he didn't even know existed now. Being a parent was a challenge. Being a lone parent was bloody terrifying.

When she eventually got out of the car he waited until she'd disappeared through the school doors before driving off. As he crawled through the Carrickbawn rush-hour streets, as eight more stultifying hours in the estate agency beckoned, James felt the familiar dread seeping under his skin.

He yearned to be his own boss again, to be in control, to be able to stand over every decision he took. He wondered if he'd ever get back there, if he'd ever manage to steer his life back onto its original course. No—not its original course, that was gone forever, but something he could be proud of, something he could look forward to.

He parked in the little yard behind the estate agency and took his jacket from the backseat.

"Belshazzar, is that you?" His mother's voice was as clear as if she were phoning from the house next door.

Zarek's heart stopped. "Mama—what's wrong?"

His father dead, his sister in a horrible accident. Someone in hospital, on life support. He wondered how much a last-minute flight to Wroclaw would cost, and whether he could borrow from Pilar or Anton.

"We got the money," his mother said. "It arrived this morning." The money. Zarek had forgotten the money. Relief flooded through him.

"You are a good boy," his mother said. "Another son would get a bonus from his job and say nothing to his parents."

The bonus fib had been a necessary evil—any form of gambling was frowned on in the Olszewski household. Zarek figured it was a perfectly acceptable fib under the circumstances— admirable, even, in its credibility. As well as €150, he'd given his mother something to boast about to Kasia Zawadzka, who lived across the street, and whose daughter Margeta worked in the Polish embassy in London.

"Buy yourself something nice," he told his mother, knowing he was wasting his time. His father's shoes would be replaced, or the kitchen windows would get new curtains, or €50 would be slipped silently to his sister.

"Any news?" his mother asked.

Zarek thought. You had to have news when someone phoned you from Poland. "Work is busy," he said. "Weather is mixed. Anton is cooking Irish stew for dinner. Pilar still hates her job."

He wouldn't mention the drawing classes. Keep it simple.

"Have you met anyone nice?" his mother asked.

"Lots of nice people here in Ireland," Zarek replied. "So many nice people, like Polish people but with more freckles."

"Belshazzar," she said, "you know what I mean."

He knew what she meant.

"I must go, Mama," he told her. "The doorbell is ringing. Kiss Papa and Beata for me."

He hung up and walked into the galley kitchen, where Anton, who came from Brittany, had just begun to peel carrots for the Irish stew.

"Want to 'elp?" he asked.

Zarek rolled up his sleeves. "Yes, I want."

"You got a new dog."

Audrey started, her trowel slipping from her hand. "Kevin, you gave me a fright." So quietly he moved, like a cat. She should be used to it by now, but his sudden appearance on the other side of the dividing hedge startled her every time. She sat back on her hunkers and smiled up at him.

"Did you have a nice time in Cork?"

"Yeah." His piercing green eyes were still fixed on Dolly, who was looking up at him from Audrey's side of the hedge, tail wagging. "You got a new dog," he repeated.

Audrey stood up and lifted the pup towards him. "Yes, I did. I bought her in the pet shop. Isn't she lovely? Do you want to hold her?"

"No," he said, flinching back.

"Just pat her head so, to say hello."

He reached cautiously toward Dolly, but jerked his hand back quickly when the little dog lunged at it.

"It's okay," Audrey assured him. "She won't hurt you, she just loves licking things. It's her way of being friendly."

But he kept his distance, regarding her warily. "Where did you get it?" he asked.

"In the pet shop," Audrey told him again. "She was sitting in the window, in a special kind of box, and I thought she was gorgeous."

"Did you pay money?"

"Oh, I did, a lot of money. She was very dear."

"More than a euro?"

"Oh yes, much more."

Kevin was forty, with a beautiful unlined face and the mind of a young child. He'd been living next door with his mother, Pauline, when Audrey had bought her house three years previously. He rarely smiled, but would occasionally give a sudden bark of laughter, gone as quickly as it had come.

"Her name is Dolly," Audrey told him. "After Dolly Mixtures, because she's a mix of two different dogs."

"Why?"

"Her dad was one kind of dog, and her mum was another," Audrey explained. "So she's a mix of the two."

"I don't like Dolly Mixtures," he said, still watching the dog intently, "except the jelly ones. I like Mars bars better."

"Me too." Audrey bent and released Dolly, who raced down the garden.

"Where's it going now?" Kevin asked.

"Just for a little run," Audrey said. "She has lots of energy, doesn't she? Look how fast she can run."

"She's jumping in the flowers," Kevin said disapprovingly.

Audrey sighed. "Yes, she is."

Every morning Kevin and his mother walked to the local shop, Pauline holding him by the hand, for the daily paper and whatever other bits and pieces they needed. Twice a week Kevin was collected by mini bus and taken to a day center in the grounds of the local hospital, where he socialized for a few hours with other disabled residents of Carrickbawn.

"Audrey, there you are."

Pauline emerged from her house, holding a package wrapped in yellow paper. "We brought you a tiny little present from Cork, didn't we, love?" She handed it to Kevin. "Why don't you give it to Audrey?"

He passed it solemnly over the hedge.

"Ah, you didn't." Audrey unwrapped the package and lifted

out the blue plastic mug with her name spelled out on the side in colorful cartoon letters.

"It says *Audrey*," Kevin said. "I saw it."

"Well, that's just wonderful." Audrey smiled at him. "That's a lovely present, Kevin—thank you so much."

"And you got a new little dog," Pauline said. "Isn't he—" She stopped, her smile fading. "Oh, Audrey, what happened to your lovely dahlias?"

"I got a dog," Audrey said. "That's what happened."

"Oh no, isn't that awful. You'll have to train him not to do that. Look Kevin, the little dog dug up poor Audrey's flowers."

"And it tried to bite me," Kevin said.

"Oh, I wouldn't think so, love," Pauline said, exchanging a look with Audrey. "I'm sure he was just being friendly."

Kevin's father had walked out when it became clear that his son would never grow up mentally. He lived about fifty miles away with his second family, and Kevin hadn't seen him in over thirty years.

Pauline had worked all her life, cleaning houses, childminding, tending gardens, taking in other people's washing and ironing. When Kevin left his special school at eighteen Pauline gave up working outside the home, but two years later she was offered the job of housekeeper for a man whose wife had just died, leaving him with two young children.

As soon as it was agreed that Kevin could accompany her to the house each day Pauline accepted the job and kept it for ten years, until the children were old enough not to need her any more. The daughter of the house, in her twenties now, still visited her old housekeeper regularly, and Audrey knew her to see and say hello.

"Did you start your evening class?" Pauline asked.

"I did, on Tuesday."

"Well? How did it go?"

"Fine, apart from my model having last-minute nerves—oh, and apparently two people protested outside the college, although they were gone by the time I arrived, because my moped wouldn't start."

"Lord, it sounds like you had your hands full. What was the protest about?"

"Oh, they objected to the nudity."

"Well, haven't some people got little to do. And what are your students like?"

"Lovely—three women and two men."

"Two men—are they unattached? Anyone interesting?"

Audrey laughed. "You're worse than my mother. One is gorgeous but far too young, and the other is…very quiet."

Have you done this before? she'd asked James, and he'd said no, never, in his soft, singsong accent. His drawings were crude but they had a charming naïveté that appealed to Audrey. He'd given no indication that he'd enjoyed the class. He hadn't attempted, as far as she knew, to make conversation with any of the others throughout the evening, and he'd gone missing at the break. Hopefully he'd open up a bit over time.

When Pauline and Kevin left her to finish their unpacking, Audrey rinsed her gardening tools at the outside tap and returned them to the shed. Back in the kitchen she lit the oven and took a low-calorie pizza and a bag of oven chips from the freezer. She set the pizza on a baking sheet and added cubes of pineapple and strips of ham, and grated more cheese over the lot. No wonder it was low-calorie, with the tiny amount of topping they put on. She shook a generous handful of chips onto the tray beside the pizza. She wasn't overly keen on oven chips—much too dry, you had to *drown* them in vinegar—but they were so handy.

As she closed the oven door Dolly pattered in from the garden, soil scattering from her paws across the tiles. Audrey looked at her. "What am I going to do with you? When are you going to stop ruining the garden—not to mention the house? There isn't a thing left you haven't chewed."

At the sound of Audrey's voice the little dog wagged her tail. She trotted to her water bowl and began to lap noisily.

"I'm bringing you to the vet on Saturday," Audrey went on. "You might need a few vaccinations, and he might give me some tips on how to train you. You'll have to walk there, and it's quite a long way, but I've got no carrier." None of the supermarkets stocked them, and she was damned if she was going to darken that man's door again.

Dolly wandered away from the water bowl and pushed her head into the log basket, knocking two blocks onto the floor. She looked up at Audrey and barked happily.

Audrey smiled. "That's the trouble," she said, retrieving the blocks. "You're just so adorable."

"You're kidding."

Jackie spooned foam from her cappuccino and shook her head. "Swear to God."

"You stripped? Everything?"

"Every stitch. I was totally naked. *Totally*."

"*Jesus*." Her friend blew on her tea. "Weren't you mortified to have them all staring at you?"

"I was at the beginning, I thought I was going to throw up. But once I realized they weren't, you know, getting turned on by it—" she giggled "—I kind of relaxed."

"*Jesus*...I'd have *died*."

"Ah no, it's grand." Jackie ran her spoon around the rim of her mug, gathering more foam. "It's just art. There's nothing sleazy about it."

"I know, but still."

"And you can't breathe a word, remember. Not to anyone. Imagine if my folks got to hear."

"I know, don't worry."

"And…"—she licked the spoon—"…there's something else."

"What?"

"There's this guy in the class…it's nothing really, I haven't even talked to him—"

"But you fancy him, and he's seen you naked."

Jackie giggled again, her eyes on the steady stream of people passing the café window. "Well, yeah, I suppose—" She broke off abruptly. "Oh my God, I don't believe it."

Her friend swung around. "What? What is it?"

"He's just walked past," Jackie said. "Just this second, while we were talking about him. How weird is that?"

Looking different today, striding purposefully along the path in a dark shirt and grey trousers. Two nights ago he'd been in blue jeans and a white T-shirt, and a navy jacket had been slung across the back of his chair.

But it was him, she was sure.

"Go after him," her friend was urging. "Go on, just pass him and say hello."

"Ah no." She couldn't, not when she'd been sitting naked in front of him the night before. Not when he'd been looking at her breasts, and her thighs, and everything in between. "No, I'll leave him off."

But there were five more Tuesday evenings to go. Who knew what might happen in five evenings?

———————

The mechanic took Irene's business card from his wallet and looked at it. *Personal trainer*, he read. *All levels covered from beginner to advanced. Fully personalized fitness programs to tone and strengthen.* And below, a mobile telephone number and an email address.

He could see her in a leotard, or sweatpants and a T-shirt maybe. No high heels in the gym, a pair of runners. She wouldn't look bad in those either. A bit older than him, but in good nick—and game for a bit of fun, he was sure.

The toaster popped and he slid the card back and spread the warm slices with butter and gooseberry jam. The kettle boiled and he poured water onto the tea bag in his mug and added two spoons of sugar and a generous amount of milk. Using the bread board as a tray, he brought his supper into the sitting room and pressed "play" on the DVD remote control, and *Reservoir Dogs* came out of its freeze and swung back into action.

He ate his toast and watched the characters on the screen, and he thought about ringing the number on the little white card and booking a free trial with the personal trainer. He had tracksuit bottoms somewhere, they'd do if they didn't have paint on them, and if his wife hadn't thrown them out. His runners were a bit ancient, but he wasn't getting a new pair for just one session in a gym.

He lifted his mug and drank the hot, sweet, milky tea. He could use a bit of exercise, he wasn't doing anything wrong. He'd stayed late on Tuesday to finish off her car. It was just a little thank-you she was offering, along with the €50. Fifty euro—she must be loaded.

And if she came on to him, and if he took her up on it, and if nobody got hurt in the process, where was the harm?

He heard his wife's key in the door and he took his feet off the coffee table.

The Second Week

September 28—October 4

---

*An uncharacteristic outburst, an
unexpected encounter, and an
impulsive decision.*

Friday

"Can I go to Eoin's house to play? He says I can go."

James regarded his daughter over his not-very-good cheeseburger. "We'll see. Are you going to eat those chips, or just play with them?"

She bit the top off a skinny chip. "He lives with his granny and granddad."

"Who does?"

"Eoin."

"Oh."

"And his dad is in heaven."

"Ah." James lifted the lid on his burger and sniffed the bright orange slice of cheese. It smelled of nothing. "That's a pity. So his mum brings him to school."

"Yeah."

Charlie never talked about Frances now, never mentioned her at all. James remembered the incessant questions, right after it happened: *Where's Mummy? Why isn't she coming back? Where did she go? Why is she taking such a long time?* He remembered not knowing what to say, how he'd wanted to be honest with her. But how could he be honest, how could you explain "disappeared" to a four-year-old?

He tried to recall when the questions had finally stopped, when she'd given up trying to get answers. He wondered if she remembered her mother at all now, if she recalled her face, or her voice, or her smell. Two years in the life of a six-year-old would, he supposed, be long enough to banish a whole lot of memories.

"She has purple boots."

"Who?"

"Eoin's mum."

James smiled. "Has she? Maybe she's a witch."

Charlie threw him a pitying look. "She's not a witch, she works in a shop."

"Maybe they sell magic spells."

"*Daddy.*"

He heard voices and looked across at the counter. The girl who'd served them was in conversation with a man who'd just appeared, and who seemed to be taking over from her. James caught his eye and nodded at him. The man nodded back, giving a brief grin, but James wasn't sure if he remembered him.

"Do you know that man?" Charlie asked.

"I do," James told her. "He goes to my drawing class."

Charlie studied him. "Is he your friend?"

"He is. He's very good at drawing."

What had surprised James was how much he'd enjoyed the class. Oh, not that he'd produced a single worthy specimen—his efforts had been laughable, although the teacher had done her best to be encouraging. He seemed to remember her talking about the energy of his drawings, which he suspected was the kind of phrase people used when there was absolutely nothing positive to say.

But the clean smell of the paper, the tiny scratching sounds of his pencil, the squeak of the charcoal, the comforting squidgy feel of his putty rubber, the peaceful atmosphere in the room as everybody worked—all this he'd found wonderfully soothing. In fact, when the teacher had announced a break, he hadn't been able to believe that they were halfway through.

Not that it had started off well. Her late arrival had been annoying—was she going to make a habit of this, were they going to be twiddling their thumbs every Tuesday waiting for her? James had found himself obliged to make some effort at conversation with the Pole, who sat next to him. Thankfully, the man's broken English meant that they were limited to the smallest of small talk.

But when she'd eventually shown up, the teacher's obvious discomfiture aroused his sympathy—they could hardly blame her for a moped breakdown. All things considered, the evening had been much more pleasant than James had anticipated.

He'd still kept his distance from the others—although he couldn't avoid the odd glance at the Polish man's work, and he'd registered the much more accomplished drawings there. He'd also noted the nervousness of the model—you could hardly miss it, she'd looked like she was about to throw up. Clearly her first time, poor thing.

He had to admit that it felt good to be in the company of others who made no demands on him. It was the first step he'd taken towards having a social life in two years, and while he recognized the need to be part of society again, if only for Charlie's sake, he was wary at every turn.

He was glad now he hadn't signed up for French. In a language class there'd be conversations to be had, and probably other oral exercises to tackle. Inevitably, attention would have been focused on James from time to time—whereas in the drawing class he could work away on his own, with little need for conversation for the whole two hours.

The rest of them probably thought he was antisocial, which didn't bother him half as much as it probably should have. Over the past two years, he'd become adept at dismissing other people's opinions. When anonymous letter writers had sent him messages that were soaked in hate, when whispered conversations had stopped abruptly every time he walked into a shop, when people he'd known all his life had crossed the street to avoid him, he'd learned quickly enough to ignore it all, and he now realized how much it had hardened him.

"Finished," Charlie announced, pushing three chicken nuggets under her serviette.

"I saw that."

"What?" Smiling, not at all disconcerted. He was far too soft on her. "What, Daddy?"

"Wrap them up," he told her, "and we'll bring them home to Monster."

Monster was Eunice and Gerry's aptly named black cat. He carried out regular forays of the neighborhood gardens, demolishing birds and mice alike. Maybe a few pieces of processed chicken would get a stay of execution for the thrushes.

"When can I go to Eoin's house?" Charlie asked again as she bundled the nuggets into a clumsy parcel, and James knew the subject would have to be faced sooner or later.

"When I meet his mum," he answered, getting up. "Here, give me your schoolbag."

As they were leaving he caught the Polish man's eye again, and nodded a farewell. The Pole raised a hand before turning back to the giggling teenage girls in school uniforms who were placing their order.

Someone who looked like him would have no problem getting women—and being foreign probably added to his attraction. Looked like he had to fight them off.

James wondered sometimes if he'd ever have another relationship, if Frances would be replaced in time. Would he ever be able to get past what had happened, would he find the courage to try again with someone else? Although, with his history, he couldn't imagine any woman wanting to get involved with him.

He shepherded his daughter from the café, holding the door open for a young woman and a little boy who were just coming in. It was beginning to rain.

Carmel stood to one side, pretending to read the menu, until the schoolgirls had finished flirting with the man behind the counter. When they'd gone she walked up to him and said, "Large chip." As he ladled the chips into a cardboard box she counted out the amount from the coins she'd been given at the bus station.

"Can I have a burger?" Barry asked. It sounded like "bugguh" when he said it.

"No."

"Why not?"

"The chips'll be enough, you'll be full after them."

She handed the man her heap of coins, waiting for his sigh of impatience at all the copper, but he simply counted them into the various compartments of his cash register. When he had finished, Carmel said, "There's a sign in the window: 'Help Wanted.'"

"Okay," he replied, reaching under the counter and pulling out an application form. She liked that he was polite, that he didn't look at her the way most people did, as if she had no right to ask.

He passed the form across the counter. "You fill this, please. You need pen?"

Carmel looked at the form, and then back at him. "Can't I jus' talk to the manager?"

"No, sorry—manager is gone home now. She will come back tomorrow."

She. Carmel imagined a woman in high heels and red lipstick who'd dismiss her before she opened her mouth. "Will you hang on to the chips?" she asked the man, taking the form and folding it. "I'm just going into the toilets."

"Of course."

In the toilets she put the form in the bin and washed Barry's face and hands, using soap from the dispenser, and ran wet fingers through his hair.

"Do you have to wee?" she asked him, and he shook his head. She washed her own hair with a sachet of shampoo from the euro shop and rinsed it as best she could under the tap. She held her head under the hand dryer until Barry whimpered that he was hungry.

When they went back outside she saw the man looking at her damp hair, but he said nothing. She took the chips from him and sat with Barry at a table by the wall. Her hair smelled of oranges, but she could feel that the shampoo wasn't rinsed out properly. It would look greasy when it dried.

"I'm thirsty," Barry said, and she returned to the counter.

"Can I get some water?" she asked. "Jus' from the tap."

The foreign man filled a big paper cup and handed it to her. Back at the table she ate a chip as slowly as she could, her stomach growling, and counted the money she'd left, and got €4.27. They'd go to Dunnes and she'd get another bag of the mandarin oranges if they were still on special offer for €1.50, and a pack of Fig Rolls, which they both liked.

She tried to give Barry fruit every few days but it was dear in most places, and Lidl was far for him to walk to, so they only got there about once a week. They needed toothpaste too, but she'd get that in the euro shop when the older woman who saw nothing was on duty.

She thought of how her grandmother would feel if she knew Carmel was begging, and lifting things she couldn't afford to pay for. The thought of her grandmother made her want to cry. She rubbed her face hard until the feeling went away.

"My legs are tired," Barry said.

"I know, but you're sitting down now so they'll get a rest."

She glanced around the room. Only three other tables were occupied. The window to the left of them was spotted with rain.

Most people would have finished work by now and would be on their way home, planning what to cook for dinner, and what to do for the rest of the evening.

Warm clean houses with televisions and hot running water, and families who were happy together. She felt a piercing loneliness for what she'd lost, and for what she'd never had.

She knew the odds were stacked sky-high against her. The chances of anyone giving her a job without an application form filled out were next to nil. But she still looked, she kept on asking wherever she went, hoping for some kind of miracle to get her out of this nightmare, to keep her from being sucked back into the much worse place she'd been when she'd met Ethan.

Coming off drugs as soon as she realized she was pregnant had been hard, it had nearly killed her, but she'd done it. She was ashamed that she'd turned to dealing, ashamed that she'd survived at the expense of others, but she couldn't see a different way out. And if they hadn't gotten the stuff from her, they'd have gone somewhere else.

She'd never pushed it on anyone, she'd just sold it when she was asked. She hadn't charged over the odds, she'd been charitable where she could, but still she'd been a drug dealer, she'd paid for Barry's nappies and food by feeding the habits of addicts, and that was something she'd have to live with.

And then Ethan had died, and she'd almost gone back then, she'd almost given everything up. She would have, if she hadn't had Barry.

And realizing in the past few months that he'd soon be old enough to understand how his mother made her living, she'd decided to get out. That hadn't been easy either, there had been plenty of inducements to stay, and it would be a lie to say she hadn't been tempted.

But in the end Barry had made up her mind for her again— and because there'd been no question of her going back to her own family, not when Granny wasn't there anymore, she'd taken her courage in both hands and gone to see Ethan's father.

She'd known there wouldn't be a welcome for her—Ethan had rarely mentioned his family, but the little he'd said had been enough. Carmel had had a fair idea of how his father would be with them, and she hadn't been wrong.

The way he'd looked at them that first time, as if he was afraid of catching whatever they had. She supposed she couldn't blame him, the state of them. A smell off them too, she could get it herself. And it was only her word about Barry belonging to Ethan, so why would he believe her? She should have known it wouldn't do any good going back to him a second time.

And now they were sleeping in the old shed she'd discovered at the back of a house that was boarded up, in a street full of people you didn't want to look at you, and she was scrounging money from strangers and stealing what she had to, to survive.

And winter was coming. She sank her head into her hands, weary of trying to go on.

"Mammy."

She looked up.

"I have to do wee."

She got to her feet. "Come on." She took his half-eaten chips to the counter. "Can you mind these?" she asked the man. "He needs the toilet again."

They had over two hours to kill before it would be dark enough for them to sneak into the shed. They'd have to make the chips last. And maybe the rain would stop, maybe they'd at least get that.

———

Irene walked into the kitchen, causing her daughter and the au pair to look up simultaneously. Passing the table on her way to the fridge she saw, in no particular order, a jam jar of muddy-colored liquid, a large page sitting on an opened newspaper and smeared with puddles of colors, two vivid red splotches on the table to the left of the newspaper, various opened pots of poster paints, and a scattering of brushes.

She decided to concentrate on the red spills. "Pilar, please wipe that paint off the table before it dries in."

A beat passed, not unnoticed by Irene, before the au pair got to her feet. As she reached for the dishcloth that dangled from the tap mixer Irene added sharply, "Not that—please use damp kitchen paper. The dishcloth is only for washing up." How many times did the woman have to be told?

"Sorry," Pilar muttered, reaching for a paper towel.

"Irene," Emily said, "look at my picture."

Irene took a can of Diet Coke from the fridge before turning to regard the mess of watery colors running into each other. No outline that she could see, nothing remotely recognizable. Should three-year-olds not be a little more accomplished? Surely they should make a stab at drawing objects, rather than just slathering colored water on a page?

"Very nice," she said, popping the tab on her can. "Get Pilar to roll up your sleeves, they're getting wet." Anyone with an ounce of common sense would have done that before the painting started.

Irene regarded the top of the au pair's head as Emily's sleeves were rolled to the elbow, as the spilled paint was cleared away. She couldn't see why anyone who had hair as naturally dark as Pilar's would imagine they could get away with going blonde.

"Next time you're painting, please cover the table fully with newspaper," she said before turning toward the door. Well aware, as she left the kitchen, that the atmosphere she left behind was considerably cooler than the one she'd walked into. Training in a new au pair was always such a thankless task.

_____

"'There was once a little boy,'" Jackie read, "'whose name was Charlie.'"

"Charlie is a girl's name," Eoin said.

"Well, normally it's a boy's name. Anyway, 'Charlie lived with—'"

"Why is it normally a boy's name?"

She lowered the book. "Because Charlie is short for Charles, which is a boy's name, but sometimes girls are called Charlie for short, if their name is Charlotte, or…Charlene, or something. Ask your friend at school if her name is short for something else, and I bet she says yes." She waited for another question but none came. "Will I go on with the story?"

"Yeah."

"'Charlie lived with his mum and dad in a small yellow house.'"

"Charlie's mum got lost."

Jackie stopped again and looked at him. "Did she?" The first mention he'd made of Charlie's mother.

"Yeah, a long time ago. Everybody looked for her, but nobody could find her."

"Oh…that's too bad. I'm sorry to hear that."

"Got lost" sounded like a peculiar way to explain death to a child—wasn't it a bit odd, didn't it leave the possibility open in the child's mind that the mother might suddenly reappear someday?

"I said my dad is in heaven," Eoin added, "so maybe her mum went there."

"Yes, maybe," Jackie said quickly. "Let's get on with the story, will we?"

What else could she have said when he'd asked about his father? It had seemed the simplest explanation—although she wondered what she'd do in years to come if he decided he wanted to look up his father's family. She'd deal with that when it happened.

"Can Charlie come to our house to play?"

"Of course she can, as soon as I meet her dad."

Charlie was always in the classroom by the time they arrived—Jackie dropped Eoin to school on her way to work at the boutique, and they usually made it by the skin of their teeth. Jackie's mother collected Eoin after school every day except Thursday, Jackie's day off.

But there was never any sign of the father on Thursday afternoons either—not that Jackie had been actively looking for him up to this. She supposed she'd have to make it her business to make contact with him if Eoin insisted on his new friend coming to play.

"Next time I collect you," she promised. "I'll talk to her dad then. If he comes before I get there, ask him to hang on."

But Eoin shook his head. "He doesn't come at home time—she goes to Little Rascals."

"Oh."

She'd have to think of another way to track down the elusive father. Maybe she could ask the teacher to deliver a message, or at least pass on Jackie's phone number so he could make contact. Arranging her son's social calendar wasn't proving too straightforward.

"I'll talk to Mrs. Grossman next week," she said, raising the book again. "We'll figure something out. Now come on, or we'll never get this done."

They finished the story and she kissed him good night and went downstairs, leaving his bedroom door ajar and the landing light on. In the sitting room her parents were watching the news. Jackie sat next to her mother and thought about the good-looking man from the art class again.

She wondered what job he had. He'd been well dressed in the

street: Maybe he worked in an office of some kind. He probably had a partner. Most people had found someone by the time they got to his age, which she guessed was somewhere in his late thirties or early forties.

They had yet to exchange a single word, and he'd seen Jackie fully undressed. How strange was that? Before the life drawing class she'd shown her naked body to exactly three men, and they'd all been similarly undressed at the time. And she'd had some degree of interaction with each of them before they'd taken off their clothes.

The first had been a boy she'd met at fifteen, the brother of a girl in her class, who'd walked her home from a teenage disco and become her first proper boyfriend. They'd deflowered each other when Jackie had been sixteen, late one night in the shed at the bottom of his parents' garden.

The experience had been both embarrassing and painful for Jackie, and on the two occasions they'd repeated it, there had been no significant improvement. Shortly afterwards he'd ended the relationship, and she'd done her best to hide her relief.

Eoin's father had followed, the summer she was seventeen, an encounter she could barely remember, and whose consequence understandably caused her to lose her taste for men for some time afterwards. When Eoin was three she met another man on a night out with some friends, who charmed her into his bed after a few dates, and dropped her abruptly after a few more.

Three men, a handful of sexual encounters: She was hardly what you'd call experienced in that area. Ironic, when people who heard she'd become a single mother at eighteen probably assumed she was jumping into bed with men every night of the week. In fact, the man at the art class was the first man to interest her in a long time. And chances were he was happily married.

But maybe he wasn't.

Saturday

S he's definitely got some Yorkshire terrier in her," the vet told
Audrey, scratching the top of Dolly's head. "She's crossed
with another small breed, possibly a Maltese or something similar. I can't be sure without talking to the original owner. Where
did you get her?"

Audrey named the pet shop.

"Ah yes," the vet said. "Michael Browne."

"Does Michael Browne have a beard and glasses?" Audrey
asked.

"He does."

Audrey waited, but no further comment was made. Either the
vet had only met Michael Browne on a good day, or he was being
extremely diplomatic.

"Dolly is very lively," she told him. "I find her quite hard to
manage."

The vet nodded. "You'll need lots of patience. House-training
is a slow job, unfortunately. But don't be afraid to be firm when
she does something that's not on. A smack on the nose, or on the
rear end, won't do her a bit of harm, and it'll give her something
to think about."

"Oh." Audrey doubted that she could find it in her to smack
Dolly, however much she might deserve it.

"You probably find that she chews things," the vet went on.

Audrey nodded. "Everything."

"Get her a rubber bone; that'll keep her distracted. Some people recommend an old slipper, but I feel that just gives them the idea that all slippers are chewable. Michael will have rubber bones."

"Right." One of Audrey's old slippers would do fine, if it meant avoiding a visit to the pet shop.

The vet lifted Dolly's head and examined her teeth. "She's about twelve or thirteen weeks old, I'd say—again, hard to be accurate without talking to the owner. Did Michael tell you whether she's been vaccinated?"

"No, and I forgot to ask. But even if she has, would it do her any harm to get another dose?"

The vet made a face. "Not a good idea—I'd need to know if she's been started on a course, otherwise it's very hit-and-miss. Could you call back to the pet shop and ask Michael?"

Audrey's heart sank. Was there a conspiracy afoot to get her to revisit that man's premises? "I suppose I could…" she said doubtfully.

The vet smiled. "His bark is worse than his bite, you know."

Audrey looked unconvinced. "His bark is bad enough."

It was the last thing she wanted. The prospect of coming face-to-face with him again was unpalatable in the extreme, but he was the only person who might have information about Dolly's vaccinations, so it looked like a return visit was unavoidable. Was she never to be rid of him?

She'd go on Monday, on her way home from school. And as long as she was going back, she'd pick up a pet carrier, and a rubber bone. Much as she hated giving him any more business, they would make life considerably easier.

———

Saturdays were always good, she didn't know why. Maybe the supermarket did a special clear-out on Saturdays. She lifted the lid
of the Dumpster and waved the smell away with her hand as she
ran her eye quickly over the tumble of boxes and packets and bags
inside. She pulled out a tray of dates, a few cartons of yogurt, sandwiches wrapped in plastic, a packet of cheese slices, and a box of
jellies. There were trays of kiwi fruit but she couldn't reach them,
and some tomatoes but they had furry stuff growing on them.

"Is there crisps?"

"No," she said, "no crisps." He'd live on crisps if she let him.

She stuffed most of the food into the plastic bag she'd used so
much the writing had all come off the front of it. She opened the
tray of dates and handed one to Barry. "Try this, it's nice."

They had no way of cooking, so the only hot food he got was
if they went to a chip shop. She didn't know what they'd do
when the weather got colder and he was eating mostly cold food.
And would they even survive a frosty night in that shed? She was
scared all the time of being in charge of Barry with nobody to ask
when she didn't know something.

She tried to give him different food to eat so he'd have a mix of
good and bad. She remembered the dinners Granny used to cook
for them, bacon and cabbage with white sauce, stews full of different vegetables, roast chicken sometimes on Sundays, although
everyone fought over the legs.

Barry began to make a funny noise. She looked down and saw
that his face had gone bright red, and was all screwed up.

"*Jesus*—" She reached a finger back into his throat and yanked
out the date stone and threw it away. He retched and brought up
a small amount of brown mush.

"Sorry," she said, wiping his mouth with her sleeve. "I forgot
about the stone. Are you all right?"

"I don't like them things," he whispered, his eyes wet from the
choking. "I want crisps."

Carmel hugged him tightly, her heart going wild. "Okay," she said. "Come on, we'll get crisps."

————————

"Can I get my hair dyed?" Charlie asked.

"Sure," James replied. "How about blue?"

She didn't laugh, like he'd been expecting. "No, I want purple."

He stopped and looked at her. "You're serious."

"'Course I am. Loads of people dye their hair."

He resumed walking. "Not at your age they don't. When you're grown up, you can dye it whatever color you like."

She sighed dramatically. He wondered what she'd be like at thirteen if she was beginning to show diva tendencies at six. Up ahead he spotted the hairdressing salon—and walking into the sandwich bar on the far side of it was a woman he knew but couldn't place. Dark hair, a phone clamped to her ear as she pushed open the door.

Who was she? And then he realized, and laughed softly. He hadn't recognized her with her clothes on.

"What?"

"Just saw someone I knew," he told Charlie. "Someone from the drawing class." They reached the salon and he ushered her inside.

"Come on," he said, "let's make you look like a beautiful princess."

"*Daddy*." But she smiled.

Sunday

It took a minute or two for the crying to register. Irene lowered her magazine and scanned the crowded playground, but didn't see her daughter. She got to her feet, frowning—and just then Emily appeared from behind the slide, still wailing, holding the hand of a skinny teenage girl who was leading her towards Irene's bench. A little towheaded boy trotted behind them, his eyes fixed on Emily.

Irene sat down again. When the trio got closer, she saw the blood on her daughter's knee. She laid her magazine on the bench and opened her bag and pulled out a travel pack of wipes, regretting her choice of cream jeans for the trip to the park.

When she reached her mother, Emily set up a fresh burst of sobbing. Irene hoisted her onto the bench. "Silly old thing—what have you done?"

"She fell off the ladder," the teenager said. "Her foot slipped." Her voice was flat, no inflection in the words. Her face was pale, her black top rumpled. A good wash wouldn't go astray. Close up, she also looked older than Irene's original estimate. Twenty, or thereabouts.

Irene pulled a wipe from the pack and dabbed at the cut, keeping the bloody knee and the cream jeans as far apart as possible. She was conscious of the woman's eyes on her, and of her handbag sitting on the bench within easy reach.

"Thanks for bringing her over," Irene said. "She'll be fine now."

They remained standing there, both of them watching the proceedings mutely. Irene wondered if one of them was going to make a lunge for the handbag. Maybe the boy was being trained, like one of Fagin's pickpockets.

Emily winced as her mother worked. "Ow, you're *hurting* me."

"Keep still then," Irene said, gripping the leg firmly by the ankle. "You need to be brave, I have to clean it."

She felt irritated by the continued presence of the others. Maybe they weren't thieves, maybe they were waiting instead for some kind of reward.

"I could look after her," the woman said suddenly. "If you wanted someone, I mean. I'm lookin' for a job, and I have my own child." Indicating the boy, who promptly stuck his thumb in his mouth and pressed closer to her side. "They were playin' together when it happened," she said.

Emily, playing with that ragamuffin. Irene would have to keep a closer eye on her in future. She pulled another wipe from the pack and dabbed at the cut again. "Thanks," she repeated, "but I already have someone."

When the woman still didn't move away, Irene reached for her bag and rummaged in it until she found a fiver. "Here," she said, "I appreciate your help." Tucking the bag casually between her feet as she smiled brightly at them.

For a second she thought the money wasn't going to be accepted. A beat passed before the woman put out her hand.

"Thanks," she mumbled, slipping the note quickly into the pocket of her jeans. She turned, grabbing the boy's hand. When they had gone about ten paces he looked back at Emily, but the woman immediately pulled him around again.

Talk about optimistic. Irene would want to be pretty desperate to employ someone like her to look after Emily. Much as Pilar irritated her, with her sloppy timekeeping and careless cleaning—

deliberately misunderstanding the instructions half the time, no doubt—Irene had to concede that Emily was in safe hands when she was with the au pair. And Pilar was always fairly well turned out, even if she could use a bit more deodorant at times.

But this woman had definitely been brought up on the wrong side of the tracks, in her grubby clothes and those dead eyes. Imagine the accent Emily would have after a week with her. Irene wouldn't be surprised if she was on drugs, she looked the type. And the boy, with that blank, half-witted stare—for all Irene knew he could have pushed Emily off the ladder, just so they could claim some reward.

Compared with them, Pilar was practically a saint.

"Right," Irene said, packing away the wipes, "let's go home and put you into the bath."

"I want Smarties," Emily said, sniffing.

"Well, you certainly won't get them if you ask like that."

She'd never pretended, she'd always been honest about not wanting children. Martin had known where she stood before he'd married her; she'd never lied to him. He'd probably been convinced that he'd change her mind somewhere along the way, but Irene had known it would never happen. She hadn't a maternal bone in her body.

It had been nobody's fault when the contraceptive hadn't worked. Her first instinct had been to have an abortion, but she hadn't bargained for Martin's persistence: He'd worn her down with his pleading and his promises of full-time nannies, and because Irene loved him, she'd finally given in. She'd been sick all the way through her pregnancy, as if her body was confirming what her mind had always insisted—she wasn't designed for motherhood.

She'd endured twenty hours of labor, sixteen without an epidural, despite her screams. And the baby, when it was finally placed in her arms, looked exactly like an aunt Irene had never gotten on with. She'd regarded her new daughter and felt precisely nothing, apart from an overwhelming urge to sleep.

It had taken months of crunches and lettuce leaves for her abs to recover fully. The nanny that Martin had promised had turned into six different nannies by the time Emily was three—for reasons Irene couldn't fathom none had stayed longer than a few months, and one had walked out after three days.

In between nannies, Martin was the one who stayed at home while Irene went to work. It made perfect sense: He was the boss, he could easily delegate, whereas Irene would have gone mad stuck in the house with a small child all day.

And now they had Pilar, who'd been with them for just three weeks, and who was already irritating the hell out of Irene.

"My knee hurts," Emily whimpered as she slid off the bench.

"It'll get better," Irene replied, slinging her bag onto her shoulder.

———————

Michael didn't often visit the park. The manicured lawns and ordered flower beds held little attraction for him—he preferred his nature wild—and the ubiquitous evidence of dogs whose owners couldn't be bothered to clean up after them, despite prominently posted reminders, was profoundly depressing. Further proof, not that he needed it, of the innate selfishness of the human race.

But walking home from the graveyard earlier he'd felt an uncharacteristic reluctance to return to his empty, silent house, so on impulse he'd turned in the park gates and claimed a bench that was far enough away from the play area for the shrieks of children not to irritate. He determined to sit and enjoy the sunshine, and banish the gloomy thoughts that had dogged him lately.

Easier said than done. Every woman who passed with a small

child—and who'd have guessed how many of them were in Carrickbawn?—reminded him of the girl's departure in tears from the shop four days previously. And try as he might, he hadn't been able to get them out of his head since then, hadn't been able to stop the doubts from tormenting him.

Had he done the right thing, sending them packing? What if she'd been telling the truth, and the boy was indeed Ethan's? Had Michael turned his back on his own grandson?

Oh, he had all the arguments to justify his actions. She was a drug dealer, she'd admitted that. How could he trust anything she said? He'd seen what drugs did to people, how they wiped away decency and left cunning and dishonesty in its place. He'd done what he felt to be the right thing: Why couldn't he leave it at that?

His throat was dry. He was too hot, his clothes all wrong for this unseasonable weather. The last day of September and everyone wilting in the heat. The climate had certainly gone haywire. He thought longingly of a glass of ice-cold beer, or even ice-cold water. He became aware of a repeated yapping somewhere to his left, and he turned, frowning, to see what animal was responsible.

She sat two benches away, the little dog attached to her wrist by a red leather leash, and she ate an ice cream cone. Michael couldn't remember the last time he'd eaten a cone. He watched her lips closing over the soft whiteness of it, and he imagined the cold, creamy taste in his own mouth, slipping down his throat, cooling deliciously as it went.

He watched her licking the drips from her fingers as the little dog pawed at her skirt and attempted to scramble, still yapping, onto her lap. Yes, a handful, by the looks of it. Hardly surprising that she'd come back to the shop asking for his advice.

He'd been a bit short with her, he acknowledged it. She'd caught him at a bad time, arriving just as he was throwing the other two out. Probably had him pegged as a cranky old so-and-so—which of course he was.

She seemed oblivious to the dog's demands for attention. She was totally taken up with the ice cream, and clearly enjoying it. There was something oddly appealing in her complete abandonment to the sensory pleasure the food was affording her. She ate with the greedy preoccupation of a small child, everything else forgotten.

The sweat trickled down Michael's back. The sun blazed on his face, but he was mesmerized by the scene in front of him. He watched her tipping back her head to bite off the end of the cone, and he remembered doing the same as a boy, sucking out the soft ice cream that was lodged inside, pulling it down into his mouth.

When the cone was gone, she licked the ends of each of her fingers again before rummaging in the red canvas bag that sat beside her on the bench. She pulled out a tissue and wiped her hands and dabbed at her mouth. She wore a white skirt that was splashed with giant blobs of scarlet and purple and bright blue, and a loose, flowing yellow top whose sleeves ended at her elbows.

Her face, what he could see of it, was pink with warmth. He liked to see naturally rosy cheeks, far nicer than some paint that had come out of a pot. When would women learn to leave their faces alone?

She bent and murmured something to the little dog, whose yaps increased in volume and whose tail immediately began to wag vigorously. As she got to her feet Michael ducked his head and pretended to be tying a shoelace, but when he heard no sound of their approach he glanced up and saw her walking off in the opposite direction, the little dog straining at the leash as she attempted to cross the grass towards a flower bed. Michael heard her owner say a sharp "*No.*"

When they were no longer in sight he rose from his bench and made his way to the little kiosk by the park's main gate, and he bought an ice cream cone for the first time in years.

It tasted wonderful.

Pilar reached across the table for the bowl of Parmesan cheese, her sleeve narrowly avoiding contact with Anton's plate of food. "My boss is crazy woman," she said.

Zarek twirled spaghetti around his fork and thought of the small boy who'd come into the café a few days before with a girl who looked too young to be his mother, but who probably was. Such a pinched little face he'd had, so pale and lost looking, not responding in the least to the smile Zarek had given him.

"You know what she say me?" Pilar demanded, sprinkling cheese liberally over her Bolognese sauce. "She say I must clean toilets every day—*pah!*"

And the girl had been pathetic too, in her shabby clothes and with eyes too old for her face. Zarek had known, handing her the job application form, that there was little chance of someone with her appearance being taken on by Sylvia.

"Cleaning toilets every day is waste," Pilar declared crossly. "We clean one time in week, and our toilet is okay, yes? One clean on Saturday, we are okay, yes?"

The two of them had still been sitting there when Zarek's shift had ended at seven, their single portion of chips long since eaten, the girl's newly washed hair drying slowly. He wondered how much longer they'd stayed, and where they'd gone afterwards. If she had to wash her hair in a café toilet, what kind of accommodation could they possibly have?

"I not understand," Pilar said, "how stupid woman is mama to beautiful little girl. But she is not good mama, she is very bad mama. The papa, he look after Emily, not the mama."

Zarek thought the girl in the café cared about the little boy. He'd seen the way she'd watched him as he'd eaten the chips she'd bought, how she'd hardly taken any herself, although she'd looked hungry enough to Zarek. He hoped the cardboard box of chips hadn't been their only meal of the day.

"*Zarek.*"

He pulled himself back to the present. Pilar was frowning at him.

"I ask if you want bathroom later," she said. "I need bath for one hour."

"Please," Zarek said, "remain in bath as long you like. Two hour if you want."

"Is good for skin," Anton added, "to remain in bath for two hour."

Monday

O ne missed call, Irene read when she came out of the shower. One new voice mail. She connected to her mailbox and listened.

Might take you up on that offer of a trial session, the mechanic said, and left a mobile number. No name, just a number. What did they need names for? Irene disconnected and threw her phone onto the bed. Five days since she'd given him her card, he'd taken his time. She dropped her towel into the laundry hamper and began to dress.

Martin walked in as she was putting on her skirt. "You coming in today?"

"Afternoon," she replied, crossing to the wardrobe and taking her shirt from its hanger. "Half past two."

One of the advantages of being married to the boss was that you came and went as you pleased. You made your own appointments and were answerable to nobody. Today she had just two sessions, one with Joan, who was training for the London Marathon, and the other with Bob, a successful businessman too fond of his long lunches, whose doctor had issued an ultimatum that included an hour in the gym at least twice a week.

Bob regularly left her in no doubt that given half a chance, he'd be happy to take Irene to a hotel for the afternoon. She ignored his innuendos as she put him through his paces; the thought of his sweaty, overweight body shedding its navy tracksuit made her shudder.

"Can you pick up my grey suit?" Martin asked, taking his watch from the dressing table and slipping it onto his wrist.

"I can." He was magnificent in a suit, an animal tamed with a well-cut jacket.

"Thanks." He left the room again, and Irene smelled in his wake the delicious tang of the Tom Ford aftershave she'd given him for his last birthday.

She opened the bedroom window and smoothed the sheet on the bed before pulling up the duvet. Pilar stayed out of this room when she cleaned: Irene figured the less temptation was put in the way of the Lithuanian au pair, the less likely she was to give in to it.

In the kitchen Emily was eating her usual mashed banana and yogurt mixture.

"Hi there," Irene said, resting a hand briefly on her daughter's curly hair. Martin was usually the one to get Emily up and dressed each morning. He liked getting up early, it was no big deal for him—and where was the sense in both of them running around after one small child?

"Doesn't she look pretty?" he asked, filling a little container with raisins and sunflower seeds and carrot sticks to put in Emily's lunchbox.

"Of course she does," Irene replied, pouring coffee. She opened the fridge as the doorbell rang.

"Pilar!" Emily slid off her chair and dashed out to the hall, Martin following.

Irene sipped her coffee and listened to the flurry of greetings. Pilar's throaty laugh, Emily's chatter, Martin's deep voice. When Pilar eventually appeared, Emily was swinging from her arm.

"I fell off the ladder in the park and my knee was hurted," the little girl was saying. "It was all bleeding, Irene had to clean it. Look, I'll show you."

Irene nodded. "Morning, Pilar."

"Good morning, Mrs. Dillon," Pilar replied.

"Look, Pilar," Emily repeated.

"Oh dear, my poor Emily," Pilar said. "You want I kiss it better?"

Emily nodded, and Pilar put her lips to the scratched knee and kissed it loudly.

"There—now it will get better very fast. But you must be careful in park, no climb on big things, too much danger for you. Now please, you finish the breakfast, yes? And then we go to school and you say hello to all your little friends."

Easy to see, as Emily obediently sat at the table and picked up her spoon, how good Pilar was with her, how well she handled the three-year-old. Perfectly understandable why Martin held the au pair in such high esteem. Look at him pouring coffee for her now, as if she were someone who'd dropped in socially instead of the hired help. As far as Martin was concerned, Pilar was the best thing since sliced bloody bread.

"I'd like you to take down the curtains in the sitting room today," Irene said. "I'm bringing them in for cleaning later. And you can clean the windows in that room too, both sides. There's a stepladder in the shed."

"I'll get it out before I go," Martin said immediately. Of course.

"And Pilar," Irene went on, "would you please remember to clean the base of the toilet bowls when you're doing the bathrooms?"

"Please?"

"The part underneath," Irene said, gesturing. "Under the toilet. Below."

Such a nuisance, having to explain everything. You'd think they'd take the trouble to learn the language properly if they expected to be employed.

"What's on for you this morning?" Martin asked. Jumping in

like he always did to protect the poor au pair, who was being harassed by her nasty employer.

"I'll be in and out," Irene answered shortly. "Nothing major." She disliked him asking her about her day in front of Pilar—who knew what the au pair would get up to if she thought she had the place to herself for a few hours? Irene usually said nothing when she left the house: Better that Pilar assumed she'd be back any minute.

"Right," she said, setting her cup on the draining board. "See you later everyone, have a good day." Brushing Martin's cheek briefly with her lips, keeping up the pretense that they were a perfectly normal married couple, laying a hand on Emily's head again as she passed.

Upstairs she applied lipstick and blotted it. She stroked on eyeliner and two coats of mascara. When she heard a car starting up, she crossed to the window and watched Martin backing out of the driveway and heading down the street. She sprayed perfume and slipped on her silver bangle, and checked the cash in her wallet.

A minute later the front door opened and closed. Irene listened to her daughter's chatter that floated up to the open bedroom window—"broke my red crayon, and Meg was *cross* with him"—until her voice faded and disappeared.

Irene took her phone off the bed and replayed the message the mechanic had left while she'd been in the shower. She remembered his dark eyes, the muscles popping on his arms as he'd braced himself against her car.

She took her keys from her bedside locker and left the room.

———

Jackie took off Eoin's jacket and hung it on a hook. As she crossed the classroom in the direction of the teacher's desk she waved to Charlie, who waved back.

Mrs. Grossman was bent over a bundle of copies. Jackie waited until she looked up.

"Jackie," she said. "What can I do for you?"

"I'm trying to get in touch with Charlie's father," Jackie replied. "I always seem to miss him in the morning, so I was wondering if you could pass on a note."

"Certainly."

"Thanks very much." Jackie pulled an envelope from her bag. "It's just that Eoin has been pestering me to let Charlie come and play after school sometime." In case Mrs. Grossman thought she had designs on the man with a lost wife.

"Yes, I can imagine—they've been joined at the hip since Charlie came to the school. But she's a lovely little thing." Mrs. Grossman took the envelope from Jackie. "I'll put it into her lunchbox when she's finished—that way he'll be sure to see it."

Jackie smiled. "Great, thanks again. I'll get out of your way."

She glanced in Eoin's direction as she walked towards the door, intending to wave good-bye, but he was too busy chatting with Charlie to notice her.

———

"I assume you remember me," she said stiffly.

"I do."

Not looking too happy today. Still mad at him, no doubt, for sending her off to buy a book the other day. Ah well, she'd get over it.

"I brought her to the vet on Saturday, and he needs to know what vaccinations she's had."

"I can't help you there," Michael told her. "That dog was abandoned on my doorstep."

Two lines appeared in her forehead. "Abandoned?"

"Tied to the door handle," he said, "with a piece of rope."

She looked offended. Probably blamed him for someone dumping the dog outside his shop.

"Look," he said, as patiently as he could manage, "I think it's safe to assume that she's had no shots. Anyone who leaves a dog on a doorstep isn't likely to shell out money at the vet's before-hand."

She digested this in silence. She smelled of honey—or was it strawberries? Something sweet anyway. Maybe she'd been eating more ice cream. Maybe she had one a day, to keep the doctor away.

"I also need a carrier," she said, "and a rubber bone."

"Carriers in the far aisle," he told her, pointing. "Toys there, on the left."

He watched her walk off. That was some rear view. Obviously loved her food, which was rare enough in a woman these days. Not that he saw anything wrong with a bit of flesh on a female. He'd always been trying to put weight on Ruth, but no matter what he fed her she'd never put on an ounce, and their daughter was turning out the same.

This woman liked her bright colors, in that yellow skirt and blue flowery top. Not afraid to be seen, not attempting to hide her size. Maybe she was some class of a bohemian, one of those free spirits who didn't care what anyone thought of her. Probably lit incense and meditated. Maybe that was what he'd been smelling, incense.

He bet she talked to the dog too. Probably called it Krishna.

She reappeared. "I'll take these," she said, laying the carrier and bone on the counter and opening her bag.

"Twenty-six fifty," Michael said. "I don't have a bag that size."

Her round cheeks flooded with sudden color. She dug into her handbag and pulled out €30 and slammed the notes onto the counter.

"And even if you did," she burst out, "you'd probably make a song and dance about giving it to me. You are the *rudest* man I have ever met—and have you *never* heard of 'please' or 'thank you'?"

It was totally unexpected. Michael wondered if she was going to jump the counter and wallop him with her green-and-pink umbrella. "If I had a big enough bag," he said mildly, taking her money and handing over her change, "I'd give it to you."

She made some kind of sound that was halfway between a snort and a disbelieving grunt as she snatched the change from him. "I don't *need* a bag," she snapped, "but a bit of common courtesy wouldn't go amiss."

He watched bemusedly as she grabbed her purchases, hanging on to her umbrella with difficulty as she marched to the door without another word. He made no move to open it for her, sensing it might be safer to stay where he was.

As she maneuvered herself and her goods through the doorway she glared back at him. "And *thank you* for opening the door, so *mannerly* of you."

Michael came out from behind the counter, wanting to say *I was afraid of getting a wallop* but deciding to leave well enough alone and hold his peace. By the time he was halfway across the shop floor the door had slammed behind her.

He scratched at his beard. What had he said? As far as he was aware, he'd been perfectly civil. Was she upset because he couldn't say for sure whether the dog had been vaccinated? What did she expect him to do, make the information up?

He shook his head and went back to his newspaper. Having a bad day by the sound of it, which everyone was entitled to. No call for her to take it out on him though.

———

"Cooee! Lovely day, isn't it?"

James pegged a sock before turning towards the sound. Not

for the first time, he wondered if Eunice lay in wait behind her net curtains, watching until he went out to the garden. He never seemed to manage a trip to the clothesline without her putting in an appearance across the fence.

"Hello there." He lifted a second sock from the bundle of damp washing and hung it next to its partner.

"You'd never think it was October, would you? Mind you, it's not as warm as yesterday—that was a real scorcher, wasn't it? Gerry and I went out to the lake. You haven't been there yet, have you?"

"No, I haven't."

"Oh, you must take Charlie, she'd love it. You could bring a little picnic and go for a swim; it's quite safe if you stay near the shore."

"Sounds good."

James had heard of the lake from someone at work. About ten miles from Carrickbawn, popular with families, apparently. A good place to bring children, he'd heard, with its little pebbly shore and a walking trail that went all the way around.

"So," Eunice went on, watching as James hung a shirt on the line, "you're settling in to Carrickbawn?"

"We are, Charlie has made lots of friends at school." He picked up a towel and flapped it out of its folds.

"And you're finding the job all right?"

"Grand." Two more towels, a couple more shirts, a few T-shirts of Charlie's. "Will the weather hold, d'you think?"

"Oh, it can't really, can it? I mean, it's October. Although the forecast is good for the week, but then they often get it wrong, don't they?"

"Sure do, aye."

"So you'll be off to your class again tomorrow night."

"I will, as long as you're okay to babysit."

"Oh, I am, she's no bother at all—and your bedtime story over the phone was a great idea, she went off right after it."

"I used to do it," he said, "when she was younger, and I was working late." Kicking himself as soon as the words were out, breaking his own rule of never mentioning his life before Carrickbawn.

"This was when you lived up north," Eunice said. "What part was it again?"

"Donegal."

"And was it the same kind of work you were doing up there?"

"More or less," he said, picking up the empty laundry basket. "Now you'll have to excuse me, but I'd better go and check on dinner—it's probably burned to a crisp."

Dinner had been eaten half an hour ago, but what Eunice didn't know wouldn't hurt her.

———

Audrey climbed into the steaming, scented water and settled down, positioning the little inflated pillow behind her shower-cap-covered head. She closed her eyes and breathed deeply, and waited for the feeling of contentment that her nightly bath normally afforded her.

Nothing happened.

She inhaled again, breathing in the patchouli fragrance that she'd loved since her teens. *Relax,* she told herself, *let it go.* But of course she couldn't.

You are the rudest man I've ever met. Had she really said that? In her whole life Audrey Matthews had never openly confronted anyone. When she encountered a lack of manners she made allowances, she gave the benefit of the doubt, she tried to placate, or held her tongue and offered it up.

Until today.

Have you never heard of "please" or "thank you"? She groaned aloud. What had possessed her? *A bit of common courtesy wouldn't go amiss.* How could she have lost her composure so badly? *Thank you for opening the door, so mannerly of you.* Her mother would be mortified. "Be polite," she'd drilled into her only daughter as Audrey was growing up. "Never stoop to the level of anyone who annoys you. Never forget that you're a lady."

Well, today it had been well and truly forgotten: Audrey had been more like a fishwife than a lady in that pet shop. And banging the door on her way out, like a spoiled child. She pressed hot, wet hands to her face, squeezing her eyes closed, trying to push the awful memory away.

Not that he didn't deserve it, mind. He *was* the rudest man she'd ever met. Everything he said, everything he did was designed to provoke. Look how unhelpful he'd been on her previous visit, when she'd simply asked him for advice. Get a book, he'd said—no, not said, *snapped.* As if Audrey hadn't paid an *outrageous* sum for Dolly the week before, as if she weren't entitled to a modicum of respect. The man was a buffoon; of that she was convinced.

But all that was beside the point. The point was, Audrey had lowered herself to his level; she'd been just as rude as he was. She'd let herself down badly, there was no excuse for it. She groaned again, sliding deeper into the water.

And the worst of it all was that she'd blown up at the most innocuous remark. All he'd said was that he didn't have a big enough bag for the carrier, which was perfectly understandable. It didn't even need a bag, for goodness' sake, with its own handle. In fact, she'd probably have turned one down if it had been offered.

But she'd been so *irritated* by his blithe admission that a dog he'd charged her €50 for had been abandoned on his doorstep— such a *nerve* the man had, not an ounce of shame—that she was just waiting for him to open his mouth again before she exploded. If he'd commented on the weather she'd probably have found something objectionable in that.

There was no way she could leave things as they were. *He* might have taken her outburst in his stride—she wouldn't be surprised if people verbally abused him on a regular basis—but Audrey was thoroughly ashamed of it. Her conscience, or maybe her mother, simply wouldn't allow her to move on until she'd gone back and apologized to him.

She slithered down until her head was under the water. She lay there, hearing the dull thrum of her own blood in her ears, trying to blot out the awful prospect. When her lungs felt as if they were going to burst she wriggled upwards again, spluttering and gasping and causing a wave of water to splash over the side of the bath, drenching her purple mules.

The thought of apologizing to him was horrifying—picture her humiliation, imagine his satisfaction. But it had to be done, she had to make amends and recover her dignity. Audrey heaved herself from the water—the bath simply wasn't working its magic tonight—and reached for a towel, ignoring the puddles on the floor.

She'd open a half bottle of red when she went downstairs. If she had a headache in the morning she'd know exactly who to blame.

Tuesday

Michael scrolled down the page until he found what he was looking for. He clicked on the icon and waited. After a few seconds a new screen popped up. He bent closer and peered at the annoyingly small print:

> Through a DNA grandparentage test, one or both of the biological parents of the alleged father can be tested to determine if there is a biological relationship to the child. Normally, we also recommend that the sample of the other parent is included.

He closed the website and shut down the computer and leaned back, rubbing his face wearily. What was he doing, where was the point in torturing himself with what-ifs and maybes, when in all likelihood he'd never lay eyes on the pair of them again?

And did he even want to? Was he prepared to find out that an uneducated, semi-delinquent creature was the mother of his grandchild? The thought filled him with distaste. On the other hand, the idea that Ethan might have left an issue, that there was something of him still on this earth—how could Michael not hope that was true? How could any father not yearn for some validation of his dead son's life?

Every day the pain of losing Ethan was there. The torment

that Michael had undergone with his son's slide into drug abuse and consequent death never left him. It was as much a part of him as the beard he'd grown after Ethan had died, the beard that his daughter detested, but that for some reason he couldn't bring himself to shave off.

What was he to do with these conflicting emotions? Was he never again to enjoy a night's sleep? What in God's name was he to do? He listened to the rain pattering on the window and he wondered yet again if they had a roof over their heads, if they had beds to sleep in.

He got to his feet, running a hand through his hair, and went out to the kitchen to check on the progress of a pork steak that he had no appetite for.

"Look at the negative spaces as well as the positive ones—what shape is produced in the area between Jackie's left arm and torso, for example? It's a triangle, isn't it? Can you see it?"

From her position Jackie was able to watch Audrey surreptitiously as she moved around the room, bending occasionally to murmur a comment, exchanging places with a student now and again to demonstrate a point, every so often throwing out a general remark.

"Don't forget to map out the holistic form first—otherwise you'll get bogged down in trying to get one part exactly right and then find that you haven't allowed enough space for the rest, and have to start all over again."

Jackie was amused to see that Zarek had brought along a dictionary this evening. Poor guy must have been lost last week. She'd heard Meg asking him about his family during the break, and his response had been comically full of mistakes, although you could understand more or less what he was trying to say.

No problem with his drawings though—from what Jackie could make out, he seemed to be doing just fine. She supposed you didn't really need language if you had artistic ability.

Thankfully, she felt a lot more relaxed this evening. Not that she'd been totally nonchalant when it had come to peeling off the dressing gown—there had still been a degree of embarrassment, she'd had to steel herself not to meet anyone's eye again—but really it had been nothing compared with the awfulness of the previous week. And now, nearly an hour into the class, she thought she might actually be starting to enjoy the experience.

I am an artist's model, she told herself as she draped her limbs over the table that Audrey had covered with the sarong. *Yes, I pose nude for art students. It's nude, you know, rather than naked. That's the artistic term. No, I don't find it in the least intimidating—there's nothing shameful about the nude body.*

And none of the five people who were studying her looked at all concerned about her breasts not being very full, or how many ripples they could count across her abdomen, or whether she had too much pubic hair. To them she was an object, a shape to be reproduced on the pages in front of them, nothing more. Which was fine by her, of course, and which made it so much easier not to be embarrassed.

Or which would be fine, if she didn't want one of them to see her as something other than just an artist's model.

"I run my own playschool," Meg said. "Just opened it last month. Still trying to catch my breath."

"Gosh, I'm sure that's demanding," Audrey replied, eyeing the Jersey cream biscuits and wondering if it would seem greedy to take a third. Meg hadn't had any at all.

Not that Meg would notice if Audrey polished off the entire plate of biscuits, the way she kept looking across at Zarek and Fiona.

———————

"In Poland I work with computers," Zarek said. "I make the programs. Here I work in chip shop."

"That must be a big change," Fiona replied.

He shrugged. "Is okay, but sometimes at night is not so good. Lots of drunk peoples."

"I can imagine."

"And you? What is your job?"

"I'm a teacher," she told him. "Primary school."

"Please, what is primary?"

"A school for young children. I teach the youngest of all, Junior Infants. My students are all four- and five-year-olds."

"Ah yes—you are lady who say, 'Welcome to my school, please enjoy your stay.'"

Fiona laughed. "I suppose so, except that it's not really my school—I just work there."

Zarek nodded. "Yes," he said. "I make small joke."

In Ireland, nobody got his jokes.

———————

"What do you think of Zarek?"

Jackie looked at Audrey. "I hope you're not trying to matchmake."

"Oh come on—he's lovely. And he's just about your age."

Jackie turned to regard Zarek, who'd just been approached by Meg. "Ah no, he's a bit too pretty for me…and anyway, it looks like someone else might be interested." She scanned the rest of the lobby, which also contained students from other classes. "I see James has disappeared again."

"Has he?" Audrey asked, hoping her face wasn't going pink, but suspecting it might be. "I hadn't noticed."

"Personal trainer," Irene said. "It's actually my husband's gym—I was working there when I met him."

Fiona's eyes widened. "He owns a gym? Lucky you—he must be well off."

Irene was half amused, half annoyed. The woman wouldn't know how to be tactful if her life depended on it. "Actually," Irene told her, "I didn't marry him for his money."

The smile slid from Fiona's face. "Oh no, I didn't mean—"

"My family owns Happy Shopper."

Fiona's mouth dropped open. "The supermarket chain?"

"Yup." Irene took another sip of the horribly strong tea. "I believe the expression is 'filthy rich.' If anyone was a gold digger, it was my husband. So what do you do?"

"I'm a primary school teacher," Fiona said faintly. "I teach Junior Infants."

"How nice." Irene wondered how many more minutes of break were left.

"I take some life drawing classes in Poland," Zarek said. "In the university in my town."

"Thought so," Meg replied. "You're definitely not a beginner. So what other talents have you got?"

"Please?"

"What do you like to do, when you're not working?"

"Well, I like listen to music, and sometime DVD watch, and I like also to swim."

"Swim? You go to the pool here?"

"Yes, I go sometime, on Thursday in the night. If I no have to work."

"Thursday," Meg repeated. "I go there sometimes too. I'll keep an eye out for you."

———————

Jackie wandered outside, needing to move around after sitting and lying still for most of the past hour. Thankfully there had been no sign of the protesting couple this evening—presumably they felt they'd made their point last week. Jackie had had visions of them bursting into the room, calling her all sorts of names, and throwing a blanket over her.

She walked briskly around the car park, enjoying the feeling of her muscles stretching themselves. As she approached a black Volkswagen she saw that there was a man sitting in the driver's seat. He seemed to be on the phone.

By the time she recognized him it was too late to swing around, so she pretended not to notice him as she walked past, but there was no way he could have missed her. She hoped he didn't think she'd gone looking for him.

Which of course she hadn't.

———————

Had she seen him? She gave no sign that she had. It didn't matter anyway, he was entitled to spend the break as he wanted.

"The frog climbed up the wall and—"

"Frogs can't climb walls," Charlie said.

"This one could, he was a magic frog. So he climbed up

the wall and jumped onto the windowsill and looked in at the princess."

The model had turned back towards the doorway. Break must be nearly over.

"He decided that such a beautiful princess would never love an ugly frog like him, so he hopped back down and lived sadly ever after in his pond."

"Is that the end?"

"It sure is. Don't forget to brush your teeth. Hugs and kisses."

Shame you couldn't change the endings as easily in real life. He hung up and got out of the car.

———————

"I let you off last week because it was your first," Audrey said, "but now that you've all settled in, it's time for a little home-work."

"Homework?" Irene repeated. "You're not serious."

Audrey smiled, not at all put out. It was an evening class; no big deal if they chose to ignore her homework. "It won't take long, and it would be good to do a little bit of drawing during the week—like anything, the more you practice, the better you'll become."

"So what should we do?" Meg asked.

"Just find a subject and get them to sit for you. I want you to try doing a few short poses, like we did at the start. Four minutes maximum for each pose, no longer."

"Do they have to be, er, naked?" Fiona asked, and a titter went around the room.

"If it's in the privacy of your own home, why not?" Irene sug-gested. "Could get interesting."

More laughter.

"No, not at all," Audrey put in hastily. "Fully clothed is fine—

and if you can get a few different subjects, even better. Just put them in fairly uncomplicated poses, and remember that all you're trying to get down on paper is the overall shape that they make. Forget about details, we'll concentrate on them later."

The students began to gather their things. Jackie went off to get dressed. Audrey unplugged the fan heater and packed it into her basket.

"Excuse?"

She looked up to find Zarek standing by her side. "Yes?"

"You want we draw at home?"

Lord, she'd forgotten to make sure he understood. "Sorry, Zarek—yes, I would like you to try doing some drawing at home. Do you have someone who would sit for you? A friend maybe?"

"Yes," he said, "I have two friend in my flat."

Sharing a flat with two others. It didn't tell her much; one of them could be a girlfriend. She hadn't gotten to chatting with Zarek at the break yet, he was still very much an unknown to her.

But she still had hopes of him for Jackie, whom she was pretty sure was single. Not that Audrey would dream of trying to manipulate anything, but it didn't hurt to keep an eye open, did it?

When he'd left, Audrey put on her jacket and walked through the empty classroom to the door. She switched off the horrible fluorescent lights and made her way up the corridor to where Vincent was sweeping the lobby floor.

"So how's it coming along?" he asked. "Settling into it, are you?"

"Oh yes, I'm enjoying it," she told him. "And I think the students are too."

She was glad she'd gone for the evening classes, nice to have something to look forward to on Tuesday evenings. And it seemed that the group was gelling—apart from James, of course. Definitely the dark horse of the class—and if that was what he wanted, there wasn't a thing she could do.

Plenty of time though, Audrey the optimist pointed out. Only two classes gone, four more to go. You never knew what might happen. She said good night to Vincent and stepped out, buttoning her jacket against the lashing rain.

So loud the rain sounded on the roof of the shed—but miraculously there seemed to be only one place where it was actually coming in, and they could avoid that by moving nearer to the other end.

Carmel had put plenty of newspapers underneath them, but her hips still had bruises in the morning. They slept in their clothes, and used their jackets for blankets. She'd gotten two pillows in the charity shop for thirty cents. One smelled of cats, and was lumpy.

But it didn't matter, none of it mattered. She had Barry, whose warm little body curled up into hers as he slept. She loved him so fiercely it terrified her. What if she couldn't always look after him, what if someone tried to hurt him and Carmel couldn't stop them? What if some drunken monster like her father found him?

She pushed the thought away, she refused to let it grow. Nothing like that would happen. Things would get better, she had to believe that. Something would come along—no, it wouldn't come along, she'd have to find it. But she *would* find it, she'd never give up, no matter how many people told her to get lost.

She stroked Barry's head softly and listened to the rain thumping on the roof.

Wednesday

Jackie's phone beeped as she brought the empty cereal bowls to the sink. She fished it out of her pocket and read **Private Number**. She opened the message and the words appeared on the screen:

Tnks for invite, Charlie away next wknd—J Sullivan

He'd gotten her note on Monday, two days ago. It had been very polite and not at all pushy. Jackie had suggested that Charlie come to play with Eoin on the following Sunday. She'd offered to collect Charlie and drop her home again, she'd said they'd give her dinner. Nothing that he could possibly take offense at.

And this was his response. No mention of possible alternatives, no number so she could get back to him. Clearly he wasn't interested in his daughter making any friends in her new home. Poor girl, with a dead mother and a father who didn't seem to give a damn.

Jackie deleted the message as Eoin walked into the kitchen with his schoolbag. She'd say nothing, she'd wait until he asked again and then she'd tell him Charlie's dad was too busy. What else could she do?

"Did you get your PE gear?" she asked. "I left it on the chair on the landing."

"Forgot." He disappeared again.

J Sullivan. He couldn't even be bothered to write his full name.

"I've come to apologize," she said as soon as the customer before her had left the shop. "I was rude to you the last time I was in here." The pink in her cheeks almost matching the little circles that dotted her white blouse.

She was the last person Michael had expected to see in the shop again. He was bemused that she felt it necessary to apologize. Her conscience was clearly a lot more active than his.

"Don't worry about it," he said. "I've been called worse. You may have noticed I'm an antisocial bastard. Excuse my French," he added, thinking she was probably the type who didn't appreciate bad language.

He didn't think he was being funny, but to his surprise her features relaxed, and he fancied he saw the ghost of a smile cross her face. He thought a smile was probably easy enough to coax from her, if you wanted to. He remembered the ice cream cone in the park, and decided she was probably predisposed to being happy.

He wondered what that felt like.

"Well," she said, turning towards the door, "that's really all I wanted to say."

"How's the dog settling in?" He had no idea where the question came from.

"Getting a little easier to manage, thank you." She paused. "I asked the vet for advice, and he was very helpful."

The significance of the remark didn't escape Michael, but he sensed no malice in it. He didn't think she was trying to make him feel bad—or maybe she was, a little, but not in a nasty way. Just giving him a gentle nudge.

"Glad to hear it," he said. "They can be a bit tricky at the start. Dogs, I mean," he added, "not vets."

No harm to coax another smile from her. Had a pleasant effect on her face, causing two small dimples to crease her cheeks. Smiling suited her a lot more than frowning—but maybe that was true of everyone.

"Well," she said, "good-bye then."

"Good-bye." It occurred to him as she walked out that it was the first civil conversation they'd had—and quite possibly the last. He didn't imagine she'd be in again, now that she'd said her piece and was coping with the dog.

He put her from his mind and began making out a pet food order.

James squeezed toothpaste onto Charlie's brush and handed it to her. "Up and down, remember, not sideways."

Charlie took the brush and began to scrub. It had been Frances who'd taught her to brush her teeth, Frances who'd cut her nails when they got too long, Frances who'd washed her hair and bathed her, and bought new pajamas when the old ones didn't fit anymore.

The first time James had taken Charlie to get new shoes, he hadn't had a clue what size her feet were. How would he explain his ignorance to a shop assistant? Would she think it strange that he didn't know? He'd been vastly relieved when he hadn't even been asked for a size before the assistant placed one of Charlie's feet into some kind of a measuring device. He'd had no idea that every child's shoe shop had a similar facility, that children's feet grew so quickly that sometimes they skipped a whole size between one pair of shoes and the next.

Of course he knew that now; talk about a steep learning curve.

Since Charlie had started school he'd learned not to panic over playground bumps and bruises, and he'd become pretty good at removing paint and other stains from her clothes. He'd learned to check her schoolbag each day for lunchbox spills and notes from teachers, and he'd also mastered the art—after a few unpleasant head lice encounters—of tying up her hair in two vaguely symmetrical bunches. Braids, he felt, could wait until she was able to do them herself.

But there were some things he was still unsure of, and one of them was bedtime. Was half past eight too late for a six-year-old? Charlie never seemed tired before then, but maybe he shouldn't wait until she started yawning. He'd feel stupid asking anyone such a basic question, so he didn't.

"Finished."

She handed him the toothbrush and he ran the head under the tap and filled the plastic tumbler with water. "Rinse."

Their nightly routine, never varying except on Tuesdays when he went to drawing class, and Saturdays when he gave her a bath. It suddenly occurred to him that at some stage in the future it wouldn't be appropriate for him to be bathing his daughter, but when? So many minefields ahead of them.

"Will you read *The Cat in the Hat*?" Charlie asked.

He made as if to collapse. "Again? That'll be six million zillion times."

"But I love it, Daddy."

"I know you do."

The note from Eoin's mother had taken him by surprise, although he probably should have been expecting some sort of approach. "What's this?" he'd asked, pulling the envelope out of Charlie's lunchbox.

"Mrs. Grossman gave it to me," she'd told him—but it wasn't her teacher's handwriting, and Mrs. Grossman wouldn't write *Charlie's Dad* on the envelope. He'd opened it and pulled out the single sheet and read *Hello—wondering if Charlie would like to visit Eoin next Sunday. I can collect and deliver her back if that suits. (And we can provide dinner, as long as she's happy with roast beef!)*

She'd signed it *Jackie*, and added *Eoin's Mum* in brackets. And below the signature, a mobile phone number.

Jackie—whose partner, according to Charlie, was dead; and hadn't grandparents been mentioned? So chances were she was currently unattached, if she and Eoin were living with her parents. And if James knew that Eoin's father was no longer around, this Jackie was probably aware that Frances wasn't on the scene anymore either.

He couldn't help wondering if there was a hidden agenda here. What if she was looking for a replacement father for her son, or maybe just a new partner for herself? Was he being ridiculous, thinking like that? Had what happened to him made him paranoid, along with everything else?

He appreciated that parents needed to make contact with each other in order to manage their offspring's friendships; but even if the invitation was entirely innocent, he discovered he simply couldn't face the prospect of having to socialize with another adult to such a degree.

Because this would just be the start, wouldn't it? He'd have to reciprocate, and before you knew it there'd be sleepovers and trips to the park together, and he and Eoin's mother would of necessity become a couple, of sorts.

He supposed it was the same reluctance he felt for mixing with the four other students in the art class. Mixing meant talking about yourself at some stage, mixing meant surrendering your secrets, sooner or later.

He knew, of course, that he couldn't avoid Eoin's mother, or any other parents of Charlie's friends, indefinitely. For one thing, it wasn't fair to Charlie, who had every right to a social life. And for another, she'd surely wear him down eventually. For somebody who still had trouble tying her shoelaces, and who needed him to check for trolls under her bed each night, his daughter was surprisingly good at getting what she wanted.

But not yet; he wasn't ready yet to risk it all coming out again. He couldn't face another round of unasked questions, hostile looks, whispers behind hands. He couldn't go through all that again, not when they'd barely settled into Carrickbawn.

He'd texted a response to the mobile number, knowing how unfriendly it would sound to Eoin's mother. No doubt she'd be put out by his blunt refusal, but there was nothing he could do to help that. He hoped he wasn't jeopardizing Charlie's friendship with Eoin, who sounded like a nice boy. Surely the mother wouldn't take it out on the children if she was annoyed?

It was a chance he'd have to take. He sat on the edge of his daughter's bed and opened her bedtime story.

Not a single sarcastic comment, not a look or a gesture Audrey could object to. On the contrary, he'd been quite civil—almost pleasant, in fact. Even making a joke about the vet.

Of course his language had been a little choice, but considering how much more objectionable he'd been on previous occasions, Audrey was willing to overlook that. And he had excused himself afterwards, which had been gratifying.

Anyway it didn't matter, it was all over and done with. She was glad, though, that they'd parted civilly. And she'd apologized for her outburst, so her conscience was perfectly clear. She could put him out of her head now with no hard feelings.

She strode happily along the path, enjoying the soft warmth of the September sun on her face—no, October now, could you believe it? The year was flying by.

She was looking forward to a pleasant hour in the garden when she got home. That bed near the patio badly needed to be weeded—she'd change into her old blue trousers and set to it. And then she'd make dinner, and after that there was her bath and the usual Wednesday-night telly to look forward to.

She turned onto her road and saw a slender, dark-haired young woman coming out of Pauline's next door. They smiled at each other as they passed.

"The weather is holding," Audrey said cheerfully.

"Certainly is," the other agreed.

It was the first time they'd said more than hello to each other.

After letting herself in, Audrey went straight upstairs and changed quickly into her gardening clothes, ignoring for once the frantic scrabbling at the kitchen door. From her bedroom window the signs of Dolly's presence were all too evident in the garden, from the little piles of upturned earth here and there to the ruined dahlia bed at one side and the complete absence of foliage on the lower parts of the hydrangeas.

Back downstairs she received her usual rapturous welcome in the kitchen. She opened the back door and Dolly tumbled into the garden, yapping joyously. Audrey went to the shed and collected her gardening tools and made her way back to the flower bed, Dolly snuffling busily into all her favorite places.

As Audrey positioned her green foam kneeler Pauline emerged from the house next door holding a mug.

"You're putting me to shame."

Audrey smiled. "You clearly haven't noticed that my garden has been demolished lately. This is just a little damage-limitation exercise." She pulled on her gloves. "I saw your visitor leaving when I was coming home."

"Oh yes, Valerie was here. She wanted the recipe for my chicken and pineapple dish. She's inviting people to dinner at the weekend."

Audrey dug around a dandelion. "It's lovely that she still keeps in touch with you. How long did you say since you stopped keeping house for them?"

"Ten years, just about." Pauline shook her head, cradling her mug. "Poor things haven't had it easy."

The wife had died, which was why Pauline had been recruited as housekeeper, but there'd been a second tragedy in that family, some months after Audrey had moved in next door. She'd forgotten the details now, but she dimly remembered Pauline being terribly upset at the time.

"She doesn't say much about it, but I gather that things between herself and her father haven't been good for quite a while," Pauline went on. "That's the last thing she needs now, with only the two of them left in the family."

Kevin emerged from the house next door just then, looking warily over the hedge for Dolly, and the subject was dropped. As the plot of a Disney film he'd just watched was being recounted to them in great detail, Audrey dug and poked and filled her trug with weeds, and found her mind wandering.

He mightn't look too bad if he smartened himself up a bit, if he bought a few nice shirts and shaved off that awful beard. It might be hiding a receding chin or something, but honestly, the state of it—as if he went at it every so often with the bread knife.

"Audrey, you're miles away."

She looked up at Pauline, and at Kevin's handsome, empty face. She felt the heat rising in her cheeks.

"Sorry, I was thinking about…school."

Lord, trying to smarten up the man in the pet shop—she really must be getting desperate.

Irene pulled her phone from her bag. "Irene," she said.

"I called a few days ago, about taking you up on the free trial."

"Who is this?" But she knew who it was.

"I did the panel beating on your car," he said. "You gave me your card, said I could have a trial."

"Oh yes…well, I'm pretty much booked up for the rest of the week, but I could squeeze you in on"—she flicked the pages of her magazine—"Friday, around half past three."

"I work till five," he said.

"In that case"—another flick—"it'll have to be Monday. Say five thirty?"

"Okay."

"What's your name?" she asked.

A tiny pause. "Ger Brophy," he said.

It didn't escape her, the second it took him to make up a name. Not surprising, though, seeing as how he probably had a wife at home. Irene scribbled *Ger? Mon 5:30* in the margin of the magazine page and gave him directions to the gym and told him what to wear.

"How long will it last?" he asked.

"About an hour. You'll need a shower afterwards, so bring a towel and stuff."

She tried to remember what he looked like, and couldn't. Dark anyway, but his features were gone. She'd know him when she saw him.

Monday at five thirty, later than she normally worked. She'd ask Martin to leave the gym early, to make dinner for Emily and to let Pilar go home.

As her hairdresser approached Irene tore the page from the magazine and slipped it into her bag.

Thursday

As he approached the library Michael saw a girl sitting on the ground outside, her back against the stippled wall, her head bent, a cardboard cup in her outstretched hand. The town was becoming overrun with beggars. He'd mention it to the library staff, maybe they could move her on.

When he was still some distance away he saw that there was a small child with her, sitting on her far side. He tightened his grip on the books under his arm.

Was it her, was it them? Hard to be sure. He kept walking—and as he drew near, as the likelihood that he knew them grew stronger, she lifted her head and stared straight at him.

Michael stopped. "What the hell are you doing?" he said quietly.

She looked defiantly back at him. "What does it look like?" There were a few copper coins in the cup, nothing more.

"Get up," Michael said, making an effort to keep his voice low. A woman passed, looking curiously at them. He resisted the impulse to advise her to mind her own business.

The girl got unhurriedly to her feet, pulling the boy with her. She faced Michael sulkily.

"You didn't give me no choice," she said. "I told you we didn't have nobody else."

He shook his head fiercely. "Don't you blame me for your miserable life—you made your choices long ago."

"I'm not blamin' you," she said, "I'm jus' tellin' you, you're all we got."

It wasn't his fault—so why did he feel responsible for them? He couldn't leave them here, he couldn't have her begging, it was out of the question. He went on glaring at her, wondering what on earth to do, and she tossed her head and looked away in the distance.

He turned and regarded the boy. If it was possible, he looked worse than the last time Michael had seen him. His hair was unkempt, his face streaked with dirt. He gazed straight ahead, his eyes empty.

"When did he eat last?" Michael demanded.

"A while ago. What do you care?" Sullenly, her eyes on the ground again.

"Have you a place to stay?"

"We're in a shed," she muttered. "We're sleepin' on the ground, in a shed."

On the ground in a shed. He had to do something. He took a pen from his breast pocket and tore a blank page from the back of one of his library books and began to scribble rapidly.

"If that's for me, you're wastin' your time."

He lifted his head. "What?" he barked. Was she going to suddenly develop some pride and decide she didn't want his charity after all?

"I can't read," she said. "I never learned it."

Michael supposed he shouldn't be surprised. God knows how much—or how little—schooling she'd had.

"Walnut Grove," he said clearly. "You know it? Behind the cathedral."

"I know the cathedral."

"Number seventeen," he said, checking his watch. "Come at eight o'clock, not before."

For the first time the sulky expression left her face. "You want us to come to your house?" She looked younger, less sure of herself.

"That's why I'm giving you my address," he said in exasperation. He pulled out his wallet and took a €10 note from it. "Go and get something to eat," he said. "Something hot. No more begging. What's my address?"

She repeated it, looking slightly dazed. She took the money without comment. Michael turned on his heel without waiting for a reply. What had he just done? He walked rapidly away, retracing his steps, the library forgotten. Eight o'clock, and it was heading for seven. So little time.

———

"Zarek!"

He turned towards the sound of the voice and saw a raised arm in the water about five meters away. The face looked a little familiar, but with her hair hidden under a navy rubber cap Zarek couldn't immediately place the woman.

She swam over, using a clumsy breaststroke. "Fancy meeting you here," she said—and as she rose to her feet Zarek realized it was Meg from his art class, an inch or two taller than his five-foot-ten height, even in bare feet. Minus her distinctive purple-framed spectacles now, of course, which was why he'd been slow to recognize her.

"You're a real pro," she said. "That dive was magnificent. I can just about keep myself afloat, as you've probably noticed." Laughing, her eyes flicking over his bare shoulders, down to his chest. "Maybe you could give me a few lessons sometime."

Zarek felt slightly uncomfortable. Coping with the teenage girls who came into the café was one thing, but someone older, someone he was going to meet regularly over the next few weeks, was another. Maybe he was imagining it—but she'd chosen the desk next to his in the life drawing class, and during the coffee breaks she was rarely far from his side. And he remembered mentioning the pool last Tuesday evening, and now here she was.

He hadn't noticed if she wore a wedding ring in the class. She wasn't wearing one now, but maybe she'd taken it off for the swim.

"So you come here a lot?" she asked, straightening the shoulder strap of her red swimsuit. "Funny I haven't seen you before; I'm usually here on Thursdays."

That may well have been true. When Zarek came to the pool he took little notice of his fellow swimmers.

"I come not all the time," he told her. "Some nights I must work." He wondered how to get away without being rude. Was she going to stay talking to him for the hour? Some people did that, he'd seen them out of the corner of his eye as he swam his laps, holding on to the side of the pool, having conversations. He wondered why they didn't just go to a café or a pub instead.

"Well, I suppose you want to get back to your swimming," she said, not making any move herself.

But it was enough for Zarek. "Yes, I do my laps," he said, turning immediately. "I see you on Tuesday, yes? At the drawing class." And without waiting for her reply he cut through the water and swam continuously for eight laps, barely putting his head above water to breathe. By the time he took a break, panting, she was nowhere to be seen.

He hoped he was wrong about her interest in him, but he had an awful feeling he was right.

"I can make the hardest jigsaw in my school," Emily announced. "It's called the farm jigsaw, an' it has a farmer an' a cow an' a horse an' some chickens an' a tractor an' a duck pond with ducks. It has a million pieces."

Her grandmother smiled indulgently at her. "A million pieces? That's a lot. You're such a clever girl. What's your teacher's name again, dear?"

"Meg."

"Well, Meg must be very proud of you."

The new maid appeared and began to clear away the soup plates. Irene's mother turned to her. "How are the art classes going?"

"Fine," Irene answered. "I'm no Picasso, but it's a bit of a laugh."

Across the table Martin and her father were talking about rugby. They'd hit it off from the start when Irene had brought him home to meet them, shortly after Martin's status had changed from boss to boyfriend.

Financially secure in his own right, Martin had been undaunted by the big house or the maids or any other indications of the fortune that Irene's father had amassed over the past thirty years—and it was precisely Martin's own wealth that had convinced Irene's parents to trust him. Here wasn't just another gold digger in search of Irene's substantial future inheritance.

Her parents had bought them the cottage in Ballyvaughan as a wedding present, and when Emily was born her father had given Irene the green Peugeot, and set up a trust fund for his new granddaughter.

The lobster was served, with breaded scampi for Emily. The men's conversation switched from rugby to golf.

"Don't you think it's time, darling?" Irene's mother murmured as Irene picked up her fork. "Emily's growing up so fast, you don't want to leave too much of an age gap."

Irene cracked a claw and dug out a chunk of flesh. She dipped it into the little bowl of melted butter, automatically registering that this meal would warrant some serious work in the gym on her next visit.

"Mother, you bring this up every time we come to dinner," she replied. "You've been telling me to have another baby since Emily was one. I can only give you the same answer I give you every time, which is that you can't get pregnant to order—it's in the lap of the gods." She spoke quietly, anxious not to attract Martin's attention.

"But you are trying?" her mother asked.

"Of course," Irene answered lightly. "But I'm not exactly in the first flush, so the probability that I'll conceive again is lower. You know that."

"All the more reason."

"I'm aware of that. Now would you mind very much if we changed the subject?"

They had no idea, they hadn't the tiniest idea. Irene imagined her mother's face if she told her the truth, if she said *Martin hasn't touched me in almost two years, not since he realized that I'm never going to feel the way he does for our daughter. We sleep in the same bed but we may as well be on different continents. Now and again I have sex with men I feel nothing for, and Martin is probably having some on the side too. But in the unlikely event he ever decides to do it with me again I'm on the Pill, because I have no intention of bringing another child into the world.*

She sipped the chilled Grüner Veltliner that had come up from her father's cellar and dabbed her lips with Irish linen. She looked across the table at her husband's handsome face and thought of the tragedy of having more money than you could ever need, and not being able to buy the one thing you desperately wanted.

———

Audrey steered her trolley past the stationery and computer equipment and gardening supplies, and turned into the clothing aisle. The supermarket offerings weren't terribly fashionable or well made, but when you were looking for a nightie that in all likelihood nobody else would see, what did it matter?

She examined the rows of nightwear without enthusiasm, the black, white, powder-blue, and baby-pink polyester offerings. Why didn't they make nighties in more interesting colors? She'd love an emerald-green one with sky-blue polka dots, or a red one with orange and yellow stripes—but she supposed for €7.99 you took what you got.

She selected a blue one with tiny white flowers running around the neck and dropped it into her trolley. As she meandered through the various clothing aisles on her way to the grocery section she steered her trolley around a male customer who was frowning at a small pair of canvas trousers.

Hardly for his own child, he was a bit old for that. A grand-child then. Audrey found it difficult to picture him with a family. Maybe he was completely different outside the pet shop, maybe he was all twinkly and smiling—but the image of him with a small child sitting on his knee was still impossible to conjure up.

A few minutes later she encountered him again in the cereals aisle. He selected a bag of organic porridge and added it to the basket he carried. He probably ate all the right foods, and would no doubt disapprove of the box of Crunchy Nut Corn Flakes that Audrey was placing in her trolley.

He had a harassed air about him. She guessed shopping wasn't his favorite occupation. Then again, he frowned like that a lot of the time; it seemed to be his default expression. For some reason Audrey felt a rush of sympathy for him. He didn't strike her as a particularly happy individual, and that was a pity. She wondered if there was anything he really looked forward to.

Had he any friends, or did he live alone and unloved? *She* lived alone, of course, and she had to admit to being unloved—well, apart from her parents, who were more or less obliged to love her—but she got on with people, she had friends, and great neighbors whom she hoped thought fairly fondly of her. And of course she had Dolly.

Then again, the man from the pet shop was buying clothes for a child, so there must be some kind of family in his life. They came face-to-face briefly, as Audrey walked past his queue at the checkout. He nodded at her, and Audrey gave him a smile.

As she took her place in another queue a few checkouts away she glanced into her trolley and saw the blue nightie nestling between a tin of beans and a pound of sausages, and she hoped to God he hadn't spotted it.

Not that it would matter if he had, of course. Not that he'd have taken a blind bit of notice.

———

At ten minutes past eight the doorbell rang. Michael set the fireguard in place and went into the hall.

They looked worse, if anything, than earlier. More shabby, more pathetic. He stood back silently to let them in, wondering if any of his neighbors had seen them. She cradled a black bin bag; the same one, he assumed, that she'd been carrying the second time they'd called into the shop. The boy stood silently beside her and clung to her thigh. They brought a distinct smell of unwashed bodies with them.

Michael closed the door and folded his arms and eyed her bundle. "There better not be anything illegal in there," he said.

"D'you want to check it?" she asked.

Her face was impassive. He couldn't tell if she was trying to be smart, but he decided to ignore it. The thought of rummaging through whatever belongings she had didn't appeal to him in the least—and the fact that she'd offered to let him probably meant she had nothing to hide.

"If you brought any food, leave it in the kitchen," he told her. "No food upstairs."

"Where's the kitchen?" she asked.

Michael led the way and indicated the table. "Leave it there."

She reached into the black bag, drew out a small white one, and placed it on the table. "You live in this big house on your own?"

"That's none of your business," he retorted. "I don't appreciate questions about my private life." She wouldn't last long if she didn't remember her place.

The color rose in her face, and for a second he thought she was going to cry. All he needed.

"Sorry," she mumbled. "I didn't mean nothin', I was jus' talkin'."

He turned for the stairs. "This way," he said shortly, wondering what had possessed him. On the landing he took two towels from the airing cupboard and showed her the bathroom. "You will both have a bath," he said, "tonight, before you go to bed." He'd debated moving his toiletries out of sight, and then decided that she'd probably rummage and find them, so he'd left them where they were. He supposed he could bear the loss of some shower gel and toothpaste.

"Have you got a hair dryer?" she asked.

"No," he said shortly. "Dry your hair with the towel." Next thing she'd be looking for breakfast in bed.

He brought them into the room that had been Valerie's and watched her taking in the double bed, the twin lockers, the big wardrobe, the dressing table with its three-sided mirror. The maroon carpet with tiny beige flowers, the cream wallpaper with its paler rectangles above the bed where Valerie's posters had hung. The heavy curtains on the two long, narrow windows.

He saw her looking at the clothes he'd laid out on the bed.

"You'll both sleep in this room," he told them. "You will put all your clothes in the laundry hamper in the bathroom, and wear what I have put out."

He'd gone through the few pieces Valerie had left behind, assuming his daughter wouldn't look for them again, and he'd selected a skirt and blouse and cardigan. They wouldn't be a perfect fit, far from it—Valerie was a good three or four inches taller than this girl, and a stone or so heavier, at least—but they'd do her while her own were in the wash.

He hadn't thought of nightwear, for either of them—or underwear, he suddenly realized. He'd bought no underwear. Not that he could have provided for the girl, of course, but he could have gotten something for the boy. They'd just have to wear something unwashed until he could find alternatives.

She picked up the small trousers and sweatshirt. Michael had removed the price tags, but they were obviously brand-new.

"You bought these for him?" she asked.

"Yes," he answered curtly. What choice did he have, with the boy practically in rags?

She pointed to Valerie's clothing. "An' they're for me?"

"Yes," he repeated impatiently. Who did she think they were for? The next down-and-out he was planning to take in?

"Can we keep them?" she asked. "Are you givin' them to us for keeps?"

Michael stared at her. Could she possibly imagine he would want them back? She blinked rapidly, and for the second time since they'd arrived he sensed imminent tears. He was no good with crying women, never had been.

"They're yours," he said quickly, shifting his gaze away from her. "Do what you like with them. You will leave the house with me in the morning at half past eight, and you will stay away until seven o'clock tomorrow evening. I will give you a packed lunch and I will provide dinner when you get back here, so you won't need to beg."

She blinked another few times as he spoke, pressed her fingers to her eyes.

"Is that understood?"

She nodded.

"Tomorrow I'm sending off for a paternity test," Michael went on. "It will show if Ethan is the father, as you claim. You can stay here until the results are known—provided you behave yourselves."

He paused. She was still holding the clothes, and the boy was hanging on to her leg. "I want no trouble here," Michael went on slowly. "Nobody turning up here who shouldn't. You understand what I'm talking about."

She laid the clothes on the bed. "You mean dealers." No defiance, the words stated flatly.

"I do—and any other of the undesirables you hang around with."

"I don't hang around with nobody," she said. "I don't have no friends since I stopped dealin'. I got nothin' to do with them people no more."

Michael decided not to comment on that. "It will probably take a week or ten days to get the test results," he said. "Until then you will leave the house with me every morning at half past eight and stay away until seven. There will be no begging. If you need… toiletries you will let me know." He paused. "Any questions?"

"Thank you," she said, her face flushing again. "Really. You dunno what you done for us."

He looked at her. He took in the shabby clothing, the greasy hair, the whole undernourished, unkempt, neglected appearance of her. He regarded the small white-faced silent boy, nose running, dirty thumb plugged in his mouth, cowering beside her.

He must be mad.

"I'll say good night then," he said, turning for the door. "Don't forget to have baths. I'll call you at eight o'clock."

"I do have a question," she said then.

He stopped in the doorway.

"Was this Ethan's room?" she asked. "Can I jus' ask that?"

A beat passed.

"No," Michael said. "It wasn't."

He closed the door behind him. Back in the kitchen he opened the plastic bag and found an almost empty liter bottle of Coke and half a packet of supermarket-brand Fig Rolls. He resisted the impulse to pour what remained of the Coke down the sink, and instead stowed the bag in a press.

When he went upstairs again two hours later, the landing smelled of soap. Their bedroom door was closed, no sound from behind it.

The bathroom mirror was steamy, the air warm and damp. Underlying the scent of soap—his, probably—was the unmistakable odor that had accompanied them into the house. He slid the window open and lifted the lid of the laundry hamper cautiously—and closed it quickly.

The bath looked as if she'd attempted to clean it after them. No hairs, no suds, no soap scum. Michael spotted a grubby pink nylon toilet bag perched on top of the cistern, next to his can of air freshener.

He peered inside and saw two toothbrushes and an almost new tube of toothpaste. The bristles on the child's brush were splayed to an alarming degree, but at least it existed. Not that brushing the boy's teeth would make much difference, if all she was feeding him was Coke and biscuits. A wonder he had a tooth left in his head.

There was a small blue sponge in the bag too, and a thin bar of white soap wrapped in a grey facecloth, a pair of tweezers, and a sachet of shampoo. He remembered her asking if he had a hair dryer, and his lie in response. He supposed it wouldn't have killed him to hand it over, but wasn't it enough that he was putting a

roof over their heads, was he expected to provide whatever gad-
getry she demanded too?

He should have though. He remembered the housekeeper he'd
employed after Ruth's death making sure that Valerie and Ethan
never went to bed with wet hair. He'd leave the hair dryer outside
their bedroom door tomorrow. He'd say nothing about it, and if
she had any sense she wouldn't comment either.

He zipped the toilet bag closed. He brought the laundry basket
downstairs and pulled on rubber gloves before dumping its contents into the washing machine, turning his face from the thick,
cloying smell. After switching on the machine he warmed milk
for his usual nightcap and made his way back upstairs.

He cleaned his teeth and washed his face. He changed into pajamas and set his alarm, wondering as he did if he should lock his
bedroom door. But the key was downstairs in the bottom drawer
of his bureau with all the rest, and to get it he'd have to put his
clothes on again or go down in pajamas and risk meeting her on
her way to the bathroom.

When he was asleep—if he fell asleep—she could do what she
liked in his house. She could traipse around and open presses and
poke into drawers. She could steal things, not that he'd left any
valuables lying around. She could leaf through his books, help
herself to his food. She could sneak into this room and smother
him with a pillow, or stab him with one of his own kitchen
knives.

He caught sight of himself in his dressing table mirror and felt
weary. He was fifty-one years old with a dead wife and son, and a
daughter who avoided him. For forty-eight hours every week he
stood alone behind a counter surrounded by pet food and rubber
toys and nesting boxes and goldfish. He had few pleasures and
fewer friends. Was it any wonder he was an irritable bastard?

You're the rudest man I ever met. Out of nowhere it popped
into his head. Her usually smiling round face on fire with indig-

nation—and her subsequent visit to the shop to apologize. He remembered her in the park with her ice cream, and in the supermarket earlier this evening. He kept bumping into her.

He wondered if she'd spotted the child's clothes in his basket, and what she'd thought if she had. He'd probably looked like some class of a child catcher, buying clothes for one of his captives. She might have been tempted to call the police.

He grinned at his reflection. For no reason that he could think of, he felt his mood lifting. He got into bed and switched off the lamp and closed his eyes.

And for the first time in weeks, he slept soundly all night.

The Third Week

October 5–11

A change in fortune, a mistaken assumption, and a confrontation.

Friday

"My nose is itchy."

"Scratch it then." James waited while Charlie rubbed at her nose.

"I'm tired of sitting," she said. "I want to go in."

"Nearly finished," he promised. "Just another tiny bit."

Barely two minutes she'd lasted so far. Talk about a short attention span. He regarded his efforts to capture her on paper, and had to admit that it could have been any child, of either gender. Still, at least he was making the effort, doing his homework.

"Can we go to Granny and Granddad's tomorrow?" Charlie asked.

"Not tomorrow, poppet," he told her, "it's a bit too far away. But we'll go soon again, I promise."

"You always say that," she grumbled. "And you never let Eoin come to our house to play. You never do *anything* I want, it's not *fair*."

She looked so woebegone, sitting with her schoolbag trapped between her feet. James closed his sketch pad and reached across to open her door.

"Tell you what," he said. "Tonight we'll go to the movies after dinner, how's that?"

"Can we go to *Horrid Henry* again?" she asked immediately, and James's heart sank. *Horrid Henry* had been horrid enough first time around, last Saturday afternoon in the company of what must surely have been the entire population of Carrickbawn's under-sixes, each of them loaded up with sugar and firing on every one of their little cylinders.

"We'll go to whatever you want," he said. He'd bring his iPod and try to tune the whole thing out, offer it up for the sake of his daughter. At least in the early evening the under-fours would be gone to bed—hopefully.

He waited until Charlie had disappeared into the school before driving off.

———————

Michael locked the shop door and turned the sign from OPEN to CLOSED. In the small back room he perched on his step stool and unscrewed the cap from his bottle of milk and undid the tinfoil wrapping on his lunchtime sandwich. As he bit into it, he wondered if the other sandwiches he'd made this morning had been eaten yet.

Probably the first brown bread the boy had ever seen, and possibly the first ham too. Maybe it would be new for her as well; God knows what kind of diet she'd grown up with. Bit of a change from Coke and biscuits, and whatever other junk they normally ate. Had the lad ever seen a piece of fruit, or a vegetable? Had he ever drunk a glass of milk?

Or maybe they'd dumped Michael's sandwiches in the first bin they'd come to. Maybe she was defying him right now, begging for enough to cover a bag of chips each, and a new bottle of Coke. He had no way of knowing, and he didn't much care. He'd done his bit for them, his conscience was clear.

At least they'd gotten a good breakfast into them—although the porridge hadn't exactly been a roaring success. Michael had served it up to them as soon as they'd appeared in the kitchen. No alternative had been offered. Milk was in a jug on the table, along with a bowl containing a small amount of brown sugar. Without waiting for a reaction, Michael had left them to it and taken the basket of damp laundry out to the clothesline.

When he'd come back in, her bowl was empty and she was attempting to coax the boy to eat from his. Michael had turned his attention to making the sandwiches, his back to them.

"Come on," he'd heard her whisper, "just another bit, for me. Good boy."

Porridge not sweet enough for him. Looking for a few Fig Rolls, presumably. At least she had the sense not to go looking for them. Michael had spread butter and ham and cheese on the brown bread and cut the sandwiches into triangles and wrapped them in tinfoil before turning to face them.

The child's expression was sullen but his porridge bowl was half empty, and the sugar Michael had put on the table had completely disappeared.

Valerie's clothes hung loosely on the girl's thin frame, the skirt too long to look anything but dowdy. The boy's trousers and top seemed a surprisingly good fit, seeing as how Michael hadn't had much of a clue. Ruth had been in charge of all that when their children were small; Michael didn't remember having to buy so much as a hair slide or pair of socks. And after Ruth, the housekeeper had taken over, and Michael had been relieved to let her.

He'd sent his visitors packing at half past eight, along with her plastic bag of junk food, the sandwiches he'd made, and a pint of milk. After seeing them off he'd sprinted upstairs and opened the door to Valerie's room, which smelled of sleep but nothing stronger. The bed was made, surprisingly neatly. Apart from the black plastic bag that lay in a crumpled heap in the corner of the room, the only sign that anyone had moved in was a dog-eared Winnie-the-Pooh book and a battered tin box sitting side by side on one of the bedside lockers. Otherwise it was pretty much exactly as Valerie had left it.

Valerie. Should Michael tell her about all this, was she entitled to know that someone had come along claiming to be the mother of Ethan's child—which, if true, would make the boy her nephew? How would she react if Michael admitted that he'd taken them in? Even to himself, it was hard to explain his actions.

No, he'd wait. He'd do the test and wait for the result. Time enough to tell Valerie then, if it was as the girl claimed. Time enough for them all to come to terms with it then. He'd closed the bedroom door and left the house.

He checked his watch and saw that the half hour he allowed himself for lunch was almost over. He took another bite of his sandwich and drank his milk.

———————

Irene pulled her key from the lock and walked into the hall. From the kitchen came the sound of Emily's laughter. She smelled fried onions. Pilar had forgotten to use the extractor fan again.

She went upstairs and stripped off her gym clothes and stepped into the large rain forest shower in their en suite bathroom. She never used the showers at the gym, opting to wait until she got home to the greater comfort of her own. She scrubbed and lathered and massaged, inhaling scents of eucalyptus and rosemary and mint. For some reason, a session in the gym with Bob always made her feel in greater need of a thorough clean.

Back in the bedroom she sprayed dry oil onto her warm, damp skin. She pulled on a pair of loose silk lilac-colored trousers and a pale pink cashmere wrap top, and slipped her feet into soft camel leather pumps. She brushed her hair and wound it into a loose twist and secured it with a long gold clip.

She dabbed perfume on her wrists and made her way downstairs. In the kitchen Emily was doing a jigsaw at the table and Pilar was emptying the dishwasher.

"Hi, Irene," Emily said, looking up briefly.

"Hello, sweetie." Irene trailed a hand across Emily's shoulders as she walked to the coffee machine. "Did you have a good day?"

"Yeah."

Irene nodded at Pilar as she spooned coffee into the machine. "Everything all right?"

Pilar returned plates to their shelves. "Yes, Mrs. Dillon. Everything fine."

Silence descended on the kitchen. Irene stood by the coffee machine as it bubbled and gurgled into action, and decided that there was little point in mentioning the extractor fan. The au pair would nod and promise to use it, and more than likely forget again.

Pilar closed the empty dishwasher and began to clean the tiles behind the sink.

"Pilar, I finish," Emily announced.

"It's not 'I finish,' it's 'I've finished,'" Irene said.

Emily looked at her mother. "Pilar says 'I finish.'"

"Well," Irene said lightly, "Pilar is wrong." She turned back to the coffee machine, conscious of the silence behind her. What was she expected to do, ignore her child's broken English?

She heard Pilar crossing the room and murmuring to Emily— "Oh, that is very good. You are very clever girl. You like do it again?"—and she gritted her teeth and said nothing.

"No—I want a story." Irene turned to see Emily scrambling off her chair in search of a book as Pilar replaced the jigsaw pieces in their box. Great, now the written word was going to be mangled too.

When the coffee was made she took a cup from the press and filled it. She leaned against the worktop and sipped the hot black liquid, watching as her daughter curled into Pilar's body, listening as the au pair began to read *The Three Billy Goats Gruff* in the worst possible accent.

After a minute she walked from the room, aware of the other woman's eyes following her.

They arrived back at five past seven. Michael let them in. "You have ten minutes before dinner," he said.

She nodded. She looked tired. "Where will we wait?"

"In the bedroom." He had no intention of giving them the run of the house.

In the kitchen he lowered the heat under the potatoes and pulled out the frying pan to put on the sausages and filled a saucepan with water for the peas. He set the table with knives and forks, and put the butter dish and saltcellar in the center. He should be getting her to help, do a bit in return for her keep, but helping out might make her feel too settled. Better to maintain their visitor status, even if it meant waiting on them hand and foot.

It was going to take roughly two weeks to discover if the child was Ethan's. As soon as he'd gotten home from work Michael had applied online for a grandparentage test kit, which was supposed to arrive within three working days. Allowing for the vagaries of the postal service, he should have it by Wednesday or Thursday. The test results, according to the website, would be sent out seven to ten days after receiving the samples.

Two weeks, give or take. Michael would put up with them till then, unless they gave him reason not to.

And after that?

He wouldn't think about after that. He couldn't think about after that.

He drained the potatoes and added butter and black pepper and a splash of milk, and plunged the masher into them. As he filled a jug with tap water—if they thought they were getting Coke here, they had another think coming—there was a soft tap on the kitchen door.

"Come in."

They ate silently and rapidly. Nothing wrong with their appetites. Michael had eaten before they arrived, but he sat at the table with them, pretending to read the paper. Out of the corner of his eye he saw her cutting up the boy's sausages. Neither of them touched the jug of water.

At one stage a few peas rolled from the boy's plate onto the table and from there to the floor, and he looked immediately in Michael's direction as his mother bent to gather them up quickly and lay them by her plate.

They ate everything. When they'd finished she stood and took their plates and cutlery to the sink. "Is it okay if I wash these?" she asked.

Michael looked up. Yes, better to let her do something. "Fill the basin. Wait till the water gets hot. Washing-up liquid is in the press underneath. Don't use too much."

The boy remained seated at the table, as silent as ever. After their dishes had been washed and dried she hovered by the sink.

Michael eventually lifted his eyes from the paper and looked at her.

"I dunno where they go," she said.

Michael stood. "Leave them. You can go back upstairs now."

She lifted the boy from his chair and they walked to the door.

"Thank you for the dinner," she said. "It was lovely. Good night."

"Good night."

Michael replaced their crockery and cutlery and listened to the sound of their footsteps going back upstairs.

As they queued for popcorn, Eoin suddenly said, "Hey."

"What?"

"I see Charlie."

Jackie scanned the knots of people milling around the cinema lobby. "Where?"

He pointed. "There. Can I go and talk to her?"

There was a girl in the crowd with Charlie's hair color, but it was impossible to make out who she was with. "Just for a second," Jackie said. "If you're not back by the time I get the popcorn I'm going in without you."

"Okay."

He sped off, threading through bodies, and she watched him until he vanished.

Not gone away for the weekend then, like Charlie's father had claimed. Of course they might be leaving in the morning, maybe he hadn't actually lied—but he'd implied, hadn't he, that they'd be gone all weekend? And even if he hadn't meant to mislead her, he'd still been abrupt and dismissive, and hadn't suggested any future arrangement. She hoped Eoin wouldn't bring them back with him—the last thing she wanted was to have to make small talk with a man who'd made a very bad first impression.

Her turn arrived and she bought the popcorn. As she replaced her purse Eoin reappeared, thankfully alone.

"Just in time." Jackie scanned the lobby quickly again. "Was Charlie with her dad?"

"Yeah—they're going to see *Horrid Henry*."

"Good for them."

She was glad Eoin had chosen a different film: Now all they needed was for the finishing times not to coincide.

But even if she'd rather not meet him, you'd think he'd bother to come over to say hello to the woman who'd offered to entertain and feed his child and give him a few hours off on a Sunday afternoon.

Talk about antisocial.

Saturday

James sloshed water around the bath, rinsing off the cleanser he'd scrubbed in. He wiped down the tiles around the shower and poured bleach into the toilet bowl. He cleaned the sink and swiped halfheartedly at the taps.

He hated housework, hated the sheer pointlessness of it all. You cleaned everything, and it got dirty again, and you cleaned it again. The mind-numbing boredom of it all, the grinding monotony of it. He'd been happy to leave all that to Frances, and she hadn't complained. It had made perfect sense to James—he'd been out working all day, she'd opted to stay at home and keep house and look after Charlie.

Now, of course, James was doing everything. Working nine-to-five with the rest of the rat race, coming home and sorting the damn house. Cleaning, cooking, washing, ironing—somehow it all got done, albeit in his slapdash, amateurish way. The dust was ignored where he could get away with it, cobwebs gathered in corners and trailed from ceilings of lesser-used rooms. He couldn't remember the last time he'd cleaned a fridge, or defrosted a freezer.

His grasp of ironing was precarious. He'd lost count of the cotton shirts he scorched before his discovery of synthetic fabrics that felt awful but never needed ironing. For everything else he kept the iron on its lowest setting. Less effective, but far safer.

Laundry was another disaster area, colors running willy-nilly into one another until he learned what went together in the machine and what definitely didn't. A wool sweater of Charlie's didn't survive its first wash, barely big enough for any of her dolls afterwards. Like the iron, the washing machine temperature was set to just above cool, and rarely moved.

James's efforts at cooking were marginally more successful, thanks to a book he'd been given as a joke Christmas present by Frances, just a few months before her disappearance. *Cooking for Dummies*, it was called, and James had laughed and put it aside—and afterwards it had become his bible.

This morning they'd had French toast, which seemed to have become their regular Saturday breakfast, and this evening he was planning a vegetable omelette. He wrote a shopping list in his head as he mopped the bathroom floor.

"Dad."

He looked up. Charlie stood in the hall, holding up two halves of a plate. "It fell out of my hands when I was drying it."

James dropped his mop and took the pieces from her. "Don't pick up broken stuff, poppy—you could cut yourself. Just come and tell me, okay?"

"Okay."

"And you didn't have to dry them."

"But I wanted to help you," she said, and his heart turned over. She was a good kid, she was turning out fine, despite his parental fumblings, despite their awful tragedy.

"Tell you what, let's go to the lake when I finish the jobs," he said. High time they saw it, and the day was fine.

Her small face lit up. "Can we bring a picnic?"

"Of course we can—have a look and see what we have in the fridge."

"And can we go to the park tomorrow?"

He smiled. "Yes, if you want."

"Yaaay!"

She spun around the hall, the broken plate forgotten. So easy to make her happy. He wondered how long that would last.

———————

The girl wasn't really trying to hide what she was doing. Maybe she didn't realize that you weren't supposed to pick flowers in a public park. Audrey wondered whether she should say anything. Could she point out politely, in a nonconfrontational way, that the flowers had been planted for the enjoyment of everyone?

The girl wasn't taking very many though, just the odd one here and there. She wasn't leaving any gaps in the display. And Audrey was well aware that her remarks, however well meaning, could be resented. Someone who looked quite harmless, like this girl in her baggy skirt and long cardigan, could turn on you and become quite nasty.

And there was a little boy with her, which you had to take into account too. He might be upset if Audrey intervened, she might startle him if she approached them. Such a small, pale little child, no bit of life about him at all.

Audrey would leave them alone. What were a few flowers? It wasn't as if the girl were snatching handbags or breaking into houses.

She pulled gently on Dolly's leash and walked on.

———————

Irene waited until Martin's program had begun before opening her sketch pad and pulling her pencil quietly from the little zipped case she kept it in. She hated using the charcoal, blackening fingers and clothes and anything you touched afterwards. Luckily, Audrey left it up to her students to use whichever medium they preferred.

From her position on the smaller of the two couches Martin's profile was clearly visible to Irene, and she could work unobserved by him. She sketched him in quickly, trying to remember Audrey's instructions. He leaned back against the couch, hands resting loosely across his abdomen as he watched the television screen.

His lips were parted, a tiny space between them. His long legs extended, knees bent slightly, one ankle resting on the other. He wore sweatpants and a T-shirt, socks but no shoes. At one stage he reached up to rub under his nose with an index finger.

Irene mapped in the overall shape of her husband. She positioned his head, indicated the angle his torso made against the back of the couch, scribbled in his arms, his pelvis, his legs. She regarded the drawing, and decided it was what Audrey had asked for: a quick pose with no detail.

She turned a page and studied what she could see of Martin's face. She drew the curve of his cheek, the upward tilt of his top lip, the line of his near-side eyelash, the globe of his eyeball. She rounded out his head and sketched in his chin, added his ear and shaded in his hair.

The man in her drawing looked nothing like Martin. Her proportions were off, his features all wrong, his nose too long, his eye too small. She turned a page and began again, and her second attempt was only marginally better.

She tried his hands, and then his feet. By the time his program ended, ninety minutes later, she'd filled a dozen pages with her useless, yearning drawings.

He glanced across as he picked up the remote control. "Want to watch anything?"

Irene shook her head.

He noticed her sketch pad. "What are you at?"

Irene closed the book. "Nothing much, just scribbling."

"How you want me?" Pilar lay on the couch. "Like this?"

"Yes, okay." Zarek's charcoal flew across the page. Pilar lay placidly, humming a tune Zarek didn't recognize. He mapped her form in quickly.

"Okay," he said, "now you change."

Pilar lifted her head. "Change? You finish so quick?" She sat up. "I see."

Zarek held out the pad.

Pilar regarded it doubtfully. "This is me?"

"Just quickly," Zarek told her. "Is short pose, no small detail."

"Where is face?"

"No face with short pose," he explained. "Just some shape and line." He turned the page. "Now you sit, please. Just few minutes."

Pilar sat stiffly on the couch, arms folded, a small crease in the skin between her eyes. No humming.

Zarek sketched quickly "If you want," he said, "I do better drawing of you another day." He assumed next week's homework would involve a more detailed study.

"With face?"

"Yes, with all things."

"And color?"

"Yes, if you want."

She considered. "Yes, I like." She thought some more. "I wear my new dress. And hair up."

"Okay."

"And not on couch; outside, in garden."

"Okay." He looked up. "I finish now, thank you."

Better stop before she thought of anything else.

"A gym? You?" His wife laughed. "That's a good one."

The mechanic pulled off his T-shirt. "I'm serious." He balled it up and aimed it at the laundry basket in the corner of the bedroom. "They're offering free workouts, not every day you get something for nothing."

She plumped up her pillow, still smiling. "Yeah, but a *workout*— when have you ever gone near a gym?"

He unzipped his jeans and let them drop and stepped out of them. "First time for everything. Just thought I'd give it a go, that's all."

"Fine—go ahead. Just don't come crying to me when you can't walk the next day."

He pulled off his underpants and stood, hands on hips, before her. "Want to draw me?"

She giggled. "Not just now, thanks."

He lifted the duvet and slid in beside her and slipped a finger under the strap of her nightdress. He pictured the rich blonde woman in bed. *Bet she wears nothing at all.* "Exercise gives you more energy," he said softly, sliding the straps off her shoulders. *Bet she'd love this, bet she's gagging for it.* "You won't be able to keep up with me," he murmured, easing the nightdress down, imagining other, fuller breasts. *Bet she'd like my hands on her, bet I'd drive her wild.* "I'll drive you wild," he whispered. "I'll be after you day and night."

His wife drew in her breath as he dipped his head. "In that case," she said, her hands gripping his dark hair, "forget the free workout—just join up."

Sunday

Carmel loved the first few seconds after waking, when the miracle of it hit her afresh, even before she opened her eyes. The sheets that smelled of flowers, the soft pillow under her head. The wonderful peace, broken only by birdsong from the garden just outside the window.

She breathed deeply, stretching her legs under the duvet, luxuriating in it all, feeling the warmth of Barry's small body pressed up against her, the rapid breathing that caused his chest to rise and fall under her hand. She could stay in this bed nonstop for a week, no problem

She opened her eyes slowly and saw the soft white glow of his hair in the dim light that filtered through the curtains. She bent and put her nose to his head and inhaled the minty shampoo smell of him. Her gaze traveled around the room, taking in the dark bulk of the wardrobe, the chest of drawers that held their clean clothes (clean clothes!), the little press by the bed on which she'd set Barry's book and her treasure box, the pale ribbons of light that framed each window.

She had no idea what time it was—her watch had been exchanged, years ago, for a Saturday-night fix—but she figured it was still early enough; she never slept that late. Another hour she might have, maybe more, of simply lying here with her son safe beside her. Ethan's father would call them in due course, she had no doubt of that, but until then they could relax.

And maybe, since it was Sunday, he'd let them stay in the house, maybe he wouldn't kick them out. Maybe they wouldn't have to walk the streets all day, with security men giving her filthy looks whenever they went into a shop. Maybe for once she wouldn't have to ask the time from people who walked past as if they hadn't heard her.

She'd offer to clean the house for him when they were having breakfast. Clean, or cut the grass, or pull weeds, or anything he needed doing. She knew he might take it the wrong way, he might get offended at her offer, thinking she meant that the house was dirty or the garden was neglected, but that was a chance she'd have to take. She wanted to pay him back in some way, and this was the only thing she could think of.

She turned slowly onto her back, trying not to wake Barry. She lay looking up at the white ceiling with the fancy lamp shade over the bulb. She listened to the repeated chirruping of a bird that must have been just outside the window.

He was checking out her story, he wanted to know if Barry was his grandson. She'd thought he didn't care, that he didn't want to know, but he did. He was letting them stay here until he found out, and they hadn't even done the test yet. It mightn't come for another few days, and then it had to be sent back and they'd have to wait some more. They could be here for ages.

She could still hardly take in what had happened. When she thought about sleeping in the shed—lying on the newspapers, listening to people screaming in the nearby houses and hoping to God none of them found her and Barry—it was like a miracle that he'd come along. He was like some kind of superhero who had rescued them. She pictured him flying through the sky like Superman, and smiled at the ridiculous image.

She'd been so sure they'd never lay eyes on him again—or if they did, that he'd just look through them like most people, pretend he'd never met them. She'd been completely gobsmacked when he'd approached them outside the library. What had changed his mind, why had he suddenly decided to help them?

And handing her a tenner, just like that. She still had eight of it left. She had about €12 altogether, she was hardly spending anything these days now that he was feeding them. Although Barry wouldn't touch the ham in the sandwiches they got for lunch, and she had to promise him a pack of sweets from the euro shop to get him to eat the brown bread.

He wasn't mad about the milk either, always asking her for Coke, but Carmel had persevered, and eventually he'd given in. It felt wrong not to eat and drink what they were getting for nothing. And she knew milk was better than Coke, she wasn't stupid—it was just that Coke was cheaper, and Barry loved it, and she liked seeing him happy. But that was before free milk.

The €5 she'd got from the snotty woman in the park had helped a lot, although she'd hated taking it. The way the woman had looked down her nose at Carmel had made her feel more of a beggar than when she was sitting on the side of the street holding out a cup.

And making sure her handbag was out of reach, as if Carmel was just waiting to grab it. As if Carmel was someone who'd rob a handbag. She felt sorry for the little girl too, with a mother who looked cross when her child hurt herself.

She thought of Ethan's father buying clothes for Barry. Going into a shop and buying them specially, brand-new. She'd nearly made a fool of herself when she'd seen them on the bed, the first clothes he'd had that weren't from a charity shop, or found in a Dumpster. Nobody had been nice to them in so long, it had been all she could do not to bawl her eyes out in front of Ethan's father. He would have loved that.

And when they'd come back to the house on Friday a hair dryer was on the floor outside the bedroom door, and a new child's toothbrush in her toilet bag, and no sign of the old one. She hadn't said anything when they'd gone downstairs; something told her not to mention it, although she really wanted to say thank you to him.

Barry stirred beside her. She stroked his hair. "Shh," she whispered.

She wished Ethan could see the two of them, all cozy in his father's house. She wondered if she'd ever be able to think about Ethan without wanting to cry. She pressed her eyes closed until the stinging went away.

It wasn't all good, of course. There was the problem of getting a job when she couldn't read or write. And even if another miracle happened and someone did offer her work, what would she do about Barry? What was the point of even looking for a job, with no one to mind him?

No—she wouldn't think like that, or else she'd want to give up, and she couldn't give up.

Then there was the problem of what Ethan's father would do when the test results came out. He was probably hoping they didn't show Ethan as the father, so he could be rid of them once and for all. What would he do with a grandchild, where would Barry fit into his life? Where would Carmel fit in?

She looked around the room again, everything becoming clearer as her eyes grew accustomed to the dimness. This must have been Ethan's sister's room. Ethan had mentioned a sister when Carmel had asked him about his family, but she'd gotten the feeling it was hard for him to talk about her.

She assumed the clothes she'd been given had once belonged to the sister. They weren't new, but they were in better condition than anything Carmel had. The skirt was too long and she had to gather the top of it into her knickers to keep it up, but she liked the blouse, and the cardigan was really soft. It was the nicest thing she'd ever owned.

She wondered where the sister was now, and what she'd think of Carmel if they ever came face-to-face. Imagine if they met by accident, and the sister recognized her clothes on Carmel. Hopefully she wouldn't be too mad; she mustn't really have wanted them if she'd left them behind in her father's house.

"I don't want no powwidge," Barry murmured then, his eyes still closed.

"Jus' a little bit," Carmel whispered. "It's nice with sugar, isn't it?"

He shook his head. He rarely wanted to eat first thing in the morning, so she'd gotten used to letting him ask for something when he got hungry later on. Now they were being presented with porridge much earlier than he normally ate, and it was taking all Carmel's powers of persuasion to get him to take it. She knew it wouldn't go down well if he refused it.

"I'll get you crisps later if you eat it all up."

"Why can't we go to a diff'went house?" he asked then, burrowing his fist into her stomach.

She grabbed his hand and held it. "Do you not like this one?"

His head went from side to side again.

"Haven't we a nice bed? It's better than our last one, isn't it?"

"No."

"Oh yes it is. An' a nice carpet on the floor, an' two nice windows, look. One, two." Stroking his hair back from his forehead as she spoke. "An' a nice wardrobe."

Barry pushed his head into her chest. "I don't wike it," he mumbled.

Of course it wasn't the bedroom he was objecting to. Carmel kept stroking his hair. "Don't worry about your granddad," she said. "He's a bit grumpy, but he don't mean it really. Didn't he buy you nice new clothes?"

She heard a door opening on the landing. Ethan's father was up, which probably meant they'd have to get up soon too. After a minute the toilet was flushed. She felt Barry go still, and knew he was listening for more sounds.

She squeezed his hand. "It's okay," she whispered. "I'll mind you, we'll be fine. Don't I always mind you?"

His bark is worse than his bite. She remembered learning that proverb years ago in school. He was grumpy and he never smiled, but he'd given her €10 and bought clothes and a toothbrush for Barry, and he was letting them stay in his house and cooking breakfast and dinner for them, and giving them sandwiches for lunch. And he'd left out a hair dryer, because she'd asked him for one.

And he was Ethan's father. It was important to keep remembering that.

———————

James sat on a bench and watched his daughter climbing the metal frame, reaching for the highest bar. With an effort he resisted the urge to rush over and stand underneath, arms spread to catch her. Charlie was fearless, always had been. He remembered her at eighteen months, trying to clamber over the gate they'd put at the top of the stairs every time their backs were turned.

"*Daddy!*"

She waved triumphantly from the top and James waved back, his toes curling at the thought of her plummeting to the ground. *Put your hand down, stop waving, hold on tight.*

Frances had never been half as nervous about their daughter. "You'll stifle her, watching her like that all the time," she'd say. "Let her off, give her a bit of free rein. What's the worst that can happen to her in the back garden, for goodness' sake?"

James would list the hazards—choking on grass, stung by a wasp, attacked by a wild dog that had managed to jump the fence—and Frances would laugh.

"Listen to you," she'd say. "I don't know how you sleep at night with that imagination. Come on in and drink your tea, she'll be perfectly safe."

And James would make himself turn away, and nothing bad would happen to Charlie in the ten nervous minutes it would take him to finish his tea. And in the end, of course, the horrible irony had been that it was Frances who hadn't been perfectly safe.

"Daddy, will you push me on the swing?"

James got up and crossed the playground after her, and stood behind a swing as she clambered up. This is what his life was now, working at a job he hated from Monday to Friday and entertaining his daughter at the weekends. He began to push.

"Higher, Daddy."

He'd known there was a chance they'd run into Eoin and his mother at some stage. Carrickbawn wasn't that big, they were bound to meet up sooner or later. He just hadn't expected it to be two days after he'd texted her to say they weren't going to be around for the weekend.

When the boy had materialized in the cinema James had braced himself for a meeting with the mother. She couldn't be far behind, she'd surely appear at any moment. He'd already been casting around for an excuse—their weekend trip canceled, her number mislaid—when Eoin had vanished again, and James had been spared an awkward moment.

But of course she'd know now that Charlie hadn't gone away after all. What must she think of him? First the abrupt text, and then to be found out in his lie. Served him right.

And what was he doing anyway, skulking off as soon as someone made contact, someone who'd committed the cardinal sin of inviting his daughter to play with her son? Wasn't it a bit ridiculous to be running scared when his whole reason for moving was so that he and Charlie could have a normal life, or as close to normal as it could ever get for them?

And how presumptuous of him to suspect Eoin's mother of having an ulterior motive—as if any woman in her right mind would choose him.

He still had her number. He'd text her and suggest another day for the children to get together. She might tell him to get lost, and he could hardly blame her if she did, but he'd take the chance for Charlie's sake. He'd wait a few days, he'd text her next week sometime.

"Daddy—watch me!"

Charlie swung away from him, waiting until the arc of the swing had reached its highest point before leaping off, landing unhurt on the springy surface of the playground, but causing considerable palpitations in her father.

———

There was a scatter of wilting flowers by the headstone. Valerie must have stopped by. Bit of a climb down from her usual offering; this lot looked as if they'd been robbed from someone's garden.

Michael placed his far more presentable bouquet in the center of the grave. The headstone needed cleaning, the stone spotted with a greyish-green lichen. He'd get on to someone next week. He stood back and regarded his wife and son's final resting place.

RUTH BROWNE, BELOVED WIFE AND MOTHER, he read. Underneath were the dates of her birth and death, just twenty-seven years apart. And below that, separated from the first entry by a couple of inches, ETHAN BROWNE, BELOVED SON, and his dates, even closer together than Ruth's.

Ethan *had* been beloved, whatever Valerie might say. He had been loved fiercely and completely from the moment he'd been placed in his father's arms, minutes after his birth. Michael's love for his son had been immense.

"There's a girl," he told Ethan now, "who says you're the father of her child. I don't know whether to believe her or not. Wish you could enlighten me."

There had been no sign of his two visitors when he'd left the house for eleven o'clock Mass. He'd left them alone, figuring they might as well have a lie-in one day of the week—and what real damage were they likely to get up to, left alone in the house for an hour? The worst that could happen was she'd try to make breakfast and burn a saucepan.

When he got back from Mass they were up, sitting at the kitchen table. She had a cup of tea in front of her and she told him they'd already eaten, although there was little sign of them having had anything at all.

Michael hadn't pursued it. The boy clearly wasn't a fan of porridge. Probably prefer one of those sugar-laden concoctions that had the cheek to call themselves cereals. If they'd rather eat nothing, that was their lookout. Michael had no intention of feeding them junk.

Her offer of help in the house or garden had touched him oddly. He supposed it was a good thing she was attempting to do something in return for her keep. He'd brought her out to the garden and shown her how to clear the weeds from between the paving stones with a trowel. The child had sat on the garden seat with his Winnie-the-Pooh book, which seemed to be the only one he possessed.

When he'd left for the cemetery Michael deliberately didn't say where he was going, or when he'd be back, still reluctant to get too familiar. She made no mention of Mass: probably hadn't seen the inside of a church in years. The child in all likelihood not even baptized.

He pulled grass from the sides of the grave and threw it into a bin. The graveyard was busy on Sundays, particularly on fine afternoons like this one. Families mostly, some older people, a few lone younger adults, some with a young child or two in tow. Widowed early maybe, like himself.

"I might be a grandfather," he told Ruth. "Can you imagine me with a grandchild? I'm only fifty-one, for crying out loud."

Walking home, it occurred to him that the girl knew where Ethan was buried, if her story was to be believed. She said she'd seen Michael at the funeral, so presumably she'd come to the graveyard. He wondered if she ever visited Ethan's grave. Maybe she did, maybe she'd been the one to leave the flowers he'd seen. If that was the case, he dreaded to think where she'd swiped them from.

The patio was spotless, not a weed to be seen. She'd put them into the green refuse bag he'd left out for her. She'd cleaned the trowel under the outdoor tap and replaced it in the shed. As far as Michael could see, neither she nor the boy had moved from the garden since he'd left.

They sat side by side on the wooden seat. The boy cradled his book and she held a scratched tin box in her lap. Michael recalled seeing it on the bedside locker by Valerie's bed, the morning after they'd moved in.

"Will you tell me when it's ten to six?" she asked Michael. "I want to take him to evening Mass."

"We can't go on like this," Irene said to Martin.

She was on her third very strong vodka and tonic, or she wouldn't have said it. She would have known, if she hadn't been a bit drunk, that there was no point.

Martin looked at her over his iced water. Martin was stone-cold sober. "Irene," he said, "let's just enjoy ourselves."

They were at Chris and Pamela's end-of-summer barbecue, which usually happened earlier in the year, the first week of October hardly qualifying as the end of summer. The delay had been caused by Chris surprising Pamela with a monthlong cruise for their twentieth wedding anniversary, from which they'd returned just the week before.

"You haven't come near me in two years," Irene said. "You're punishing me."

"Don't do this now," Martin replied calmly, glancing around the crowded lawn.

"You're punishing me because I—" Irene broke off as one of the caterers approached with a plate of barbecued banana slices wrapped in bacon. She waved him away but Martin took two and held one out to her.

"You need to eat," he said.

Irene ignored the food. "You always knew I didn't want children," she said. "I'm doing my best with Emily. I can't give what I haven't got."

Martin ate the two canapés. He wore a black shirt, sleeves rolled to the elbows, and grey jeans. He was easily the best-looking man in the garden. Irene had spotted two women checking him out earlier.

"Our marriage is a sham," she said. "Everyone thinks it's perfect but it's a sham. Are you seeing someone else? Are you sleeping with—"

"Irene," Martin said, an edge to his voice now. "Don't."

"Daddy?"

Emily appeared beside them, her cheeks flushed, her dress stained with grass. Martin crouched and hoisted her into his arms.

"You having fun, baby? You want a drumstick?"

"I'm thirsty," she said.

"Come on then—let's get you a drink."

Irene watched them walk towards the patio, her head spinning gently.

Wondering if Eoin would like to meet Charlie next wknd—James Sullivan

Short and to the point. Clearly not a man given to small talk. At least he'd put his full name to this one.

Not surprisingly, no mention of the children's encounter in the cinema on Friday night, no explanation as to why he hadn't come over and introduced himself. But he'd changed his phone setting to allow his number to be displayed when his text had come through.

Jackie saved the number under Charlie. She wasn't responding before Thursday at least. And she wouldn't invite Charlie to their house again. If they did meet up let it be in the park, or let him offer to do the entertaining.

But at least he was making an effort, he was showing some concern for his daughter's well-being. Maybe he wasn't as bad as he seemed, maybe he was just shy. Or maybe Charlie had badgered him into it.

"Not at the table, dear," her mother murmured.

"Sorry." Jackie slid her phone back into her pocket. She'd say nothing to Eoin until arrangements had been made. Her father cut more slices from the roast beef joint and Jackie held out her plate for seconds.

She lifted the boy onto the couch and whispered something to him, and then she vanished. Michael heard her running lightly upstairs. He sat in his usual armchair, already regretting his impulse to let them come into the sitting room for half an hour after dinner. It had seemed churlish to insist that they go straight upstairs to bed, particularly with her spending the afternoon doing his weeding, but now he had to put up with them. And once he'd made the offer for one night, they'd probably expect it all the time.

He and the boy regarded each other warily. That hair was a disgrace, all crooked fringe and ragged ends.

"Who cuts your hair?" Michael asked.

The boy's mouth opened and he seemed to be saying something, but no sound came out.

"Speak up," Michael ordered. "I can't hear you."

"Mammy," the boy said in a tiny voice, shrinking away from him.

"Don't be so frightened," Michael said impatiently. "I'm not going to eat you."

The boy stuck his thumb into his mouth and looked pointedly at the door.

"What's your name?" Michael asked.

The boy whispered something around his thumb.

"What? Take out your thumb."

For a second Michael thought he was going to bolt. He kept his eyes firmly fixed on the sitting room door and said nothing.

"I think you've forgotten your name," Michael said. "I think we'll have to find you a new one."

Still looking away, the boy shook his head slowly.

"You haven't forgotten it?"

Another shake.

"What is it so?"

He slid out his thumb and whispered, "Bawwy."

Barry, the same name as Michael's father. Ethan had only been ten when his grandfather had died—did ten-year-olds even know the first names of their grandparents?

And anyway, Ethan would hardly have remembered his own name, probably, by the time this boy had been born, never mind a dead grandfather. It was coincidence, nothing more.

The girl reappeared with the Winnie-the-Pooh book in her hand and settled on the couch next to the boy, who immediately clambered onto her lap, his thumb drifting again into his mouth. She opened the book and whispered, "Who's he?"

The boy murmured a reply that was lost on Michael. He shook his newspaper open again and turned to the crossword page.

"And where does he live?" the girl whispered. Another inaudible response.

As Michael took a biro from his breast pocket he remembered her saying that she couldn't read. So they were just looking at the pictures and talking about them. Better than nothing, he supposed.

"Look, that's his friend—what's his name?"

Ethan had loved Winnie-the-Pooh. Someone had given him a book of stories for his third birthday and Michael remembered reading it to him at bedtime, sometimes the same story night after night. There had been one story about a game that involved throwing sticks over a bridge into a river.

"The donkey looks sad, don't he? Why's he sad?"

Poohsticks: The name of the game jumped abruptly into Michael's head.

"Oh look, there's the kangaroo."

Ethan used to suck his thumb too. They'd tried everything to get him to stop but nothing had worked. And then he'd stopped overnight, all by himself, a few weeks after he'd started school.

"Look—the umbrella is goin' down the river."

The boy's eyes were beginning to close. He leaned against his mother and yawned hugely, showing a row of tiny even teeth. The girl stroked his hair absently as they went through the book.

Michael returned to his crossword and attempted to concentrate, but he was distracted by the low whispers on the couch. He threw a couple of briquettes into the fire, causing a small shower of sparks to fly upwards.

He wondered if it had ever crossed her mind to look for a job. Of course there was the problem of the child—who would look after him if she went out to work? Would she have to wait until he started school? And even with him off her hands, what job could she hope to get, an ex–drug addict with no literacy skills and precious few qualifications, if any?

And what about a place to live when they left Michael's house? How was she going to afford that? As a single parent, surely she'd be entitled to some kind of rent allowance; there must be a state handout for the likes of her. Not that she'd have the wit to go about claiming it on her own.

He read the same clue for what must be the sixth time. They weren't his problem, not yet anyhow.

After a few minutes the girl closed the book and began to maneuver herself and her son off the couch, trying not to wake him.

Michael got up and lifted the boy from her arms, ignoring her look of surprise. "Open the door," he muttered.

The boy weighed nothing, or next to nothing. He felt like a bird in Michael's arms. His hair smelled of the mint shampoo Michael had seen in her toilet bag. They climbed the stairs silently, the girl in front. She opened the bedroom door and pulled back the sheets, and Michael laid the boy onto the bed.

For the first time, a tiny smile flitted across her face.

"Thanks," she said. "His name's Barry," she added.

Michael turned and left the room without responding. She probably thought he was getting all grandfatherly now. Back in the sitting room he plumped the couch cushions that their bodies had flattened, and returned to his crossword.

Barry. It was a coincidence, that was all.

I am nothing to write home about, Audrey Matthews had entered in her diary on her seventeenth birthday. *I have frizzy hair that looks red in the sun and my eyes are too pale and I'm big-boned. I have never had a boyfriend or got a Valentine card, or even had anyone whistle at me in the street. Nobody looks twice at me.*

Of course she'd hoped, at seventeen, that she wouldn't be alone for much longer. She'd woken each morning with a sense of expectation: Maybe today it would happen, maybe someone would catch her eye on the bus, or in the library after school, or walking home for dinner. Maybe today someone would look twice at her, and see beyond the frizzy hair and big build.

But it didn't happen at seventeen, or at eighteen or nineteen either. When she was twenty and a student in Limerick's College of Art, Audrey answered an ad in one of the local papers and arranged to meet a twenty-six-year-old man—*GSOH, honest, romantic*—for coffee. She sat for half an hour in her pink jacket and blue skirt, sipping a cappuccino and trying not to watch the café door.

Three weeks later she tried again, this time choosing a man who described himself as easygoing and down to earth. He turned up, but ten minutes into their stilted conversation his phone rang and he left, full of apologies—his friend's car had broken down. Promising, as he walked away, to call her again.

When the third man made it quite plain, before his latte arrived, that he wanted a lot more than coffee, it was Audrey's turn to make an excuse and leave.

She decided to try singles holidays. The first one, a week in Rome, was truly awful. Audrey was the youngest by twenty years, and most of the other females were leathery-skinned divorcées who spoke bitterly of their exes to Audrey, and dropped her immediately whenever any of the men in the group appeared.

By the end of the week Audrey had had a single conversation with Frank, who invited her to his room after he'd downed several glasses of Prosecco, and another with Victor, who broke down in the catacombs as he described being left at the altar by the love of his life.

"She was my soul mate," he wept, oblivious to the dark, earthy passages through which they trailed. "I'll never find someone like her again." Audrey felt like pointing out—kindly, of course—that someone like his ex-fiancée might well leave him standing on his own at the altar for a second time, but she held her tongue and tried to ignore the curious glances from nearby holidaymakers.

After two similarly unromantic breaks, she gave up on the idea of singles holidays and decided to let nature take its course. At that stage she was twenty-five, and she'd recently gotten a job as an art teacher in the larger of Carrickbawn's two secondary schools. She was heartened to see a number of single men among the staff: Surely one of them would regard Audrey as a viable proposition.

She was well aware that not much had changed in terms of her appearance since her seventeenth birthday. Her hair had improved somewhat, thanks to the arrival of de-frizzing products, but her weight had increased, food being her chief comfort in times of loneliness. She regarded herself as more curvy than obese, and while she'd never been overly bothered about not having a size-four figure, she wouldn't have minded more shapely knees, and at least the suggestion of a waist.

All her life Audrey loved color. She adored bright, primary shades and filled her wardrobe with patterns and swirls and bold designs that she knew many a similarly built woman would have balked at. She wore scarves and ruffles and layers, and she chose fabrics that tended to float around her as she walked. She was conscious of sniggers from the meaner girls in her classes—and the disparaging looks of some of her slimmer female colleagues—but she did her best to ignore them.

She felt she was fairly popular with her students in general, and she was on cordial terms with the entire staff. She made an effort to be pleasant and good-humored with everyone, as her mother had always urged her to be.

"Audrey, you're like a ray of sunshine," one of her colleagues declared once. "Never in a bad mood, always smiling."

But none of the men asked her out. Nobody even suggested going for a coffee after school, or lunch on the weekend. She was a regular attendee of staff outings, but there was never a hint of romantic interest from anyone. One by one she signed their engagement cards and contributed to their wedding presents, and as the years went by she struggled to keep her hopes intact.

And now she was thirty-seven, and twenty more Valentine's Days had come and gone without a visit from the postman. Her thirty-eighth birthday was only a few weeks away, and she was at home alone on another weekend night. And it was becoming harder and harder to believe that there was still someone out there who was destined to fall in love with her.

She put another briquette on the fire—she must be the only person in Carrickbawn with a fire lit on this balmy evening, but she hated sitting in front of an empty fireplace. Back in the kitchen she made tea and took a packet of Ritz crackers from the press. She topped ten of them with a square of cheddar cheese, a wedge of apple, and a blob of whole-grain mustard with honey.

She brought her supper back into the sitting room and switched on the television, selecting a documentary on blue whales in favor of a repeat of *Love, Actually*, normally one of her favorite films. The last thing she wanted to watch this evening was several people falling blissfully in love.

As she settled back on the couch Dolly opened her eyes, grunted contentedly, and closed them again. Audrey lay her supper aside quietly and reached for the sketch pad and charcoal stick that sat on the little end table. She opened a page and began to draw the curve of Dolly's head, the round black nose, the tiny pink pads beneath the paws, the short hind legs that quivered abruptly every so often.

Her charcoal flew across the paper as her subject began to appear. When the drawing was finished she regarded it critically. She flipped through the pad and looked at her other efforts— Pauline standing by her patio table, cup in hand; a view of Kevin from Audrey's bedroom window as he stood, lost in thought, in his garden; a couple of women deep in conversation outside a house across the road; some children playing by the lake a few weeks ago; the school caretaker, sitting in the sun outside the staff room window one lunchtime, enjoying an illicit cigarette while the principal was away.

Audrey was an observer, grabbing moments from other people's lives and capturing them in her sketch pad. Maybe that was as good as she was going to get; maybe there was nobody waiting to meet her after all.

Oh, stop it, she told herself impatiently. *You could be so much worse off. You could be homeless, or bereaved, or the victim of a crime, or dying of starvation in some third-world country.*

But she wasn't any of those things, she was just lonely. Which of course was less of a hardship than not having a roof over your head, or not knowing where your next meal was coming from, but which was still quite enough to leave you feeling fairly desolate every now and again.

She laid aside her pad and went back to her supper.

Monday

They ate their porridge as silently as ever. After making the lunchtime sandwiches Michael stood by the window and considered the sudden change in the weather that had caused the heavens to open. The garden was saturated—it must have been raining for most of the night. What was he to do? He could hardly throw them out in this rain, but he was equally determined not to leave them in the house all day on their own.

He turned and regarded the boy, his porridge half eaten, a dribble of milk at the corner of his mouth. He wondered what on earth he'd do with him in the pet shop. A small child would be bored to death. Still, it looked like he had little choice.

"He can come to the shop with me until it clears up," he said to the girl. "You can call and collect him." Let her sort herself out, she was old enough.

Before she could respond, Barry pulled at her sleeve and she leaned and put her ear to his mouth. He whispered something and she whispered back, and he shook his head vehemently. She whispered again, and again he shook his head.

Michael waited, his arms folded. Of course the boy didn't want to spend the day with a grumpy old man: What child in his right mind would? He waited to see if she managed to persuade him.

She lifted her head eventually. "Can he bring his book with him?"

"Yes." The more distractions he had, the better.

"An' can I call in at lunchtime an' see him?" she asked. "If it's still rainin', I mean."

"You can." Hopefully the rain would have stopped long before lunchtime. "We leave in ten minutes," he told her, assuming she'd want to go as far as the shop with them. Assuming that the boy would insist on it.

Upstairs he pulled a suitcase from the top of his wardrobe and rummaged through the children's books that were piled in there. He hadn't looked at them in years, not since his children had stopped demanding bedtime stories. He pulled out half a dozen and packed them in the small rucksack that usually held just his lunch. He brushed his teeth and went downstairs.

They were sitting where he'd left them, the boy's face turned into his mother's chest. Michael added the three wrapped sandwiches to his rucksack. In the hall he took a black umbrella from the hall stand and handed it to the girl. She accepted it wordlessly.

"Don't lose it," he warned, taking his golf umbrella from its hook. The three of them walked out and Michael unfurled the big blue-and-green umbrella over them. A gift, his bank had called it, rather than something that Michael had paid for several times over in bank charges.

As they turned onto the path outside, one of Michael's neighbors emerged from her house two doors up. Michael nodded as she passed them, noting the curious glance she threw at his companions. Let her think what she liked. They made their way along the wet streets and he wondered, with a mixture of apprehension and irritation, how the morning would go.

———

Dear Mama and Papa, Zarek wrote. He stopped and stuck the end of his pen into his mouth. Writing his weekly letter home—

phone calls were for special occasions—was a task that he approached with mixed emotions.

The weather here has been unusually fine until today, he wrote. *Now it is raining heavily, and the sky is full of cloud.*

He had the apartment to himself on weekday mornings, with Pilar and Anton both gone to work. The café didn't open until eleven, and some days Zarek's shift didn't begin until well after that. He relished the peace of the empty apartment.

The café was busy last week. The good weather brought many people into town. This week will be quieter, I think.

As he wrote, he imagined his mother coming out to the hall in her dressing gown, sliding open his envelope and pulling out the sheets and unfolding them. He saw her tucking the bank draft into her pocket as she called to Zarek's father that there was a letter from Ireland.

I have bought my plane ticket for Christmas. I will see you all, God willing, on December the twenty-third, and I will stay for five days.

He missed Poland deeply. He missed the different smells and tastes and sights, the different quality of the air. He missed his family and friends—and of course he missed being surrounded by his own language, where he could speak without struggling to be understood.

I was glad to hear about the new bookshelves. I look forward to seeing them when I am home.

That was what his €150 had bought. He was happy it was something that everyone would benefit from, but sorry that they hadn't chosen something more frivolous than a bookcase, like a gas barbecue that would keep his father happily occupied, or one of those garden seats on a swing that his parents could enjoy on fine evenings.

Pilar and Anton are both well. Pilar found a €5 note on the street a few days ago and she bought a coffee cake, which we all shared. It was good, but of course not as good as your poppy seed cake, Mama.

The previous evening Anton had cooked a fish dish that was halfway between a soup and a stew, which he said was a specialty of Brittany. He was the first Frenchman Zarek had ever met, and in addition to producing delicious meals he played guitar and sang mournful French songs, and the words sounded like they'd been soaked in honey.

I was glad to get the photo of Beata's new hairstyle. The shorter length suits her, I think.

Zarek finished the letter and added the bank draft. He made no mention of the art classes. It was the smaller by far of the two secrets he kept from his parents, and it caused him a lot less torment than the greater one.

As they approached the pet shop Carmel recalled their last visit there. Ethan's father threatening to call the police, reducing her to tears as she and Barry had left. She'd called him a bastard—did he remember? She glanced at him but he appeared to have nothing more on his mind than getting in from the rain.

He took a bunch of keys from the front pocket of his rucksack and turned to her. "We're going in the back way," he said. "We'll see you later."

Telling her to get lost. She crouched and gave Barry a quick hug. Immediately his bottom lip began to quiver.

"I'll be back soon, promise," she whispered. "I'll bring you a surprise, like I said. Be a good boy, okay? An' don't forget to say if you have to make a wee, don't wet your new pants, okay?"

She turned and left them before Barry had a chance to protest. How would they be, the two of them together without her? As she made her way to the main road she struggled to open the umbrella Ethan's father had given her, her eyes swimming with sudden tears. She blinked them away and stood at the edge of the path and waited for a break in the traffic. This was the first time she and Barry would be parted for longer than a few minutes since he'd been born.

She crossed the street, the rain still pelting down. Already her shoes were soaked, and the hem of her skirt was sticking unpleasantly to her legs. She longed for a hot bath, and tried to imagine lying in the scented water, her hair spread out like a halo around her head.

Maybe Ethan's father would let her have a bath this evening, after Barry had gone to bed. Maybe she'd swipe a bottle of bath stuff in the euro shop, just in case. And she could let her hair get as wet as it wanted, and dry it with the hair dryer afterwards.

A woman came towards her in a motorized wheelchair. Carmel stepped off the path to avoid her, almost colliding with a cyclist who swore loudly before swerving around her and cycling on.

She pulled her jacket more tightly closed and plodded on, tears running freely down her face, not caring who saw. Knowing none of them would give a damn.

———————

From behind the vertical blinds of the gym's floor-to-ceiling windows Irene watched the mechanic locking his car and jogging through the rain towards the front door, holding a sports bag over his head. While she waited for him to make his way to her she drank water and gathered her hair into a pink elastic loop.

The gym was almost empty, the afternoon members mostly gone home, the evening crowd not yet arrived. A man jogged steadily on one of the treadmills and two women worked their way around the circuit of resistance machines. A bank of televisions high on one wall displayed frighteningly thin models sauntering along a catwalk as music pumped from speakers on the ceiling.

The door opened and he appeared. He wore navy tracksuit bottoms and a blue T-shirt, and sneakers that had definitely seen better days. Irene walked across to him, her hand out.

"Hello there. You made it." She pretended to think. "It's...Ger, isn't it?"

He shook her hand, his grip firm. "That's right." No sign of discomfiture. "Go easy on me."

She smiled. "Not a chance."

She'd forgotten how dark his eyes were, how solidly built he was. The T-shirt strained across his chest. He was slightly shorter than Martin, but just as broad. "Let's see what you're made of," she said, leading him towards the bicycles.

He was strong, but not terribly fit. As Irene guided him through the workings of the various machines a sweat broke out on his forehead, and the fabric of his T-shirt began to darken, but he didn't protest. He was pushing himself, trying to impress her with his strength and stamina, but most of her male clients did that.

Towards the end of the session the last of the other gym users left the room, and they were alone. "You'll be rushing home after this," Irene said as he replaced the weights he'd been using for the bench presses.

"I have a late job on," he said, his back to her.

Expected home for his dinner, the wife slaving over a hot stove for him. Irene led him to the final station and demonstrated the correct rowing position. "Back straight," she ordered. "Bend from the hips."

He straddled the machine and put his feet into the stirrups and began to row. "Keep your back straight," she repeated.

He was nothing to her, he was just her way of coping. Any

man would do—any man had done in the past—but he was here
now. If he asked, she'd accept.

He finished rowing and sat, breathing heavily. Irene tore paper
towels from the roll by the water station and handed them to
him, and he wiped the sweat from his face and behind his neck.

"Well done," she said. "You put up a brave fight."

He got to his feet. "That was good," he said, still panting.
"You're good at this."

"I like to see people working up a sweat," she said.

"We might do it again sometime." He ran a hand through his
damp hair. His face was flushed, and it suited him. "When you're
not working."

"Sure," she said. "You have my number."

———

Barry sat hunched on a chair behind the counter, book clutched
in his arms, an occasional dry sob lifting his thin shoulders.
Whenever the shop door opened he looked at the floor and made
no response if any of the customers spoke to him.

Michael had ignored the earlier tears, preoccupied as he was
with the normal Monday-morning chores, and also reluctant to
unnerve the child any further. Maybe never separated from the
mother before; not surprising that he was upset now, if that was
the case.

When the tears had turned finally to sniffles Michael had
pulled out his handkerchief. Barry had flinched at his approach.

"Just wiping your face, that's all," Michael had told him, in as
gentle a voice as he could muster. "Just mopping you up before
you turn into a puddle." He'd put a hand under the boy's chin
and repaired the damage as best he could, and Barry had looked
steadfastly over Michael's shoulder and endured it.

"I'm not going to hurt you," Michael had continued in the

same low, even voice. "I'm just a bit grumpy sometimes, that's all." He'd been struck by a sudden inspiration. "I'm a bit like Eeyore, you know, the donkey in Winnie-the-Pooh?"

Barry's eyes had jumped to Michael's face for a second, and slid away again.

"Eeyore is a bit grumpy sometimes, isn't he?"

No response; but at least the tears had stopped. Michael had returned the handkerchief to his pocket. "Why don't you have a look at Winnie-the-Pooh?"

But Barry had pressed the book to his chest and made no effort to open it, and Michael had given up. He'd told anyone who asked that he was looking after the child for a friend, and thankfully, nobody had pursued it.

Now, at half past ten, it was still raining heavily. Barry yawned and shifted slightly in his chair. Michael decided to give it another go.

"This is my shop," he said. Leaning against the counter, a good six feet away.

No response.

"It's a good shop, isn't it?"

Nothing.

Michael indicated the tank by the wall that housed a dozen or so goldfish. "See the fish swimming around? They're called goldfish, because they're sort of gold in color."

The boy turned towards the tank and regarded its occupants solemnly, his thumb drifting to his mouth.

"Have you any more story books?" Michael asked.

He shook his head slowly.

Michael went into the back room and brought out his rucksack. He set it on the counter and pulled out a book.

"See this?" he asked, holding it up. "It's about a train."

Barry let his thumb slide out of his mouth. "Thomas the Tank Engine." A tiny whisper.

Michael looked at him in surprise. "You know it?"

A small nod. "I seen him."

"Where?"

"On telly."

Michael laid the book on the shelf next to the boy. "You could look at the pictures if you like." He walked off and stood by the tins of cat food for a minute or so. When he returned, Barry was turning the pages.

It was what anyone would do. Children needed stimulation if they were to grow up with any bit of intelligence. Michael would have done the same for any child, particularly one as silent as this boy. It was unnatural for children to be that quiet.

He watched the white head bent over the book. He heard the small rustle as the pages were turned, and the shallow, rapid breathing. He thought there was something heartbreaking about the vulnerability of small children. Whatever tomfoolery the girl might be up to, her son was wholly innocent.

The shop door opened again and he turned his head towards it.

———————

"Come on in," the mechanic called.

His wife walked into the bathroom. "What are you up to? Didn't you have a shower at the gym?"

"Yeah," he said, "but it was a bit rushed." He swirled a hand through the foamy water. "I could do with some company in here."

She smiled. "I don't need a bath, I'm not dirty."

"'Course you are," he said. "You're the dirtiest girl I know. Come on in, there's loads of room."

She giggled. "Go on then." She pulled her dress over her head and laid it on the stool.

"Keep going," he said.

She undid her bra and dropped it on the floor.

"More."

She hooked her thumbs into the waistband of her panties and pushed them over her hips and let them fall. "Here I come," she said, stepping over the side and lowering herself into the water.

"See?" He squirted shower gel into his palm. "Jesus, you're filthy," he said, massaging it into her thighs. "I'll have to give you a good scrub."

"Wow." She closed her eyes and lay back. "You weren't kidding about a workout making you more energetic."

"Baby," he said softly, inching his way upwards, "you have no idea."

———————

"Teeth, love," Pauline said, and Kevin took his toothbrush from its mug and waited while she ran a line of paste onto the bristles. He wore the blue pajamas he'd always worn—or rather, the latest version of the only shade and style he would tolerate.

He spat into the sink, and Pauline handed him a glass of water. His teeth were cream in color, and in perfect condition. In his entire life he'd never needed a single filling, despite the chocolate and sweets he ate whenever he got a chance. He'd gone through adolescence without a spot, his hair had never been greasy.

You had to wonder about a God who paired such a perfect body with a damaged mind. Was it supposed to be compensation, or the cruelest of jokes?

She waited while he took off his slippers and climbed into bed, and then she tucked the blankets up to his chin. He'd never been a fan of duvets; he preferred something that could be wrapped snugly around him.

"Can we go to the lake tomorrow?" he asked as she smoothed the sheet. Since he'd learned to swim as a teenager the lake was one of his favorite places. Pauline had taken him there several times over the summer, usually bringing a picnic and spending the whole day.

"Well, the forecast isn't great for the next few days," Pauline answered, "but if it picks up again we'll go. You'd like another swim before the winter, would you?"

"Yeah." He loved the water, he was like a fish in it. "If it's not too cold."

"We'll see." She bent and kissed his cheek. "Good night, love, sleep well."

She left his night-light on and padded downstairs. In the kitchen she made a cup of tea and took two Jaffa Cakes out of their pack to go with it. She brought them into the sitting room and raised the volume on *Fair City* before taking her knitting from the basket at her feet. She didn't really follow *Fair City*, she didn't follow any of the soaps, but she liked the sound of it while she knit.

She'd be finished with the front of the sweater by the end of the week, and then it was just the sleeves and the neckband, and putting it all together. She had plenty of time, his birthday wasn't for another three weeks. Forty-one, could you believe it? And her heading towards sixty-six in February, and eligible for the free travel.

They'd make good use of the free travel. Kevin loved the train. They could go to Dublin to see the zoo and the wax museum. Or Galway, and transfer to the Salthill bus for him to have a swim. Next summer they could do all that.

But the free travel was the only good thing Pauline could see about getting older. When she thought of the future it was with huge anxiety. What would become of Kevin when she wasn't around to look after him anymore?

She couldn't expect her sister to take him in. Sue had her own responsibilities, with a father-in-law down the road who was becoming more dependent on them every year and a daughter who'd just taken herself and her three small children out of an abusive marriage.

Where would Kevin end up, what alternative was there for him but a home where he would probably be left sitting in an armchair for hours every day, and given pills if he made a fuss? Pauline couldn't bear the thought. Her needles clacked as she worked along the row, the pale blue wool unraveling jerkily from its ball as it was gathered up.

She tried to banish the gloomy thoughts. She'd go on for years yet, she was as healthy as a horse. And by the time Kevin was eventually left alone, there might be some kind of nice sheltered accommodation for him, with enough supervision to keep him safe.

When the ads came on she put down her needles and dipped one of the biscuits into her tea. She wouldn't worry. It might never happen.

Tuesday

There was a large brown envelope sitting on the hall tiles when Michael came downstairs. He picked it up and turned it over—and realized, by the complete absence of return address, no indication anywhere of the sender's identity, that it must be the paternity test kit. At least they were quick.

He pushed a finger under the flap and slid it across. Inside he found an information sheet, a return envelope, and three smaller envelopes, each a different pastel color and each containing two cotton swabs colored to match their envelopes.

He scanned the information sheet rapidly and saw that it repeated what he'd already learned on the website. He pushed everything back into the big envelope and brought it into the kitchen while he made the porridge.

When the other two came down he waited until they were sitting at the table.

"That test came," he said, watching her face.

She looked unconcerned. "So what have we to do?"

"It's just swabs," he said. "Like cotton wool buds, like things people clean their ears with."

"What do you do with them?"

"You rub them on the inside of your mouth. We'll do it this evening."

She poured milk on their porridge. "Okay."

Michael turned to look out the window. A weak sun shone,

hardly there at all, but a vast improvement on yesterday morning's rain.

He began to make the sandwiches. "I'll take the boy," he said, spreading butter thinly. "It's better for him than dragging him around the streets all day. You can come and get him at lunchtime."

"Okay," she repeated. Michael turned and saw that Barry was poking at his porridge and not looking unduly concerned at the thought of spending more time in the shop.

Today he'd show him *Where the Wild Things Are*. That had been one of Valerie's favorites. He'd read it to the boy. Children needed to be read to.

———

"I'm lookin' for work," she said. Aware of how she must appear, although she'd put on a bit of lipstick from the samples in Boots and combed her hair outside the door.

The man behind the newsagent's counter barely glanced at her. "Nothing at the moment."

"Any jobs goin'?" she asked in the stationery shop next to the newsagent's.

"No." The girl, younger than herself, was filing her nails. A white powdery film sat on the pages of the magazine that was open in her lap.

"Can you ask your boss?"

The girl gave Carmel an icy look. "He's my father," she said. "There's no jobs."

"I'm lookin' for work," she said to the woman behind the ticket desk at the cinema.

"Well, don't look at me," the woman said. "Manager comes on duty in the evenings. Next."

"I need a job," she said in a pub.

The barman looked her up and down. "Have you worked be-hind a bar before?"

"No, but I—"

"Can you pull a pint?"

"No, but—"

"Sorry." He didn't look sorry.

"I'm a quick learner," she said.

"I'll bet you are," he said, his eyes on the front of her blouse.

Carmel turned and walked out.

———————

Irene picked up her phone. "Yes."

"It's Ger," he said. "I was at the gym yesterday."

She said nothing. He was keen.

"I was wondering if you're free some evening this week."

"Friday," she said. Martin got home at six on Fridays. "Seven o'clock," she said. "Where?"

"You could come to the garage. There's a room."

The garage: Talk about slumming it. But the notion was mildly exciting.

"Make sure you have a shower before I get there," she said, and hung up.

———————

"When you're drawing hands," Audrey said, "map in the overall shape first, like you do for the short poses, then find the line of the knuckles, using your pencil to give you the angle like I showed you last week, and from there draw in the fingers, noting their relationship to one another, which one is longest, et cetera. It might be helpful to think in terms of fingerless gloves."

Hard to believe this was the third class, they were halfway

through the course. The weeks were dashing by, and still she felt that she hardly knew any of them. Of course it was hard to get to know someone while the class was going on, when she was the teacher and trying to spread herself evenly among the five of them.

And it wasn't as if she could launch into a conversation when they were all trying to concentrate on their drawing—which was what they'd paid her for, after all.

So getting to know them was confined to break time, and then it depended largely on who happened to be standing nearby when she filled her cup and moved out of the queue. Up to this, the only people she'd spoken to properly had been Jackie and Meg, and all she really knew about Meg was that she ran her own playschool.

The fact was, all of them were still practically strangers to her—and of her five students, James Sullivan remained the most unknown quantity. He was quiet, but it was more than that. For whatever reason, he didn't seem in the least interested in getting to know anyone. Look how he kept disappearing at break time, and he barely opened his mouth the rest of the time. Shame, really, given that he'd been her only hope among the males—not that the choice had been exactly wide.

Zarek, though, was a delight. Always good-humored, always eager for Audrey's advice, even if he was the one who needed it the least. She hadn't been surprised to learn that this wasn't his first attempt at life drawing.

"I like to draw," he told her, "is good for relaxing." Poor man, probably catching about a quarter of what she said, despite her attempts to make sure he understood.

Sadly, her efforts to bring him and Jackie together were proving useless. When she did manage to draw him into conversation with Jackie he made polite small talk with both women, not appearing remotely interested in letting Audrey slip discreetly away.

Irene clearly was no artist, but she was easily the liveliest in the class, keeping the rest of them amused with frequent deprecatory comments on her own efforts. For all her wisecracking, though, Audrey knew virtually nothing about her life outside the classroom. She knew nothing about any of their lives.

She stood behind Irene's latest drawing. Jackie's hand had been drawn at such an improbable angle to her arm that she'd have to have severely dislocated her wrist to achieve it.

Irene looked up and grinned. "What d'you think, Audrey? Will they be looking for it in the Louvre?"

Michael swept the pale blue swab gently around Barry's mouth. This was it, he told himself, this would give him the answer. The child held his mother's hand and kept his eyes on her face as Michael worked.

"Good boy," she murmured. "See? I told you it wouldn't hurt."

Michael removed the swab. "Wait here."

In his bedroom he placed it on the edge of his chest of drawers to dry, careful not to allow the tip to come into contact with anything. He had to do this right, it had to be perfect.

He took one of the pink swabs from its envelope and returned to the bathroom and handed it to Carmel. "Roll it against your cheek and under your tongue and behind your bottom lip, and don't stop till I tell you."

He counted slowly to ten in his head. Barry stared as she moved the swab around her mouth. She kept her eyes fixed on the middle of Michael's chest. At ten he held out his hand and she gave him the swab.

"Dinner in ten minutes," he told them.

Back in his room he used the green swab to collect his own sample. He regarded the three swabs sitting side by side on the chest of drawers. He wrote their three names on the appropriate envelopes. In the morning when they were dry he'd pack up the swabs and post them off, and then they'd wait.

And then what? His mind still refused to go any further. What a turn his life had taken, Ethan still creating turmoil from the other side of the grave. Michael closed his bedroom door gently and went downstairs to take the shepherd's pie from the oven.

"Working in café is okay," Zarek said. "The other peoples are friendly, it is not so bad."

"And if you get hungry you can help yourself, I suppose," Audrey said.

He looked mildly shocked. "Oh no, Audrey, I do not like the fast food, the chip and the burger. It is not good, and very full with the fat. I like to eat the food that is healthy for the body."

And Audrey, who had a hard time resisting food that was full with the fat—a bag of salty, vinegary chips, say, with a generous dollop of ketchup—decided that a polite smile was the only possible response.

"My flat mate Anton is from France," Zarek went on. "He is very good cook. He cook very nice food, very healthy."

"Your own French chef—lucky you."

"Yes," Zarek replied. "I am very lucky."

"Do you have kids?" Fiona asked.

Irene nodded. The boredom of small talk. "One. You?"

"Actually"—Fiona smiled, the color rising in her pale face—"I don't have any children yet, but I've just found out that I'm pregnant."

Irene raised an eyebrow. "And you're happy about it?"

Fiona looked at her in surprise. "Oh yes, very happy. Delighted. Of course."

"In that case, congratulations." Irene sipped her coffee and grimaced. "Jesus, I thought the tea was bad till I tasted this."

"Weren't you?" Fiona asked.

"Wasn't I what?"

"Happy—when you found out you were pregnant, I mean. Sorry," she added quickly, reddening again, "it's just that you asked me, and I thought you sounded as if…well, as if you weren't—happy I mean, when you found out. Sorry," she repeated, "maybe I'm being too personal."

What a little mouse she was, tiptoeing around Irene, stuttering and stumbling as if she were going to be taken out and shot if she said the wrong thing.

"I was as sick as a pig for the whole nine months," Irene said. "Couldn't wait for it to be over."

"But then your baby was born, and it made it all worthwhile," Fiona said, and Irene hadn't the heart to tell the silly cow the truth.

"Of course," she said. "When are you due?"

"Oh, not for ages, not till next May."

Irene sipped more horrible coffee. Barely pregnant and over the moon about it, dying to be telling the world. Took all sorts.

"I was wondering if you'd like to come to a birthday party—well, it's really a children's party—" Meg laughed and pushed her red braid behind her ear "—it's my daughter actually, she'll be five. But I thought it might be interesting for you, you know, an Irish birthday party, just to see what it's like."

Zarek struggled to keep his polite smile in place. "Er…when is party?"

"Friday, around three o'clock. You wouldn't have to stay for long, just a glass of wine, or whatever...you know, just to experience it."

"Oh, sorry, on Friday I work all the day."

"Oh...well, no harm, just thought I'd ask." She smiled brightly before lifting her mug to her lips.

"Sorry," Zarek repeated, watching her glasses fog up from the coffee's steam. Another lie, but he felt it was unavoidable. The invitation had perplexed him. He had no experience of Irish children's parties—but surely it was rather odd to invite a man to a party for a little girl?

Coupled with Meg's presence at the swimming pool the previous Thursday, the invitation suggested rather more to him.

He might be wrong, he reminded himself, he might be misjudging her. Maybe she genuinely felt it would be interesting for him to witness an Irish child's birthday party.

But he thought not.

"It's between the fire station and the library," Irene said. "Red-brick building, two stories. Floor-to-ceiling windows."

"Oh yes," Audrey said vaguely. She must have walked past it umpteen times—she went to the library every two weeks or so—but she had no memory of seeing a gym on that street. Or maybe she'd seen it and blotted it out.

"I should have known you had a job that involved lots of exercise," she told Irene. "You're so lovely and slim. You must be really fit."

"Anyone can be fit," Irene replied. "All it takes is a bit of willpower. You'd be amazed at how quickly people change once they start to eat right and take some exercise."

"Oh, I'm sure you're right," Audrey said, attempting to suck in her stomach, and ignoring the last custard cream on the plate beside her.

"People come in for a free workout, and most of them are pleasantly surprised by how much easier it is than they were expecting. We tailor our programs to suit the person's ability, and then adjust them as they start to get fit."

"Really? That's so interesting," Audrey said, beginning to edge away. "And now you'll have to excuse me, I need to run to the loo before we go back in."

She made her escape, vowing to avoid Irene in future during the breaks.

"Night-night, sweetie," James said, and hung up. He'd wait until their model went in—the class couldn't very well resume without her.

He could see her from the car, sitting on the low wall to the side of the front door. He'd momentarily forgotten her name; he'd always been useless with names. Frances often had to remind him who was who at dinner parties.

He supposed she wasn't unattractive, in a girl-next-door kind of way. Nice, pleasant face, the kind that seemed ready to break into a smile at any moment—after she'd gotten over her first-night nerves. Couldn't be easy, taking off your clothes for strangers—he didn't think he could do it, whatever incentive he was offered.

He saw her standing up and turning towards the door. Give her a minute and he'd follow.

"Well done," Audrey said, "you all made great efforts with your homework."

"I sense another lot coming on," Irene said.

Audrey smiled. "How right you are, Irene. For next week I'd like you to forget about the whole body and try a few detailed studies, hands and faces in particular."

"Hands are impossible," Fiona said. "I can never get them right."

"Everyone finds them tricky," Audrey assured her. "Just persevere. Remember what I said—map in the whole hand first, then find the line of the knuckles and work from there. Watch the length of the fingers, measure them against one another."

"How long should we spend on a detailed study?" Meg asked.

"Not too long, certainly no more than ten minutes."

Packing up her things a few minutes later, watching her students pulling on jackets and gathering pages together, Audrey thought with pleasure of the slice of cheesecake that she'd bought on the way home from school, waiting for her now in the fridge at home.

Better not mention it to Irene.

———

As Zarek walked out the front door of the college a sudden downpour caught him unawares. He stepped back into the doorway, buttoning his jacket, hoping it wouldn't last.

A car approached him. "Sit in," Meg called, and Zarek's heart sank. He'd rather get soaked—a hot shower when he got home would soon put things right—but how could he refuse without appearing rude? He opened the passenger door.

"Thank you," he said, getting in and pulling it closed.

"You couldn't walk home in this," Meg said—and indeed the rain was coming down in sheets now. "Where do you live?"

Zarek told her. "Maybe," he said, "it is far from you—you can put me anywhere."

"Not at all," Meg assured him. "Nowhere's far really, in Carrickbawn."

She drove out of the college and turned for the town center.

"So," she said, "you're enjoying the class?"

"Yes, I enjoy a lot. And you?"

"Oh yes, it's good fun," she said, "but I'm certainly no artist. Unlike you," she added. "You're definitely the star."

Zarek demurred, turning to look out the window.

"Of course you are," she went on. "I saw your homework when you were showing Audrey—who was that woman you drew? Those sketches were amazing."

"My flat mate," he told her.

"Girlfriend?"

Zarek glanced at her, but she was looking off to the right as they approached a junction. He was tempted to lie again, but reluctant to implicate Pilar.

"Good friend," he said instead. That might be suitably ambiguous.

Meg made no reply. Zarek thought suddenly of her daughter, whose party he'd narrowly avoided. A safe topic, surely.

"You have more children?" he inquired.

"Nope—just the one."

Silence fell as she negotiated a roundabout and approached a red traffic light directly afterwards. The rain lessened slightly but continued to fall steadily.

"I love being in the car when it's raining," Meg said, pulling away as the light turned green. "So cozy, isn't it?"

"Yes." He wasn't sure what "cozy" meant, but thought it easier to agree. He calculated that his street was two minutes away.

"You can direct me when we get nearer." She drove with one hand on the steering wheel and the other on the gear stick, slightly faster than Zarek was comfortable with.

"James is a bit strange, isn't he?" she said then, taking a hand off the gear stick to push her glasses farther up on her nose.

"Please?"

"Well, he talks to nobody, and then he disappears at break. You'd wonder why he signed up, wouldn't you?"

"Maybe," Zarek suggested, "he like to draw."

To his surprise, Meg burst out laughing. "Yes," she said, "that must be it." She drove through another roundabout. "Friend of mine lives down there," she said, indicating a road off to the left. "Her husband left her last week, out of the blue. He'd been having an affair for years, apparently. She's devastated, as you can imagine."

Zarek was bemused. If he'd understood it correctly—and he thought he had—it seemed an incongruous piece of information to share with a near stranger, particularly when he didn't know the unfortunate woman in question.

"Wouldn't mind if my husband walked out," Meg said then, turning to flash a smile in Zarek's direction. "He's not what you'd call an exciting man."

"Next turn on left please," Zarek said with relief. He had never been so happy to see his street appear.

As soon as Meg pulled in, Zarek leapt from the car. "Thank you," he said, "is very kind of you. See you next week."

"Maybe we'll meet before then," she said, "at the pool, on Thursday?"

"Maybe I work, I am not sure," Zarek answered, easing the door closed. "Thank you," he repeated, "have good birthday party."

Backing away, waving and smiling as he willed her to move off. No doubt in his mind now, her interest in him was plain. As he took his door key from the pocket of his satchel he wondered briefly what her reaction would have been if he'd told her where his interest lay.

———————

"You wouldn't by any chance be going my way, would you?" Jackie asked, holding her rucksack over her head. "I normally walk home, but in this rain…"

He didn't look as if it was the best thing that had happened to him all day, but he reached across to open the passenger door. "Hop in."

She hopped in. "Thanks a million. I don't live too far away, just along by the canal and then behind the hospital, about ten minutes. I hope it's not out of your way."

"No problem," he said, putting an arm on the back of her seat as he swung around to reverse out of the space. "You don't drive yourself then."

"Actually I do, but I haven't got a car. I'm still on a provisional license and the insurance would cripple me."

"Aye, it's very high down here."

His accent was soft, not harsh like Belfast. "What part of the North are you from?" she asked.

He didn't answer right away. He waited for a green Peugeot to move out of a space ahead of them, and Irene waved as she straightened up and drove off.

"Donegal," he said. "Have you lived in Carrickbawn all your life?"

"Yes—I was planning to go to college in Dublin when I left school, but…my plans changed."

He smelled nice. There were no rings on either of his hands. He drove slowly along by the canal.

"When did you move here?" she asked.

"Few months back," he said. "How did you get roped in to sit for us?"

She laughed. "I answered an ad, and then I met Audrey, who persuaded me. I was a bit nervous at first—no, I was *very* nervous at first, you probably noticed—but I'm okay now. It's right at the next lights," she added.

Was it her imagination, or was he giving away as little information as possible? Were her questions so intrusive, or was he so reluctant to talk about himself that he felt the need to counter her inquiries as quickly as possible with a question of his own?

She felt something on the floor by her feet. She bent and picked up what appeared to be a child's plastic hair band. Her heart sank as she placed it on the dashboard. "Someone will be looking for that."

He glanced across. "My daughter…thanks."

He had a daughter, so chances were he also had a wife or partner. Jackie waited until her road was approaching, and then she said, "Thanks very much, you can drop me anywhere here. I'm just around the next corner."

He pulled in and waited in silence as she got out.

"Thanks again," she said. "See you next week."

"Aye," he said, "you will," and pulled the door closed.

She turned onto her road, listening to him driving off. So that was that. He hadn't shown the slightest interest, because he was already happily attached. Par for the course, as far as her love life was concerned.

She reached Number 6 and opened the gate, rummaging in her bag for her key.

Wednesday

I assume," he said, "that you're looking for work."

She glanced up from her porridge. Surprised at him bringing it up, no doubt. Happy to take free bed and board for as long as it lasted, and let tomorrow go to hell.

"I am lookin'," she said. "But nobody will give me a chance."

"Where have you tried?"

She shrugged. "Everywhere. Anyplace I pass."

"Shops?"

"Yeah, everywhere."

"What about the hospital?"

She looked blankly at him. "The hospital?"

"They might be looking for cleaners."

"Oh. Yeah," she said, poking her spoon into the porridge. "I'll try there."

"Do you have a CV?"

Another blank look. "A what?"

He should have expected that. Of course she wouldn't know what a CV was. How could she?

"You need some kind of a form, telling people what experience you've had, or what your strengths are…" But even as he spoke, he knew it was useless.

"I don't have no experience," she said.

"You never had a job?"

"No."

He changed tack. "Did you do your Leaving Cert?"

She shook her head. "I left school at fourteen. I failed the Junior Cert." She hesitated. "I missed lots of time—my family…" She trailed off.

Michael felt it wiser not to pursue that avenue. "And you never had any kind of a job, not even part-time?"

Another shake of her head.

Michael raised his eyes and regarded the kitchen ceiling. "Well, you're certainly a challenge, but that's not to say nobody will employ you. Have any of the places you've tried given you application forms?"

She shrugged again. "Forms aren't no good to me. I told you I can't read."

"But you did get some."

"Yeah." Her expression was sullen. "I threw them away."

Michael turned back to the last sandwich, forcing himself to breathe deeply. *Patience*, he told himself as he spread butter. *Shouting at her will get you nowhere.* By the time he'd wrapped the sandwich in tinfoil he felt marginally calmer.

"Go back to wherever gave you a form," he said. "Tell them you're very sorry but you spilled a cup of tea over it, and please can you have another one. Be polite, say please. Bring them back here and I'll help you to fill them out."

She nodded. "Thank you." But her thanks were automatic; her face showed no gratitude. Probably, he felt, because even she could see that the possibility of anyone giving her employment was so remote as to hardly exist.

"Five minutes," he said, leaving the room. A given now that the child would start the day in the shop, that the three of them would walk there together. Upstairs he packed up the dried swabs for posting at lunchtime, trying to ignore the fact that the subject of what would become of the boy if she did manage to get work hadn't been broached by either of them.

It was such a nice morning, fresh and clear after last night's rain, that Audrey decided to leave the moped at home and walk to work. She called Dolly in from the garden, pulled on her jacket, and headed off.

Autumn was in the air, a hint of crispness, an advance warning of the frost she'd surely see on the lawn in a few weeks. But today the sky was blue, the breeze not too strong. The leaves were just beginning to turn, a few early droppers dancing along on the path in front of her, rusty orange and yellow and red. A perfect autumn morning. She walked along the familiar paths, smiling at fellow pedestrians like she always did, her thoughts on the day ahead.

The closer she got to Carrickbawn's main street, the busier her surroundings became. Everyone seemed to be in a hurry: the young sharply dressed man talking rapidly on his mobile phone; the woman pulling a dark blue suitcase behind her, heels clicking sharply on the pavement; the older man up ahead with a small leather rucksack on his back; a slight young woman by his side holding the hand of a little boy, both of them trotting briskly to match the man's pace. Everyone rushing along, places to be, things to do.

At length Audrey turned off the main street and into the lane that connected it with the road that led eventually to the secondary school where she worked. Quieter here, nothing much happening at this early hour. She glanced in the few shop windows—balls of wool piled into pyramids, brightly dressed mannequins, bathroom tiles in various shapes and colors. A selection of birdcages with twittering occupants in the window of the pet shop; no pet carrier, no new four-legged animal to replace the one Audrey had bought.

She recalled seeing Dolly for the first time, pressing her palms to the window, watching the little pup yapping soundlessly on the other side of the glass. Now, not even three weeks later, it was hard to remember a time when Dolly didn't live with her. For all the challenges the little dog presented, Audrey had no regrets about acting on her impulse of that morning. The unconditional love Dolly showered on her was worth any amount of frayed blind cords or ruined dahlias.

She passed a young woman sitting on a bench by a bus stop—the same one, Audrey thought, who'd been walking ahead of her a few minutes before. There was something familiar about her, but Audrey couldn't think where they might have met. She smiled at the woman as she passed.

"D'you have the time?" No answering smile on the pinched face. Her shoulders hunched as though she were cold.

Audrey pushed up her sleeve. "Five past nine."

The woman nodded and Audrey walked on. It wasn't until she'd almost reached the gates of the secondary school that she remembered.

Picking flowers in the park just a few days ago, accompanied by a little boy.

———

"Think I'll go back to that gym," the mechanic said.

His wife glanced up. "You're going to become a member?"

"Not a full one. They have this casual membership thing where you can pay for ten sessions and use them whenever you want."

She looked surprised. "Never heard of that before. Thought you'd have to sign up for at least six months."

"Yeah, must be the recession—probably not getting the usual membership. I think it's a good idea."

"Mm." She smiled. "Maybe I'll come too."

"Yeah," he said, returning her smile. "Maybe you should."

Another beat passed.

"Might go on Friday," he said. "Start the weekend off with a bang—I mean a workout."

"Very funny," she said, still smiling.

He sat unmoving for another scatter of seconds. "Is this going to take long more?" he asked eventually.

"Done." She held up her sketch pad, and he regarded her attempt to draw his hands.

"Fantastic," he said.

Thursday

"When Jack woke up in the morning,'" Michael read, "'he couldn't believe his eyes—just outside his bedroom window was a giant beanstalk, reaching all the way to the sky.'"

Barry studied the picture, sucking absently on his thumb. Michael remembered Ethan, sweet smelling and pajama-clad, curled up in bed as Michael read, making the same moist rhythmic noise as this boy.

Barry reached out and touched the beanstalk with a small finger. His nails could do with a clip, and a scrub.

"Beanstalk," Michael said. "It grew from the magic beans the man gave him."

Barry's finger trailed the beanstalk's length.

"It's very long, isn't it? Look how it goes right up to the clouds."

The previous night he'd remembered the fairy-tale collection that Valerie had gotten from someone for her fourth birthday. Shabbier now, of course, but still more or less intact. Six books, nested together in a little cardboard folder at the bottom of Michael's wardrobe, because they hadn't fit into the suitcase with the other books.

Not surprisingly, Barry didn't seem to have come across Jack and the Beanstalk before.

He took his thumb from his mouth. "Where's his mammy?" Little more than a whisper.

"Still asleep," Michael said. "She doesn't know anything about the beanstalk. She'll get a big surprise when she wakes up, won't she?"

A nod, thumb slipping back in.

Their fourth morning together in the shop, the child still with far too little to say, but each day inching towards a fraction more communication. Michael imagined the kind of life he'd endured up to this: traipsing the streets with his mother when they weren't holed up in some hovel, or sitting on the ground beside her as she held out a paper cup. No interaction with other children, no stimulation beyond one tattered book that she couldn't even read to him.

"'Jack jumped out of bed and dressed quickly. He ran outside and began to climb the beanstalk.'"

It wasn't ideal. They had to stop every time a customer came in. There wasn't much room behind the counter, the light wasn't great for reading, and they had only a single chair and a step stool for sitting on, but they did the best they could.

"'Up and up and up he went, all the way to the top.'"

The girl came at lunchtime if it was dry and took Barry away for the afternoon, and Michael didn't see them again until seven. He wondered again if there was any possibility of someone giving her a job. She was presentable enough now, with regular showers and clean clothes, but she was still illiterate with no qualifications and no experience. If someone like her came looking for work from him he wouldn't be long sending her packing.

She should still try, though. If she managed to get a few application forms he'd make some attempt to fill them in, and a CV might help if he could somehow magic one up out of thin air. She could hand it in at the job center, and someone might be desperate enough to take her on. Unlikely, but not impossible.

The shop door opened. Michael handed the book to Barry and got to his feet—and saw, with a jolt of surprise, his daughter crossing the floor towards him.

"Hello," she said. The same wary look on her face that he got now whenever they met, a flick of a smile, gone as quickly as it had come. He couldn't remember the last time she'd smiled properly at him. She held a white envelope.

"I just dropped by to give—" She spotted Barry and stopped. "Who's this?" Half smiling at the child.

Michael was completely thrown. It happened so rarely, the possibility of her visiting the shop while Barry was here hadn't even crossed his mind. He hadn't worked out what to say, he had nothing ready.

"His name is Barry," he said, his mind racing, taking a few steps away from the boy. His tone conversational, not wanting to alarm his charge. "I'm looking after him for someone."

She stared at him. "*You're* babysitting? Who for?"

"His mother," he replied, in the same careful voice. "You don't know her."

She shot another glance at the child, whose attention, thankfully, had returned to the book.

"It's just temporary," Michael said. "Just for a short while."

"It's weird," she said. "It's not like you."

"It's no big deal," he replied. "It's nobody you know."

But it was a big deal, or it might be. He had to tell her, now that she'd seen the boy. She was Ethan's sister, she had a right to know.

"What?" she asked, watching his face. "What are you not telling me?"

He stepped away from the counter and beckoned her out of earshot of the boy. She followed him into the aisle, her expression becoming increasingly wary.

"Valerie," he said quietly, "I'd rather not have this conversation here. It's complicated, and this isn't the time or place to go into it. Why don't I give you a call this evening?"

She didn't move. "Just tell me now," she said. "What's going on?"

Michael glanced back at Barry, whose head was still bent over the book. Her book. He turned to face her again. "It's complicated," he repeated.

"I've plenty of time," she said.

He remembered how stubborn she could be. He rubbed his face, hunting for the right words. *Just tell her, don't make a big thing of it.*

"His mother came to me out of the blue, a couple of weeks ago," he said quietly. "She told me that she'd been…with Ethan, and that the boy was his."

Valerie stared at him, her mouth dropping open. "He's *Ethan's?*" Her head swung back towards the boy.

"He might be, I don't know," Michael said quickly. "It's only her word I have."

"But why is he here now?" she demanded. "Where's his mother?"

"She's…looking for work," he said. "She can't do that with a child in tow."

"Looking for *work?*" Valerie's frown deepened. "How long has this been going on?"

"Not long," he said, "I told you, a week or two."

"Where are they living? How did she find you? Why did she wait till now to make herself known?"

"They're staying with me," he told her shortly. "She came because they were being evicted from—"

"They're *staying* with you? They're *living* with you?" Her voice rose in disbelief, and Michael glanced again in Barry's direction, but the boy didn't react. "You took them *in*, without even checking out their story?"

"I *am* checking it out," Michael told her, his impatience beginning to rise. "We've done a paternity test, and I'm—"

"You've done a *paternity* test," she repeated incredulously. "You've taken in two strangers to live with you, and you've done a paternity test. Had you any intention of telling me about all of this?"

Keep calm, he told himself, *nothing to be gained by losing your cool*. "Of course I would have told you, but I thought I should wait until the test results came through, in case it wasn't true. I'm doing the best I can here. I couldn't leave them on—"

"Doing the best you can?" She shook her head angrily. "You're giving bed and board to two people you don't know from Adam, after throwing your only son onto the street at sixteen—"

"For God's sake," Michael said impatiently, "not this again. I had no—"

"You're showing a boy you didn't know existed up to a few weeks ago more attention than Ethan or I ever got from you. You failed as a father so you thought you'd try your hand at being a grandfather, is that it?"

"Valerie," Michael said tightly, "please, you need to understand—"

"*Jesus*," she breathed, "you didn't even try to contradict me."

"Oh, for God's sake—of *course* I gave you attention, I did as much as any father could do."

"Until our mother died maybe—and then you switched off, and dumped us on Pauline." Her face hard as she flung the words at him. "No wonder Ethan went astray."

Michael felt the anger hot inside him. "You can't possibly blame me for that—I had this shop to run, I had to get help. What was I expected to do, send you to an orphanage?"

"Maybe you should have, maybe we'd have been better off." She tossed the envelope she held onto the counter and turned abruptly and strode towards the door.

"Valerie," Michael called, "don't leave like this, please—"

The door banged behind her. He stood immobile, shoulders hunched, chest tight. He took a breath and then another. He returned to the counter and picked up the envelope.

The front was blank. He slid a finger under the flap and pulled out the card. *Happy birthday*, he read, above a painting of a sailboat.

Best wishes, she'd written inside, *from Valerie*.

His birthday. He'd completely forgotten it.

————————

After turning on the oven she typed the text.

> Bringing Eoin to the park at 4 on Sunday—we'll be in the playground if you and Charlie want to join us.

He'd see they weren't making any special arrangement, that there was no dinner on offer this time. Let him take it or leave it. Jackie pressed *send* and off it went.

She took flour and castor sugar from the press, eggs and margarine from the fridge. She brought a mixing bowl to the table and switched on the radio. She loved having Thursdays off, when most people were working. She usually made a batch of buns on Thursday, and topped them with the coconut icing that Eoin liked. She weighed flour and tipped it into the bowl, and let her mind wander.

Three life drawing classes down, three to go. She wouldn't be sorry when they were over. Whatever Audrey might say about all bodies being beautiful, Jackie was still very conscious of her less beautiful parts. And holding a pose for longer than three or four minutes wasn't as easy as it looked—if it wasn't an itch it was pins and needles, or a muscle spasm, waiting to torture her.

She added sugar to the bowl and stirred it through the flour. The money would come in handy, though; she'd already put a deposit on the Wii console in the toy shop. Eoin would be thrilled.

She cracked eggs into the mixture, and cut the margarine into cubes. She plugged in the electric beater and worked it through the ingredients, watching as they came together into a creamy, gloopy mix.

Shame about James being attached, but she'd get over it. She filled a bun tray with paper cases and dolloped spoonfuls of the mixture into them. Nothing to distract her now, though, from the tedium of sitting still for as long as Audrey dictated.

Zarek didn't interest her, too much of a pretty boy. She'd never gone for the Colin Farrells or Brad Pitts, preferred more rugged features on a man. Give her Harvey Keitel any day. And anyway, she didn't think she could handle the language barrier that would go along with dating Zarek, always having to think of the easiest way to say something.

It was funny that Audrey kept trying to match them up, but she was completely wasting her time—and Zarek showed as little interest in her as Jackie felt for him.

But just three more nights and it would all be over. And who knew—maybe Charlie's father would turn out to be a pleasant surprise.

She opened the oven door and slid the tray inside. Talk about clutching at straws.

———

"You're good at cookin'," she said. "I'm useless."

Michael poured white sauce onto his chicken. "Did your mother never teach you?"

Her face immediately closed. "No." She cut up Barry's chicken. "She never cooked nothin', she hadn't a clue."

"Or any of your family? What about your father?"

As soon as the question was out, he recalled her insinuations about her father. He willed his words unsaid, but of course it was too late.

Her mouth twisted. "Him? He couldn't hot up a tin of beans. He was a waste of space." She reached for the salt, and added far too much to both their plates. Michael held his tongue.

They ate in silence for a few minutes. A mother who didn't cook, a father who might have interfered with her. Was it so surprising that she'd turned to drugs?

"My granny cooked," she said then in a different voice.

"Did she live with you?"

"Yeah, but she died." She bent her head over her plate, not looking at him.

A week ago they'd come to him, seven nights already spent under his roof. He couldn't truly say he was unhappy with the arrangement. They were easy, a lot easier than he'd been expecting. He made no allowances when he cooked dinner, and they ate whatever he put in front of them, more or less. Barry balked at some of the vegetables—presumably, Michael assumed, because he'd never come across them before—but the girl generally persuaded him to give them a go.

She cleaned up after each meal. She washed the dishes, she swept the kitchen floor, she wiped down the table. And the bathroom was always tidy—towels hanging on the rail, no puddles, no hairs in the plughole. Somewhere along the way she'd learned how to do things right. Maybe that had been down to the grandmother.

And much to his relief, they hadn't attempted to come into the sitting room after dinner since the night he'd invited them in himself. Once she'd tidied up they went straight upstairs, and he didn't see them again until breakfast time.

Not that he'd mind too much, he supposed. They hadn't unduly bothered him, that one time.

They ate in silence for a few minutes,

"My daughter called into the shop this morning," Michael told her then. "She wasn't too pleased to find the boy there."

Her fork stilled on the way to her mouth. "Did you tell her about us stayin' here?"

"I did."

"Does she want you to put us out?"

"It's not up to her," he said shortly. "You'll leave when I say so, and not before."

She laid her fork down, the food on it uneaten. "When the test comes back," she said, "you'll see that I wasn't tellin' no lies."

Michael regarded her pinched face, hair held off her face with a cheap plastic band. "Maybe so."

She made no attempt to resume eating. "But what'll you do if the test says that Ethan is the dad? Will you still kick us out an' send us back on the streets?"

Michael glared at her. "Will you stop going on about it? I'm not going to decide something that hasn't happened yet."

Silence. She looked away.

"Right?"

"Yeah." Quietly.

After a minute she picked up a fork and began eating again. He felt the room full of all the things that had been left unsaid.

Post a photo, the website urged. Clients who post a photo are far more likely to receive attention.

"Clients" sounded so official. And "receive attention"—how horribly clinical. When had looking for romance become such a business? When you resorted to the Internet, Audrey supposed, and paid €100 a year to become a member of a site that just might help you to find what you were looking for.

She regarded her almost-completed membership form on the screen. All that remained was to input her credit card details, and off she could go in search of love. She'd decided against a photo, knowing that her size could put off a lot of possible suitors. Better that they get to know her first, better that they connect mentally, and then it mightn't matter that she didn't have the perfect figure.

She took her credit card from her wallet and began entering the numbers in the box on the screen. Halfway through, she stopped.

What if nobody made contact, and what if any messages she sent were ignored? Did she really want to pay €100 to discover, maybe, that nobody at all was interested in getting to know her?

And was this really the way she wanted to find him, by filling in a form that asked for her hobbies and interests, by ticking a box to indicate her age group, and another for her gender preferences, by doing her best to sound normal, and desirable, and not a bit desperate? Had it really come to this?

No. She closed the screen and shut down her computer. Internet dating might suit others, but it wasn't for her; she wasn't comfortable in cyberspace.

"I'll stick to more old-fashioned methods," she told Dolly. "He's out there somewhere and I'll find him, or he'll find me. It's not too late."

She picked up the TV remote control and switched on the news, and turned her attention to the latest banking crisis.

The Fourth Week

October 12–18

A dangerous liaison, a surprising discovery, an angry impulse, and an indiscretion.

Friday

Zarek indicated his sketch pad. "Is okay I draw you?"

Anton nodded, eyes half closed as he plucked the guitar strings and hummed gently.

Zarek sat opposite his flat mate and began to stroke the charcoal onto the page. He echoed the curve of Anton's shoulder, the angle of his elbow, the folds of his shirtsleeve. He drew the lock of shiny dark hair that tumbled over Anton's right eye, the long narrow nose, the full bottom lip, the square chin. The shadow of dark chest hair at the open V of his shirt.

Eventually Anton laid the guitar aside. "Time to check ze dinner," he said. He crossed the room and regarded the drawing, one hand resting lightly on Zarek's shoulder.

"Is good," he said. "You 'ave ze talent."

Zarek blew the loose charcoal off the page. "I like to draw," he said.

Anton turned and left the room, and Zarek remained sitting for some minutes as he regarded the image he had created.

———

Dolly trotted off the path and made purposefully towards a group of teenagers who were clustered around a drinking fountain.

"No—" Audrey pulled firmly on the leash, and Dolly veered back onto the path and nosed into an approaching child's crotch.

"*Dolly!*" Audrey yanked on the leash again. "Sorry about that," she added to the boy, who scuttled out of Dolly's reach, "she's just being friendly." She wondered, as they walked on, if the ongoing struggle to keep her pet's behavior within the limits of social acceptance would ever be over.

They came to a bench and Audrey opened the bag of licorice allsorts she'd treated herself to on the way to the park. She ate contentedly, telling herself that by the time they'd walked home she'd have worked up a fresh appetite for the wedge of deli-bought lasagne she was planning to reheat for dinner.

As she rummaged for her favorite sweet—the coconut wheel with a licorice hub—a young woman and a small towheaded boy approached and sat on the other end of the bench. This was the third time Audrey had seen them in a handful of days, but neither of them showed any sign of recognition.

She caught the eye of the little boy and smiled. He regarded her impassively, his gaze drifting to the licorice allsorts. She extended the bag towards him. "Would you like a sweet?"

He darted a look at his companion, who nodded. He dipped his hand into the bag and took out Audrey's least favorite, the jelly circle covered in tiny licorice bubbles.

"Say thank you," the woman told him, and he murmured his thanks before cramming the sweet into his mouth.

"Do you want some?" Audrey asked the woman.

She shook her head. "I don't like them sweets."

The boy sucked his licorice noisily, his attention caught now by Dolly, who was sniffing at his feet.

"What's your name?" Audrey asked him.

"Bawwy." So quietly she nearly missed it, his eyes on Dolly as she nosed at his shoe.

"She won't hurt you," Audrey assured him. "She's very nice and doesn't bite at all. She's just curious, she wants to sniff everything."

"What's she's name?" he asked timidly.

"Dolly. You can pat her head if you like. She'll probably try to lick your hand, but she definitely won't bite it."

But he made no attempt to pat her, watching her warily as she continued to nose into his shoes.

Throughout his exchange with Audrey the young woman he was with sat quietly, seeming detached although she continued to hold the little boy by the hand. Audrey wondered if she was the mother, or maybe a big sister charged with his care. Her face was pale and drawn, her hair caught at the back of her head by a rubber band. Whether by nature or through circumstance, she gave the impression of someone who didn't smile easily.

It was hard to know if they were in need. The woman's clothes looked clean enough, if a little shabby, and the boy was decently clothed too, but there was something about them, some suggestion of neglect in their peaky faces that made Audrey wonder.

She held out the bag again, and the boy put in his hand. "Take a few," Audrey urged, and he pulled out two and stuffed them both into his mouth. Was he hungry, or was that just a normal childish greed for confectionery?

"They're nice, aren't they?" Audrey asked, helping herself to another wheel. "This one is my favorite," she said.

He looked at it, his cheeks bulging.

The woman turned to Audrey. "Have you got the time?"

Audrey pulled up her sleeve and looked at her man's watch. Anything feminine looked ridiculous on her wrist. "Twenty past five," she told the girl, who nodded her thanks.

Audrey regarded the half-empty bag of sweets. "Oh dear, I'm too full to finish these now," she said aloud. "I wonder if I could find anyone to give them to." She looked at Dolly, pattering around at their feet. "What do you think?"

Dolly yapped, as she did every time Audrey spoke directly to her.

"Who? Really? You think so?"

Another yap.

"Hang on, I'll ask him."

She glanced at the woman. *Okay?* she mouthed.

A silent nod, the suggestion of a smile at the corners of her mouth.

Audrey offered the bag to the boy, whose gaze was fixed on Dolly. "Would you like these?" she asked. "Dolly says you might."

He threw another look in his companion's direction. "Say thank you to the lady," she ordered.

"Thank you," he breathed, more to Dolly than to Audrey.

"You're very welcome," Audrey told him, getting to her feet. "Well, it was nice to meet you. Bye."

"Keep them for later," the girl was saying as Audrey left. "Granddad will have dinner ready soon. You can have some after."

So there was a granddad on the scene. Audrey remembered the man from the pet shop buying clothes the other day for what she'd presumed was a grandchild. She felt a brief familiar stab of longing for a family of her own, for a child or two she could dress in miniature colorful clothes. A scenario, she had to admit, that became less likely with every year that passed.

She tugged Dolly away from a little girl's choc ice and walked towards the park exit.

––––––––––

Although his attempts were hopeless, completely without artistic merit, this didn't take in the least from his enjoyment. It was the act of drawing that he found satisfying, however ham-fisted the images that he produced.

He balanced his sketch pad on his knee and observed his sleeping daughter, and compared her with the girl he'd attempted to draw on the page. No resemblance whosoever; but it didn't matter. Audrey wouldn't have the real thing to hold up against his drawing—and anyway, Audrey didn't judge a work by its accuracy, she set much more store by the artist's enthusiasm. James wasn't sure it was the best criterion, but it was certainly the kindest for non-artists like himself.

He went back through his sketch pad, trying to see any improvement in his drawings as the classes had gone on. His first few attempts were disastrous, hardly recognizable as human at all, and the later ones really weren't much better. Jackie would not be impressed if she could see what a mess he'd made of her, he was sure.

He realized that hers was the only female adult body he had seen in the flesh, so to speak, apart from Frances's—if you didn't count the bare-breasted women on French beaches that they'd seen on their honeymoon. "Don't look," Frances would order, shielding his eyes as they'd walked by. "No comparing."

The model's shape was very different from Frances's. Her breasts were smaller, her hips more rounded, her thighs heavier than his wife's. Of course, after having Charlie, Frances's body had changed, but James had loved the evidence of their daughter's birth in the new soft fleshiness of her stomach, the fuller breasts.

He groaned quietly, the sadness reaching out at him. He gave in to it, he recalled his wife's smell, the texture of her skin and hair, the sounds of her pleasure. He pictured them entwined—and despite his sorrow he felt a minute twitch of arousal.

He closed the sketch pad and got abruptly to his feet and walked quickly from his sleeping child's bedroom.

"You've some body," he said, running his fingers lightly across the ridges of her rib cage. "Not an ounce of fat on you. You must spend your life in that gym."

Irene lay with eyes closed, wishing he'd shut up. She hadn't come here for a conversation. She concentrated on the feel of his hand as it traveled over her body, as his fingertips explored her. The sex had been gratifying, it had filled its own space, but this was what she had come for, to be touched and stroked by a man's hand. This was what she yearned for.

He bent and put his mouth to her throat. "You smell really good," he murmured, and she felt his tongue in the hollow of her clavicle as his fingers found a nipple and began to play with it, and as it grew stiff her desire returned and she ran her nails lightly along his spine, traveling down to the curve of his buttocks, arching up towards him and pushing his head down to her breast.

And as their movements became more urgent, as her breath quickened and her skin grew damp, Irene blotted out the grubby blanket and equally grubby cushions he'd laid on the lino-covered ground, the fly-spattered lamp shade on the dim ceiling bulb, the smell of grease and the cobwebs in the corners and the scatter of rusting screws in the battered tin lid by the door.

She closed her eyes and pictured Martin's face above hers, Martin's hands, Martin's touch on her skin, Martin whispering that he loved her, wanted her, would never leave her.

And from beneath her closed eyelids the tears trickled.

Saturday

C an you believe this weather?" Pauline stood by her back door, shading her eyes against the sun. "The middle of October."

"I know. It's wonderful." Audrey tightened the belt of her dressing gown as she approached the dividing hedge. "I'm a disgrace, not dressed yet. Any news?"

"Not really, things have been quiet. You?"

"Nothing much. Looking forward to the midterm break in a couple of weeks. Not that I've any big plans, but I've two rooms that need painting, and I was thinking of bringing Dolly out to the lake at some stage, see what she's like in the water."

"Oh, we're going there tomorrow. Kevin has been pestering me, and the forecast is good. Why don't you and Dolly come with us?"

Audrey shook her head. "Thanks, but I've earmarked tomorrow to stain the shed. I've been putting it off long enough, and the weather mightn't hold."

They both turned to regard the shed at the bottom of Audrey's garden, and Pauline tactfully didn't comment.

"Well, I'd better see what that fellow is up to," she said, turning towards her house. "Talk to you later, Audrey. Enjoy the sunshine."

In the kitchen Audrey wrote her shopping list: *wood stain, dog food, milk, custard, chicken, steak and kidney pies, veg, tooth-*

paste, eggs, bath oil. She tore the page from her notebook and tucked it into her purse, then pulled it out again and added *chocolate.*

Her biscuit jar had a supply of little Kit Kats and Penguin bars to have with a cup of coffee, but it wasn't Saturday night without some proper chocolate.

"I did the first bit," she said, handing over the form. "I put in my name."

Her name, he read, was Carmel Ryan. Her writing was childish, the letters carefully but unevenly formed, the *C* of Carmel not quite large enough. Michael scanned the rest of the form.

"Date of birth," he said, unscrewing his fountain pen, and she told him. Her birthday was in September, a couple of weeks before his, and she was just gone twenty-two. He wrote *Irish* after *Nationality* and ticked the small box beside *Female.*

Address. He filled in his own, aware of her watching as the words flowed across the page. *Telephone.* He looked up.

"I take it you don't have a mobile phone."

"No."

He filled in his number.

Qualifications. He left it blank. Nothing he could make up there.

Previous Employment. He paused, and then wrote *Housekeeper,* and put his own name and the shop address under *References.*

Additional Information. He looked up again. "Anything you were good at in school?"

She shrugged. "I didn't mind art."

He wrote *Hobbies: painting, walking.* For all the good that particular piece of information would do, but it was something to fill an inch of space.

"I like children," she said then, her color rising. "I like bein' with them, I mean."

"Have you any experience of being with them, apart from Barry?"

"I minded another boy, in the squat. When his mother was—" She broke off abruptly, and then added, "sick."

Michael wrote *Childcare experience*, aware of the inadequacy of the claim. Keeping an eye on an addict's child now and again when the mother was high on whatever substance she pumped into herself hardly qualified as childcare in the proper sense of the word. But the girl had also raised her own son for three years in difficult circumstances, which must count for something.

To be sure, Barry was overly quiet and not exactly bursting with energy, but with so much stacked against him it was probably a minor miracle that the lad was still breathing.

"Anything else?" he asked, without much hope. "Any holiday jobs when you were younger? Waitressing, shop work?" *Before you went near drugs, and left the real world behind.*

She shook her head.

Michael scanned the form, well aware of how pitifully sparse the information was. It would have to do; they had nothing else.

"Bring me the other ones," he told her. "Put your name on the top again and I'll fill in the rest."

"Thanks," she said, getting up quickly and leaving the kitchen.

Michael felt—what? Pity, he supposed. If she was to be believed—and the more he got to know her, the more he felt that she might be—the odds had surely been stacked against her from the start. A dysfunctional family, an abusive father, and an education system that had failed her. If she was to be believed.

But she was drug-free now, that much of her story at least was true. Michael would know if she wasn't; he'd had painful first-hand experience of what being high looked and sounded like, and since her arrival here she'd exhibited none of the signs he'd seen in Ethan.

And he had to acknowledge that she looked after her son as far as she was able; he had to give her that. The way she looked at the boy across the kitchen table sometimes reminded Michael poignantly of how Ruth had looked at Ethan. She might be wincingly rough around the edges, but she wasn't incapable of tenderness.

Maybe, after all, she'd done the best she could with the hand she'd been dealt.

When the interval between popping sounds began to stretch, Zarek took the saucepan off the heat. He tipped the pile of warm popcorn into the large blue bowl that normally held their fruit supply, and sprinkled it with salt. In the living room he placed the bowl on the couch, between Anton and himself.

"*Merci.*"

Anton dipped his hand into the bowl as Zarek inserted the DVD and pressed *play*. After the usual preliminaries, the opening credits of *The Remains of the Day* began scrolling up the screen.

On the Saturday nights when Zarek wasn't working, the two men's routine of DVD and popcorn rarely varied. They took turns to choose and rent the DVDs, but Zarek consistently popped the corn, it being tacitly agreed that Anton, after cooking dinners all week, deserved a break.

Now and again Pilar joined them, but tonight she'd gone for a drink with a fellow Lithuanian, much to Zarek's, and he was pretty sure Anton's, quiet relief. Pilar seemed unfamiliar with the concept of silent watching, preferring to keep up a steady, full-volume commentary anytime she sat in front of a screen.

Zarek stretched an arm along the back of the couch and

watched the butler interacting with the recently arrived house-keeper. The subtitles they'd selected were in French, Polish not having been among the offered languages, so Zarek did his best with the spoken word.

At first the nuances of their exchanges were largely lost to him—he generally aimed for the bigger picture when he watched a film in English—but as the film progressed, by studying the body language and facial expressions he slowly became aware of the butler's unspoken feelings for the housekeeper, and of the man's tragic inability, or unwillingness, to recognize until too late that his feelings were reciprocated.

And as the closing credits rolled, Zarek Olszewski could appreciate the exquisite irony of watching that particular film with Anton.

Sunday

There they are."

Eoin darted away from her and disappeared into the throng of people massing around the play area. Jackie followed, keeping her eyes peeled for his orange T-shirt—but it was Charlie she spotted first, bouncing on a metal horse as it wobbled on its coiled spring. And there stood Eoin next to her, talking to a man who crouched on his hunkers beside them.

As Jackie approached, the man looked around—and she experienced a sharp lurch of dismay as she recognized Charlie's father. She felt the heat rising in her face, and she saw the surprise in his as he realized who she was. She waited in dread for him to give the game away. Whatever he said now, her cover would be blown.

"Hello," he said, standing up and putting out a hand. "You must be Eoin's mum. I'm James Sullivan—nice to meet you finally."

James Sullivan. James from the drawing class was James Sullivan, father of her son's best friend. She'd never heard his last name in the class; she didn't know anyone's last name, apart from Audrey's. It had never occurred to her that the two Jameses might be one and the same.

Even when—the memory flashing back to her—she'd found a girl's hair band in his car, and he'd mentioned his daughter, she hadn't put two and two together. But why would she? There were surely several men named James in Carrickbawn; a few of them at least must have daughters.

She became aware that he was looking inquiringly at her.

"Jackie," she said faintly. "Moore." Thanking her lucky stars that he'd somehow divined—or decided to assume maybe—that her son wasn't aware of her part-time job. He was pretending he didn't know her, and Jackie went along with it gratefully.

His handshake was firm, his skin warm. Jackie struggled to assimilate this new situation. He was the father of her son's friend, and he'd seen her naked three times. And she fancied him, no point in denying it. And it felt distinctly weird to be meeting him in her role as Eoin's mother now.

"Nice little park," he said, not seeming to notice that she'd been struck dumb—or maybe filling the space while she recovered her wits. "Good facility for families, especially when the weather obliges. Isn't this weather something in October?"

He didn't appear to be at all discomfited. Not that there was any reason for him to be embarrassed—*she'd* been the naked one, after all. And he hadn't shown any sign that he was interested romantically in her, so why should the fact that she was the parent of his daughter's friend cause him any awkwardness now?

"So," he went on, "you've lived here all your life?"

The same question he'd put to her in the car the other night. Still letting on that they'd never met before—because wasn't that exactly the kind of question you'd ask someone new? Or maybe he'd simply forgotten.

"All my life," she answered, turning to watch their children, who were now rushing towards the slide, "born and bred." She turned back to him. "Thanks for not giving the game away."

He smiled. "I guessed you mightn't have mentioned your evening job."

"No." The image of her sitting naked in front of him slid into her head, and she searched for a change of subject. "So Charlie's settling in well here?"

He nodded. "Kids are resilient," he said.

The remark struck her as strange. Resilient was something you needed to be if you were up against some problem or obstacle. Had they moved from the North to escape from a bad situation? Abruptly she remembered the "lost" wife—who may, she realized now, not be dead as Jackie had assumed, but divorced, or estranged in some other way. Maybe he'd left a bad marriage behind him; maybe he and Charlie were fleeing from a woman who'd made their lives miserable.

Or maybe Jackie just had a vivid imagination. She was acutely conscious of him standing next to her, in faded black canvas jeans she hadn't seen before and a white T-shirt. He was ten years older than her at least, and there may or may not be some kind of skeleton in his cupboard.

And he might still be attached, either to a wife who for whatever reason didn't live with him now, or to a new partner here in Carrickbawn. Really, he was far from ideal boyfriend material—and yet, tragically, he was the first man she'd been attracted to in years.

"How about ice cream?" he asked suddenly. "Why don't I go and get some?"

Ice cream; they could eat ice cream like any group out together on a sunny day. Doing something as normal as eating ice cream might make her feel less tongue-tied. "That'd be lovely," Jackie said.

"Cones? Does Eoin like cones?"

She smiled, already feeling more at ease. "What do you think?"

They'd been thrown together, thanks to their children. Might as well make the best of it.

———————

James paid for the four cones and pocketed his change before gathering them into his hands. Her face when they'd met, the look of shock on it that had puzzled him in the split second it had taken him to recognize her. Long time since he'd seen anyone blush like that.

What were the chances, even in a town the size of Carrickbawn? Eoin's mother, the life drawing model. It was clear that she was terrified, waiting for him to blurt it out in front of her son. She looked too young to be the boy's mother, must have had him early. He remembered that she lived with her parents—Eoin's father having scarpered, probably.

James had done his best, pretended they'd never met. He was pretty sure the kids noticed nothing, despite her badly hidden embarrassment. The ice cream was all he could think of, something to get him away for a few minutes and give her a chance to get over it.

Funny, in a way. Going to meet Charlie's friend and discovering that you'd already met his mother, and she'd had no clothes on at the time. He grinned as he made his way back to the noisy playground, imagining Charlie's horror—and Eoin's—if either of them knew.

Maybe he'd tell Charlie someday though, share the joke with her when she was old enough not to be mortified. One of the cones dripped onto the back of his hand and he bent to lick it off. Long time since he'd had a cone. Long time since he'd had a reason to buy more than two of them.

Might be an okay afternoon. For Charlie's sake, he'd do his best to enjoy it.

Despite her shower, the sharp tang of the wood stain was still on Audrey's hands. A long, hot bath would be top of the agenda when she got home. Dolly strained at the leash as usual, impatient to explore everything she encountered as they moved through the park. Audrey avoided the play area, chock-full, on this sunny day, of shrieking toddlers and young children. The last place an excitable little dog needed to be.

A man came from behind and hurried past her, carrying a pair of ice cream cones in each hand. Something about him looked familiar, but without seeing his face Audrey couldn't identify him.

Dolly veered suddenly off the path, heading purposefully towards a bed of hard-pruned rosebushes. "Come back here, you monkey," Audrey called, pulling sharply on the red leash. A man sitting on a nearby bench turned his head at the sound of her voice.

"Hello," Audrey said, spotting him. "Isn't the weather gorgeous?"

"Very nice," he replied.

His beard as unkempt as ever, which quite spoiled his whole appearance. She wondered how he didn't see it when he looked in the mirror. He wore dark blue trousers that reminded her of bus drivers, and a pale grey shirt whose sleeves he'd rolled to the elbows. His lower arms were very white indeed.

He nodded at Dolly. "You're getting the hang of her then," he said.

"Yes, she's doing fine. Still needs a firm hand, but I'm learning as I go along."

"Glad to hear it."

Audrey began to move off. "Well, it was nice to—"

"You wouldn't happen to know of any playschools in the area, would you?"

The question was totally unexpected. Audrey stopped. "Playschools?"

"Yes, for a three-year-old."

What an odd inquiry, out of the blue like that. "I don't

think—" she began—and then abruptly remembered someone telling her lately that she'd opened one. Who was it?

"You know one?" he asked.

"Hang on." She searched her memory. One of the people in the life drawing class—Fiona? Meg? Oh, which of them? "Somebody mentioned that they'd recently started a playschool," she told him, "but I can't quite remember who—"

He stood up abruptly, and for an instant Audrey thought he was going to stalk away because she hadn't given him the right answer. Instead he slid his wallet from his trouser pocket and pulled a card from it while Dolly sniffed around his ankles.

"This is my number," he said, handing it over. "You might let me know, if you think of it. I'd appreciate it."

"Certainly."

And as Audrey took the card he crouched and scratched under Dolly's chin. "Hey," he said softly. Dolly nuzzled into his hand, grunting with pleasure.

Audrey looked down. Clearly, he had no trouble getting on with dogs. There was a small patch at his crown where the scalp was just beginning to show through his greying hair.

After a few seconds he got to his feet. "Thank you," he said. "I'm grateful to you." He nodded at Audrey and moved off in the opposite direction.

Audrey recalled the children's clothes in the supermarket. Now he was looking for a playschool. Clearly, there was a child in his life that he cared about. Maybe all he needed was the rough edges smoothed off him a little.

She looked at the card he'd given her and read *Michael Browne* and the shop name and address, and a telephone number. No decoration, no unnecessary words. Short and to the point, exactly as she'd have expected of him. She put the card in her bag and gave a little tug on the leash, and Dolly trotted beside her as they made their way towards the exit.

Without the beard he might be quite pleasant looking, and it might take a few years off him too. He might not be that old at all, in fact; some people went grey very young. And if he got out in the sun more instead of being cooped up in that shop all day, he wouldn't look so pasty.

They walked through the streets of Carrickbawn until they got to Audrey's road. Dolly's pace quickened as they approached the gate. Audrey thought of the chicken and pasta bake in the freezer. Ten minutes for the oven to heat up, and twenty-five for the dish to cook. Did she want to wait that long?

Maybe she'd do an omelette instead, if she hadn't eaten the last of the Emmentaler. An omelette without cheese was like a soft-boiled egg without salt.

On the other hand, she could uncork a half bottle of wine and sip a glass on the patio while the chicken was cooking. Yes, that sounded like a plan.

She waited until she'd closed the gate behind them before crouching to unclip the leash from Dolly's collar, and the little dog darted away and skidded around the side of the house, yapping joyously.

No doubt about it, Audrey thought, the sun made everyone happier. He'd been quite pleasant today, even if he was looking for something.

———

The notion of a playschool had come to him in the night, when he'd woken to visit the toilet and was waiting to drop off again. He'd been pondering the problem of what to do with the child in the unlikely event of the girl being offered work. Of course it might be none of his business by then; the test results would probably have come back, and depending on the result the two of them could be out of his life.

But what if they weren't? If there was a positive result he'd feel some responsibility, wouldn't he? Like it or not he'd have to look out for them, to a certain extent at least. And the girl couldn't take up the offer of a job without provision being made for the child. It was as simple as that.

One option would be for Michael to continue bringing him to the shop, but that couldn't go on long-term, it wouldn't be fair to the child to have him cooped up behind a shop counter with just a few books for company.

A playschool then; some setup that would take him for part of the day at least, give him a chance to mix with other kiddies, leave the mother free to get some kind of a job. Yes, a playschool was what was needed. He'd look into it if the test results bore out the girl's claim.

He'd fallen asleep soon after he'd made the decision, and he'd thought no more about it until he'd dropped into the park on his way home from the cemetery and met the woman with the little dog again.

There she'd been, strolling happily along the path in the sunshine, dressed as usual in bright, summery colors. And for some reason the playschool idea had resurfaced in his head. She might be a good one to ask; he sensed she'd try to help if she could. And it was no harm to make inquiries, didn't tie him to anything if the information turned out not to be needed.

And sure enough she'd done her best, her forehead wrinkling as she tried to recall who'd mentioned playschools to her. He'd left his card with her; all he could do now was wait and see if she got in contact.

He recalled her eating an ice cream, on another sunny day. He remembered the pleasure she'd taken from it. He wondered suddenly what she'd have said today if he'd offered to buy her a cone. Probably would have taken him for a right nutcase, would have gathered up her little dog and run a mile in the opposite direction.

He sliced a turnip, another dilemma turning itself over in his head. Would it be feasible to simply turn his back on the other two if it transpired that there was, after all, no connection—if they were, literally, nothing to him? Would he be justified in sending them away, maybe to a life on the streets, with the possibility strong of her eventually returning to the easy money of drug dealing?

He put the turnip chunks into water and began to peel potatoes. Of course he'd be justified; he wasn't responsible for them. In fact, if it turned out that she'd been lying about Ethan, Michael would feel like a right fool. He wouldn't be long showing them the door. Might even call the police, have her done for fraud. Get that child put into care. Might be for the best.

He turned his attention to his daughter, forcing himself to recall the words that had sliced into him in the shop. Was she right, was Michael trying to salve his conscience after the way things had gone with Ethan? *You failed as a father*, she'd said. Michael had loved both his children deeply—he still adored Valerie—but he'd been preoccupied with grief after Ruth, and there'd been the shop to manage. Most of the time, he had to admit, he'd left the parenting to Pauline, who'd been so good at it.

Had he done it all wrong, had the upbringing they'd gotten damaged his children? He'd provided for them, they'd never been short. He'd gone to work every day so they could have school trips and new clothes and birthday parties, even if he'd missed more parties than he'd attended.

He'd put Valerie through nursing, he'd never even suggested she get a part-time job like a lot of other students did. He'd helped her out with the deposit on her apartment. He'd helped her move in.

But his son had turned to drugs and was dead at twenty-four, and his daughter was hardly speaking to him anymore. Was it really his fault?

And was it so bad now if he tried to show some kindness to two people in need? So what if it was more out of a sense of duty than a genuine desire to help them? The fact remained that he was putting a roof over their heads and feeding them well. What right had Valerie to criticize him for that?

He'd thought about phoning her. He'd picked up the phone a few times in the shop, but he'd put it down again. He'd say it wrong, it was sure to come out different from the way he wanted. He was no good with words, he rubbed everyone up the wrong way without even trying.

The doorbell rang and he put down the potato peeler and went to answer it.

Monday

Irene walked into the main bathroom. Pilar was buffing the bath taps with a pink chamois.

"Please make sure you clean around the plughole," Irene said. "That wasn't done yesterday."

Pilar looked up. "Please, what is plughole?"

Irene sighed. "This part here. You really should try to improve your English, Pilar; it's very tiresome having to explain everything."

Pilar turned back to the taps and muttered something.

"Pardon? I didn't quite catch that."

"I say thank you, Mrs. Dillon," Pilar replied.

"I *said*, not I say."

"Yes, Mrs. Dillon."

Irene remained standing behind her, watching as Pilar squeezed a few drops of water from the chamois and resumed her efforts with the taps. Just being in the same room as the au pair irritated her.

"And another thing," she said. "I distinctly remember asking you to clean the base of the toilets, but clearly this is not being done—the downstairs one hasn't been touched in a week."

Pilar straightened up slowly, the chamois still in her hand, and turned again to face Irene.

"Mrs. Dillon," she said, two pink spots appearing in her cheeks, "I try the best I can do, but always you are not happy."

"Did you clean the base of the toilets yesterday?" Irene persisted. "You didn't, did you?"

"No," Pilar admitted. "I forget. There is many—"

"I *forgot*," Irene said through gritted teeth.

"I *forgot*," the au pair repeated, the pink in her face deepening, "because there is too many work in this house. You give me too many work every days. Everything I do, and still you give me more."

Irene regarded her steadily. "Well, Pilar," she said slowly, "maybe this job is too much for you."

Pilar frowned. "No, Mrs. Dillon, I can do, but you give too many work for one person. It is not possible—"

"Nonsense," Irene said crisply. "A hardworking person would clean this house in half the time it takes you. The only reason I keep you on is because for some reason my daughter likes you."

Pilar met her gaze, eyes blazing. She raised her arm slowly and let the chamois plop into the bath.

"Yes, Mrs. Dillon," she said quietly. "Emily love me, and I love her. A pity her mama not feel the same."

Irene narrowed her eyes. "I beg your pardon?"

"You hear me, I think." Pilar reached around and untied the white apron Irene liked her to wear in the house, and draped it carefully over the side of the bath. "I go now," she said, and walked out of the bathroom.

Irene listened to her footsteps on the stairs. She heard Pilar going into the kitchen, and a few minutes later the front door opened and closed softly. She crossed the landing to the main bedroom and stood at the window and watched Pilar walking unhurriedly down the street, her jacket swinging from one shoulder.

She took her phone from her bag and walked downstairs. She riffled through the phone book until she found the number of the employment agency. She spoke to Triona, who told her that they had no au pairs available at the moment, but that she'd let Irene know as soon as the situation changed.

"Thank you," Irene said coldly, and hung up. Of course there were au pairs available. There were always au pairs available, now more than ever. The agency had evidently decided that Irene had had her quota and wasn't entitled to another.

She called her mother.

"My au pair has just walked out," she said. "Are you free to take Emily for the afternoon? I have a full schedule in the gym that would be very awkward to change at this stage."

"Of course I'll take her," her mother replied. "Why did your lady leave?"

"Probably got a better offer," Irene said. "Will you ask around for a replacement?"

Her next call was to Martin. "Pilar has just walked out," she said. "I have an appointment at half past twelve, so can you pick Emily up from playschool and drop her at my parents' house?"

"Pilar walked out?"

Irene bristled at the disbelief in his voice. "Yes, Martin, your perfect au pair just turned on her heel and left. Can you collect Emily or not?"

"Of course I can, but—"

"Sorry," she said, "another call coming through." She hung up and dialed Pamela's number.

"Just checking that lunch is still on," she said.

"Absolutely. Twelve thirty sharp," Pamela told her. "I assume you're going to the tennis club afterwards for Miriam's thing?"

"You assume right," Irene said. "Are you wearing your Chanel?"

As they talked she took a Diet Coke from the fridge. Pilar wouldn't be hard to replace. Her mother would probably have found another by the time Irene collected Emily later. There was always someone available if you knew the right place to look.

She decided to assume he was unattached. No mention of a partner, no ring, no talk of having to be home for dinner, no remark at all that would suggest the presence of a third party in his and Charlie's lives. His wife, if he'd ever had one, was out of the picture. And surely if there was a new partner she would have accompanied James to the park, particularly when he was meeting another woman? He was unattached.

After their shaky start, the afternoon in the park had passed off well enough. By the time he'd returned with the ice cream Jackie had gotten over the shock of discovering who he was. Their conversation had been mostly small talk, with his side of it more questions than answers—she hardly learned anything about him, except that he was an estate agent, and by the way he said it she intimated that he didn't like it—but all the same there hadn't been too many awkward pauses.

And he was gorgeous, and he didn't wear sensible shoes. And she loved his accent, all those soft, rounded words, and saying "aye" instead of "yes." And the way his cheek dimpled when he—

Listen to her.

She dipped her facecloth in the hot bath water and squeezed it out, and pressed it to her face to soften the avocado mask before washing it off. *Calming*, it had said on the pack, but she felt anything but calm right now.

She lay back in the bath and breathed in the warm, wet air and imagined kissing him. Imagined lying beside him.

Their children were friends, so they'd doubtless be seeing each other regularly. She'd deliberately mentioned living with her parents, and she wore no ring on her wedding finger, so it was quite obvious she was unattached. He might not fancy her now, but that could change. She might grow on him. It was perfectly possible.

"James," she whispered, under her facecloth. "James Sullivan."
Pause.
"Jackie Sullivan."
Giggle.

All of a sudden it came to her, as she rinsed shampoo from her hair. Meg, it was Meg who'd opened the playschool. Audrey would ask her on Tuesday if she could take on another child.

She towel-dried her hair and massaged in conditioner. Funny to have waited till October to find a playschool; surely he knew they all started in September, the same as the regular schools?

Still, nothing to do with her. She'd make inquiries like she'd promised and leave it at that. She pulled her plastic shower cap over her head and went downstairs to watch the Monday-night soaps.

"But *why* did she go?" Emily asked.

Leaning against the wall outside, Irene registered the short silence that followed this question. Trying to explain Pilar's abrupt departure to a three-year-old couldn't be easy, particularly as Martin didn't understand it himself.

"We're not sure, lovie," she heard him say eventually. "But maybe there was another little girl who needed her more than you did."

"But I wanted her to stay here," Emily said, her voice wobbly. Irene imagined the eyes brimming with tears, the trembling chin.

"I know you did, but she had to go. She was very sorry to leave you."

"Was she?"

"Oh, she was. She said she'd miss you very, very much."

He was doing his best, like he always did. Trying to be everything for his daughter, trying to compensate for her mother's inadequacies. Irene pushed herself away from the wall and went downstairs. In the kitchen she filled a glass with ice and brought it into the sitting room, where she poured herself a gin and white.

As she switched on the television her phone rang.

"Darling," her mother said, "I've just got a call from Barbara Keane. Her sister-in-law has a Spanish girl who'll be leaving them in a week or so. Quite legit, the husband is taking up a job in Dubai so the family's moving over, and apparently the au pair isn't taken with the Middle East. Have you got a pen?"

Irene wrote down *Katerina* and a mobile number. As she thanked her mother and hung up, Martin walked in and dropped wearily onto the couch.

"Is she asleep?"

He nodded, his eyes closed.

"Do you want a drink?" Irene asked.

"No thanks." He opened his eyes. "So what happened?"

She picked up her glass and the ice clinked. "I told you, Pilar decided that the work was too much, and she opted to go. That's it."

"That's it? No row? She just walked out?"

Irene shrugged. "That's it."

"What about giving notice? I can't see her just deserting us like that."

"Well, she didn't say anything about notice to me."

Martin folded his arms. "We never seem to hold on to an au pair for long," he said. "They never seem to last."

That's because I get rid of them. The words sounded clearly in Irene's head. *I get rid of them as soon as I can because I'm jealous. I'm jealous of how they are with Emily, and I'm jealous of how you are with them, all friendly and chatty because they can do what I can't.*

They sat in silence for a while. Irene sipped her drink.

"So what now?" Martin asked eventually.

"Now," Irene replied lightly, "we find someone new. I just got a name from my mother. I'll give her a ring tomorrow."

He reached across and took her hand. "Irene, love," he said, "do we really have to get another au pair?"

She looked down at his fingers entwined in hers. The feel of his skin on hers was so rare, and so precious. She squeezed his hand, she stroked his wrist with her thumb.

"Would you not give it a try?" he asked softly, pleadingly. "Just for a month, just to see. You could still do the gym in the mornings if you want, while Emily's at playschool. You're her mother, you're better than any au pair."

He would never understand, never.

"I can't," she said. "I just can't. I'm sorry."

He released her hand, as she had known he would, and picked up the remote control. They watched *Questions and Answers* in silence.

———————

"I am very happy," Pilar declared, "to be finished with that *kalè*."

Zarek made an educated guess as to what *kalè* meant.

Pilar tipped back her head and emptied the rest of her M&M's into her mouth, and cracked the shells loudly.

"But I will miss Emily," she went on, her cheeks full of chocolate, her face mournful. "I could not say good-bye, and that is very terrible for me."

"Yes, it is terrible."

"Maybe," she said, crumpling the M&M's bag and flinging it at the wastepaper basket, "there will be a job at your café for me."

Pilar at work, Pilar at home. No more quiet mornings in the apartment, before the café opened. The scenario was one that did not appeal to Zarek. "But you are so good with the childrens, I think you must find another job like this one."

Pilar made a dismissive gesture. "Yes, yes, I try for au pair job of course, but also I look in your café, and at Anton's job. I must try everywhere."

"Yes," Zarek said, his heart sinking. "You are right."

"I will come," she said, "when you are in work, and I will speak with your boss. You will say I am good worker, and very honest, because of course is true."

"Of course," Zarek said faintly.

"Tomorrow I come. What time your boss come in work?"

"Tomorrow is Tuesday," Zarek told her, clutching at the reprieve. "Is my day off."

Pilar shrugged. "So I come on Wednesday. You text me when boss come in work."

"Yes, I text."

Doom. He sensed doom, quite close by.

———

Carmel sat on the bed and flicked through the job application forms Ethan's father had filled in for her. Ten, she'd gotten, for all the good it would do. Even if she couldn't read what he'd written, she could see how little there was on every page. But he was trying to help, so she had to do what she could. Tomorrow she'd bring them back to the places they'd come from.

She looked at the top sheet and read *Carmel Ryan*. Ethan's father had never once asked her for her name, he'd been happy to have her living in his house without even knowing what she was called.

He wasn't getting involved with them in case she was lying

about Barry being part of his family. She could understand it, she wasn't blaming him. He couldn't be expected to believe her without some proof.

Well, he knew her name now; and he knew Barry's, because she'd told him. She wondered if he ever used it when the two of them were in the pet shop. She knew he read stories to Barry. She couldn't imagine him doing it, but Barry had told her about Jack and the Beanstalk and Thomas the Tank Engine and Cinderella, so it had to be true.

He wasn't the monster he made himself out to be. It wasn't surprising that he'd gone a bit grumpy with his wife dying so young and then his son going on drugs. And what was the story with Ethan's sister? There must be a problem there too, when she never came around to visit her father, never even phoned him up for a chat in the evening. And it sounded like she'd gone mad when she'd walked into the shop and seen Barry.

She slid the pages back into the big brown envelope he'd given her. Better keep them clean or he'd have something to say. She set the envelope on the bedside locker, next to her tin box. Her treasure box.

She undressed slowly and got into bed beside her son.

Tuesday

rene tapped on the playschool door.

"Come in."

She turned the handle and walked in. "Sorry I'm late," she said—recognizing, as she spoke, the woman who sat beside Emily at one of the low tables on the other side of the big bright room.

The woman regarded Irene in mild astonishment. "Hi there. You're here for Emily?"

Irene crossed to the table, her heels tapping softly on the lino or vinyl or whatever it was on the floor. "I'm her mother. Small world."

Meg from the life drawing class was her daughter's teacher. Showed how little they knew about each other, after three evenings spent together.

Emily looked up briefly before continuing with her jigsaw. "Where's Pilar?" she asked sulkily.

Irene crossed the room and sat on the edge of the table beside her daughter. "You know Pilar's not with us anymore," she said. "Daddy told you. Come on, get your jacket."

Emily didn't budge.

"She's almost finished," Meg said. "Just another minute."

Irene felt a twitch of annoyance. She sat and watched as Emily unhurriedly selected a wooden piece and tried to insert it into the wrong place—on purpose, she suspected.

"Emily," she said, "it's time to go, and Meg is waiting to close up. Go on, get your jacket."

"Pilar always gets it for me," Emily said, choosing a different jigsaw piece. "Or Daddy does."

Before Irene could respond Meg rose and crossed swiftly to the row of plastic hooks and lifted off Emily's yellow jacket. "Here we go," she said brightly, holding it out to Irene.

Irene took the jacket without comment. Why couldn't she mind her own business? "Come on," she said, turning back to Emily, "time to go home."

Emily picked another piece from the pile. "I'm not *finished*," she said.

"I think Mummy is in a hurry, lovie," Meg said.

"She's not Mummy, she's *Irene*," Emily said. "I just have to finish the jigsaw."

"No, you don't." Her patience spent, Irene grabbed her arm and pulled her to her feet. "It's time to go home now."

Emily's face crumpled as Irene maneuvered her arms into the yellow jacket, acutely conscious of the other woman watching silently. Let her think what she liked; Irene wasn't about to be dictated to by a three-year-old.

She lifted a hand in farewell as she propelled her crying daughter to the door, and Meg smiled briefly in return.

"See you tomorrow, Emily," she called.

Emily made no response, which gave Irene some small satisfaction.

———————

The day was crawling by. Each time James looked at his watch he was frustrated all over again by how little time had passed since he'd last checked. Lunch had been hours ago surely, and yet here it was, not even three o'clock.

By half past three he'd had enough. He locked the door of the house he'd been showing and phoned the receptionist to say he was going home with a headache. It was the first time off he'd taken since he'd started the job ten weeks ago, so his conscience didn't prick him unduly.

He drove to a shopping center on the outskirts of the town and whiled the time away getting a hot-towel shave and a haircut, which took all of half an hour, and buying what his grandmother would have called fripperies—biscotti in the little Italian delicatessen, a pair of sparkly green hair slides for Charlie, a milk jug with a row of fat smiling cats around the rim and a matching sugar bowl for Eunice, who refused to accept payment for her babysitting, and two pairs of black socks to add to the dozen he already had.

He arrived at Little Rascals ten minutes early and waited for Charlie to finish the butterfly collage she was working on, aware of the appraising glance of the manager, who hadn't ever asked him about Charlie's mother.

"Want to go for pizza?" he asked Charlie as they drove off.

Her face broke into a delighted grin. "Pizza? But it's not Friday."

"I know, but I thought we might have a special treat," he told her, "just this once."

"Yaaay."

He couldn't explain the restlessness he'd felt all day, the sense of impatience that had dogged him since he'd woken. He wanted to race through the day, he wanted the hours to flash by without taking a breath. By the time they finished their pizza it would be six, a quarter past when they got home.

He'd get Charlie cleaned and settled into pajamas and dressing gown, and while she was sitting in front of the telly he'd shower and change, and then it would be close to seven, not long to wait at all until Eunice arrived to babysit. And after that he'd kiss

Charlie good night and get into the car and drive to Carrickbawn Senior College.

He enjoyed the drawing, that was it. He looked forward to the classes, he was glad he'd signed up for them. He found them relaxing, and a nice break from the weekly routine.

That was all there was to it.

―――――――――

From the minute they'd left the playschool Emily had been impossible. After lunch, which she'd refused to eat, Irene had dropped her into the shopping center crèche while she did her usual round of the boutiques and shoe shops. Within twenty minutes Irene's name was being called over the center's public address system.

"Sorry," the crèche supervisor said when Irene returned, fuming. "She's being very aggressive and upsetting the other children. We're not prepared to look after her if she can't play nicely."

"What did she do?" Irene asked, regarding her daughter, who stood in the corner, red-faced and glowering.

The supervisor indicated another little girl who was sniffling on the lap of a second adult. "She bit that child, and was physically aggressive with several of the others, pinching, pulling hair, and so on."

Irene approached Emily and crouched beside her. "What's going on?"

"Nothing," Emily mumbled. "I don't like this place."

"Well, they don't like you either." Irene marched her outside. "You'll have to come around the shops with me. Don't touch anything."

"When is Pilar coming back?" Emily demanded.

Irene gritted her teeth as she steered Emily through the doors of a shoe shop. "Pilar is never coming back—you can forget about her. How could she come back to such a wicked girl?"

That evening Emily refused to eat dinner. She sat at the table regarding the mashed potato, sausage chunks, and little pool of baked beans Martin placed in front of her.

"Don't want it."

"You're getting nothing else," Irene warned, but Emily refused a single bite.

"I want Pilar."

Irene threw an exasperated glance at Martin, but he was studying Emily thoughtfully, and Irene knew his sympathies lay wholly with his daughter.

"Pilar had to leave," he said. "I told you she was very sad, but she had to go."

Emily's eyes filled with tears. "Was it because I was wicked?"

Martin shook his head, frowning. "Of course not, darling. Why on earth would you think that?"

Irene held her breath, but Emily didn't mention their earlier conversation. "Can you ask her to come back?"

"I don't think we can do that—but we'll get someone else, just as nice," he promised, pulling a tissue from the box on the sideboard and dabbing at her eyes. "Now, why don't you have a little bit of sausage, just for me?"

And just for her father Emily began to eat her dinner, observed by her mother, who could do nothing right.

At quarter past seven Irene left them to it—Emily taking longer than usual to go to sleep, demanding a second story from Martin—and made her way to Carrickbawn Senior College. She parked the car and pulled out her mobile phone and dialed the number her mother had given her. She hoped the Spanish woman's English was better than Pilar's.

"Allo?"

"Hello—is that"—she checked the page—"Katerina?"

"Yes." She pronounced it "jes." "Who is this please?"

"My name is Irene Dillon. I was given your name by, er"—what had her mother said?—"someone who knows you."

"Jes?"

"I'm looking for an au pair, and I believe—"

"Oh, sorry," the voice said, "but I have new job, very sorry."

"Thank you," Irene said crisply, and hung up.

So much for that. Could immigrant workers really be that hard to come by? Irene seriously doubted it, but where were they all? Martin had made it clear that a new au pair wasn't the route he wanted to take, so he was going to be no help at all. It was up to Irene to find one.

Maybe she could put it to the class this evening, maybe one of them would have some kind of a lead. Maybe Zarek would know someone; he must have immigrant friends.

So degrading, to have to rummage around like this for a maid. She slipped her phone back into her bag and opened the car door—and was startled to receive a broad smile from the anti-social Northern man, who'd just pulled up beside her.

"Lovely day," he said, "isn't it?"

———————

The mechanic listened to the sound of his wife leaving for her art class. Her footsteps on the path, her car door opening and closing, the engine starting up, the car moving off. He waited until the sound had disappeared completely. Then he waited another five minutes before pulling out his phone.

When can we do it again? he typed. Short and to the point, she wasn't one for chitchat. She saw what she wanted and she went for it.

She was dynamite. The thought of her made him hard. He pressed *send* and off it went.

"I'm looking for an au pair," Irene said. "Someone for a bit of housework and childminding. I was wondering if any of you know someone who might be interested."

"Yes," Zarek said immediately, grasping at his escape from the possibility of having Pilar as a co-worker. "My flat mate is looking for new job," he told Irene. "Very nice person, very friendly. Loves the little childrens. Very good worker."

"Sounds perfect. Would you happen to have her number?"

Zarek tore a corner off his page and scribbled Pilar's name on it, and copied her number from his phone. Maybe he should phone Pilar during the break, tell her to expect a call. No—better not get her hopes up, just in case nothing came of it. Although Irene certainly sounded interested.

He handed the piece of paper to her. She glanced at it before putting it into her handbag.

"Thanks a lot," she said. "Much obliged."

The door opened and Audrey hurried in, looking flustered.

"So sorry," she said, shrugging off her jacket. "I do hope I'm not late. My little dog escaped from the garden and I had to go looking for her."

"Relax; it's only two minutes past," Irene told her.

"Oh, that's a relief." Audrey dumped her canvas bag on the table at the top of the room. "Anyone seen Jackie?"

"She's on the way," Fiona said. "I met her in the corridor when I was coming in."

"Good." Audrey pulled a cardboard tube from the bag. "While we're waiting for her, I'll show you what we'll be doing tonight."

"Have you find your dog?" Zarek asked.

Audrey smiled warmly at him as she eased the top off the tube. "Yes, I got her, she'd only gone as far as the next garden. She's still a puppy, she's very lively and curious."

She reached into the tube and eased out a rolled-up sheet. "Now, I want you to look at this drawing and see what you notice."

She unrolled the sheet and stuck a blob of Blu-Tack to each corner and attached it to the blackboard. Her students regarded the charcoal image in silence.

The female subject was nude and seated on a stool with her back to the artist, but she was turning from the waist to look over her shoulder. Her arms were raised, piling her hair onto her head, the curve and nipple of the near-side breast just visible. A towel was draped loosely at her hips, her buttocks rising from its folds. Her face was in three-quarter profile, her lips slightly parted in a half smile.

The rolled edge and claw feet of a bath were visible to the right of the figure. The impression was given of someone just about to step in—or maybe just out.

The proportions and perspective were perfect, the lines gracefully and confidently executed. There was a wonderfully sensual feel to the image.

"Tell me what you notice," Audrey repeated when nobody spoke.

"It's like a negative," Meg said. "Like it's reversed, or something."

Audrey nodded. "Exactly right—"

Jackie entered just then, wearing her usual dressing gown and carrying her rucksack. *Sorry*, she mouthed at Audrey as she dropped the rucksack and began taking off her shoes. Audrey smiled at her briefly before turning back to the class.

"That's exactly what it is, a drawing in reverse. It's called a tonal study. What we do is cover the whole section first with pencil or charcoal"—she indicated the sheet—"and then we pick out the figure using our putty rubbers. It's like you're doing the opposite of what you normally do. You're rubbing out the figure instead of drawing it."

They were silent, their eyes still on the drawing. Jackie tucked her rucksack under a chair and undid the belt of her dressing gown.

"It's a useful exercise," Audrey went on. "The object is to pay attention to the tones and planes of the figure, to see where the light hits, and what shapes are created by it. Once Jackie is in position I'll go through it in more detail."

"Who did it?" Irene asked.

Audrey blushed a little. "I did, actually, at a life drawing course I attended last summer. In Tuscany," she added.

"It's great," Fiona murmured, and the others chimed their agreement.

"You are very good artist," Zarek said.

Audrey's cheeks grew pinker. "Oh, well, thank you...anyway, that's what we'll be trying out tonight. I think you'll enjoy it."

Jackie came to the center of the room and stood by the chair, looking questioningly at Audrey.

And the fourth life drawing class began.

Michael sat in the gathering dusk and remembered his wife laboring over the flower beds, easing up weeds or thinning seedlings or dead-heading flowers. Ruth had loved the garden; she was happiest when she was making things grow, or simply sitting on summer evenings where Michael sat now, surrounded by the scents and colors that she'd created.

He'd let the place go after she died. He'd never been any good in a garden anyway, better at admiring flowers than growing them. Everything had faded away without Ruth to water and weed and nurture, and he hadn't cared. What good were flowers to him, what did he want with scents and humming bees and flapping butterflies, when she was gone?

He'd like it now, he'd like to have something to look at when he sat out here. Maybe he should employ a gardener, couple of hours a week, put a bit of a shape on it. The girl had started things off, with her weeding. Maybe she—

He shut the thought off and turned his face to the sky, ribboned with grey and orange and purple. Wouldn't mind being able to paint, like to try and capture that. Maybe he could do a class. He watched a bird flitting across the lawn, home to bed. He turned to glance up behind him and saw the curtains drawn in Valerie's room.

After another few minutes, when the darkness began to draw in, he rose and went indoors, and locked the door for the night.

"I didn't see you at the pool on Thursday."

"Yes, I must work. One of the other worker on holiday, so I work for her."

"Oh." Meg sipped her tea.

"How was birthday party?" Zarek asked.

She rolled her eyes, pushing her glasses up in a gesture that was becoming familiar to him. "Well, busy, of course, and noisy. She invited all the girls from her class—she wanted all the boys to come too, but I had to put a limit on it. I think thirteen came."

Zarek imagined thirteen little girls full of sugar, leaping and shrieking around the house. "Lot of fun," he said, thanking the gods that he'd escaped.

Meg made another face. "Fun for the kids, sure—but I was exhausted at the end of it. Of course," she added, "my darling husband wasn't there—he *said* he had a meeting at work that he couldn't get out of, very convenient. So I had to do the whole thing myself."

Zarek laid down his cup. "Please excuse," he said. "I need toilet."

"So this is your first year of the playschool," Irene said.

"That's right. I was a teacher before I went on maternity leave with my daughter, and basically I never went back. She's just started school, so I thought I'd try this."

"And how do you like it?"

"Well, it's hectic, but I love working with children, especially really young ones. They're a joy—most of the time."

Irene laid down her half-full cup. "Frankly, I don't know how you do it. No offense, but I have to say it would be my idea of hell."

"None taken; each to his own," Meg replied lightly. "What is it you do again?"

"My husband and I own Fitness Unlimited, next to the library."

"I know it." Meg ran a finger around the rim of her cup. "And I have to say that going to a gym would be *my* idea of hell."

Irene grinned. "*Touché.* By the way," she went on, "what do you think of Zarek? He's gorgeous, isn't he?"

"Zarek?" Meg's hand drifted to her braid. "To be honest, I hadn't really noticed."

Pathetic; what a bad liar she was. Couldn't she see how everyone knew she was mad for him? Irene debated telling her that she was wasting her time, but then decided not to. Let Meg find out all by herself.

———————

"Would you mind if I told you something?"

"Not at all," Audrey replied. She never minded being taken into someone's confidence. The very question, cloaked in a vague secrecy, usually suggested that the something in question was fairly interesting.

"It's just that…I'm pregnant."

Audrey's face broke into a wide smile. "Oh Fiona, good for you. Your first?"

"Yes, and I'm dying to tell everyone."

"Of course you—"

"But my husband says we should wait, you know, until it's safe."

"How far gone are you?" Audrey's knowledge of pregnancy and all it entailed was limited to staff room chat among the teachers who found themselves in that condition. Nevertheless, she'd picked up a respectable amount of information over the years.

"Only a few weeks; I suppose he's right." She glanced at the hand Audrey was using to hold her cup. "You don't have children yourself?"

"Not yet," Audrey told her cheerfully, "but I live in hope."

"I think," Fiona said, her blush deepening again, "you'd make a very good mother"—and it was with the greatest difficulty that Audrey resisted the impulse to hug her.

———————

"So how are you feeling?" Irene asked—compelled to show interest, since Fiona had shared her big secret the week before.

"Fine—no morning sickness at all so far." She crunched into a custard cream. "If I hadn't done a test, I'd wonder if I was imagining things."

Irene remembered the awful queasiness that had begun barely three weeks into her pregnancy and lasted right through, making breakfast, and often lunch too, an impossibility. Her stomach churning, as if her body were rejecting the fetus as much as Irene's mind had been.

"You're lucky," she told Fiona. "Not everyone sails through. And you're tiny, so you'll probably get your figure back in no time."

"Maybe," Fiona said, smiling brightly, "you should give it another go. I mean, I know you said you had a tough time before, but you never know, a second pregnancy might be a lot easier."

Irene wanted to slap the smile off her face. A few weeks' pregnant and already an expert. Assuming that everyone was just dying to go through the horror of bringing another screaming baby into the world.

"I have no intention of having another child," she said. "I'm having far too much fun having sex with whomever I please. Why would I want to stop that?"

Fiona looked half amused, half shocked. "No—I don't believe you."

"True as I'm standing here," Irene said. "Right now I'm having sex with the man who repaired my car a couple of weeks ago. He's a bit less polished than I'm used to, but very enthusiastic, if you get my drift." She scanned the room. "There's Audrey on the move, looks like we're going back."

She walked away, leaving the silly cow to follow.

"So you had Eoin when you were what—twelve?"

Jackie laughed. "I was eighteen, and very innocent. It was a one-night stand in Greece, after far too many beers."

"Oops. Bet your parents were delighted."

"Don't remind me. I'd say they came this close to throwing me out on the street. They're fine now, thankfully, and mad about Eoin."

"I'm assuming," he said, "that the father isn't on the scene."

"You're assuming right; I never laid eyes on him again. We weren't exactly intending to keep in touch." She pressed her hands to her cheeks. "God, I sound like a total slut, don't I? I'm not, honest."

James laughed. "I believe you, honest."

They sat on the low wall that flanked the college entrance. He'd cut short his bedtime story—the prince and princess had married with indecent haste—as soon as he'd seen her coming out. Their conversation was easy, more relaxed than it had been in the park. She'd had time to get used to him being who he was.

She hadn't looked in his direction all through the first half of the class, and he supposed that made sense. She was naked, he was her son's friend's father. Awkward. And for his part, he'd tried to concentrate on the fact that her body was an object to be drawn, and nothing more. Awkward too.

Okay now, though. Enjoyable now, to be sitting in the dusk with her. Eighteen when Eoin was born, so twenty-four or -five now. Nine or ten years younger than him.

Not that her age mattered in the least. They were only chatting. They were just friends, or parents of friends.

"Lord, I almost forgot," Audrey said, falling into step with Meg as they returned to class. "Someone was inquiring about playschools and I promised them I'd ask you if you had any vacancies."

Meg laughed. "'Vacancies'; that makes me feel like a B and B… is it for a friend of yours?"

"No, not at all—at least, it's someone I hardly know really, I just bought my dog from him. But I met him in the park on Sunday and he was asking me about playschools, goodness knows why, and I thought of you."

"Well, thanks for that, I'll certainly talk to him. I have ten on the books, which is as many as I want really, but there is a boy who comes just two days a week, so maybe I could take this child the other three…look, pass on my number and ask him to give me a call."

"I'll do that, thanks."

———————

"So," Audrey said, taking the picture from the blackboard, "I'd like you to try one or two tonal studies this week. Think negative spaces, think light direction, pick out the highlights. See how it goes."

Two classes to go, and so far so good. Her students weren't particularly artistic, apart from Zarek, but hopefully they were enjoying the experience. At least nobody had dropped out.

She waited until the classroom had cleared and then left, pulling the door closed. As she walked down the corridor Jackie hurried up behind her.

"Is everyone gone?"

"Yes, all gone. You look like you're in a rush."

"Just wanted to catch a program on telly—see you next week." She waved as she flew up the corridor.

She'd certainly gotten over her nerves: sitting didn't seem to faze her at all now. Nice girl, Audrey had been lucky to get her. Thank goodness she hadn't had to take Terence the science teacher up on his offer; imagine him ogling Irene as he sat there without a stitch on.

In the lobby Audrey stopped to exchange a few words with

Vincent, and by the time she walked outside, a minute or so later, her model was nowhere in sight.

All through the first half she'd done her best to ignore him. Hadn't once looked in his direction while they were drawing, had kept her eyes firmly on the floor in front of her, or off into the distance. Just once, as she'd been going from one pose into another, she'd given a lightning glance towards his table, but he was turned away, saying something to Zarek.

Not that she expected anything to be different, of course. Just because they'd spent a couple of hours together over the weekend didn't mean anything would have changed between them. Particularly not here, where she was just the model again, and nobody's mother.

She'd wandered outdoors at break—not looking for him, really not, just needing some fresh air—and he'd appeared a minute later, and they'd had a lovely chat, with her feeling no embarrassment or shyness at all. He'd asked about Eoin's father—didn't that mean he was interested, just a bit? Wasn't he trying to find out if she was with anyone?

She hadn't mentioned Charlie's mother, something had stopped her, some sense that he didn't want to talk about that. But they'd gotten on well, they had.

And now the class was over, and she'd rushed getting dressed, and there was no sign of his car in the car park.

No matter. She hadn't really expected anything to be different—except he could have offered her a lift home, since he'd as good as chatted her up at the break, and since she was his daughter's friend's mother, and since it wouldn't have killed him.

No matter. She walked quickly down the driveway towards the college gates—needing to keep up the pretense, at least until

Audrey motored past her, that she was rushing home to the television.

———————

What were the chances? Irene reread the name on the slip Zarek had given her, but it still said *Pilar Okrentovich*, and Irene very much doubted that there were two Pilars in Carrickbawn, let alone two with the same unpronounceable surname. She'd just gotten the number of the last au pair in Ireland she intended calling.

She screwed up the slip and threw it out the car window. She took out her phone to call her mother—surely she'd have some other leads—and saw a text message waiting to be read. She opened it.

When can we do it again?

She closed the message and scrolled through her contacts till she found her mother's name.

Wednesday

Michael Browne."

As abrupt as ever. Snapped out, as if Audrey was interrupting something important.

"It's Audrey Matthews," she said.

"Who?"

"You were asking me about playschools," she said briskly. Really, you'd think at this stage he'd recognize her voice. "I met you in the park. On Sunday. You sold me my dog."

"Oh…yes," he said.

"You asked me about playschools," she repeated.

"Yes?"

Was that a note of *impatience* in his voice? When *she* was doing *him* the favor, he had the *gall* to sound impatient? What was it about this man that he could make her feel so cross so easily?

"Hello?"

"I'm still here," she said stiffly. "I got you a number." She could just picture him standing behind his counter, as grumpy as ever. Easy to be polite and pleasant when you were looking for something.

"Her name is Meg Curran." She recited the number.

"Many thanks," he said.

"Good-bye then," she said shortly and hung up without giving him a chance to say any more. She walked off in the direction of her class, feeling prickly.

Zarek cleared the table of crumbs and cardboard cartons and cups and scattered salt packets, and wiped the surface with his cloth. So many people eating such unhealthy food, filling their bodies with fat and salt and sugar. Not for the first time, he wished he worked in a shop that sold nothing edible. Art supplies maybe, or musical instruments. Or sports equipment, like the shop Anton worked in.

The café door opened and Pilar walked in. It was the first time they'd met since the previous evening, Pilar having gone to her room before Zarek had returned from the art class, and not yet up by the time he'd left the apartment to come to work.

"Hello," he said. "I have good news."

Pilar's eyes widened. "You say your boss I look for work, your boss say for me to come?"

"No," he said, "my boss not here yet."

Her face fell.

"No, no," Zarek said, "I have better news, about better job for you. Lady in my life drawing class looking for new au pair, she ask everybody."

Her hopeful expression returned. "Lady in your class?"

"Yes—I give her your number. She no call you this morning?"

"No." Pilar took out her phone and inspected it. "Nothing. She nice lady?"

"Very nice. She make the jokes, she is funny."

"She have many childrens?"

"I don't know."

"What her name?"

"Irene."

Pilar's smile faded. "Irene? Irene what? What her last name?"

"I don't know last name."

"What she look like?" Pilar demanded. "She short hair, white hair?"

Zarek nodded. "Yes, she very pretty."

"She wear the short skirt, the high shoe?"

"Yes; but she—"

"Aaiiie!" she cried, throwing her arms up to clutch at her chest, causing a few heads to turn in her direction. "She Mrs. Dillon! She my old boss! She Irene Dillon, she mother of Emily! Zarek, what you do? You give my number to my old boss? Aaiiie!"

Zarek regarded her in alarm. "Pilar, please no shouting. How you be sure she same person?"

"She same, she same," Pilar hissed. "I know she same. She Mrs. Dillon, with the white hair and the pretty face and the short skirt. She look for new au pair now, because I leave. Why she not call me, if she not Irene Dillon?"

Zarek had to acknowledge the logic of that. He felt his hopes slowly dissipating.

Pilar thrust a hand towards him. "You give me form for job in café now. My God," she added vehemently, "I not believe you give my number to Mrs. Dillon. You try to give me old job back. You try to kill me."

"But work is hard here," Zarek said desperately. "Lots of drunk peoples at night, lots of fighting. Maybe other ladies look for au pair—"

"Give me form," Pilar demanded. "Job is job. If other ladies look for au pair, I go for job. If no other ladies, I take job here. If work okay for you, work okay for me."

Zarek reached under the counter and took out a form, his excuses exhausted.

———————

As she left the boutique, Jackie's phone beeped. She took it from her bag and looked at the screen. Charlie, it read.

Charlie, which of course was James. Her heart skipped. She pressed *open* and his message popped up:

> Taking Charlie to the cinema on Fri, wondering if you and Eoin would like to join us—J

She read it through three times. He was inviting them to the cinema. She should wait before replying, not seem too eager. She replaced her phone and walked to the end of the street. She pressed the button to summon the green man on the opposite side and stood waiting at the edge of the pavement.

It wouldn't seem eager if she replied. It was a play date for their kids, that was all. The green man lit up. She pulled her phone out and typed Sounds good. What time? She signed it J, the same as his. She pressed *send* and off it flew to him, as the green man turned red again.

She liked the way they were both J. She liked that he hadn't made it sound all about the kids—although of course that was why they were meeting. She pressed the traffic signal button again.

Wasn't it?

She wished she knew for sure that his wife was dead. She wished he'd say something, make it clear what the situation was.

Her phone beeped again as the green man reappeared.

> 7:00. We'll bring the popcorn. See you then.

No J this time. You didn't need to put your name if you knew the person well enough. She dropped her phone back into her bag and hurried across the road as the green man disappeared for the second time. She walked the half block to the coffee shop where she normally got her lunchtime sandwich, listening to the Lady Gaga song that had been playing in her head all day.

Love, love, love, I want your love, she heard.

———————

Carmel turned as quietly as she could, pulling her pillow farther under her head and nestling into it. The novelty of lying in a clean, comfortable bed hadn't worn off; she didn't think it ever would. She stretched her legs, enjoying the crisp, smooth feel of the sheets that he'd changed over the weekend, even though they'd only been sleeping in them a little over a week.

In the squat they'd had no sheets at all, and she had no idea how long the blankets had been on the bed that she and Ethan, and later Barry, had slept in. Here they had hot showers every evening, and still he changed the sheets.

But that was the trouble, wasn't it? It was so good here, so much better than anyplace she'd been, even her own home. Especially her own home, with every night full of menace, never knowing when her bedroom door was going to open. This was so different, they were so safe here.

And she knew it couldn't last, nothing like this lasted. And then what? Where could they possibly go from here? Whenever she thought about leaving this house, it felt like someone was shoving a fist into her stomach.

She'd spent the morning dropping back the job application forms, and everywhere she'd gone she'd gotten the same reaction. Nobody had said anything, but their faces had said enough. Their faces had said *Is that it?*

"We'll let you know if something comes up," they'd told her, and it had sounded, each time, like a thing they said to make her go away.

Was it a week since they'd done the test to see if she was telling the truth about Ethan? She couldn't remember what day that had been, but it felt like a week ago. Ethan's father had said the results would take a week to ten days. That meant they could come any day. Maybe tomorrow.

She knew what the results should show, but maybe they weren't always right, maybe they got it wrong sometimes. And even if they got it right, how did she know what he'd do when he read them? Even though she did everything she could think of not to make him sorry he'd taken them in, he might still be tired of having them living in his house. He might give her some money for Barry and then throw them out. She turned over again and closed her eyes and tried to stop tossing it all around in her head, but it was impossible.

———

It was for Charlie, he was just doing it for his daughter's sake. He was responsible for her happiness, and meeting her friend in the cinema would make her happy. And he and Charlie went to see a film most Fridays, it wasn't as if he was arranging a special trip. He was just inviting the other two along to join them, that was all.

It was for Charlie.

Thursday

I come to Ireland two year ago," Pilar said to the woman who sat on the other side of the coffee table. "I clean the houses and look after the little childrens, and also I cook a little bit."

The woman's red hair was almost exactly the same color as the coat on a dog Pilar had once had. Pilar had never met a human whose hair was that shade of red. There were magazines on the coffee table that didn't look as if anyone read them.

"When you say you cook, what exactly do you mean?" the woman asked, clasping her topmost knee with fingers that were tipped with purple varnish. "I mean, can you actually *cook*?"

Pilar had never had more than a passing acquaintance with recipes and saucepans. Her mother had thrown her hands up in despair at her daughter's leathery dumplings and stodgy blinis and haphazardly seasoned borscht.

Happily, since her arrival in Ireland, Pilar had managed to avoid jobs that involved producing anything more challenging than sausages or beans on toast—and since moving in with Anton, she was enjoying the luxury of having her own meals cooked for her.

"Um…my cooking is simple," she said. "I do the sausages, the fingers of fish, et cetera"—a sudden image of Emily's mashed banana and yogurt breakfast jumped into her head, and her heart twisted as it always did when she recalled the little girl—"and also the boiled potatoes and the, er, beef burger."

The woman turned her nails upwards and inspected them. "I see…and do you drive?"

Pilar assumed what she hoped was a regretful expression. "Sorry, no driving."

In fact she'd driven happily, if a little erratically, in Lithuania from the age of seventeen, but the thought of driving on the wrong side of the road, in a car where nothing was where you expected it to be, terrified her.

The woman sighed. "So you clean and cook basic children's food, and you don't drive, and that's it?"

"Also I can iron the clothes," Pilar said, casting about for inspiration. "And…um, walk with the dogs. And a little work in the garden also." Fresh inspiration struck. "And perhaps the childrens like to learn a little Lithuanian?"

"Lithuanian," the woman repeated flatly.

"Yes—maybe they go for holiday."

The woman stood and smoothed her blue-and-white skirt. "Well, thank you for coming. I'll be in touch."

Pilar shook the hand that was extended to her and walked towards the door, knowing before she was past the threshold that she wouldn't be returning.

But there may be other women in need of an au pair, not quite as demanding as this one. And of course, failing that, there was always the café. Even if it wasn't her first choice of employment, it would be very nice to work with Zarek, with whom she got along so well.

Perhaps *he* would like to learn a little Lithuanian, as they stood together behind the counter.

When Emily had been positioned in front of the television and Irene had the kitchen to herself, she looked up a number in the phone book. She took her credit card from her bag and made a short call. After disconnecting she scrolled through her messages until she found the mechanic's last text.

She pressed *reply* and typed Bradshaw's, 3:30, Sunday. Room 12.

Bradshaw's was a smallish country hotel about eight miles outside Carrickbawn. Irene had no intention of revisiting that garage. By three o'clock the Sunday lunchtime drinkers would have gone home for their roast beef, and a person slipping upstairs after that wouldn't be noticed. Irene would check in at three fifteen; let the mechanic make his own way up when he arrived.

Might be awkward escaping from his wife on Sunday afternoon, but Irene was fairly confident that he'd make the effort. Sex with her in the comfort of a hotel bedroom—few enough men would turn that down, and he'd certainly seemed to enjoy his first encounter.

Twenty minutes there and back, and an hour or so in the room. She'd be home by five to take over from Martin and boil an egg for Emily's tea.

Unless she'd found a new au pair by then, in which case they could take their time at Bradshaw's.

———

"I'd be able to take him three days a week, Wednesday to Friday," Meg said, "if that's any good to you."

"That would be fine, thank you," Michael replied. Three days was better than no days.

"So you'll bring him along next Wednesday?"

"Not me," he told her. "I have to work, but his mother will take him."

"And I assume you're the father?"

Michael wiped at a smear on the counter with his sleeve. "No,

I'm not the father." He didn't think she'd pursue it, and she didn't.

"Right, so," she said. "Did Audrey give you my address?"

"No."

She called it out and Michael wrote it down.

"And it was Barry you said, wasn't it?"

"Yes."

"And the surname?"

"Ryan." He paused. "And I will be paying, so I would appreciate if you could furnish me with a bill for the remainder of the first term. Let me give you my address."

She was probably wondering what his relationship to the boy was. Imagine if he said, *I may be his grandfather; we're just waiting for the outcome of the paternity test.*

"That's fine," Meg said when he'd called out his address. "So I'll see him at half past nine on Wednesday. But let's wait to make sure he settles in first, before I bill you for anything. Not every child is cut out for playschool."

She sounded pleasant and capable. Michael pictured Barry building a tower with bricks, or doing a jigsaw, or drawing a picture maybe, surrounded by children his own age. Doing normal things for the first time in his life.

"He's quiet," he told Meg. "He's had little contact with other children. It may take him a while to find his feet."

"Don't worry," she said. "I'll have a fair idea in the first few days if he'll settle. You'd be surprised how quickly most of them adjust."

Neither of Michael's children had gone to playschool. He didn't think they'd existed then, and even if they had, Ruth wouldn't have wanted them to go. She'd been a stay-at-home mother, glad of the excuse to give up her office job once Ethan was on the way.

Playschool would probably have been good for Valerie. After

her mother died the little girl had become terribly clingy, first to Michael and then to Pauline, as soon as the housekeeper had arrived on the scene. It had taken her several weeks to settle when she'd started school.

Michael remembered the tears every morning as Pauline was putting on her uniform. If it hadn't been for Ethan, two classes ahead, and blessedly willing to hold his little sister's hand on the way, they'd never have gotten her there.

After he'd hung up Michael looked around the silent shop. Strange how empty the place felt in the afternoons, even though the boy made such little noise when he was here.

They'd gone through the fairy-tale collection and moved on to a set of Mr. Men books that Michael had spotted on a special-offer stand in the local bookshop. Barry's favorite was Mr. Bump. The first time Michael heard him laugh was when Mr. Bump walked straight into an apple tree and knocked several apples off. Barry's laugh was short, more of a high-pitched shout than a laugh really. Michael supposed he hadn't had much practice.

He thought it was probably then, when he'd heard that first laugh, that he'd decided to go ahead with the playschool without waiting for the results of the test. It had suddenly seemed petty to be waiting, to be making a small boy's development dependent on a blood connection.

Whatever their relationship, Michael had decided that he would fund a year of playschool for him. He would do it because he could, and because the boy needed it. It would give him a start in life, try to make up for what had gone before. Even if it turned out the girl was trying to pull a fast one, the child was still the innocent party.

He'd wait till tomorrow to tell her what he'd done. He wondered what her reaction would be. He was aware that he was interfering. Even if he was putting a roof over their heads it was still none of his business how she raised her son. But he hoped she'd have the intelligence to see how it would benefit the boy. The fact that it wasn't going to cost her a penny might help.

He went into the back of the shop to bring out more tins of puppy food.

I am sorry to tell you that Pilar is out of work, Zarek wrote. *On Monday she had an argument with her boss and she walked out. She has been looking for more work but so far she has not been lucky. Yesterday she came into the café and filled out an application form.*

He couldn't mention the fact that Pilar's boss just happened to be in his life drawing class, and that he'd inadvertently offered Pilar as a replacement for herself. It would be a good story, it would be funny were it not for the fact that he'd kept the art classes from them up to this.

Here the weather is mixed, some good sunshine but also very wet days. I hope it is not getting too cold at home yet. Have you had the chimneys cleaned this autumn?

Weather in Poland could be cruel from November to March, with the temperature often plunging to minus twenty. He wondered how his first Irish winter would compare: If the weather he'd experienced here so far was any indication, he wasn't expecting anything too predictable.

I am fine, thank God. No complaints, I am enjoying my time in Ireland.

He dropped his pen and sat back and pondered the truth of that remark. Certainly he wasn't unhappy here. His job could undoubtedly be more interesting, but most of the time it wasn't unpleasant.

His accommodation was comfortable, if not luxurious, and he got on well with his flat mates. There were no arguments, nobody had fallen out. The three of them ate together on the evenings Zarek wasn't working, and often spent time in one another's company outside mealtimes.

Really, he couldn't complain. Life in Ireland had been good since his arrival. And if he sometimes longed for more, maybe he was simply looking for too much.

The Fifth Week

October 19–25

———

*A result, a group invitation, a
tragedy, and a new beginning.*

Friday

His stillness was absolute. Audrey had no idea how long he'd been there—she'd just gotten home from work and come upstairs to change into her gardening clothes—or how long he'd stay in that position, but she decided to take a chance. She grabbed her sketch pad and began to draw, her pencil flying across the page, her eyes flicking rapidly between the scene outside and the pad.

Kevin squatted on the lawn, feet planted solidly, forearms resting on his thighs, upper body tilted slightly forward. He peered downwards, totally preoccupied with something in the grass.

"He can watch something for ages," Pauline had told her. "Ants, worms, a few earwigs—I've no idea what he finds so fascinating."

His face was hidden from Audrey, her view of him foreshortened by her elevated position at the upstairs window. It was a challenging posture to capture, but Audrey did her best, scribbling busily until his head lifted suddenly and turned towards the house—and here came Pauline making her way across the lawn to him, bending to see what was engaging his attention.

Audrey closed her pad and dropped it on the bed. She began to change into her gardening trousers, hearing Dolly's demanding yips from the kitchen. Another weekend, two lie-ins to look forward to, and only another week to the midterm break. She'd bring Dolly to the park after dinner; a quick trot around it would tire her out for the evening.

The park reminded her of Michael Browne. She wondered if he'd followed up on the playschool. She wouldn't ask Meg on Tuesday, it was none of her business, but Meg might well mention it herself.

Audrey was just interested, that was all.

———————

"A playschool?"

Her expression wary, which immediately irritated him. Couldn't the silly woman see what he was offering?

"He needs to mix with other children," he said briskly. "It's not good for him to be with just you or me all the time. And there'd be lots of books, and jigsaws, and other toys. He'd be learning, you'd be giving him a good start."

She nodded slowly, biting at the nail of her index finger. Michael itched to tap it away, like he'd always done with Valerie as a child.

"It would be three mornings a week," he said. "Wednesday to Friday. She's doing us a favor, taking him in. I was lucky to find any place at all, this late in the year."

She gnawed at the cuticle now with her teeth.

"Please stop doing that," Michael said sharply, and she dropped her finger quickly.

"She's holding a place open for him," he said. "He could start this coming week, next Wednesday."

It didn't matter to him, it was nothing to him whether the boy went or not. So why did he feel like shaking her right now until her teeth rattled? What the *hell* was wrong with her?

"Well? What do you think? Are you happy to let him go?"

"It's jus' that…you don't know yet." Her color rose, her hand drifted to her mouth again until she saw him looking, and she let it fall.

"I don't know what?" But he knew what she was talking about.

"If I'm tellin' you the truth," she answered, her face aflame. "About Ethan, if he's the father."

"Are you telling me he isn't?" Michael asked quietly.

Suddenly, shockingly, he realized that he didn't want to hear her admit that she'd made it all up.

She shook her head rapidly. "No, I'm not sayin' that. I *told* you the truth—but you don't *know* it's the truth yet. So why are you doin' this big thing for us? What if you change your mind in a few weeks, or a few months, after Christmas or somethin', an' Barry has to drop out because I can't pay, an' he got all that learnin' that might just stop, an' then we have to go back to nothin' after all that?"

She stopped abruptly, pressing her lips together. Michael left the table and walked to the kitchen window and stood looking out at his excuse for a garden.

"I'm not going to change my mind," he said evenly, keeping his back to her. "I'm prepared to pay for the full year. I'm doing it to help the boy, because I can afford it, and because I want to, and because he deserves a good start in life, whoever he is. Everyone does." Looking at the old stone wall at the bottom of the garden, not looking at her.

"I'm sorry," she said then, "if I don't sound grateful. I *am* grateful, you done so much for us. I'm jus' scared, that's all. Nothin' like this ever happened to us before. I jus' think…it's too good to be true, an' it can't last."

Michael made no reply. What could he say to that?

"You read him stories," she said then. "In the shop. He told me."

He nodded, watching a robin dropping from the top of the wall to land lightly on the grass. "Yes," he said. "I do."

"He likes them."

Michael tapped his fingers on the edge of the sink. "It's good for him," he said. "Stories feed the brain."

A short silence followed, and then she spoke again. "When we met you first," she said, "I thought you were really mean, but you're not. You're a good man. I knew Ethan would have a good father."

Michael had no idea how to respond. He studied a cracked tile on the margin of wall above the sink.

"Thank you," she said. He heard her getting up. "I'll never forget what you done for us."

She turned and walked out of the kitchen and up the stairs, to where Barry had already been put to bed.

Later, when he went up himself, Michael heard soft singing coming from Valerie's room.

―――――――――

She sat in the darkened cinema beside Eoin. On his far side was Charlie, and beyond her, James. The air was thick with the smell of popcorn. The volume was too high—why was it always set so high? Did the cinema staff think they were all deaf, or were they just trying to make them deaf?

The film, about a car that seemed to think it was human, didn't interest her in the slightest. The plot was paper-thin, the ending apparent in the first two minutes. The acting was mediocre, the dialogue as predictable as the plot.

But if she closed her eyes she could pretend the children were at home, fast asleep. She could imagine that she and James were out on a date, his arm around her, his thigh touching hers. She could picture them leaving the cinema when the film ended and going to a restaurant for dinner. Or maybe they'd have eaten before the film, maybe they'd just go somewhere quiet for a drink afterwards.

His hand reaching across to touch hers as they chatted, the wine making her feel beautifully woozy. Going back to his place, or her place—her apartment, which of course existed in her imagination—

"Mum."

She opened her eyes. Eoin was pulling at her sleeve. She dragged herself out of the apartment. "What?" she whispered.

"I have to go to the toilet."

"Okay." She stood up.

Back to reality, where James was three seats away from her, and they were on a play date.

———

"We might go to the park on Sunday," he said as they were getting out of the car. "Just if you're around."

She smelled of oranges, her shampoo maybe. She wore pale pink lipstick, and the neckline of her top sat just above her breasts, a hint only of cleavage visible, the suggestion of a shadowy dip, that was all.

But he knew what her breasts looked like, he knew the shape and color of her nipples. He had studied the dark triangle of pubic hair at the top of her legs, he had attempted to reproduce her body on paper.

"If the weather is fine," she was saying, "we'll see you there."

"Grand," he said, putting the car into gear.

"Thanks for this evening," she said. "Eoin, what do you say to Charlie's dad?"

Charlie's dad, that's what he was. If she only knew the thoughts Charlie's dad had been having about Eoin's mum. He drove off, leaving them waving on the path.

Saturday

D essert?"

The mechanic's wife shook her head. "I might have some Ben and Jerry's at home."

He raised his hand for the bill. "Must drop into the gym again tomorrow afternoon." He patted his stomach. "Work some of this off."

"Ah, not Sunday, it's our only day together."

"I'll be a couple of hours, that's all. We'll get a DVD on the way home that you can watch while I'm gone." He entered his PIN in the credit card machine and took the receipt from the waiter. "Come on, don't you want me to be fit?"

"Okay—two hours, not a minute more." She stood up. "I have to use the loo—I'll follow you out."

He took his jacket from the chair and walked towards the exit.

———

He was standing by the door as they approached the restaurant. Irene could have pretended not to know him, but then she thought, *Why not say hello to the man who repaired your car?*

"Hi there," she said. "Fancy meeting you here." She turned to Martin. "This is the man who did the panel beating on my car."

Martin shook his hand. "Martin Dillon. Nice job, thanks."

"No worries." The mechanic looked down. "And who's this?"

"This is Emily," Irene replied. He hadn't given his name to Martin, because it wasn't Ger, like he'd told her.

"Hey." He waggled his fingers at Emily, who stuck her thumb into her mouth and moved closer to Martin.

"Well, take care," Irene said, pulling the door open—and a woman coming out walked straight into her path.

"Oh—sorry," the woman said, drawing back. "Oh," she said again, smiling, "hello there"—and Irene recognized Fiona from the life drawing class.

Fiona, whose hand curled around the mechanic's arm. Fiona, who was married to the mechanic. Fiona, who was pregnant.

"One of my satisfied customers," the mechanic said, indicating Irene with a tilt of his head. Not seeming to have noticed the fact that his wife seemed to know Irene. Not seeing the danger, not knowing what Irene had told his wife on Tuesday night.

Right now I'm having sex with the man who repaired my car. Not as well polished as I'm used to, but very enthusiastic.

And Fiona was remembering too, the smile fading from her face as the mechanic turned and led her away.

Jesus, she would have to be his wife. And now she knew what he had done, because Irene had told her. Irene had told her that her husband had been unfaithful.

And Fiona was pregnant, and had been delighted about it.

"She seemed to know you," Martin said.

"She used to come to the gym," Irene replied, walking ahead of him into the restaurant.

Michael dialed his daughter's number and listened to the soft double *brr* of her phone ringing. Over a week since she'd called to the shop and found Barry there, and no word from her since. He suddenly couldn't let it go any longer.

He had nothing ready to say when she answered, nothing new to tell her. He simply wanted to make contact, to feel that he was connected to her in some way, even if it was only by the sound of her voice traveling to him through the earpiece of his phone.

The rings stopped and her answering machine clicked on. Michael looked at the ceiling and listened.

Sorry I can't get to the phone right now. Please leave a message and I'll get back to you.

"It's Dad," he said. "I'd really like to talk to you; please let's not fall out. Ring me anytime, or drop into the shop if you're passing." He paused. "And thanks for the birthday card, it was thoughtful of you."

He hung up. He shouldn't have said drop into the shop, she might think he was trying to keep her away from the house. But he couldn't imagine a meeting between the two women, couldn't picture how that would go. He walked back to the kitchen, where Carmel was washing up and Barry was flicking through the pages of Mr. Bump.

"If you want to watch television, come into the sitting room when you've finished," he said.

It was Saturday night, and he didn't feel like sitting on his own in there.

———

"How's your meal?" Martin asked.

Irene took another forkful of the Thai green curry she didn't want. "It's very nice."

He'd been willing to meet another woman in a hotel when his wife was pregnant with his first child—which meant that in all likelihood he'd done it before, probably with other women who'd brought their damaged cars to him.

Martin refilled her wineglass and she watched the pale cream liquid flowing in. She brought it to her lips and drank, feeling the icy sharpness of it running down into her.

When Irene had been unfaithful in the past, she'd been well aware that some of the men she'd been with had had wives at home; of course they had. But Ger, or whatever his name was, had a pregnant wife, and Irene knew her. And she saw their little encounter in the garage for the horribly sleazy act that it had been.

She watched Martin pouring more water into Emily's glass. She saw her daughter eating noodles with her fingers, slurping them into her mouth, laughing with her father at the noise it made.

Fiona wasn't a pretty woman. She was nondescript, with a personality to match. Irene recalled the couple of conversations they'd had at the break times, Fiona all eager puppy, blurting out inanities. She must have been delighted when a good-looking man like him had shown an interest in her.

"Look at that for a mucky face," Irene heard Martin say, his voice full of tenderness. It had been his idea to go out for dinner. "We need to cheer up Emily," he'd said, and it seemed to be working. Anyone looking at them would take them for a normal happy family out on a Saturday night.

Irene ate some more of her curry, and drank more wine. As she set down her glass she felt a prickling sensation behind her eyes, an obstruction in her throat.

"Excuse me," she said, getting up and walking towards the bathroom, where she pressed a cold, wet tissue to her eyes until the impulse had passed.

No crying. Tears didn't solve anything.

"She told me."

"Told you what?"

"That she had sex with you." Hating the words, forcing them out because she had to see his reaction.

"What?" He looked shocked, but it was easy to look shocked if you'd just been found out.

"She didn't know you were my husband, she was just showing off." She kept watching his face. "She said you were...very enthusiastic." Her voice broke on the last word. She pressed her hand to her mouth.

He looked at her in disbelief. "Hang on—let me get this right. That woman told you she had sex with some man, and you assume it's me. She doesn't even know my name."

"You fixed her car. She said it was the man who fixed her car. Why would she make it up? She didn't know I knew you."

"Because she's a bloody liar, I don't know. Maybe she fancies me—I can't help that, can I?"

But Fiona heard Irene's voice in her head. Irene, who could have any man she wanted. Irene, who only had to bat her eyelashes for them to come running, wives forgotten.

"Look," he said, "nothing happened. Yes I repaired her car, and yes she offered me the free trial in the gym, but—"

"The gym?" Fiona frowned. "What's she got to do with—" She broke off, the awful realization dawning. "Oh God," she breathed, remembering Irene telling her about the husband who owned a gym, her own response that he must be loaded. "Oh *God*—"

The last hope that it wasn't him fell away. It was all true, the pieces sliding into place, the full ugly picture sitting there in front of her. She covered her face with her hands.

"Fiona," he said, "you're only upsetting yourself. I told you she offered me a trial when she collected her car, I told you all that." He reached for her shoulder but at his touch she twisted away from him, lowering her hands.

"You didn't tell me that. You said they were offering free workouts, you didn't mention Irene." Her hands clammy, her face cold. "You never said someone offered you a workout for fixing their car, that's news to me."

"What does it matter who offered it to me?" he said. "All I did was get a workout. That's not a crime, is it?"

She put it together again in her head. Maybe, after all, she'd added it up wrong. Irene had brought her car to him, he'd repaired it, and she'd suggested a workout. He'd gone to the gym, a week or so ago.

"But you've been back," she said.

"No," he said, "I haven't, I—" He stopped. "At least, I have been back, but she wasn't there."

She remembered the night he'd mentioned the gym for the first time. He'd nearly torn the nightdress off her, so turned on he'd been that night. Hard as a rock before she'd touched him.

And the evening he'd come home from the workout, how he'd gotten her into the bath with him. Insatiable again, mad for her the minute she'd stepped in. Had he been thinking of Irene then, was that the effect she'd had on him?

She felt too full, the pizza she'd eaten sitting uncomfortably in her stomach. "So," she said, hating where they were going, but unable to stop bringing him there, "where's your card?"

"What card?"

"You must have some kind of membership card for the gym, something to show when you go there."

"There's no card, just my name on file. I just sign in when I get there." He pushed a hand through his hair impatiently. "Jesus, what's with the third degree?"

Fiona said nothing.

"*Jesus*," he repeated angrily, "I love the way you believe me. Great that you have such trust in me. Thanks a lot."

But Fiona thought of Irene, who'd had no reason to lie, who wouldn't need to lie about men, looking like she did. And he didn't have a membership card, and he'd never been remotely interested in gyms before.

"Okay," she said.

"Okay? That's it?"

"That's it."

On Monday she'd walk home from school by the gym. She'd go in and ask about a membership that allowed you to pay for ten sessions. And if they said she couldn't do that, if they told her they didn't offer that kind of membership, she'd know for sure.

But she knew already, didn't she? She was sure already.

Sunday

It was a very different day from the previous Sunday. It wasn't, in fact, a day for the park at all, with a chilly breeze blowing pink into Eoin's cheeks, and the threat of rain present since morning.

"I'm cold," he said, burrowing into the new jacket that Jackie had bought him. He was suddenly growing so fast, everything too short or too tight.

"We won't stay long," she said. "Charlie would be disappointed if we didn't show up." Her insides were fluttering, her face warm despite the chill.

And there they were, James sitting on a bench behind the swings, Charlie hanging off the nearby roundabout. There were only four or five other children dotted around the playground, and a couple of huddled mothers in the far corner.

"You're squeezing my hand too tight," Eoin said crossly, and Jackie released him and walked towards the bench while he went to join Charlie.

"Hardly cone weather," James said as she approached. He wore an army green woolly hat with a fat black stripe, and a black hooded parka. He rubbed his hands together. "We must be mad."

Jackie laughed. "I think we must." She sat beside him and stuck her hands into her pockets. "The sacrifices we make for our children."

"They grow up that fast," he said, his eyes on Charlie and Eoin, who were swinging side by side now.

"Sure do." And right then she felt the first spatter on her cheek. "Damn, there's the rain."

"Come on," he said, getting up and signaling to the others. "Let's find someplace that sells the opposite of ice cream, whatever that is."

"Hot chocolate?" Pulling up Eoin's hood and tying it under his chin.

"Exactly."

The four of them hurried from the park as the rain began in earnest. It occurred to Jackie that to a casual observer they probably looked like the perfect family grouping: father, mother, son, daughter.

The thought was delightful.

Audrey wondered if she should do anything to mark the end of the life drawing course. Never having taught an evening class before, she wasn't sure of the protocol. Was she supposed to take them all out for a drink on the last night? She didn't think she'd fancy that much. She wasn't a big fan of pubs herself—and maybe they were all rushing home anyway, to babysitters or neglected spouses.

She could invite them here though. She could have a little thing in the house. Oh, not a party, nothing fancy like that. She couldn't imagine organizing a whole party. But she could serve finger food, couldn't you buy boxes of frozen nibbly party things that you just heated up in the oven? And she could get a few bottles of wine, and some juice in case there were some who didn't drink.

The more she thought about it, the more the idea appealed to her. Saturday night maybe, from six to seven. No, six was dinnertime for families, she'd make it from eight to nine.

Just a little get-together, she'd say, *at my house. Nothing fancy, just an hour before you go out.* That would make it clear she wasn't asking them to come for the whole night. It would be like a cocktail party, somewhere to go before you went off and had your normal Saturday night out. The warm-up act, she could be.

Yes, she'd invite them on Tuesday for the following Saturday night. She took a page from her notebook and began to jot down what she'd need, feeling quite excited, now that she'd decided, at the thought of being a hostess.

Monday

"A brief return to warm weather for tomorrow and Wednesday, with highs of twenty-two degrees in places, and the west of the country getting the best of the sunshine."

Weather forecasters always sounded relieved to Irene when they predicted fine weather, as if they were being held personally accountable when the rain came—which they probably were by some.

"That's good," Martin said, folding his newspaper and getting up, "a bit of sunshine for my little Miss Sunshine." Tickling Emily under the chin, making her squirm away from him, giggling.

Irene crossed to the percolator and refilled her coffee cup.

"You busy today?" Martin asked.

"Not terribly. I can collect her, if that's what you're asking."

"That would be good."

Since Pilar's departure Martin was dropping Emily at play-school every morning and collecting her again at lunchtime any day he could manage it. Since Pilar's departure Emily had grown increasingly quiet, particularly around her mother. Since Pilar's departure Emily spent more time at her grandparents' house.

Since Pilar's departure the distance between Emily's parents had grown. Now Martin only spoke to Irene when he had to.

After they'd left Irene cut a pineapple into slices and cut the slices into chunks. Her hand shook slightly as she transferred them from the chopping board into a bowl. For the second night in a row she'd woken before five and been unable to get back to sleep.

When she'd eaten half a dozen chunks she pushed the bowl away and went upstairs and brushed her teeth and made up her face. Then she phoned the employment agency again.

"It's Irene Dillon," she said. "I called you last week looking for an au pair. Haven't you got anyone yet?"

"I'm sorry." The voice on the other end held little regret. "Nothing at the moment, it's a busy time. As soon as anyone becomes available we'll let you know."

Irene hung up and put her phone into her bag as she walked out to the car. The bookstore this morning, she'd almost finished her thriller. The dry cleaners to collect her red suit. The off-license for gin and wine. The deli for prosciutto, and a jar of those feta-stuffed olives that Martin liked. The health store for rose water and bulgur wheat. Bananas, yogurt, mayonnaise in the supermarket on the way to the playschool to pick up Emily at half past twelve.

The whole endless afternoon trying to keep Emily amused until Martin got home, because Irene's mother had a golf game at two.

As she drove, Irene thought about the coincidence of Pilar sharing a flat with Zarek. She wondered what Pilar's reaction had been when Zarek told her he'd passed on her number to someone who was looking for an au pair. Had Pilar put two and two together and realized who Irene from his art class must be? If she hadn't, she must be wondering why she'd gotten no call.

But Pilar had probably guessed—she might be lazy, but she wasn't stupid. She must have hit the roof: the woman she'd walked out on a week earlier being offered Pilar's number by poor, ignorant Zarek.

Imagine ringing her old au pair, imagine the groveling Irene would have to do to get her to come back. Or maybe she wouldn't have to grovel at all, maybe Pilar would jump at the chance to return to her darling Emily.

Martin probably still had her number. Not that Irene had any intention of asking him for it.

She reached the end of her road and turned left for the town center.

———

Michael opened the back door of the shop and walked in, pressing the alarm code as Barry pulled off his jacket and let it drop to the floor.

"Jacket," Michael said, and Barry picked it up and set it on top of a box of cat litter. They walked through to the shop. Michael unlocked the front door and bent to pick up the post, which lay scattered on the floor.

He found the usual mix. Menus from fast-food restaurants, two bills, a bank statement, and an invitation to subscribe to *National Geographic* for just 35 euro for the entire year. He bundled them all together and brought them back to the counter. He handed the menus and the *National Geographic* mailing to Barry.

"Put those in the bin, would you?" he asked, and Barry dropped them into the wastepaper basket in the corner.

Michael laid the rest of the post on the shelf under the counter. He'd deal with it at lunchtime. He turned back to Barry.

"Want to feed the fish?"

Barry nodded, like he did every morning now. Michael opened the tub of flakes and allowed him to take out a pinch and scatter it into the tank.

"Want to feed the birds?"

Another nod.

When the various creatures had been tended to, Michael

walked to the end of the counter and back again. He crossed the shop floor and opened the front door and looked out. He closed it and came back and paced the length of the counter again, and then stood drumming his fingers on the countertop.

Eventually he turned to regard Barry, who'd taken his usual seat and was looking expectantly at Michael.

"Yes," Michael said. "A story, yes. Just give me a minute."

He turned away from the boy and reached inside his jacket and drew out the plain brown envelope that had been sitting on the hall floor this morning, waiting for him when he'd come downstairs. More than an hour ago now since he'd bent and picked it up.

He turned it over in his hands. He tapped it against his palm. His name and home address were typed; no other information on it apart from the postmark. A minute oval stain—grease?—just beneath the flap on the reverse. *Open it*, he commanded himself. *Just open the damn thing.*

He took his penknife from his pocket and pulled out the blade. He slipped it under the flap and drew it slowly along the edge. He folded back the blade and returned the knife to his trouser pocket. He pressed apart the sides of the envelope and pulled out the sheet inside and unfolded it with hands that were suddenly unsteady.

Positive.

The word, sitting in the middle of a sentence, jumped out at him. He leaned heavily against the counter and worked his way back to the start of the paragraph, forcing himself to read slowly.

Following a DNA test having been carried out on the samples we received on Friday October 12, a positive result has been recorded in terms of the male bloodline. A definite DNA link has been established between Michael Browne and Barry Ryan, and paternity of Barry Ryan has been confirmed within this bloodline.

A definite DNA link has been established.

He was a grandfather.

His son had fathered a child.

Michael rubbed a hand across his face. He needed to sit down.

The door opened and a woman he knew slightly walked in and smiled hello. Michael dropped the letter under the counter and braced trembling hands on the counter, and made a sterling effort to smile back.

"Are you all right?" she asked, approaching the counter. "You're looking a bit pale."

"I'm fine," Michael said. "Never better."

"Glad to hear it." She took two tins of cat food from the shelf and brought them to the counter. Barry caught her eye.

"Oh hello," she said, smiling. "Who's this now?"

"That's my grandson," Michael said. "His name is Barry."

"What are you doing?"

Audrey swung around, almost toppling off her stepladder. Kevin, appearing out of nowhere as usual.

"I'm taking down my hanging basket for the winter," she explained. "I'm going to empty it and put it into the shed until next year."

"We're going to the lake tomorrow," he said, "if it's hot."

Audrey scanned the early-evening sky, which was striped with pink. "I think you might be in luck. See those red bits in the sky? That means it'll probably be nice tomorrow."

"We have pink lemonade and chicken wings and apples, but not the green ones, the red ones."

"Mmm, sounds yummy. I love chicken wings."

"I'm going swimming," he said, his eyes on Dolly, who was attempting to scrabble her way through the hedge, "if the water isn't too cold."

"That's nice, a swim would be lovely. *Dolly*," Audrey added sharply, "stop that."

"I got new togs," Kevin said. "They're blue."

Audrey smiled. "They sound very smart. I was saying to your mum I must take Dolly to the lake sometime."

He regarded the animal doubtfully. "Can he swim?"

"Oh, I'm sure she can—I think all dogs love the water. And even if she didn't want to go in, we could still walk around it, couldn't we?"

"You could come with us, but the dog would go in your car. And he couldn't eat the chicken wings."

Audrey smiled. "Thanks, Kevin, but I have to go to work tomorrow. We might take a trip out there over the weekend—and maybe you and your mum would like to come too."

"Yeah. I have to go now."

He turned abruptly and made for the back door. The curious gait he had, arms held rigidly at his sides as he walked. Audrey wondered, not for the first time, what would become of him if anything happened to Pauline. Who would take him in, who would want the responsibility of a fully grown man who was still a child? It must worry Pauline desperately.

She unhooked the hanging basket from its bracket and carried it carefully down the steps. She upended it onto the compost heap and broke up the earth with her rake. The weather was really gone crazy if tomorrow was going to be warm enough to go swimming. Nearly the end of October, almost winter really.

She put the empty basket on a shelf in the newly stained shed, next to half-full paint cans and old flower pots. She replaced the ladder, propping it against a wall in the shed, next to a growing bundle of newspapers she really must recycle soon.

And afterwards, try as she might, she couldn't remember the last thing she'd said to Kevin.

Michael waited until they'd finished the fish pie, until she'd begun to stack the empty plates.

"Will you stop that for a minute?" he asked. "There's something I need to talk to you about."

She looked at him, the plates still in her arms. "What is it?"

"Just sit down for a minute."

She perched on the edge of her chair. "Are you cross about
somethin'?"

Michael shook his head. "It's not—"

"Did Barry do somethin' in the shop?"

"Stop interrupting me," he said irritably. "It's nothing like
that." He reached into his inside pocket and brought out the
brown envelope. "The result came today. It's positive."

"*Oh*—"

She made a sound between a gasp and a moan, her face crumpling. She laid the plates down and sank her head into her hands
and began to weep quietly, and Michael realized he'd been too
abrupt. He should have led up to it, not blurted it out like that,
but all he knew was how to be direct.

He glanced at Barry, who was regarding his mother anxiously,
his own lower lip trembling.

"It's okay," Michael said quickly, "she's fine, she just got a surprise, that's all." He put out a hand and patted Barry's shoulder
awkwardly. "She'll be fine, don't worry."

"I *told* you it was Ethan," she said brokenly, her voice muffled
behind her hands. "You wouldn't *listen*."

"It's all right," Michael said, not sure now which of them he
was addressing. "It's all right."

Carmel got up abruptly and crossed the floor and pulled a
sheet off the roll of kitchen paper. She buried her face in it and
blew her nose noisily.

"Mammy?" Barry said tremulously, and she went back to him and scooped him up. She sat and rocked him as she pressed the wadded paper to her eyes.

"Sorry," Michael said quietly. "I shouldn't have sprung it on you like that." He felt awkward. His hands didn't know what to do with themselves. "I suppose whatever way I'd told you, it would have been a—"

He stopped. Not a shock, because she'd known already. A reminder then, maybe, the past coming back to slap her in the face. Ethan's ghost, here in the kitchen with them.

Ethan's son. Michael looked at Barry, and the little boy looked back from the safety of his mother's arms. They were Ethan's eyes, of course—how had he not seen that before? Or had he seen, and chosen to ignore? Ethan's son, sitting across the table from him. His grandson.

Valerie's nephew.

"I must make a phone call," he told Carmel. It would give her a chance to pull herself together if he left for a few minutes. In the hall he dialed Valerie's mobile, but after half a dozen rings her voice mail clicked on. Michael hung up. This wasn't something you could tell a machine.

Tomorrow he'd try again. She'd have to be told, even if she didn't want to know. Even if she cut him off for good. He'd have to tell her she was an aunt.

He walked into the sitting room and put a match to the fire he'd set earlier. They'd have a bit to talk about this evening.

———

Happy Monday, he typed. He was about to press *send*—and then he stopped.

What was he doing, flirting with a girl years younger than him? Where did he imagine it was going to go? There was nowhere it could possibly go, not while he was still in the no-man's-land he'd been catapulted into two years ago.

They were parents of children who were friends. That was all they could be, he needed to remember that. When they met, it was for the children.

He deleted the message and laid his phone back on the arm of the couch, and reached for the TV remote control.

Tuesday

A tap on the door. "Eight o'clock," he called, like he did every weekday.

Her eyes still closed, Carmel smiled. "Okay," she called back, and listened to his footsteps going back down the stairs.

It wasn't all sorted, far from it. He hadn't said they could stay with him for good, he hadn't said anything like that. What he'd said was *for the moment*, which could mean anything. She couldn't relax, not completely.

And there was still the question of her getting a job. There was still no sign of anyone wanting to take her on. She would just have to keep on trying, every day until she found something.

But Barry had a granddad, it was official. And his granddad seemed to be okay with Barry being his grandson—not that he'd said anything, but she thought he was okay with it. And tomorrow Barry was going to start playschool, which would be good for him, even if thinking about it made her feel horribly lonely.

And his granddad knew now that Carmel had been telling the truth—which had somewhere along the way become the most important bit of all this.

She leaned over and kissed the top of Barry's head. "Good mornin', sleepyhead," she said. "Time to get up."

"The thing is," Irene said, lowering her cup, "Martin and I have been having some…difficulties."

"Difficulties?" Her mother's perfectly shaped eyebrows rose. "What kind of difficulties?"

Irene dabbed at her lips, leaving an imprint of cherry-red lipstick on her heavy linen napkin. "It's hard to explain," she said, wondering what had triggered her sudden impulse to confide—in her mother of all people. "We seem to have…drifted apart a bit lately."

Her mother picked up the coffeepot and refilled Irene's cup. "Darling, that's perfectly normal in any marriage. Your father and I regularly drift apart. I shouldn't worry about it."

"You're right," Irene replied, adding a few drops of cream to her cup. "It's nothing, I'm sure."

"Put on your best outfit and get him to take you out to dinner," her mother said. "Flatter him a bit, men love that."

"I will," Irene promised. "I'll do that."

The bleakness pooling inside her as she sipped coffee and nibbled almond biscuits so thin you could see right through them.

The day at the lake must be going well, past six o'clock and no sign of Pauline's car. Maybe they'd stopped for tea somewhere on the way home, decided to make a real day out of it, even though the sun had slid behind a cloud at around three and hadn't been seen since. Hopefully Kevin had gotten his swim in early, before the chicken wings.

She hurried indoors, hauling her shopping bags with her. Barely enough time to put something together for dinner before she'd need to get ready for the art class. She opened the front door, thinking about beans on a toasted bagel, with a couple of rashers and a soft poached egg.

That would do nicely.

As Zarek tucked his sketch pad into his bag the apartment door opened and Pilar walked in.

"You have luck?" he asked hopefully. Her third interview since the previous Monday.

She made a face as she unraveled her scarf. "Five childrens—*five*! How I look after five childrens and clean house too? How? She think I am machine?"

"Five is big family," Zarek agreed, zipping his bag closed, "but maybe childrens all good, maybe they help with jobs."

Pilar flapped an arm out of her jacket sleeve, almost whacking him in the face. "*Pah*—no childrens help with jobs, childrens make *more* jobs."

Zarek edged towards the door, hoping to make his escape before the subject of the café could be raised. "Well, I must—"

"Your boss say about me today?" Pilar demanded. "She give me job?"

"Not yet," Zarek answered, his hand on the doorknob. "She very busy. Maybe tomorrow." He opened the door and fled, Pilar's indignant voice following him all the way down the stairs.

A quick glance around the room confirmed what Irene had assumed—there was no sign of Fiona. Of course she hadn't come, she wasn't the type for confrontations.

Not that Irene had been planning any kind of confrontation. In the unlikely event that Fiona had shown up at the life drawing class, Irene had planned to say nothing, to pretend their meeting on Saturday night hadn't happened. She doubted very much that Fiona would approach her, let alone mention the encounter.

But now there was no need to pretend anything. She nodded

at the others and took her usual place and began to lay out her materials as Audrey plugged in the fan heater and their model entered the room in her blue dressing gown.

"Anyone seen Fiona?" Meg asked, and Irene shook her head along with the other four.

———————

"By the way," Audrey said just before the break, as they laid down pencils and pulled sheets off their boards, "I wanted to invite you all to my house for a little drinks party, as we're finishing up next week. Just a glass of wine and some nibbles, nothing fancy. I was thinking Saturday night, say from eight to nine, so you'll still have plenty of time to go out afterwards."

"That'd be lovely," Meg said. "Count me in."

Zarek looked uncertain. "Maybe I work Saturday, I am not sure."

"I don't think I'll manage it either," James said. "It's not that easy for me to get out in the evenings."

Audrey's smile slipped. "Oh, that's a shame. Do try, both of you." She looked at her one remaining student, uncharacteristically silent. Was she imagining it, or was Irene a little subdued this evening? "Irene? Can you make it?"

"Should do," Irene said lightly. "Sweet of you to invite us."

"I just wanted to do something small." Audrey turned to her model, who was slipping on her shoes. "Are you free, Jackie?"

The girl looked pleasantly surprised—did she imagine Audrey would have issued an invitation in her company that didn't include her?

"Thanks," she said, "I'd love to."

"Great, that's settled then, Saturday it is. I'll give Fiona a ring, hopefully she'll be able to come too. Remind me to give you my address before you go home."

The class trooped out for coffee and Audrey wrote *Ring Fiona* in her notebook before following them. Her first party, or whatever you wanted to call it, was officially on—even if the attendance might be less than she'd expected, only three definite guests out of a possible six. Still, she'd make the best of it, and maybe they'd all get there in the end, or most of them.

She walked slowly down the corridor towards the muted buzz of conversation in the lobby and joined the queue at the coffee station. Drinks, nibbles, music. A fire if the evening was chilly—no, a fire either way; it made the room look much better. Dolly would have to be banished to Audrey's bedroom in case anyone was allergic. Maybe softer lighting for the sitting room, get a few low-watt bulbs, add a bit of atmosphere.

She filled her cup with coffee. When you thought about it, it should hardly take any effort at all.

———————————

The fabric of her sweatshirt was textured, like waffles, and colored the same shade of blue as tiles on swimming pools. Her eyes weren't blue, they were grey, and fringed with dark lashes. Her eyebrows were thick and dark.

"Hello," he said. "Fancy meeting you here."

She smiled. "Only on Tuesdays."

He sat next to her on the low wall. "I tell Charlie a bedtime story at break time," he said. "That's why I go to the car, she made me promise." Feeling the need to explain, not wanting her to think he was avoiding everyone.

"That's nice. Make sure she doesn't tell Eoin though—I'd hate the pressure."

He laughed.

And then she said, all in a rush, "By the way, if you wanted to go to Audrey's thing on Saturday night you could bring Charlie over to my house and my parents would babysit. She could sleep over, I mean. Just a thought, just if you fancied it."

James glanced at her, but she was poking at something on the ground with her shoe. "Well," he said, "that's…nice of you." And then he stopped.

"We have a camp bed," she said, still intent on whatever had taken her attention on the ground. "We could drop her back in the morning. Just, if that was all that was stopping you, I mean. Feel free to say no."

Wasn't it the last thing he wanted, to get involved with other people? To put himself into a position where someone might start asking questions, looking for the reasons that had brought himself and Charlie here, forcing him to revisit the past, when he'd vowed to leave it behind them?

Hadn't he been dreading something like this ever since he'd moved to Carrickbawn?

Evidently not.

"Thanks," he said. "I'm sure Charlie would love that."

———————

As she listened to Fiona's phone ringing Audrey wondered belatedly if she should have waited till the morning. Just gone half past nine, not very late—but Fiona could be sick, probably *was* sick, since she'd hadn't turned up to the class. She was about to hang up when the phone was answered.

"Hello?"

Low, barely audible. Audrey pressed the phone to her ear. "Fiona? It's Audrey, from the life drawing class."

"Oh…hi."

"I was hoping you weren't sick, when you missed the class. I hope you weren't in bed just now."

"No, I mean, yes, I have…some bug, but I wasn't in bed."

She certainly sounded below par. "Oh dear," Audrey said, "I'm sorry to hear that, with the baby coming and everything—but hopefully you'll be better by Saturday, because I'm having a little get-together at my house—you know, just because we're getting to the end of the classes. Next week is the last one, if you can believe it."

"Oh…right."

"About eight o'clock, just for an hour or thereabouts. I'd love if you can make it."

"Yes…thanks. I'll see how I feel, thank you."

"Great—well, I won't keep you. Take care, get well soon." As she hung up Audrey realized that she hadn't passed on her address. No matter, she'd phone Fiona again on Saturday morning, see if she was feeling up to it.

She hoisted her bag onto her shoulder and left the empty classroom.

Wednesday

The playschool was warm, with miniature tables and chairs scattered about, and children who chattered and played with toy cars or scribbled with crayons on pages or pulled on dress-up clothes from a big plastic box in the corner. A few of them stared at Barry but most ignored him.

The teacher, who was very tall and who wore purple glasses and had a nice smile, crouched in front of him.

"Hi there," she said. "My name is Meg, and I'm delighted to meet you."

He pushed himself closer into Carmel's side, his thumb stuck in his mouth. "Sorry," Carmel said, "he's a bit shy."

"That's fine, that's no problem," the teacher said, straightening up. "Can you stay awhile with him? Are you rushing away?"

Carmel shook her head. "I can stay as long as you like," she said. "I don't have no job." Maybe she shouldn't have said that, maybe it sounded bad to say that.

"Perfect," the teacher said, pointing to one of the tables where two of the other children were sitting. "We'll put Barry over here, with Ciaran and Emily. Ciaran never stops talking," she added under her breath to Carmel as they walked across. "He'll be perfect for Barry."

She pulled out a small chair and Barry was persuaded to sit, as long as Carmel crouched beside him. The little girl with the blonde curly hair looked familiar.

"This is Barry," the teacher said to her and the little boy. "He's just arrived and he doesn't know anyone yet, so I'm hoping you'll be really nice to him, okay? And this is Barry's mammy, who's staying for a little while."

"I saw him in the park," the little girl said, looking at Barry, "when I hurted my knee from the ladder."

"You met Barry?"

"Yeah, an' his mammy too."

The teacher looked inquiringly at Carmel, who nodded, remembering the mother in her white jeans who'd given Carmel a fiver to go away.

"Maybe you and Barry would do a jigsaw together," the teacher was saying, and Carmel watched as the little girl began to assemble the jigsaw, picking up pieces and slotting them into place. Barry watched her too, but clung tightly to Carmel's arm and made no attempt to join in.

"I'll leave you to it," the teacher whispered, disappearing to another group. Carmel reached for a book that lay on the table. She opened it and saw a picture of an apple with a word underneath.

"Apple," she murmured, looking at the shape the word made.

Michael pressed the bell beside V BROWNE and waited. After a few seconds the intercom crackled.

"Yes?" A man's voice, which threw him for a couple of seconds.

"I'm looking for Valerie," he said. "I'm her father."

"Please come up," the man said, after the tiniest of pauses.

The door buzzed and Michael pushed it open and ascended the stairs to the second floor. Valerie was waiting for him in the doorway, wearing her nurse's uniform.

"I haven't much time," she said. "I'm due at work."

No hello, no how are you.

"This won't take long," he said, following her into the apartment's cramped hallway. She led him through to the sitting room, where a man was standing by the window. As soon as they walked in the man crossed the room, holding out his hand.

"Tom McFadden," he said, gripping Michael's fingers tightly. "Good to finally meet you."

Good to finally meet you? Michael had no idea who the man was, or what he was doing in Valerie's apartment, appearing very much at home. Older than Valerie, a good dozen years older, maybe more. Receding slightly above his temples, well-cut suit, shiny shoes. He smelled of some aromatic wood.

"Can I make you tea or coffee?" he asked.

"There isn't time," Valerie put in, before Michael had a chance to respond. She made no attempt to explain who Tom McFadden was. "What was it you wanted?" she asked Michael.

Not even inviting him to sit, for God's sake. Michael decided to ignore the other man's presence. "It's about the boy in the shop," he told her. "The paternity test results have come back, and it turns out that he is Ethan's child. Your nephew," he added.

Her blank expression didn't change. The man stood off to the side, his hands thrust into his trouser pockets. Michael hoped he felt uncomfortable.

Valerie gave a tiny nod. "Okay."

Okay? Was that it, was that all she had to say about the fact that her brother had fathered a child before he died? Michael stood his ground, watching her face, willing her to add something, to ask him something.

She turned abruptly. "I won't keep you," she said. "Thank you for letting me know."

"That's it?" The words were out before he could stop them. "That's all you have to say?"

She opened the door. "That's it."

"You don't want to meet them?"

But she'd vanished into the hall. Michael followed her.

"Valerie," he said, lowering his voice, "I'm trying to make amends here. Don't you see that? I'm trying to do good by Ethan."

She held the front door open. "You're a bit late," she said, looking past him.

Michael shook his head. "You don't mean that," he said. "You're not cruel like that."

No response, her gaze steadfastly refusing to meet his.

"You know where I am," he said, "if you change your mind."

He walked out and turned towards the stairs, and the door clicked shut before he'd taken half a dozen steps.

There was an unfamiliar yellow car parked outside Pauline's when Audrey got home from work. It had a Cork registration number. Audrey wondered if it belonged to Pauline's sister. She knew the sister's daughter had split from her husband not so long ago: Hopefully there wasn't another family crisis. And where was Pauline's red Escort?

She walked up her driveway and let herself in, and hung her blue jacket on the banister post, on top of the two others. She really must invest in some kind of a hall stand.

She opened the kitchen door and as usual, Dolly leapt at her ecstatically. Did she think, every morning when Audrey went to work, that she was being abandoned forever? The joyous reunion every afternoon seemed to suggest it.

Audrey bundled the newspaper sheets from the kitchen floor and stuffed them in the bin, and let Dolly out to the garden. The weather had definitely turned chillier, but as yet there was no sign of rain. She inspected the lawn and decided that a final cut would be needed at the weekend.

Back in the kitchen she switched on the local radio station and heard *"...late last night. The man's name has not yet been released."*

That didn't sound good. She'd have to wait for the next news to hear the full story. She filled the kettle and plugged it in. She took coffee from the press and milk from the fridge. She lifted down the biscuit jar that sat on an open shelf and chose a Kit Kat from the selection inside.

When the kettle boiled she made coffee. She was taking the Kit Kat out of its wrapper when her doorbell rang. She went out to the hall and opened the door, and smiled inquiringly at the woman with the very pale face and pink-rimmed eyes who stood on the step. She looked like a diluted version of Pauline.

"You must be Sue."

"Audrey," the other said quietly—and Audrey's smile faded at the hollow sound of her voice.

––––––––––

Pilar was not happy. Nine days of unemployment had taken their toll. "When?" she demanded. "When I get job?"

"Soon," Zarek assured her. "Few more days, you find job."

"I have forty-seven euros," Pilar announced, pulling an onion from its net bag. "When it is gone, I have nothing. I hate this bugger country."

Zarek considered suggesting a move back to Lithuania, and decided against it. "You find job soon," he repeated. "I am sure."

"How you sure?" she asked, pulling a knife from the block. "How you know? You have big ball that say what happen in future?"

"Er—"

"Why your boss not phone? Why she not want me?" Pilar sliced off the ends of the onion and yanked away the skin. She'd taken to frying onions at odd hours of the day. The apartment smelled constantly of them. "You tell her about me? You say I am honest, and work hard?"

"Yes, I tell, but many other peoples also looking for work," Zarek told her. "Very little job in Ireland now." Keeping his eyes on the knife, just in case.

"You say I your flat mate, you tell this?"

"Yes, yes, I tell everything."

She sliced the onion furiously, sending slivers flying. "*Pah!*" She flung the onion slices onto the pan and they began to sizzle loudly. "I am fed up bored from the waiting, I am *sick* from the waiting."

"One more day, maybe," Zarek said. "I go for walk now. You like something from shop—some chocolate?"

Pilar shook the pan, making the onions jump. "No chocolate," she cried, "I want *job*, not chocolate."

"Okay, I go, I see you later." He made his escape and approached the front door just as Anton walked in, sniffing the air.

"Pilar is frying ze onion?" he asked.

Zarek nodded. "I go for walk."

Anton dropped his bag of groceries. "I come too," he said.

"Well? Did you like your new school?"

Barry nodded. Michael looked at Carmel.

"He got on okay," she said, taking off her jacket before bending to remove Barry's. "But I had to stay all the time."

"Did he mix with the others?"

"A bit. An' he made a snake out of plasticine, didn't you?"

"Yeah."

"An' he drew a picture, didn't you?"

"Yeah."

"Will we show—" a pause "—your granddad?"

Granddad. The first time the word had been said aloud. Michael thought it best not to react.

She took a folded page from her plastic bag and held it out to him. Michael unfolded it and saw a very wobbly blue circle with a few wavy lines radiating from it.

"It's the sun," Carmel said.

"It's very good," Michael said. He looked at Barry. "Will we put it on the fridge?"

Barry nodded.

Granddad.

Michael turned to Carmel. "I have something for you." He took a ring with two keys on it from his pocket and held it out.

She looked at the keys but made no attempt to take them.

"Go on," Michael said. "Just make sure you don't lose them."

She looked up at him. "I never had no key to no place, never."

"Well, you have them now," he told her. "It's just to make things easier, that's all. Take them, it's no big deal."

She took the keys from him. She held them in her palm and studied them.

"It is a big deal for me," she said, still looking down at them. "It's a huge deal."

———

"No, it's better this way," Pauline said, her fingers pleating and releasing the hem of her skirt, over and over as she'd been doing since Audrey's arrival half an hour earlier. "It's the best way, it is really."

Not a tear, not a tremble to her lip, her face a greyish white. Her hands working ceaselessly on the blue cotton hem, her voice hardly there, barely above a whisper. And a terrible calmness, an awful acceptance of the fact that she'd just lost her only child.

"What would he have done, when I was gone?" she asked

them. "He'd never have managed, never." Pleating, releasing, frowning at the hem as if that was the only thing she had to concern herself with.

"I left him alone, you see," she told Audrey, "while I went to the toilet. And when I got back to the rug there was no sign of him. He'd left everything very tidy, all the leftovers back in the box. And his clothes in a lovely neat bundle. He was always such a tidy boy, right from the start, never a mess."

Listening to the broken words, Audrey felt so helpless. What could you say, what on earth could possibly be of any use to Pauline now? Better to listen maybe, just to let her go on talking about him, and listen.

"But it's for the best, it really is," Pauline said, ignoring the cooling tea on the table in front of her. "He'd have had to go into a home, you see, after I was gone. He'd have hated that, it would have killed him."

"I'd have looked after him," her sister Sue put in, weeping, a sodden piece of kitchen roll clutched in her hand. "You know I'd have done that, Pauline."

But Pauline shook her head in a way that suggested she wasn't even considering it, that she'd never considered it. "Ah no," she said softly. "No, you couldn't have done that, not at all. You've enough on your plate, dear."

Kevin's body hadn't been found for eight hours. Pauline had refused to leave the lakeside, refused anything to eat or drink, had stood with a blanket around her shoulders until two police divers had brought him back to her.

A doctor had been summoned by the policewomen who had brought Pauline home. He'd given her some Valium, which Pauline had refused to take, and a prescription for more. Kevin's body had been transported to the hospital mortuary, where a postmortem was being carried out.

All this had been conveyed tearfully by Sue on the way back

to Pauline's house. "We got a phone call at one in the morning," she'd told Audrey, blotting her eyes with the end of her sleeve. "We couldn't believe it. It was a nightmare."

"He's better off now," Pauline repeated, smoothing her skirt over her knees before starting to pleat it all over again. "He's happy now, nothing can happen to him."

Audrey had cried too, the tears coming in waves with each fresh memory of him. Standing on his side of the hedge, telling her in great detail about a program he'd seen on television, or a pizza he'd eaten the night before. Reaching out warily to pat Dolly, snatching his hand back when the little dog had lunged at it.

Handing Audrey a blue plastic mug that spelled out her name on its side. Walking to the shop with his mother each day for milk and bread and the paper, and a packet of Jelly Tots.

The idea that he was gone forever, that Audrey would never see him or talk to him again, was too sad to take in. But for Pauline's sake she had to pull herself together. She pulled a fresh sheet from the kitchen roll on the table and blotted her eyes and blew her nose.

"Dear," she said, putting a hand on her neighbor's shoulder, "would you take a small brandy maybe?" She had no idea if there was brandy in Pauline's house, but she'd had a bottle in her own house for years. She couldn't recall the circumstances that had led to its purchase—or maybe she'd gotten it as a present—but it lay on its side in the drawer under the DVD player, barely touched.

"Ah no," Pauline replied, pleating and pleating. "I couldn't look at it, dear."

Outside the window the rotary clothesline whirled lazily in the gathering breeze. Audrey recognized three or four of Kevin's T-shirts among the towels and socks and underwear. The colors blurred together as she looked out. Her eyes felt swollen and stinging, her face tight with dried salt.

She pushed back her chair and stood. "I'll get the clothes in from the line," she said, not waiting for an answer before opening the back door.

The sharp air felt wonderful on her hot face. As she unpegged the bone-dry clothes—out since yesterday morning, they must have been—and bundled them into one of the towels, she felt a spattering of drops.

She hurried back inside, where Pauline sat in exactly the same position. Sue was pouring water into the teapot, making more tea that nobody wanted. Audrey stood by the worktop and folded everything into a wobbly pile, shielding the clothes from Pauline with her body. What might the sight of Kevin's T-shirts do to his mother now?

The rain fell steadily and the kitchen darkened slowly as the three of them sat on. Biscuits were produced and left untouched. Tea cooled once again in cups. Now and again Sue and Audrey would conduct a short back-and-forth of murmured conversation—the weather, Sue's family, the life drawing classes—but mostly they sat in silence, the only sound the steady patter of drops on the window and the sudden rattle, every several minutes, of the fridge.

Pauline went on pleating, and said once, apropos of nothing, "His birthday is coming up, I was knitting him a jumper." And neither of them knew how to respond to this heartbreaking item of information, so it drifted away into the silence.

At eight o'clock the doctor phoned, and Sue held a short conversation with him in the hall, the kitchen door closed so the words were inaudible to Audrey. At half past eight the doorbell rang. Sue went to answer it and returned with her husband and daughter, just up from Cork. In the ensuing flurry of tearful embraces Audrey whispered to Sue that she'd be back after school the following day, and slipped out quietly.

In her own kitchen she poured away her cold coffee and returned her chocolate biscuit jar to its home on the shelf. She toasted bread and opened a can of beans, and then found she couldn't manage more than a mouthful. She went into the sitting room and took the brandy from its drawer and raised the bottle to her lips and took a large gulp, and spluttered and coughed for several minutes afterwards.

Later in bed, Kevin's face was there when she closed her eyes and tried to sleep. He stood at the other side of the hedge and regarded her as calmly and unblinkingly as he always had.

She thought of Pauline's life, changed utterly in the space of a few hours. She couldn't imagine the nightmare of losing a child. How did anyone survive it, how could each new day be endured without that part of yourself? How would Pauline find the strength to go on, now that her beautiful, damaged son was gone?

At two o'clock Audrey gave up trying to sleep and went back downstairs with Dolly trotting at her heels. She heated milk and added a dessert spoon of brandy and a pinch of nutmeg, and drank it curled on the sitting room couch, wrapped in a red-and-green-tartan mohair blanket she'd brought home from a short break in Scotland a few years before. She began watching a black-and-white Hitchcock film and fell asleep before the first ad break.

She woke at eight, stiff and chilled and headachy, and when she turned off the television all she heard was the continuing rain.

Thursday

"Well? Which is it?" She held her hair on the top of her head and twirled in front of the dressing room mirror in one of the two dresses she'd selected from the bargain rail. "Hair up or down?" Letting it tumble over her shoulders, then gathering it back together again. "Up, I think."

Her friend leaned against the wall, arms folded. "I thought you said he wasn't interested."

Jackie smiled at her reflection in the mirror. "He's not. What about the hair?"

"Down. So what are you so perky about?"

"Audrey's party, of course. I love a party. And the dress?"

"The other one."

Jackie pulled the pink dress up over her head and stood in her underwear. A side effect of being a life drawing model, she'd discovered, was that parading around in bra and knickers didn't cost her a thought now.

She slid the dress back onto its hanger. "He might be interested," she said.

"I knew it."

"But I could be wrong." She pulled on the other dress for the second time and turned so her friend could slide up the zip. "Sometimes I think he is and other times...I don't know."

"Have you found out about his wife yet?"

Jackie adjusted the sleeves. "He might not be married."

"Well, his daughter's mother so. You know what I mean."

"I figure she's off the scene."

"You figure? You still haven't asked?"

"Well, it's not something you can ask, just like that." She regarded her reflection. "So you think this dress?"

"Definitely—and of *course* it's something you can ask. You *have* to ask."

"I will, as soon as I get a chance."

But she wouldn't. James would tell her when he was ready, and something warned her not to push it. Charlie's mother wasn't around, and that was enough. All that mattered right now was that they were going to Audrey's party together on Saturday night.

She couldn't wait. He was dropping Charlie to her house just before eight and they were driving to Audrey's, which was on the other side of the park. She'd have him all to herself for at least ten minutes. Fifteen, if there was traffic.

She'd be wearing a new dress that looked pretty damn good on her, and she was down one and a half pounds this week. She'd been doing twenty sit-ups every day for a fortnight—well, most days, and mostly twenty—and she was feeling fine. And she might even sign up for Pilates after Halloween—which would be quite funny, even if she was the only one who got the joke.

She could tell James. He'd get the joke. They'd laugh together about it.

"Right, get me out of this," she said and her friend slid the zip down. Jackie pulled the dress over her head, wondering if she should get new underwear too. Oh, not because anything was going to happen—how could it, with her parents at home, not to mention their children?—but just because she felt like wearing something lacy and frivolous next to her skin.

And because, after all, maybe he wouldn't bring her straight home from the party. Maybe they'd drop by his empty house for a while.

———————

Scanning the death notices—one sure way to tell you were moving on was when you took to reading the death notices—Michael almost missed the announcement. *O'Dea*, it read, *Kevin*, and Michael's eye flew on to O'Reilly and Staunton and Tobin and—

O'Dea? Kevin? He traveled back up the page.

Suddenly, he read. *Beloved son of Pauline and Hector*—

Hector. In the ten years she'd worked in his house he'd never heard Pauline's ex-husband's name mentioned.

Removal on Friday at 7 PM from St. Martha's Hospital mortuary to the Church of the Redeemer, burial Saturday at St John's Cemetery after 11 AM Mass.

Kevin, suddenly dead. Pauline's son taken abruptly from her, like his own son had been snatched from him. He remembered—could still feel—the horror of Ethan's death, the grief that had numbed him first and floored him after. And now that grief had been visited on Pauline, who'd already, surely, had her quota of heartache. Like himself.

He was alone in the shop, with Barry gone to playschool. The two of them were going to go on living with Michael for the foreseeable future. As soon as the test results had come, all his uncertainties had disappeared. Of course they were staying with him, there was no question. They were family.

"I could show you how to cook," Michael had said. "If you wanted."

"Yeah," she'd said. "I'd like that."

"And if you wanted to learn to read, we could look into that too." Once she got the hang of reading, she might have a hope of a job. "There are classes, I could find out about them."

"Okay," she'd said, her color rising.

"And that boy could use a proper haircut. I could bring him along with me next time I'm going."

"Okay."

She was his daughter-in-law, as good as, and he would treat her as such. She had provided him with a grandson, she was his last link to Ethan. Funny the way things worked out.

He looked down at the paper again and read *O'Dea, Kevin*. He should call Valerie, make sure she knew. He lifted the phone—and put it down again. He'd drive by her apartment this evening after dinner, he'd drop a note in her letterbox, and then he'd text her to let her know it was there. He couldn't face talking to her again, not just yet.

He turned the pages to the crossword and unscrewed his pen.

"Are you all right?"

The third time someone had asked her this morning. Audrey gave him the same answer as she'd given the last two—"*I'm fine, just a little tired*"—because she daren't mention the reason she looked the way she did today, in case she made a fool of herself by bursting into tears.

She could feel their eyes on her all the same, as she sat in the staff room trying to read the newspaper during her only free period on Thursday. She could sense them wondering where the normally bubbly, happy Audrey Matthews had gone. Well, she wasn't about to enlighten them, she just couldn't.

Her eyes felt sore; it hurt to blink. The feeling was unfamiliar, Audrey being blessed with an ability to sleep soundly each night, usually within ten minutes of getting into bed. The last broken night she'd had was when Dolly had first arrived, well over a month ago.

"Audrey, there's carrot cake. Bernie sent it in," someone called from across the room. Bernie, husband of their principal, regularly sent in something delicious and home-baked—presumably to keep the troops happy.

Audrey shook her head. "Thanks, I might have some later." There, more cause for them to wonder if something was up. Unheard-of for her to say no to cake, but what could she do? The thought of food, any food, held no appeal for her today. She'd filled a cereal bowl with Crunchy Nut Corn Flakes as usual this morning—and by the time she'd taken the milk from the fridge she knew she couldn't look at them, and she'd tipped them back into their box.

She turned the pages of the newspaper, willing the time to pass. Not just the rest of today, but the rest of the week. The next few days would be horrible, the removal and the funeral. And what about afterwards, how would Pauline cope with all the time that came after that?

The bell rang, startling her. She folded the newspaper and stood, gathering her things for the next class. At the door she met a teacher she hadn't yet seen that day.

"Audrey, are you all right? You don't look so good."

"I'm fine," Audrey told her, "just a bit tired."

The Sixth Week

October 26–31

———

*A lapse of memory, a departure,
a reconciliation, and an
unexpected resolution.*

Friday

Zarek turned over and checked his bedside clock. Half past seven, and he didn't start work till eleven. He stretched each of his limbs in turn, working clockwise from his left leg. He drew circles with his ankles, three in one direction, three in the other. He cracked the knuckles on both hands. He lay on his back and studied the ceiling, and decided that he had to stop living a lie.

He was twenty-five years old, not some adolescent who couldn't see his way and didn't know what he wanted. Zarek knew what he wanted. He'd known for a long time. He'd known for years, but he'd been afraid to admit it, even to himself.

And then he'd come to Ireland, and his life had changed, everything had changed. And now he knew what had to be done, which didn't make it one bit easier. The prospect of admitting the truth was a terrifying one. Zarek had no idea what would happen once he took a step down that path, but he had to take it before the uncertainty destroyed him.

He'd do it as soon as the next opportunity presented itself. He'd say what had to be said, and he'd live with the consequences, whatever they may be.

He put out his hand and turned on the radio, and listened to a man speaking much too quickly. After thirty seconds the only

words Zarek had caught were "Dublin," "everyone" and "following."

He closed his eyes and wished the man spoke Polish.

"Carmel," Meg said, "could I have a quick word before you go?"

She was going to tell her not to bring Barry back. In the
three days he'd been at the playschool he hadn't once opened his
mouth, except to whisper to Carmel anytime he wanted to use
the toilet. He ignored the other children apart from Emily, who
built Lego towers for him and kept up a running commentary
when she made a jigsaw. "See, this is the horse, it goes here, an'
then you put the tractor in this place, or no, this one, an' the
farmer goes in here…"

Barry wouldn't touch the apple pieces that Meg fed them at
break time. He didn't join in with the singing or the dancing, or
the clapping. He listened to the stories that Meg read, leaning into
Carmel's side and sucking his thumb doggedly, but he didn't volun-
teer any answers to the questions she asked the children afterwards.

And he flatly refused, each morning, to allow Carmel to leave.
Of course Meg wouldn't be happy with that, she wouldn't want
a mother around all the time. Carmel waited for both of them to
be sent packing.

"I was wondering," Meg said, "if you'd be interested in making
this official."

"Official?"

"Yes. I wouldn't be able to pay you very much. I was thinking
sixty euro a week—twenty a day—but it would be cash in hand,
you wouldn't be paying tax on that."

Carmel struggled to understand, *sixty euro* hammering in her
head. "You're askin' me do I want a job."

Meg smiled. "Sorry, I'm not explaining myself very well. Yes, I'm offering you a job. You've made life so easy for me since you've arrived. You've everything tidied away before the kids are even collected. You tie laces and wipe noses and mop up spills, you do anything that needs to be done."

"I jus' like keepin' busy," Carmel said. "It's nothin', I don't even notice I'm doin' it."

Sixty euro.

"Well, *I've* noticed," Meg said, "and it's been a huge help to me. Since I started this playschool in September I've been struggling. It's really too much for one person; I need another pair of hands. Are you interested at all?"

Carmel licked her lips, which had suddenly gone dry. "I thought you were goin' to throw us out."

Meg looked at her in surprise. "What? Why on earth would I do that?"

"'Cos Barry is so quiet," Carmel said. "He don't mix much, and 'cos he don't let me go home. I thought you mightn't want us here."

Meg laid a hand gently on Barry's head. "He's a great boy," she said softly. "He's a credit to you. He'll just take his time, that's all, and he'll find his voice when he's ready." She smiled at the little boy. "Won't you?"

He sucked his thumb and gazed back at her.

Carmel's eyes had begun to feel hot. She blinked hard. "You'd pay me sixty euro a week," she said, "for three mornin's."

"I know it's not much," Meg said, "but—"

"It's fine, it's plenty," Carmel broke in. "I'd love to. Honest to God, I'd love it."

A job. She'd just been offered her first job, in this colorful, noisy room that was going to help Barry find his voice. She was going to come here three mornings a week and help out, doing what she'd been doing anyway, without thinking, for the past three days. What was wiping a few noses and tying a few laces, and putting jigsaw pieces back into boxes? It was nothing, it wasn't work at all.

She was going to get €60 every week for doing nothing. And she was going to be with Barry, they were going to be together.

"Thank you," she said, hearing how feeble it sounded. Wanting to throw her arms around Meg, wanting to spin cartwheels around the room. "I'd really love it."

"That's great," Meg said. "I'm delighted. And I can't promise anything, but if it works out we might take on a few more children after Christmas, when there'd be two of us, and Barry could come five days a week, and I could pay you a bit more. How does that sound?"

"Fine, that sounds great." Carmel felt the happiness erupt in her. She got to her feet quickly, afraid that Meg was going to change her mind. "We'll be goin'," she said. "Let you finish up."

"Hang on a sec," Meg said, walking to the door. "I'll be right back." She left the room.

Carmel crossed the floor and lifted Barry's jacket down from its red plastic hook. A white label had been fixed to the wood above the hook, and it said BARRY. The room was full of white labels, all with a word written on them in black marker, all stuck with squidgy blue stuff to various objects.

Carmel had copied *table* and *chair* and *door* onto a page with a crayon as Meg had read a story earlier. She'd drawn a corresponding picture beside each word, and the page was folded in her pocket now. Next week she'd do *window* and *blackboard* and *wall*, and after that she'd start on the books that had a different word and picture on every page.

Meg reappeared. "Your first week's wages," she said, holding out three €20 notes.

"Ah no." Carmel backed away. "I wasn't started yet."

"Of course you were; we just didn't know it." Meg folded the notes and pushed them into Carmel's hand. "Go on, I insist. I won't feel I've been taking advantage."

On the way home—home!—Carmel bought a biro and a ruled copybook, a book with a chicken on the front and a small tube of jellies for Barry, a packet of flower seeds, a bag of potatoes, a turnip, a chicken, and a bottle of whiskey. She'd seen whiskey at the back of a kitchen press, so she knew what kind he drank.

She reached the house and stopped at the gate. Barry looked up at her.

"Jus' a sec," she said.

She gazed at the redbrick façade, at the place where they lived now. Number 17, Walnut Grove. The house where Ethan had grown up. The house she had keys for.

"Tell you what," she said, "let's have a quick lunch and then go to Granddad's shop, okay? I have to tell him somethin'."

She was bursting with it, she couldn't wait till he got home from work. She was dying to see his face when she told him. She wanted him to be glad he'd taken them in, to be glad she was the mother of his grandchild.

———

She was alone, leaning against the radiator under the window, arms crossed over her chest, looking towards Pauline's ancient orange carpet that was patterned with tiny brown stars, her dark hair curtaining her face.

The small room was crowded with Pauline's neighbors and friends, stopping off on their way home from Kevin's removal. They stood around or perched on chair arms, balancing cups and glasses and plates. The air was thick with perfume and coffee and hard-boiled egg, and humming with various subdued conversations.

Audrey threaded her way through the room with Pauline's biggest teapot, topping up cups as she went. She reached the radiator.

"A hot drop?"

The woman lifted her head, and Audrey was struck by how lost she looked. She regarded Audrey dully for a few seconds before recognizing her.

"Oh, hello…no, thanks."

Her cup sat by her feet on the carpet, hardly touched. A whitish film had settled on the surface of the tea. Audrey cradled the teapot and leaned against the wall next to the radiator, and the two of them remained silent for some time.

When the woman eventually spoke, Audrey had to lean sideways to hear her.

"Kevin was like a second big brother," she said. "He didn't talk to me as if I was a child. He taught me how to tie laces, just before I started school. I didn't know there was anything different about him, I just thought he was wonderful." She stopped then, and shook her head. "It's so unfair."

Audrey said nothing. In the far corner of the room a sudden laugh erupted, and was cut off abruptly.

"How is Pauline?" the girl asked, raising her head to look at Audrey again. "I can't talk to her properly, with all the…"

Pauline was in the kitchen, surrounded by Sue and her family, and more callers. "She's bearing up," Audrey said, hearing how pathetic it sounded. What else could you say though? This girl didn't want to hear that Pauline was completely shattered, that when she looked at you she didn't see you, because her grief blocked everything out.

Kevin, it turned out, had suffered a massive heart attack in the water. He'd died from that, not from drowning. Not that it made any difference now.

"It's not *fair*," the woman repeated, her voice still low but urgent now. "Why *Kevin*, for God's sake? Where's the sense in that?" She rubbed her face. "God, sometimes I just…" Her voice trembled and she trailed off, bowing her head again, breathing deeply.

"I know," Audrey murmured, putting a tentative hand on her arm. "There's no sense to it."

"My brother died," the woman said then, "a few years ago. He was twenty-four."

"Oh," Audrey said, recalling Pauline's upset at the time. "Oh, I'm so—"

"It's just *cruel*, to snuff out somebody's life, just like that. What kind of a God does that? Ethan didn't deserve it—and Kevin didn't deserve it either."

"No."

"I blamed my father," she said, half to herself. "On some level I think I still do, but…" She stopped again, and looked apologetically at Audrey. "Sorry, I shouldn't be saying all this, we hardly know each other."

"I'm Audrey." Putting out a hand, which the woman took.

"Val," she said. "I know your name, Pauline often mentioned you. You were good to Kevin."

Audrey demurred, but the woman said, "No, you were. She was very thankful. He used to chat to you over the hedge all the time, she said."

The tears rose in Audrey's eyes then, and she fished a crumpled tissue hurriedly from her sleeve and pressed it to her face. "He did," she whispered.

"I'm sorry," Val said. "I didn't mean—"

"No, no, no—" Audrey blew her nose and got to her feet,

pushing the tissue back up her sleeve. "Well," she said, attempting a smile, "I'd better get on. So nice to finally meet you."

She left the room as quickly as the crowd allowed and set the teapot on the draining board in the kitchen. She walked straight out the back door, avoiding anyone's eye, hoping nobody was taking any notice of her as she pulled it closed.

She took great gulps of the night air, feeling the frosty nip of it steadying her somewhat. Winter on the way. She walked to the hedge that divided Pauline's garden from her own, and she stood where Kevin had so often stood—and the thought of him undid her again, and she bent her face into her hands and allowed the tears to fall.

Val was right, it was cruel. It was senseless and tragic and so *unfair*. Audrey cried in noisy, messy sobs, leaning up against the hedge where Kevin had stood so often.

When her tears eventually abated, when her sobs lessened, she inhaled deeply again and again, trying to steady her breath. Her nose ran, her face was wet, everything inside her head felt heavy and cloddy. As she rummaged for a tissue again—not that it would be much use at this stage—the kitchen door opened behind her.

She turned to see a man coming out, his frame silhouetted against the light from the kitchen, his features indistinguishable in the darkness of the garden. She swiped at her eyes quickly with a sleeve, willing him to go away and leave her alone.

Instead he walked straight over to her. She attempted to regain her composure as he approached, as she recognized him. He reached silently into the breast pocket of his jacket, drew out a large white handkerchief, and handed it to her.

Audrey accepted it wordlessly and wiped her eyes and blew her nose. Eventually, when she felt a little steadier, she looked back at him.

"What are you doing here?" Her voice was thick, as if she had a heavy cold. Her throat hurt from sobbing.

"Paying my respects," he replied mildly—which, of course, wasn't what Audrey was asking at all. Had he taken her literally just to annoy her?

Oh, who cared? She folded his handkerchief and pushed it into the pocket of her skirt. "I'll wash it and return it."

"Keep it," he said, his gaze directed now towards the bottom of the garden. "I have lots more."

The air was becoming steadily chillier, but Audrey didn't feel ready to return to the house. She looked a fright, she was sure, her hair every which way, her eyes swollen, her cheeks burning, but out here in the dark it didn't matter.

"I assume," he said then, "what you were asking was how do I know Pauline."

"It doesn't matter," Audrey replied. It felt surreal, holding this quiet conversation with him in the darkness.

"She was my housekeeper," he said, as if she hadn't spoken. "After my wife died she kept house for me and my children. She was with us for ten years. They both were, her and Kevin."

In her befuddled state, it took several seconds for the implications of his words to sink in. Audrey was dumbfounded. *This* was the man Pauline had worked for, the man she'd held in such high regard?

He was so good to us, she'd often said to Audrey. *So generous. He paid me well over the odds, and insisted on us eating dinner with them before we went home in the evening. Up to his eyes with his business, but always a kind word for Kevin.*

Good? Generous? Kind? The man who'd been cranky and—yes, downright rude, the first few times Audrey had encountered him? Of course he'd changed a bit since then, he'd mellowed somewhat, but still.

"And you?" he asked, turning to face her. "What's your connection?"

"I live next door," she told him, indicating her house absently, still astounded at his revelation. Still piecing it all together. "So Val is your daughter."

A beat passed. "You know her?"

"Only to say hello to, if I passed her on the road when she visited this house. I met her properly just this evening. She's in the sitting room."

"Yes," he said—and Audrey remembered that Val had given the distinct impression that father and daughter weren't on the best of terms. *I blamed him*, wasn't that what she'd said? She blamed her father for her brother's death, whatever she meant by that.

His son had died. First his wife, then his son—and somewhere along the way, he'd become estranged from his only remaining child. If anyone had earned the right to be grumpy, it was him.

"My grandson has started playschool," he said then, "thanks to you."

It took her a second to switch subjects so utterly. She'd completely forgotten about his asking her if she knew any playschools. "That's good," she said.

His grandson. Yes, the small clothes she'd seen him buying. But he wasn't Val's child, was he? Whenever Val had come to Pauline's she'd been alone—surely if she had a little boy she'd have brought him to visit her old housekeeper?

Oh, it was too complicated to figure out, and none of Audrey's business anyway. She gave a slight shiver, and immediately he said, "You should go inside."

But Audrey couldn't face it yet. She still felt fragile, as if the tears might erupt again at any second. "I'll stay out here a little longer," she said, "but you go in if you want."

To her great surprise he took off his jacket. "Here," he said, "throw that over your shoulders."

"No, really, I—"

"Go on," he said, "it'll keep you warm. I don't feel the cold."

Audrey took it, too weary to argue, and draped it across her shoulders, and the warmth of it—the warmth of him—settled into her. It smelled of peanuts.

"Thank you," she said. They stood in silence for a few minutes, listening to the muffled buzz of conversation from the house. When the silence between them stretched, Audrey stole a glance at him. His hands were in his pockets and his gaze was off down the garden again. Was he remembering his son, or his wife?

She thought of her irritation with him, how she'd dreaded each visit to his shop. Well, she'd had reason enough, she supposed, not to want to meet him.

But look at him now. Look at the two of them, standing together peaceably, if not exactly happily. Nothing like a tragedy to remind you what was important, and what didn't matter at all.

Eventually she slid his jacket from her shoulders and handed it back. "Thank you. I think I'll go in now."

He accepted the jacket wordlessly. She left him there and went through the kitchen, squeezing Pauline's shoulder on the way and telling her she'd see her in the morning. She walked back to her house and let herself in quietly, and gathered Dolly into her arms.

She stood in her dark kitchen and looked out the window, but most of Pauline's patio was hidden from her view by the dividing hedge. She turned away.

"Let's go to bed," she whispered to Dolly, and the little dog licked her face.

Saturday

Hello?"

"It's Irene Dillon," she said. "Please don't hang up."
She'd found Pilar's number in Martin's phone. She'd known it
would still be there, and it was.

Silence.

"I'm calling to apologize," Irene said. "I realize I was difficult
to work for."

Another brief silence before Pilar said, "Is okay, Mrs. Dillon."
Another pause, and then: "How is Emily?"

"She misses you, a lot," Irene said. "In fact—" she closed her
eyes "—we're wondering if you'd like to come back. For Emily."

She waited for Pilar to say that she'd gotten another job, or to
make up some other excuse—moving back to Lithuania, whatever. Or maybe just to tell Irene to go to hell, or words to that
effect. A grey-and-white cat emerged from the hedge that separated them from the neighbors and padded across Irene's lawn,
stopping to sniff at something in the grass.

"Mrs. Dillon," Pilar said, "Emily is beautiful girl, and I miss
her too. But I think I cannot work for you. I think it is too difficult for me to make you happy. I am sorry."

As Irene watched, the cat sat on the lawn and raised a hind
paw to scratch under its chin.

"Pilar," she said clearly, "just give me a minute. Let me explain."

"Dad," she said quietly.

Michael turned. They were in the church grounds, waiting for Kevin's coffin to be brought out. People were scattered in small huddles, talking quietly. Michael had seen his daughter earlier in the church and avoided her, thinking he wouldn't be welcome if he approached.

"Hello," he said. "How are you?"

She wore a purple coat he hadn't seen before, and a green scarf splashed with purple daubs. Her hair was caught up at the back of her head. Her face pale, the tip of her nose pink, a slick of something shiny on her mouth. Beautiful, she'd always been so beautiful. The sight of her made him want to weep with love.

"Dad," she repeated, "I've been horrible to you."

Michael made a small dismissive gesture.

"No, I have," she said. "I've been horrible." Her eyes welled up, and she blinked rapidly. "I know you did the best for us, I know it wasn't easy…with Ethan, I mean." She bit her lip as she waved a hand vaguely towards the church. "This has made me realize how stupid, how petty I've been…I wouldn't blame you if you didn't want to have anything to do with me again."

Michael smiled. "Well," he said, "I'm afraid that's never going to happen."

She gave a sound that was halfway between a sob and a laugh. "I was hoping you'd say that." Thumbing tears from under both her eyes, blinking again. "Dad, I'd like…can I come and meet them?"

Michael felt something lift away from him, something he hadn't even known had been weighing him down. "Of course you can, anytime you want. When were you thinking?"

"Maybe tomorrow," she said. "I'm working later today, but I'm off tomorrow."

"Tomorrow's fine," he told her. "What time would suit you?"

"Maybe around five?"

"Five would be perfect. You could stay to dinner if you liked."

Over Val's shoulder he saw the woman who'd bought the little dog. Audrey. He didn't have to think for her name, it just slid into his head. He lifted a hand and she smiled at him, a watery version of her usual smile. She wore a pink jacket and a red-and-blue flowery skirt. She looked summery, at the end of October. She probably looked summery all year. She probably didn't own any black clothes.

Val followed his gaze. "You know Audrey?" she asked.

"I do," he said. "She bought a dog from me."

"You know she's Pauline's next-door neighbor?"

"I do."

"Small world," Val said. "She seems lovely."

There was a stir at the church doorway then and they turned to watch Kevin being brought out. When the hearse began to drive away, Michael looked back at his daughter.

"Are you walking to the cemetery?"

She nodded and they fell into step with the rest of the crowd, and after a while she tucked her arm into his and he covered her hand with his, and in this way they traveled the short distance to Carrickbawn cemetery.

———

There was nothing on television until the late movie, and that was still hours away. Audrey stopped flicking through the channels and turned to the newspaper she'd bought on her way home from the funeral. It had sat untouched all afternoon while she'd mopped floors and scrubbed sinks and pushed the Hoover under beds, trying to shake off the gloom that had settled around her. She hadn't even lit the sitting room fire, so busy she'd kept herself, and now it hardly seemed worth the effort.

She leafed dispiritedly through the newspaper but nothing lifted her spirits. The letters page full of complaints, the usual spate of road accidents, the ongoing unresolved conflicts around the world, the never-ending political scandals. Really, why did anyone want the news?

She turned to the crossword and found a pen in her bag. Maybe it would distract her for half an hour. The first clue was *brief recap of material.* As she thought about it her mobile phone beeped. She took it off the coffee table and read **Audrey, I will come to your party—Zarek.**

I will come to your party. She looked blankly at the screen.

Party?

And abruptly, she remembered.

"Oh my *God*!" she cried, springing from the couch, causing Dolly, who'd been dozing beside her, to leap to the floor with a startled yelp. Audrey raced upstairs—"Oh *God*"—kicked off her slippers on the landing, dashed into her bedroom, and scrabbled under the bed for her shoes—"oh my *God*"—flew back across the landing and scrubbed at her teeth in the bathroom—"oh *God*"—ten past seven now, fifty minutes before they'd start arriving—"oh *God*"—not a *drop* of alcohol in the house, not a *scrap* of party food, impossible, completely *impossible* to buy anything now, no time to queue in a supermarket, what in God's name could she do?

She rushed downstairs again, almost tripping over Dolly, who galloped along beside her. She raced into the kitchen and began yanking open presses, riffling frantically through their contents. Spaghetti hoops, instant mash, steak and kidney pie, raisins, carrots, tomatoes—nothing, *nothing* she could possibly use. Could she phone everyone and cancel? No, she could *not*, at this late stage. But she had to serve *something*, you couldn't have a party without food, she *must* have something to give them—

She opened the freezer and pulled out drawers—and discovered, to her enormous relief, a just-opened bag of oven chips and two pounds of sausages.

"Oh, thank *God*," she muttered, scattering the chips onto a baking sheet, grabbing a scissors to cut the sausages in half. While the oven was heating she tore upstairs again and replaced the towel in the bathroom and changed her skirt and combed her hair and applied lipstick with a trembling hand.

Back downstairs she did what she could in the sitting room, put a match to the heap of kindling in the fireplace, added half a bucket of coal when the flames licked, plumped cushions, shoved magazines under the couch, bundled away her book and her reading glasses, shuffled the CDs into some sort of order, and raced back to the kitchen with two empty cups.

Twenty-five past seven. She slid the baking sheets of chips and sausages into the oven, corralled Dolly in the kitchen, grabbed her bag and moped keys, and left the house, pulling on her helmet.

The off-license was ten minutes away.

———————

Zarek hoped his text to Audrey hadn't been too late. He'd meant to send it earlier, but the café had been busy and it had slipped his mind until he was leaving work.

His initial reaction when Audrey had invited him to her party was to decline. The prospect of an hour or two of struggling to understand his classmates' conversations—not to mention forgoing his DVD night with Anton—didn't tempt him. So he'd demurred, using work as his excuse, although he'd known quite well that he was off at seven that Saturday.

But as the week had worn on and he'd prepared to send his regrets to Audrey, he'd begun to feel slightly guilty. He liked his art teacher, and she'd made a kind gesture, and he was about to reject it with a lie. And however preferable a night in with Anton and a DVD might be, they would both still be there next Saturday. And surely he should experience one Irish party, at least. So in the end he'd decided to go along.

Twenty to eight. He should leave in the next few minutes if he wanted to arrive on time—because it would be impolite, surely, to turn up late. Audrey would no doubt have everything in place by now, was perhaps having a glass of wine as she waited for her guests to arrive. Zarek knotted his tie and polished his shoes, mildly curious, now that the time had come, about what the evening ahead would entail.

Twenty to eight as she stood in line at the off-license, her heart in her mouth, her skin prickling with impatience. The wine hurriedly chosen, two red, two white—would four be enough? She had no idea, but it was all she could fit in the moped's basket, along with the cartons of orange juice and bottles of sparkling water. The white wine wasn't chilled, she'd have to put it in the freezer when she got home.

What if they all drank red, or white? What if her four bottles ran out after half an hour? Oh, what had *possessed* her to do this? But the guests would surely bring some wine with them, wouldn't they? Didn't everyone bring wine to a party?

"Next," the man at the cash register said, and Audrey hoisted her basket onto the counter and resisted the impulse to check her watch again.

They'd be late, nobody ever arrived on time. She'd be fine. She took her change and grabbed her purchases and fled outside.

Irene regarded her reflection in the full-length mirror. Pretty damn good for forty-two. She thought of the concentrated effort that had gone into ensuring that she still looked well in her forties. The punishing gym schedule, the constant calorie counting, the endless massages and facials.

She took her diamond earrings from their box and put them on. Might as well go the whole hog, even if it was only a glass of plonk at Audrey's. She remembered when Martin had given her the earrings, a week after Emily had been born. Her reward for having his child.

She dabbed perfume on her wrists and slipped her feet into the waiting silver shoes and picked up Audrey's gift bag. The thought of the party didn't exactly fill her with excitement but it would pass the time, it would distract her, and she could knock back a few glasses of cheap wine and let on she was happy for an hour or so. And if the affair was truly dire, she could make up a headache and call a taxi and leave.

She walked out to the landing and stood outside Emily's room and heard Martin singing softly, some silly song about a butterfly that Emily loved. "*Flutter by, flutter by, butterfly,*" he sang.

She stood there listening for several seconds. She let the thought of what she was planning to do float briefly into her head, and the wrench it brought caused her eyes to close.

"Again," Emily said clearly from the bedroom.

"Okay, but this is definitely the last time." The song floated out once more to the landing.

Irene went downstairs and let herself out, and made her way along the path to the waiting taxi.

———————

Jackie remained sitting at her dressing table when she heard the doorbell. Through the open bedroom door she heard her father letting James and Charlie in, and James introducing himself and his daughter, and her father's call to Eoin. She waited until Eoin came out of the sitting room and then she left the room and walked downstairs.

At the sound of her approach her father and James looked up. She saw the way James took in the dress she was wearing. She thought of how he knew precisely what was underneath, how he studied it for two hours every Tuesday evening, and the thought sent a shockingly vivid thrill through her.

The children disappeared and her mother came out from the kitchen, and the four of them made small talk in the hall for a few minutes. She knew her parents were sizing up James, the only man who'd ever shown up at the house looking for their daughter. She knew they hoped he'd turn out to be more than just Charlie's father.

"We'd better go," she said as soon as she could. She didn't want James realizing how interested her parents were in him. She went to the kitchen and took the wine she'd bought earlier from the fridge, and they said good-bye to her parents, and she thought again about having him all to herself in the time it would take them to cross the town to Audrey's house.

———

Zarek stood on the doorstep and checked the address he'd copied down from the blackboard in the life drawing classroom. The house number corresponded with the one that was stuck in brass to the yellow front door, and the street name had been displayed on the wall of the first house. So he was definitely at the right place—but where was Audrey? Had she said Friday, and not Saturday? No, he was positive Saturday had been mentioned.

He looked at his watch. Two minutes past eight o'clock. He

put his ear to the door and pressed the bell a second time, and heard it ringing inside the house. He also heard a persistent yapping, and remembered Audrey mentioning a little dog.

When there was still no response he walked to the side of the house and regarded the little passageway that led to the back. Maybe something had happened to Audrey, maybe some mishap had befallen her. Maybe she was lying unconscious within the house. Should he walk around, see if a window was open anywhere?

As he stood there uncertainly he heard the buzz of an approaching motor, and a second later Audrey zoomed into view. He watched her pulling up at the curb, and almost toppling off the bike in her attempt to dismount. He sensed an urgency about her movements that brought him hurrying back down the garden path towards her.

"Zarek—I'm *so* sorry." She yanked off her helmet and dumped it on the seat, and began pulling a canvas bag from the front basket. "I'm a little...disorganized, I'm afraid."

Zarek reached for the bag. "Please, I take." It was surprisingly heavy, and contained numerous bottles and cartons.

"Oh, thank you, dear." She rushed ahead of him, keeping up a scattered commentary as she opened the front door and led him into the hall and through to the kitchen. "Oh, you brought wine, how thoughtful, please excuse the mess, I'm afraid I've been a little...oh sorry, don't mind Dolly, she's perfectly harmless, *stop* that, Dolly, go *down*...yes, yes, just over there, thank you so much...*no*, Dolly, *bad* dog, I'll just put her outside in the—yes, if you could put the white into the freezer, I'm afraid they're not very cold—"

She broke off abruptly, her face changing. "*Oh!*" she cried, just as Zarek became aware of a burning smell. They turned simultaneously towards the oven, and Audrey threw open the door. Waves of black smoke rolled out immediately. "Oh *no*—"

To Zarek's dismay she burst into tears. "Oh, it's all going wrong," she wept, her hands pressed to her cheeks. "My neighbor, you see, he *died* on Tuesday, he was barely forty, such a *lovely* man, you have no idea"—lunging for a tea towel and swiping at the tears—"but of course it made me forget about this party, *completely* forget until I got your text, and then I had to *dash* out, and I put them into the oven *much* too soon, not thinking at *all*, and now everything's *ruined*—"

She began flapping the tea towel at the smoke, which helped distribute it about the kitchen. Zarek grabbed a pair of oven gloves that hung beside the cooker and slid out the two baking sheets and brought them to the back door. They each held what looked to him like short, fat lengths of charcoal.

Audrey looked tearfully at the burned offerings as Zarek opened the door and laid the trays on the ground outside. "I had so little *time*, you see," she sobbed, "it was such a *rush*—oh *goodness*, and everyone coming, such a *disaster*—" Dropping the tea towel and pulling tissues from a box on the worktop to dab frantically at her eyes.

"No, no," Zarek said, propping the back door open with a chair, "is no disaster, don't worry, Audrey." He searched for words to reassure her, so woebegone she looked. "Important things for party is friends, and wine, and…perhaps little music, that is plenty." He decided to assume that Audrey possessed some sort of sound system.

"But it's a *party*," she cried, "and all I have is, oh, I don't know, maybe some *popcorn*, and *that's* not going to be much help."

"You have popcorn?" Zarek asked. "I make every Saturday in my apartment, I am popcorn king. Popcorn is perfect food for party. Where is popcorn?"

Audrey blew her nose, regarding him doubtfully. "You think that would do?" She reached into a press and drew out a box that contained bags of microwavable popcorn. "Oh, but it's only—"

"Perfect," Zarek repeated firmly, taking it from her and lifting out a bag. "Healthy food." Which may have been pushing it a bit, but no matter. He put the bag into Audrey's microwave and switched it on.

"See?" he said, smiling. Choosing to ignore the little dog, who seemed to be enjoying the charcoal. "Simple as pie."

"Oh, and I think there are crackers," Audrey said, sniffing as she opened another press, "and there's cheese in that—"

The doorbell rang, causing her to start violently. "Oh *Lord*, someone else," she wailed, practically throwing the box of crackers at him as she pulled out another tissue and dabbed at her eyes again, "and we're still in such a *mess*, and I must look an absolute *fright*—"

Her face was certainly blotchy, the skin around her eyes puffy, the shiny pink lipstick he'd noticed earlier all but gone. Zarek saw no reason to point any of that out. He handed her a bottle of red wine and a carton of juice.

"You smile, you look beautiful," he told her. "Now you go, say welcome, put music, give drinks, and do talking. Go now, and I make food. I am chef."

And thankfully she went, leaving him to make the best of what he'd been given.

———

In the end, five of the six guests showed up. Fiona, it would appear, hadn't yet recovered. Audrey felt a twinge when she remembered that she'd intended calling her on Saturday morning, but if she'd felt able to come she would have rung, presumably, to get the address. Audrey would ring her in the morning, see how she was. Hopefully her husband was taking good care of her.

Remarkably, the guests who'd come seemed to be not unhappy with the proceedings. Could they possibly not have noticed how thrown-together the party was? They could hardly have missed the distinct smell of burning in the hall, but none of them had commented, bless them—and now, an hour into the affair, she'd caught nobody looking at a watch or stifling a yawn.

And poor Zarek had outdone himself on the food front, appearing within minutes with a mountain of popcorn, a platter of crackers topped with slices of cheese and cubes of pineapple, and Audrey's fruit bowl filled with assorted chocolate bars. He'd found her supply in the jar, all by himself. It wasn't a banquet, but when you considered that it had been conjured up out of practically nothing, it was perfectly acceptable.

Audrey circulated among the small assembly, offering more drinks. She needn't have worried about running out of wine. Everyone had brought a bottle except for Irene, who'd brought two in a little wooden crate, *and* a box of Black Magic chocolates, which Audrey didn't actually care for—she found dark chocolate too bitter—but of course it was the thought that counted. She'd pass them on to poor Pauline, who preferred dark chocolate.

The food disappeared, and nobody seemed to mind that they weren't getting chicken kebabs or cheese balls or onion bhajis— or indeed, fake cocktail sausages and chips. Audrey must remember to take in the baking sheets later, or Dolly, who must be still in the kitchen, might try to eat them and end up with a stomachache.

The fire flickered, casting a soft, warm glow in the room— much better, after all, than the colored lightbulbs Audrey had originally been thinking of for her table lamps. The guests chatted, glasses were refilled, and the music was looked after by Jackie, who wore a really pretty, colorful dress.

Just after ten o'clock there was a general pulling on of jackets and collecting of bags that Audrey didn't attempt to discourage, feeling a little drained from her earlier panicked preparations, followed by two hours of trying to be the perfect hostess. Kevin's death was still much too raw for her to look happy without an enormous effort.

In the hall there was some discussion about where everyone lived before it was discovered that James, Jackie, and Irene were heading in one direction and Meg and Zarek in the other. Audrey stood on the doorstep and waved them off, thinking with longing of her bath, followed by an hour with her book in front of the fire in dressing gown and slippers.

All things considered though, despite the disastrous start, the evening could be said to have been, if not exactly the party of the year, then far from an abject failure.

As soon as they left Audrey's road Meg pushed a button and some female whose voice Zarek didn't recognize began to sing, accompanied by a soft saxophone. "*I've been waiting so long*," she sang, slow enough for Zarek to understand, "*for you to notice me.*"

Meg's perfume reminded him of Turkish Delight. He sat tensely in the passenger seat, marveling at the mischance that had led to him being her only passenger. He'd assured her that walking was no problem for him, but she wouldn't hear of it—"Not in the dark, on a Saturday night; you could meet anyone"—and to insist would, he felt, have seemed ungrateful for her offer, so now he was trapped.

"That was a lovely evening," she said. "You were good to help with the food."

"Food was easy," he said, happy to talk about such an impartial subject. "Popcorn in microwave, not complicated. Also putting cheese on biscuit, and pin-apple."

She laughed. "Pineapple."

"Yes, thank you, pineapple. And the chocolate I find in a box."

"Still though," she went on, "I'm sure Audrey was delighted to have you."

She wore a low-cut green dress that stopped at her knees, and gold sandals with lots of straps. Around her left wrist was a charm bracelet that jangled when she moved her arm.

"So," she said, "how d'you like living in Ireland?"

"Is good," he said, determined again to keep the conversation as unthreatening as possible. "I like it very much. Peoples are friendly, but my job not very interesting. In Poland I work with the computers."

"Really?" Slowing as they approached a junction. "And what do you do here?"

"I work in chip shop," he replied, hoping she wouldn't ask its name. Carrickbawn had lots of fast-food cafés. "Polish food very different to Irish," he added, attempting to steer things away from his job.

She waited for two cars to pass, and then she swung right. "And," she said, "I'm sure you had no trouble finding a nice Irish girlfriend." Turning to flash him a brief smile. "If I was single I'd be interested." Laughing lightly as she took another turn. "Or even if I wasn't."

Zarek kept his gaze straight ahead and made no response. When the silence began to stretch, Meg said, "Sorry—I didn't mean to embarrass you."

"Meg," he said. He paused, forming the words in his head before saying them. "There is something I must tell to you."

She glanced at him again. "Zarek, don't worry, I—"

"I am homosexual," he said, loudly enough to make sure she heard over her own words, and the voice of the singer.

A beat passed.

"Oh," Meg said. "Oh, I see. Well, that's…"

She shifted gears as a roundabout came into view. She negotiated the roundabout.

"I am next left road," Zarek said. "Maybe you remember?"

"Yes, sure." She turned left.

"Just here is okay," he said.

Meg pulled into the curb.

"Thank you," he said, "for the drive."

"You're welcome." She gave him a quick smile.

"See you on Tuesday," he said, getting out. "Thank you," he repeated, closing the door.

He stood on the path until her car had disappeared, feeling a wonderful release.

———————

"Well," Jackie said brightly, "here we are."

He'd been quiet on the way to the party, but she hadn't minded. She'd prattled enough for both of them, knowing that she looked good, feeling happy to be in his presence. The party itself had been okay, although Audrey's musical collection left a bit to be desired. And there'd been no dancing, much to her disappointment. She loved to dance.

But she'd done her best, she'd chatted with everyone. Even Irene, who'd been fairly knocking back the wine, and who as far as Jackie could see hadn't eaten a single thing. Throughout the evening Jackie had been conscious all the time of James and where he was in the room, and had looked forward to being alone with him again at the end of the evening.

She'd been dismayed when she'd heard him offering Irene a lift home. Dismayed but not surprised, since Audrey, attempting to organize everyone's journey, had made it practically impossible for him not to—"Oh, the three of you are going the same way; isn't *that* convenient."

And to make matters worse, Irene had gotten straight into the passenger seat. As if she had every right to sit there, as if Jackie were the child being driven home by her parents. How annoying. Jackie had sulked silently while Irene had flirted brazenly with James, commenting on his accent, asking him what he thought of the social scene in Carrickbawn, telling him he had to try her favorite Thai restaurant. Pathetic.

Thankfully, Irene had been dropped off first, at a grand-looking redbrick house. Jackie had slipped into the front seat as soon as it had been vacated, resisting the impulse to wave Irene's sickly perfume away.

For all the good sitting beside him had done her.

He'd responded to her questions and comments cordially enough, but there was a distance between them that Jackie hadn't been expecting, and couldn't bridge. He didn't meet her eye, he made no attempt to move the conversation beyond her prattling small talk. He gave no indication that they were anything more than cordial acquaintances.

Before they reached her road, Jackie realized that she'd been foolish to suppose there was anything between them. Wishful thinking, that was all it had been, a product of her fertile imagination. And now they were here, and all she wanted to do was get out of his car.

"I'll pick Charlie up at ten," he was saying. "That's not too early, is it?"

The engine still running, his fingers all but drumming on the steering wheel. Looking out the front windscreen, not even glancing her way. Another car whooshed by, some awful music booming out.

"Ten is fine." Jackie felt for the door handle. "Well," she said, "good night then. Thanks for the lift."

"Good night," he replied, turning to look at her finally, smiling now that she was getting out. Now that he was getting rid of her.

"See you in the morning," he said.

"Sure."

She took her key from her bag and let herself into the house as he drove off. She closed the door gently and leaned against it and listened. The television was still on in the sitting room, so at least one of her parents was still up. She took a deep breath and crossed the hall, and put her head in.

Her father half rose when the door opened, but she whispered, "No, stay there, I'm going straight up. I'll see you in the morning."

Without waiting for his response she closed the door and hurried up the stairs. Ten minutes later she was in bed, her makeup only half removed, her teeth carelessly brushed. She closed her eyes and waited for sleep, and refused to dwell on the fact that he wasn't interested in her.

Not in the slightest.

She was disappointed, anyone could see that. He'd probably ruined her night. He'd made a mess of it, trying to let her down gently and getting it all wrong instead.

He drove through the streets that were becoming increasingly familiar to him. His fault, all his fault, chatting to her at the art class breaks when he should have kept his distance, taking her up on the offer of babysitting arrangements for Charlie when he should have turned it down. Inviting her and her child to the cinema, when asking Eoin to join them hadn't even occurred to Charlie.

Weak-willed, that's what he was. Wanting what he had no right to look for, and now she was suffering for it. He'd skip the last art class, that would be best. No doubt Charlie would be looking to meet Eoin after school again, now that they'd started, but maybe it wouldn't happen for a while.

He was so bad at this, so clueless. But he had to keep his distance, he couldn't get involved with anyone. He turned into his road, dreading the empty house that was waiting for him, alone for a whole night with his miserable thoughts.

He let himself in and made straight for the press in the kitchen where he kept the whiskey bottle. A single glass of wine all evening surely entitled him to a nightcap now.

Sunday

A udrey unlocked the back door and Dolly raced out, yapping, and galloped about the garden. She had so much energy; keeping her cooped up in the kitchen all day was far from ideal. Maybe if she was on a long leash she could be left in the garden while Audrey was at work. But if she was outdoors, wouldn't she need a kennel to shelter in if it rained? Such a small animal, so many bits and pieces required. Just like a baby.

Audrey sat on the garden seat and sipped her tea. It had taken no time at all to clean up after last night's party. Only five guests after all, hardly a big crowd. A few glasses and plates, a run-around with the Hoover. Audrey still cringed at the thought of the shaky start—the panic Zarek's text had caused, the mad dash to the off-license, the smoke that had met her and Zarek in the kitchen, her outburst—but eventually, she was sure, the memory would amuse her.

She switched her attention to the week ahead, and debated what to do with her midterm break. A whole week off, nothing in her diary apart from the last life drawing class on Tuesday. If they got a fine day she and Dolly might drive somewhere for a day out, Westport maybe, or Kilkenny. She must watch the weather forecast.

She'd been planning a trip to the lake during the week, but that was out of the question now. She wondered how long it would be before she could contemplate the lake without thinking immediately of how Kevin had died there.

She laid her mug on the windowsill and walked to the hedge that separated her garden from Pauline's. Next door's patio was as neat as ever, with its little cast-iron table and chairs where the two of them had often sat on sunny mornings. Beyond that were the shelves that held Pauline's collection of herbs in their green and blue pots, and by the far wall stood the glass-topped frame where she'd grown lettuces and cucumbers and strawberries.

She'd gone to Cork to stay with Sue and her husband for a few days. Maybe when she came back, or maybe a bit later, Audrey might suggest that she get a little dog. It would be company on the long winter nights. It might be some small comfort to Pauline.

Michael Browne should be able to help; he may well know someone with pups looking for homes. No harm in asking anyway, after Audrey had gone to the bother of finding a playschool and putting him in touch with Meg. Not that he owed her anything, of course, but he might remember her help and feel more inclined to be of service.

She'd washed and ironed his handkerchief, and despite his having told her to keep it, she felt she should return it. She'd drop it into the pet shop when she was in town tomorrow. And while she was there she could inquire about kennels. She hadn't an idea how much they cost, they could be far too expensive, but it wouldn't hurt to—

Hold on a minute.

Audrey turned away from Pauline's garden and regarded Dolly, who was throwing arcs of earth up behind her as she scrabbled under what was left of the nasturtiums.

What was going on here exactly? Was Audrey actually trying to come up with an *excuse* to visit the pet shop? The hankie, a little dog for Pauline, a kennel for Dolly? Did she actually *want* to see him again, was she developing—

Oh Lord. Oh *Lord*.

"Dolly," she said sharply, belatedly becoming aware of what she was witnessing. "Bad dog. Stop that." Dolly looked up briefly, trotted to another part of the bed, and resumed digging.

It was just because there was nobody else, that's all it was. He was practically the only unattached man she'd had any sort of interaction with in months, years even. You couldn't count the few remaining single male teachers, they were all younger and not in the least interested in Audrey.

Apart from Terence, of course, the science teacher who'd offered his services as a life drawing model, and who would probably have welcomed a date with Audrey, or with anyone. But poor Terence, with his after-dinner mints and crocodile shoes and shiny forehead, made Audrey feel vaguely queasy.

So she was latching on to Michael Browne as her last hope—that must be what it was. Goodness, how pathetic was that? Look how abrupt he'd been at the start, look how he'd done his best to annoy her.

Although to be fair he'd improved somewhat on better acquaintance. And in Pauline's garden the other night he'd been quite nice really. Giving her his hankie, and then his jacket. Quite gentlemanly, you'd have to admit.

But that awful beard made her want to run for a razor. And they probably hadn't a thing in common.

Apart from a love of dogs, of course.

Although he hadn't seemed particularly fond of Dolly.

Then again, hadn't he—

"Oh, *stop* it," Audrey said aloud, crossly. She stomped to the back door and went inside and put the kettle on, banging and clattering whatever she could along the way. She made more tea, and then discovered that she didn't want it. She looked for a chocolate bar before she remembered they'd eaten them all at the party the night before. She stood at the sink, glaring out at Dolly, who was now curled innocently under the hydrangea bush, fast asleep.

She would *not* return his handkerchief. He had told her he didn't want it, which meant he didn't want Audrey hanging around bothering him. She'd take a trip to Limerick during the week and find a kennel there, and bring it home on the back of the moped, or arrange for it to be delivered if it was too big.

And if Pauline decided to get a dog they'd find one without his help, quite easily. They could put an ad in the paper, couldn't they? That's what everyone did if they were looking for something that wasn't readily available in a shop.

She'd put this nonsense out of her head right now. She'd banish all thoughts of Michael Browne, put them down to temporary insanity brought about by a combination of grief, desire for romance, and midterm weariness.

She thumped upstairs to make her bed.

———

Valerie brought a bottle of whiskey—his second gift of whiskey in three days—and something wrapped in blue tissue paper and a coloring book and crayons. She handed the whiskey to Michael and then she turned to Carmel and put out her hand.

"I'm Val, Ethan's sister."

Carmel shook her hand. "Pleased to meet you," she said. She'd washed her hair and changed into one of the two skirts she'd gotten from the charity shop with her wages. She must have bought lipstick too, first time he'd seen it on her.

She'd disappeared into the garden straight after washing up the lunch things, and when Michael had looked out a few minutes later she'd been crouching by the weed-filled strip of earth just beyond the patio.

She'd taken the trowel from the shed again and she was

painstakingly rooting out the bindweed and dandelions and whatever else had crept in and taken root over the last several years. When she finally came back inside, over two hours later, she'd shown Michael the picture of the flowers she'd sown there instead.

"I bought these because I like the look of them," she'd said. "I asked the girl what the name was. I never tried to grow no flowers before. I hope you don't mind."

Michael hadn't minded. He thought October might not be the month to sow Sweet William seeds—well, to grow any flower seeds really—but what did he know about gardening? If they didn't come up she could try again in the spring.

"You look like Ethan," Carmel said to Val now, flushing deeply immediately afterwards. Afraid she'd spoken out of turn, Michael supposed.

Valerie didn't seem to mind. "Pauline, our housekeeper, always said we were the image of each other." She handed Carmel the tissue-wrapped package. "This is for you: If you don't like the color you can change it."

Inside was a scarf in swirling greens and blues. Carmel pressed it to her cheek. "It's gorgeous," she said. "I got nothin' for you."

"Don't worry about it." Val crouched in front of Barry. "Hi," she said. "I'm your auntie Val." She offered him the coloring book and crayons. "These are for you."

He took them shyly, after a quick glance up at Carmel.

"I can dwaw the sun," he whispered. "An' a house."

"Can you really?" Val whispered back. "Will you show me?"

Michael opened the sitting room door. "Why don't you go in?" he said to them. "I'll bring tea."

In the kitchen he filled the kettle and put cups and buns on a tray. He walked quietly back into the hall and stood outside the sitting room door, which he'd left ajar.

"Five years ago," he heard Carmel saying. "Just after I ran

away from home. Couldn't stick it no more after my granny died."

Ran away from home at seventeen. Val was learning more about her in the first five minutes than Michael knew after a month.

"Ethan was one of the first people I met on the street. He looked after me," Carmel said. "Got me into his squat." Pause. "He was funny. He could take people off, you know what I mean?"

Michael knew what she meant. Ethan had been a clever mimic, had often had them in stitches pretending to be the parish priest, or some of the neighbors. Singing "Blue Suede Shoes" exactly like Elvis.

Long pause. Michael heard the kettle singing and returned to the kitchen and made tea. While it was brewing he tiptoed back to the hall.

"He tried to give it up," Carmel was saying, "the two of us did, lots of times. But it was hard…" A rustle, some movement. "When I found out I was havin' Barry though, I stopped for good, I just made myself. Ethan tried real hard too, but he kept goin' back."

"Were you with him when he died?" So low Michael could barely hear it.

"Yeah," Carmel answered. "He jus' kind of…faded away. I was holdin' on to him"—her voice breaking, a cough—"I kept tellin' him he better not die, an' then I jus' felt him sort of…leavin'."

Michael stood motionless, his hands by his sides.

He just faded away. I felt him leaving.

"I was in bits," Carmel said. "I kept shoutin' at him to come back, not to leave me alone with a kid. Barry was only gone one."

Michael pulled his handkerchief from his pocket and bent his face into it.

———————

In the end it was all a bit of a rush. Irene had been waiting for Martin and Emily to come home from an afternoon outing: the cinema, followed by sausages and chips in the café down the road. She'd planned to wait until Emily was in bed, and then say what needed to be said. But in the end she realized that she couldn't face him.

So she wrote a note on a page from her sketch pad. The words flew across the white paper in her big, rounded handwriting.

Martin—

I can't do this anymore. I can't be who you want me to be. I've tried, but I can't. You'll both be better off without me, and hopefully in time we'll all be happier. I'll be in touch through my parents at some stage. Pilar will be back to work in the morning. Please try to be kind when you tell Emily.

I love you. Always have. Always will. Always.

I xx

When she had finished, she didn't reread it. She folded the page and left it on the kitchen table. She hauled the bags she'd packed earlier downstairs and into the boot of her green Peugeot.

When everything was done she pulled the front door closed and posted her keys back through the letterbox. She got into her car and thought about her immediate plans.

The holiday cottage in Ballyvaughan for a few days, followed by the flight to France. A few weeks in Paris to revive her wardrobe, to stand before paintings, to sip cognac in jazz bars, and to book the next flight. Winter in St. Lucia, or possibly the Seychelles.

And after that, she had no idea. Lots of travel, she imagined. Lots of men, there were always men. And maybe somewhere along the way, if she kept searching for it long enough, she would find some happiness, some peace of mind.

Remote as the possibility seemed at this moment.

She started the car and drove away without looking back. No more looking back now.

The first thing Zarek noticed as he opened the apartment door was the smell. It reminded him of long-ago laundry days at home, before they got the washing machine. His mother at the kitchen sink, scrubbing with a big yellow bar of soap at their shirt collars and sleeves, the windows steamed up, the thick, heavy smell of wet wool permeating through the house.

He hung his jacket on the hall stand and walked through to the kitchen, and was met by clouds of steam. Pilar turned from the cooker, her face damp and rosy and smeared with white. She held a large plate on which some curiously shaped objects sat, each about the size of an adult fist.

"I make kuldunai for dinner," she announced. "Special dish from Lithuania."

There was white powder in her hair. A pot bubbled enthusiastically on the cooker. Pilar began dropping the objects one by one into the pot, causing the liquid to erupt over its sides and hiss onto the gas flame below.

The kitchen table held an almost-empty bag of flour, a mound of eggshells, a Pyrex jug, two bowls, and the wooden board that Anton used to chop vegetables. Everything, including the floor, seemed to be covered in a thin film of the white powder that Zarek assumed was flour.

The larger of the two bowls was empty, but had clearly been used to make some kind of dough. The smaller one held a few shreds of minced meat. "Ah," Zarek murmured. "Pierogi."

It appeared, from the ingredients, that Pilar was making dumplings of some sort. Zarek's mother's dumplings were spicy

and delicious, the pastry made with sour cream, the filling a mixture of cooked potato and cheese, or minced meat and herbs. As
she cooked them, a tantalizing savory smell would waft through
the house, drawing the family to the kitchen.

Pilar's dumplings, on the other hand, smelled of wet wool.

"Is celebration," she announced, dabbing at her face with the
tea towel. "For new job." She laughed. "Sorry, I mean old job."

Zarek wasn't entirely sure of the facts, but it appeared that
Irene, also known as the terrible Mrs. Dillon, had phoned the day
before and invited Pilar back to work. According to Pilar, Irene
had told her that she herself was leaving, which sounded unlikely
to Zarek—what mother would abandon her child? But he wasn't
about to argue with Pilar, who was clearly delighted with the turn
of events.

"You clean up kitchen," she told Zarek, "and I finish kuldunai.
And then we eat."

Anton was out this evening with a group from his workplace,
which meant it was just the two of them for dinner. Zarek began
to clear the table, thinking of the stir-fry with noodles he'd been
planning to cook, and hoping that Lithuanian dumplings tasted
considerably better than their aroma would suggest.

Monday

"Jesus." Carmel immediately clapped a hand to her mouth. "Sorry."

Michael looked at her. "Is it that bad?"

She shook her head, still staring at him. "It's not bad, I jus' got a shock," she said. "I thought you were someone else."

Michael turned to Barry. "It's me," he said. "It's your granddad."

Barry regarded him silently, eyes wide.

"I like it," Carmel said. "You look better. You look younger."

"Dinner will be ten minutes," Michael replied—because how else did you respond to that?

In the kitchen he stirred gravy and rubbed his chin, hidden for so long under its hairy coat. His whole face had an exposed quality to it now, the part that had been covered by the beard a bit pink and raw looking. It put him in mind of a just-shorn sheep. He assumed he'd get used to it, although the thought of having to shave again each morning was mildly depressing.

Valerie would be happy. She'd never approved of the beard he'd started to grow shortly after Ethan had left home. Michael couldn't remember now why he'd suddenly decided on it. He had no idea either what had prompted him to buy a new razor on the way home from work today, an impulse he'd followed without really knowing why.

"Well," he said aloud, "it's done now."

"You look like Ethan," Carmel told him, when they were eating bacon and cabbage a few minutes later. "He looked like you, I mean. I didn't see it before."

Ah yes, Michael thought, that was why. He'd seen his absent son's face every time he looked in the mirror, and he'd covered it with a beard so it didn't keep haunting him.

"Can I show you something?" she asked when the plates were cleared away.

"What?"

"Hang on." She left the room.

Left alone with his grandson, Michael regarded him. "What did you do at school today? Did you draw a picture?"

"Yeah."

"What did you draw?"

"The sun."

Michael smiled. "Just for a change," he said.

"An' I made a Lego house with Em'ly."

"Well done."

Carmel reappeared with the tin box Michael recalled seeing on the bedside locker by her bed. Battered and dented, about half the size of a shoe box, the lid fitting uneasily. She pried it open and took out a photo, and handed it to Michael.

It took a few seconds to recognize Ethan. He looked horribly thin and he was unshaven, and he wore a shabby brown sweater whose sleeves were too short for his arms. But it was Ethan, and on his face was a smile.

And he held a baby in his arms.

Michael looked up. "Why didn't you show me this before?"

"I thought you'd get mad," she said, reaching into the box and taking out more photos. Her and Ethan, her and Barry, the three of them together. Less than a dozen images in total, a meager enough collection compared with Michael's albums of Ethan and Valerie's early years, but a record of them as a family, for the brief time they'd lasted.

"They're not very good," she said. "We only had one of them cameras you throw away."

Michael regarded the handful of photos of his son. He wasn't sure how it had come about, but he realized that somewhere over the past few weeks he'd made his peace with Ethan. He'd blundered his way through it the way he blundered through everything, but it was done now.

The sadness, of course, would always be there, but the guilt had left him. He'd done his best for Ethan, and now he was getting the chance to do his best for Ethan's son. And that was a blessing he hadn't expected—a blessing he'd never have gotten if Carmel hadn't shown up in his shop that first day.

And Valerie, Valerie had come back to him. For the first time in over twenty years, Michael Browne could honestly say he was at peace—and yes, happy. He was happy.

After dinner he settled in his usual armchair and picked up the newspaper and pretended to read it, while on the couch across from him Carmel turned the pages of the *Chicken Licken* book she'd bought with her wages and went through it haltingly, and with many mistakes, for her son.

Tomorrow he'd buy a block of ice cream on his way home from the shop. No reason why they shouldn't have dessert once in a while—and everyone loved ice cream.

Anton mashed potatoes with crushed garlic, black pepper, butter, and warm milk as Pilar filled a jug with water. Zarek set the table and thought about the fact that he'd officially come out.

Just to one person, it was true—and telling Meg hadn't really mattered, they hardly knew each other. But it was the first time he'd actually put it into words, the first time he'd said them aloud: *I am homosexual.*

He'd come out, and the world hadn't ended. Meg had been a little taken aback, but that was to be expected, given the circumstances. He presumed she wasn't too upset; he hoped there wouldn't be awkwardness at their last life drawing class.

Maybe he should have said nothing—but saying nothing had suddenly become impossible. And so he had spoken, and it had been such a relief to finally say the words, such a letting go, such a weight rolling away.

Of course there were far more difficult challenges ahead.

He thought about his mother asking him, every time he rang home, whether he'd met anyone nice. He remembered her pointed references to any suitable female in their neighborhood, once he'd reached the age where he might reasonably be expected to bring home a girlfriend. He remembered her disappointment when no girl had ever been brought home.

He tried to imagine what her reaction to his news might be, and failed. He had no idea how she would feel, what she would say to him. He thought about his father, getting up for early-morning Mass every day of the week. What would the knowledge that his only son was gay do to him?

But he had to tell them, and it had to wait until he went home at Christmas. This wasn't something that could go into a letter, or be said over the phone. He would tell them and they would cope, they would have to cope.

His sister, he felt, might not be too surprised. In her quiet way, Beata may well have figured out what Zarek hadn't even admitted to himself up to quite recently.

But difficult as breaking the news to his family would be, the person whose reaction Zarek most needed, and most dreaded, was Anton. He glanced at his flat mate, who'd begun to spoon the silky mashed potatoes into a serving bowl, and the bowed, dark head, the line of Anton's arm, the curve of his neck—everything, everything—sent a wave of love and longing through Zarek.

When he'd first begun to feel for the Frenchman what he'd never felt for any female, Zarek had done his best to deny it. He'd struggled against these new and dangerous emotions, he'd tried to pretend they didn't exist. He'd considered moving out of the apartment, even leaving Ireland altogether, but the idea of cutting ties with Anton was simply too painful.

And of course changing his location wouldn't make the slightest difference—he was who he was, a gay man. Once he accepted the truth of this, all the uncertainties of his adolescence finally made sense. And so he made the decision to stay where he was, to bide his time and wait for the right moment to say what was in his heart, and suffer the consequences.

"I 'ave something to tell," Anton announced, bringing the potatoes to the table and pulling out a chair. "Some news."

Pilar began pouring water into their glasses. "Good news?"

Zarek took a seat and picked up the serving tongs and helped himself to a rosemary-scented lamb cutlet.

"Yes, it is good news. I 'ave decided," Anton said, spooning potato onto his plate, "to return to France." He reached for the black pepper. "My uncle will open ze new restaurant in Brittany next month and he invite me to work there, as his assistant chef. So I return."

"You leave?" Pilar lowered the jug. "When you go?"

"Three weeks," Anton replied, taking a cutlet. "November fifteen."

"You become real chef," Pilar said. "With job in important restaurant. With big white hat."

Anton smiled. "I am not sure about ze 'at."

"Yes, this is good news," Pilar said. "You are good cook. I like your cooking very much. But Zarek and I will miss you—yes, Zarek?"

Zarek spooned potato onto his plate. "Yes," he said.

"Zarek?" Anton asked.

Zarek looked up.

"You 'ave nothing to say me?"

"This is good for you," Zarek replied. "Congratulation."

"You will come to France maybe," Anton said, "when you 'ave ze 'oliday?"

Zarek held his gaze. "Maybe," he said. "If you like."

"*Oui*," Anton replied, a dimple appearing in his cheek. "I like." He lifted his glass. "And maybe you stay, maybe you find ze job. Maybe my uncle need ze waiter."

"Yes," Zarek replied, hardly trusting his voice. His heart knocking in his chest. "I would like to be waiter."

"Maybe I come too," Pilar said, oblivious. "Maybe I meet nice French man with big house and plenty of euros."

———————

Meg listened to her husband and daughter laughing at some cartoon in the next room, and she thought about how foolish, how incredibly silly she'd been.

She spread the pizza base with roasted tomato sauce. What on earth had made her run after Zarek like some infatuated teenager? She didn't want another man, least of all a younger foreign one. Least of all a younger foreign *gay* one. It would be funny if it weren't so excruciatingly mortifying.

She halved cherry tomatoes and scattered them over the sauce. For the past few weeks she'd treated her husband abominably. She'd pushed him away anytime he tried to get close, and she wasn't even sure why. Maybe opening the playschool had caused it, maybe the stress of those first few hectic weeks had sapped her patience—she'd been so mad at herself for not sailing into it like she'd imagined—and her poor husband had been the one to bear the brunt.

She grated mozzarella and sprinkled it on the pizza, and

topped it with slivers of smoked salmon and spoonfuls of sour cream. Or maybe she'd been going through one of those dips everyone felt now and again, where nothing seemed to be going right. What a bitch she'd been though, snapping at him for the least little thing, turning away from him in bed—God, it was a wonder he hadn't walked out.

She shook oregano on top and opened the oven door and slid the pizza in. And then Zarek's admission in the car, on the way home from Audrey's party. Mortifying at the time, totally unexpected—but she'd realized, before she'd even gotten home, that it hadn't mattered to her in the least, because Zarek meant nothing to her. He'd been a diversion, a distraction, that was all.

She took white wine from the fridge and levered off the cork. She filled a glass and sipped it, leaning against the kitchen table. She had a lot of making up to do, a lot of amends to make. She'd start tonight, after they'd put Ruby to bed.

And she'd skip the last life drawing class. She couldn't face Zarek, knowing what a fool she'd made of herself. And anyway, she wasn't really cut out to be an artist. She couldn't draw to save her life.

"Can I go to Charlie's house? She came here, so now I should go to hers."

Jackie tipped the plastic cup, and the die hopped out onto the snakes and ladders board. "Oh good, five." She moved her yellow counter along its line. "You have to wait until Charlie invites you—you can't just go to her house whenever you feel like it. I invited Charlie here, so that's why she came. Your turn."

Eoin shook the cup and tipped out the die. "But I have no school for a whole week and you have to go to work and I'm *bored* at home by myself."

Jackie's head was fuzzy from lack of sleep, most of the past two nights spent lying on her back, listening to recycled daytime radio. "We'll see," she said, picking up the cup.

Eoin groaned. "You always say that."

"I'll ask Granny if she'll take you to Jungle Jim's, or to the park, okay?"

She'd run a bath at ten to ten the previous morning; she'd been sitting in it when the doorbell had rung. She'd heard voices downstairs, James and her father, but she couldn't make out the words. The talk hadn't lasted long, a couple of minutes only. And thankfully her parents hadn't spoken about him since—probably sensing, from the timing of the bath, that she didn't want to.

She'd make more of an effort to get out and about with her friends. She'd dress up and look happy and talk to anyone who talked to her, she'd find someone who wanted her. She was only twenty-four.

She was dreading the last life drawing class, dreading his eyes on her body. She wished it was over. If Audrey was planning another class after Halloween, Jackie would tell her she wasn't interested. She'd had enough of life drawing. Been there, done that.

And if James made contact for Charlie's sake she'd respond, for Eoin's sake. It would be hard to be in his company so she'd try to minimize that, arrange it so one or other of them took the two children. She'd manage, like she always did.

She slid her counter down a snake. And given time, she'd get over him.

Tuesday

Halfway home from town, Audrey's phone began to ring.

"Hello?"

"It's Michael Browne," he said.

Audrey stopped dead in the middle of the path, causing a minor obstruction among Carrickbawn's pedestrian population.

"Hello? Are you there?"

"Yes," she said, running a hand through her hair, tweaking her blouse collar. "Where did you get my number?"

"You phoned me," he said, "About the playschool. I had it from then."

"Oh…but didn't I call your landline?"

"I have caller ID."

"Oh."

Foolish, asking him that. What did it matter where he'd got her number? She was prattling because she was nervous, which was ridiculous. She stood in the middle of the path and people walked around her.

"I'm calling," he said, "to let you know that I'm having a sale."

"A sale?"

Did pet shops have sales? Was he ringing all his customers to tell them?

"Tomorrow," he said. "A one-day sale. Everything reduced. I just thought I'd let you know, in case you needed anything."

A kennel. She needed a kennel. Silly really, to go all the way to

Limerick if she could get one right here. "Do you have kennels?" she asked. Wouldn't kill her to go and look. Daft to turn down a bargain, if it was on sale.

There was a short silence. Had he heard?

"I do," he answered then. "Twenty percent off tomorrow."

Twenty percent off. She'd be foolish not to at least check them out.

"Right," she said. "I'll call in."

"Right," he repeated. "I'll see you then."

She heard the click as he hung up. She remained standing there, the phone still clamped to her ear.

"Excuse me." A woman with a double buggy was attempting to maneuver it around Audrey.

"Sorry." Audrey stepped out of her way and moved on slowly. He'd rung her to tell her he was having a sale.

Business must be slow. This was a strategy to boost his sales, nothing more.

But he'd rung her, he'd taken the trouble to look her up on his caller ID and he'd rung her. And she was calling in to his shop tomorrow, to check out kennels that were 20 percent off.

She paused in front of a boutique she never went into because it was too dear. There was a green-and-white skirt on the mannequin in the window. A card on the floor read *Skirt €85*.

Eighty-five euro. Scandalous.

She pushed the door open and went in.

"Hi, Audrey." Jackie smiled. "Fancy meeting you here."

It is cold today, Zarek wrote. *Winter is coming to Ireland. I will see how it compares with the Polish winter.*

In the past few days he'd taken to wearing both his sweatshirts at the same time. He'd visited the local charity shop and picked up a navy wool coat for €9. There was a small cream stain on the underside of the left sleeve, about the size of a walnut. Zarek presumed it was the reason for the coat's presence in the shop, but he was happy to overlook it.

My flat mate Anton is moving back to France soon, Zarek wrote. *He will begin working in his uncle's new restaurant. We will miss him.*

They were going to put a notice in the porch of the local church, whose priest was active in helping newly arrived immigrants to Carrickbawn, and where flat-sharing adverts could often be found. They were going to look for a replacement for Anton.

I was glad to hear that Mama's varicose vein operation went well, Zarek wrote. *I hope the bruising will quickly fade.*

Pilar had already laid claim to Anton's bedroom, which was the biggest of the three. Zarek hadn't argued. What did it matter who slept where, what did any of it matter when Anton was gone?

I am sorry to hear that cousin Ana and Mieszko are to separate, Zarek wrote. *It is sad for the children, especially Danek, who is still so young. Perhaps they will reconsider.*

Anton knew. Zarek hadn't needed to say anything because Anton knew. He had looked straight at Zarek and asked him to come to France. He'd talked about Zarek getting a job in Anton's uncle's restaurant.

Zarek finished the letter and put it into an envelope and added his bank draft, full of a shaky, terrified hope.

The last, and smallest, life drawing class. Audrey stood by the table of the only student who'd shown up and wondered what had happened to the rest. She cast her mind back to enrollment night, and her first meeting with them all.

She remembered how struck she'd been by Zarek's good looks—well, anyone would be—and her dismay when the older

couple had reacted so negatively to the notion of someone un-
dressing in the name of art. She recalled her relief when Meg had
arrived, her second enrollment. And soon afterwards Fiona had
appeared, and it began to look like the class might fill up after all.

She recalled Irene striding into the room, all glamour and confidence, and James's late arrival, practically at the last minute. She
remembered how she'd fully expected a dozen or so to enroll, and
how glad she'd been to get five in the end.

And going home afterwards, she remembered wondering how
they'd all get on. Whether any romances would strike up,
whether there would be clashes. As far as Audrey could see, nothing dramatic had happened at all. They'd interacted at the break,
they'd chatted politely with one another, and that had been that.

But she'd enjoyed the classes, she didn't regret offering them
in the least. She'd done her best and that was all anyone could
do. Maybe she'd take a break now, maybe she wouldn't think
about another course for a while. But after Christmas she was
quite prepared to give it a second go—life drawing intermediate,
maybe—and see what happened. Maybe next time she'd get more
than five, maybe she'd get ten.

Jackie looked a bit glum this evening. She might be sorry the
classes were over. They were certainly an easy way to make a few
euro, if you had the courage to let everyone see you in all your
glory. Audrey thought of how terrified poor Jackie had been on
the first evening, cowering in the toilet block, ready to bolt. How
terrified Audrey had been too, that her first class would have no
model. But Jackie had gotten over the nerves and now it was no
bother to her. She'd probably be delighted to come back for another round after Christmas.

Audrey regarded the bowed head of her single student.
"Another minute with this pose," she said, "and then we'll have
the break."

Zarek looked up and smiled. Such a wonderful smile he had.

"Listen," he said, "I know it's short notice, and I know I said I wouldn't need you tonight, but something's come up and I wonder if I could ask you to come around and sit for half an hour, forty minutes tops. Charlie's asleep so it would be just a matter of watching telly, or…whatever."

"Of course," Eunice said, "that's no trouble, dear. Let me just leave a little note for Gerry and I'll be right over."

"Thanks a lot," he said, "I wouldn't ask only it's important."

"I assumed that, dear," she said placidly. "See you in a bit."

James hung up and reached for his jacket. Determined not to analyze what he was about to do, afraid it might take away his resolve. Only knowing that he suddenly wanted to tell her everything, and see where that took them.

He had to tell her, he'd never sleep again if he didn't. And she had a right to know, hadn't she? If she ran a mile when he told her what had brought him and Charlie down from the North, so be it. And if she told his story to the whole of Carrickbawn, he'd have to live with that too—but either way, he had to tell her, and he had to tell her tonight. She was taking up too much of his head space, she was there all the time.

He paced the sitting room floor until he heard Eunice's footsteps on the path outside. He opened the front door before she had a chance to ring the bell.

"Thanks a million," he said. "I'll be back as soon as I can, help yourself to anything in the fridge, or make tea, or whatever."

Five minutes to drive to her house, and the same to get back home. That left half an hour at the most to spill his guts, half an hour for her to take it all in. Talk about mission impossible.

"I just wanted a word," James said as soon as she opened the door. "I won't keep you long."

Jackie cursed the fact that she'd already cleansed her face. Not a scrap of makeup on, not even a dab of lipstick. At least she hadn't gotten into pajamas, which she'd been tempted to do as soon as she'd come home from the art class.

She stepped outside, pulling her cardigan closed. "Maybe we could sit in your car," she said. "My parents are inside." Her palms were suddenly damp. She wiped them on her jeans as she followed him down the path.

In the car she sat upright, her back pressed against the door. James was turned away from her, looking straight ahead. She smelled licorice.

"You weren't at the class," she said.

"No." He hesitated. "I didn't think it was a good idea."

She had no idea what to make of that. She waited, but nothing more came.

"Where's Charlie?" she asked, just to say something.

"At home in bed. A neighbor is there. I said I wouldn't be long."

Another silence. She hugged her cardigan more tightly around her.

"I want to explain," he said then. "I want to tell you about... my situation."

His situation? Jackie kept her eyes fixed on his profile, wishing he'd turn and look at her.

"First of all," he said, "my name isn't James. At least, James is my second name. I started using it when we moved down here. My name's Peter."

He'd changed his name. He was a fugitive from justice because he'd killed someone up north, and now he was in hiding. He was in the Real IRA, or he was a loyalist paramilitary. Either way, she didn't like the direction he was taking.

"The reason we moved, and the reason I changed my name," he said, turning at last to face her, "is because two years ago, my wife—" He stopped.

His wife. Jackie felt a dull lurch in her abdomen. She could feel the cold of the car door through her clothes.

"Two years ago my wife disappeared," he said. "She left the house one day to go shopping, and she never came back."

Jackie drew in her breath. *Charlie's mum is lost,* Eoin had said, and she'd assumed that meant dead. But it didn't mean dead, it meant lost. His wife was lost. She gave an involuntary shiver.

"You're cold."

"I'm okay," she said, but he turned the key and switched on the heater, and in a few seconds she felt warm air at her feet and on her face.

He turned away from her again. "After she disappeared," he said, staring straight ahead, "the police launched a massive search. They dragged lakes and sent divers off the coast, and combed woodlands and mountains. They interviewed me so many times I lost count."

She thought she vaguely remembered a young mother going missing in Donegal. It had made the headlines for a couple of days, till something else had taken its place. Nothing very newsworthy about someone still missing.

Had there been a mention of it on the first anniversary? Maybe. There was usually a mention, a fresh appeal for information.

"Some people decided I'd done away with her," James went on. "I got anonymous letters, people spat at me in the street, or crossed over to avoid me. When they started asking Charlie if she knew what her dad had done, I decided it was time to move. So we came here."

"And she was never found?"

He shook his head. "Not a trace." He hesitated. "You're the

only person I've told, down here. I wanted you to know, because…"

He might have killed her. He might have killed his wife and
disposed of her body so well that nobody had found it. But he
didn't strike Jackie as a killer.

"I'm glad you told me," she said.

"I'm not free though," he answered. "Until a body is found, or
until she turns up, I'm still married. For seven years, apparently."

"I know," Jackie said. "I know that." She did know that, without having a clue where she'd heard it. One of the thousand
pieces of random information that had found a place in her head.

Was he asking her to wait? Was that what he wanted? It was
what *she* wanted, she was sure of that.

"I'm not going anywhere," he said then. "I'm staying here in
Carrickbawn."

"That's good," she said. "Eoin would be sorry if you moved."

He turned to look at her again. "Just Eoin?"

"No," she answered, her heart thumping in her chest. "Not
just Eoin."

Wednesday

He watched as Audrey pushed open the door. He waited for her reaction to his lack of beard.

She stopped dead. "Oh—" her hand reaching up to press against her chest "—goodness."

Nobody used "goodness" in a sentence like that. Michael had seen it written in old-fashioned children's books, but he'd never heard anyone use it in that way. It suited her perfectly.

He was too old, much too old to be experiencing silly little darts of pleasure, but there they were, hopping around inside him. For God's sake.

"It's *so* much better," she said, a warm smile spreading across her face. "I must admit I never really liked your beard."

"Me neither," he said. He discovered a smile on his own face, completely uncalled for. "I came to my senses," he said, "and shaved it off."

They stood grinning at each other for a while. He hoped no wretched customers would come in. She wore a green-and-white skirt and a yellow blouse. She reminded him of a daffodil.

"So," she said at last, "you're having a sale." She looked around. "I don't see any signs."

It had been all he could think of to get her to come back. He should have made some signs, he hadn't thought it through at all. He'd never had a sale in his life. He had no idea how they should look.

"No signs," he said. "Just twenty percent off everything, keep it simple. You mentioned a kennel."

"Yes, so Dolly can be outside while I'm at work. I teach art," she said, her smile widening again. "I'm on holidays this week, midterm break. And last night my life drawing evening class ended, so I'm completely free."

She stopped abruptly, as if she'd been caught doing something she shouldn't.

"In that case," he said, his heart thudding like a two-year-old's, "perhaps I could persuade you to let me take you to dinner some evening."

"Oh—" the hand flew to her chest again "—oh, well…"

She was going to turn him down. She had no interest in him. He was the rudest man she'd ever met. He was far too old, he must be a good fifteen years older than her. His chin was like a sheep's shorn arse.

"Well," she said, "I must say, that would be quite delightful."

Michael regarded her round, pleased-looking face. Not at all what he'd thought he'd go for. Nothing like Ruth, who'd been small and slight, and not given to particularly loud clothing.

"Wonderful," he replied, leading the way to his supply of kennels, which was located on the farthest left-hand aisle. "Wonderful."

———————

She'd known he'd look so much better without the beard. She wondered what had prompted him to do it. He had a good strong chin too, a bit Rock-Hudson-ish.

He'd just asked her out to dinner. She'd just said yes.

She was pleased with the green-and-white skirt. It had been worth the ridiculously high price. She wasn't entirely sure her yellow blouse was right with it though; she suspected it made her look a bit like a daffodil. Maybe she'd drop into the boutique again on her way home, see what tops they had.

He was taking her out on a date. He was going to bring her to a restaurant and they were going to sit opposite each other and eat food. And afterwards he was going to drive her home, and when he parked the car she was going to suggest that he come in for coffee, or maybe a nightcap.

And she had no earthly idea what was going to happen after that.

He bore no resemblance to the men who'd peopled her dreams for as long as she could remember, men with broad chests and full heads of dark hair who crushed her in passionate embraces and knelt in front of her with little velvet-lined boxes, and who eventually walked her down the aisle, looking adoringly at her. He was as far removed from those men as it was humanly possible to be.

But he was real. And he wanted to take her out to dinner. And she was looking forward to it with an enthusiasm that amazed her.

She followed him down the aisle, past the bird feeders and dog collars and little tubs of goldfish food, her heart flooding with happiness.

Thanks a Million

To Sara Weiss, Jen Musico, and all at Grand Central Publishing for their help and attention.

To my Irish stalwarts Ciara Doorley and Faith O'Grady, for always being there when I called.

To the Tyrone Guthrie Centre in County Monaghan, my all-time favourite writers' and artists' retreat, for taking me in whenever I need a week of pure uninterrupted writing.

To my life drawing tutor Paul, God bless him, who always found something positive to say about my, er, artistic efforts.

To my family, as supportive as ever.

To everyone who bought a copy of *Semi-Sweet*, my first U.S.–published novel, and to all who left a lovely message on my website afterwards.

To you, for doing me the honour of buying this book. Thank you so much, and I do hope it pleases you.

Roisin x
www.roisinmeaney.com

Back to the Drawing Board

by Roisin Meaney

The notion of life drawing has long fascinated me. I'm intrigued by the idea of a group of people coming together with the sole purpose of studying someone else's nude body for a couple of hours. Who, I wondered, would be sufficiently confident to pose for strangers in all their unclothed glory? I knew it wasn't something I could ever do, not if my life depended on it—thanks, I suspect, to my Irish Catholic upbringing.

And what about the students in such a class? How could anyone sit there and not feel like some kind of a voyeur? I wasn't at all sure I could even do that, shy and retiring little creature that I am, but the longer I spent pondering it all, the more curious I became.

An evening class in itself was such fruitful ground for a writer—strangers meeting up, colliding regularly for a few weeks. Things had to happen. And I suppose I could have chosen to write about an evening class in, say, car maintenance or flower arranging, but life drawing, by its very nature, seemed more open to all sorts of delicious possibilities. (I hasten to add that no offense is intended to car mechanics or florists, whose lives may well be full of scandals!)

So in the end I decided I had to investigate. I hunted down a life drawing class and went along to enrollment night. On meeting Paul, the teacher, I told him what I was up to. I had decided to come clean, as I thought my cover would be blown anyway when the book eventually got published. Paul seemed amused at the idea of his class being used for research purposes but was happy to go along with it, so I duly presented myself on the first night, armed with my pencils and putty rubber. (Paul generously provided the paper, unlike Audrey, but let's forgive her as she was such a novice in the whole area of evening classes.)

My fellow students, about a dozen, were a mixed bunch, ranging in age from eighteen to about seventy, and the gender split was around half and half. I discovered from chatting to them before the class progressed that when it came to life drawing, I was actually the only total beginner, which made me feel slightly more like an imposter.

I probably should mention at this stage that I hadn't exactly been blessed with artistic ability. I'd studied art in secondary school (high school to you), and I could copy someone else's cartoon drawing fairly well, but that was about the extent of my talent. I had no idea how my attempts to reproduce a real person would go, but I wasn't hopeful. I reminded myself why I was there—to see how a class operated and to pick up a few tricks of the trade for Audrey to pass on—and I set out my tools, trying to look as if I knew what I was doing.

In due course our model entered the room, wearing a dressing gown. She looked about nineteen or twenty, and was tall and attractive. I glanced around at my partners in crime—sorry, I mean fellow students—but none of them looked in the slightest bit embarrassed as she undid the belt of the dressing gown, quite nonchalantly, and bundled it onto a chair. Paul indicated the pose he wanted her to take up, in exactly the same tone of voice he would use, I imagined, if he was giving her the weather forecast, or telling her when the next bus was due. And off we went.

Needless to say, my efforts were disastrous. The poor girl on my page looked as if she was in dire need of immediate surgery to correct her crooked spine, misshapen legs, and distorted hips—not to mention breasts that were separated from each other by at least two sizes. My initial self-consciousness at being less than four feet from a naked female paled in comparison to the mortification I felt every time Paul passed my way and glanced at the fruits of my labor.

But he was kindness itself, bless him. His murmured comments were beautifully judged, his praise not so fulsome as to sound insincere, his criticism constructive and helpful. When he used the word "energy" at one stage, it sounded like such a positive way of looking at my offerings that I immediately filed it away and gave it to Audrey to use for James, whose artistic endeavors mirrored my own, God help him.

At break I cornered the model and interrogated her, and discovered that she was a student in the local art college, and well used to posing for life drawing groups. She admitted, when I probed, that the first time was a challenge, but she quickly became accustomed to it, and now it didn't bother her in the slightest. I made a mental note not to use an art student as the model in my story—I needed poor Jackie to be on the verge of a nervous breakdown on her first night.

I stayed the course, despite my obvious lack of talent, and I thoroughly enjoyed the classes, thanks to a combination of Paul's tact, his music choice (Neil Young, Willie Nelson, Diana Krall) and the nicely laid-back atmosphere in the room. Everyone seemed intent on the task in hand, but in a lovely, casual, nonpressurized way. This was an evening class, after all.

I can't say I progressed very much in terms of being able to reproduce a human body in 2-D form, but when it came to plotting the book, Paul and the classes were invaluable. I loved writing this one—I know I say that about all my books, but I grew very fond of Audrey, with her bright colors, enormous heart, and enduring certainty that love will find her—and I'm thrilled that *Life Drawing for Beginners* is joining *Semi-Sweet* on U.S. bookshelves.

I really hope you enjoy reading it; do visit my website and let me know if you do. Even if my artistic skills are sadly lacking, it's always lovely to hear that my literary efforts are going down well somewhere!

Reading Group Guide

Discussion Questions

1. All of Audrey's students are nervous about joining her class. Have you ever taken a night class? What was your experience like? Would you ever join a life drawing class?

2. Many characters in this book are single parents. How is parenting portrayed in the novel and how is each parent different? Are you a single parent yourself or do you know any single parents?

3. What do you make of Irene? Do you think she is a good person? Why or why not?

4. Michael kicked his sixteen-year-old son out of the house because he was a drug addict. Do you think he made the right decision? Would you have made the same choice?

5. Zarek is keeping a secret for most of the novel. What is that secret? Why do you think he is finally able to reveal it by the end of the book?

6. Do you think it is fair for Carmel to ask Michael for help? Or do you think she is asking too much of him?

7. When Valerie meets Barry for the first time she says to Michael: "You're showing a boy you didn't know existed up to

a few weeks ago more attention than Ethan or I ever got from you. You failed as a father so you thought you'd try your hand at being a grandfather, is that it?" Why is Valerie so angry? Do you think she is too hard on Michael or does she have good reason to be upset?

8. Jackie is very reluctant to model for the life drawing class, but she ultimately gives in. How do you think her experience of modeling changes her? Would you ever be brave enough to do what she does?

9. Audrey is not a conventionally attractive woman, but Michael finds himself drawn to her. Why do you think that is?

10. When does James's relationship with Jackie change? Why is he able to open up to her?

11. Irene makes a dramatic choice at the end of the book. Do you agree with her decision? Do you think she was being selfish or doing the right thing for her family?

12. When Audrey first meets Michael, she finds him extremely unlikeable, but her feelings for him slowly shift. Why?

13. How does Michael change over the course of the novel? If you were in his shoes, would you make the same choices he does regarding Carmel?

14. After the last drawing class, Audrey reflects on how the class turned out and how her students got along with each other: "Nothing dramatic had happened at all. They'd interacted at the break, they'd chatted politely with each other, and that had been that…She'd done her best and that was all anyone could do." Is Audrey's interpretation correct? Did anything dramatic or life-changing happen to her or any of her students as a result of her class?

About the Author

ROISIN MEANEY began her career when she won the Tivoli Write a Bestseller competition for *The Daisy Picker* and has written seven novels since. She has lived in the United States, Canada, Africa, and Europe, and currently resides in Limerick, Ireland. You can visit her website at www.roisinmeaney.com.

If you liked
Life Drawing for Beginners,
you'll love *Semi-Sweet*

five
spot

Hannah Robinson is about to open the doors to her new shop, Cupcakes on the Corner, when her boyfriend announces that he's leaving her for another woman. Has her lifelong dream just turned into a nightmare?

———

"Wise, witty, and wonderful. I couldn't turn the pages fast enough."   —Debbie Macomber, #1 *New York Times* bestselling author

"Roisin Meaney writes like a friend you haven't met yet— charming, insightful, and full of surprises. *Semi-Sweet* is totally delicious!"   —Claire Cook, author of *Must Love Dogs* and *Seven Year Switch*